ANDERSEN'S FAIRY TALES

HANS ANDERSEN'S
FAIRY TALES

With an Introduction by
MARGARET W. J. JEFFREY

Illustrated by
VERNON SOPER

COLLINS
LONDON AND GLASGOW

First published, 1835
This edition, 1954
Latest reprint, 1986

ISBN 0 00 424721 3

Printed and bound in Great Britain by
William Clowes Limited,
Beccles and London

HANS CHRISTIAN ANDERSEN

Hans Christian Andersen was born on April 2nd, 1805, in the ancient town of Odense, in Denmark. His father, Hans Andersen, was a cobbler who, it is said, came from a once well-to-do yeoman family; his mother was of the most humble origin. The family lived in the poor district of the town close to the penitentiary; they lived in one room, which contained, in addition to the cobbler's bench, a large bedstead, a chest-of-drawers and a bookshelf. But the atmosphere was cheerful, there were pictures on the walls, books and music in the bookshelf, pretty cups, glasses and knick-knacks on the chest-of-drawers. On the door leading to the kitchen there was a landscape, painted by the cobbler, who was a man of many talents, independent spirit and considerable self-made education. He had real appreciation for literature and a great love for the theatre, which he instilled into his son at an early age. He used to read out to him the plays of Holberg, the great Danish dramatist, the fables of La Fontaine and tales from *The Arabian Nights*, and he made all kinds of toys for him, such as cut-out pictures which could be moved by pulling strings, dolls and a small theatre in which the boy produced his own special versions of Shakespearian dramas.

Young Andersen was a delicate, over-sensitive child who preferred solitary games or the company of women to the rough companionship of the boys of his own age. He lived in his own world of fantasies and dreams, which was, no doubt, his way of responding to the superstition, magic and ignorance which surrounded him. The weird, the uncanny, the frightening—such as the local asylum for the insane—held a peculiar fascination for him.

In 1812 his father enlisted as a soldier in the hope that war—it was the height, or rather the beginning of the end, of the Napoleonic era—might provide him with a chance of bettering his lot, but after two years in which he did not see active campaigning he returned broken in health. He died in 1816 aged thirty-five.

Two years later Anne Marie Andersen married again; her second husband—also a shoemaker—took little interest in the boy, who could not easily accept the fact that he now had to share his mother's affection with a stranger.

Andersen received only the most desultory schooling at various local establishments. The lack of a proper basic education was to prove one of his most serious handicaps in later years.

Several attempts were made to place him in some trade or other, but his ambitions were of a different kind. His interest in literature and the theatre had been awakened; he wrote poems and dramas, he discovered his gift for singing and declaiming, he sought the company of people of quality and education, he yearned for a life more exalted than that to which his lowly station and lack of education seemed to have condemned him. Besides, a gipsy fortune-teller had predicted that one day his home town, Odense, would be illuminated for him. He believed in his destiny.

One morning, early in September 1819, Andersen, then fourteen years old, a gawky, overgrown lad, unprepossessing in appearance to the point of grotesqueness, mounted the stage-coach at Odense on the first lap of his journey to Copenhagen, where he was determined to make his name as an opera singer. He carried with him a letter of introduction to a well-known opera singer, some addresses, the contents of his home-safe, amounting to less than two pounds, and an unshakable faith in God's providence.

Arrived in Copenhagen, he at once proceeded in a manner which was both businesslike (in its methodic thoroughness) and utterly fantastic—being based entirely on subjective and erroneous assumptions on the ways of the world—to organise his future. After a few days he was reduced, physically, to near starvation and, mentally, to the very brink of suicide.

However, his faith prevailed over his despair and his courage over the apparent hopelessness of his plight; he found not only the means of physical survival but also the way which was eventually to lead him to his true vocation.

His first patrons were Professor Weyse, the musician, and Siboni, the Italian singing teacher of the Royal Conservatoire. They provided him with funds sufficient for his immediate needs, and Siboni undertook to give him singing lessons.

After a short while his voice proved inadequate and his general appearance quite unsuited for the stage. His next patron was the poet Guldberg, who collected further funds and gave him free lessons in Danish, German and Latin and later secured his admission at the dancing-school attached to the Royal Theatre. His failure as a dancer and small-part actor having proved complete, yet another attempt was made to train him as a singer in the chorus school of the Royal Theatre. But soon it became painfully clear to everyone except Andersen that no amount of training and perseverance would ever lead to success. But he would not give up: if he was not to reach the stage as an artiste he would do so as dramatic author. He set to work and wrote a tragedy entitled *Alfsol*, which he felt sure would be accepted. It actually reached one of the directors of the theatre who, though he considered it quite unsuited, nevertheless thought the young author deserved help and encouragement. Thus it came about that Andersen was recommended to the State Councillor Jonas Collins, a noble and kind-hearted man who obtained the King's consent to have Andersen educated at the Latin Grammar School of Slagelse at the expense of the Crown. Moreover, Collins assumed the young man's guardianship. In the years that followed Andersen virtually became a member of Collins' family, a position which he maintained for the rest of his life.

Andersen remained at Slagelse for four years (1822–26) and spent a further year at the Academy of Elsinore. He later referred to his years at school as "the years of my degradation". No doubt he was unhappy: his oversensitiveness and general emotional instability made him suffer unduly under the régime of a disciplinarian headmaster. But, no doubt also, without this belated schooling he would never have been able to give his talents articulate expression.

He left Elsinore in 1827 to complete his studies for the final university examination under private tuition in Copenhagen and matriculated with distinction in 1829.

The same year appeared his first major work, *A Walking Trip*, a collection of fantastic sketches in the manner of the German romantics. It was on the whole well received. A number of poems in the same vein followed. The same year also he wrote a vaudeville—a very slight affair—which was successfully performed at the Royal Theatre. Six other pieces (four operettas and two vaudevilles), of which he himself had the highest opinion, were rejected with accompanying criticism so severe that Andersen nearly suffered a nervous breakdown.

In the spring of 1831 he went on the first of his many journeys abroad. Travelling was to become one of the abiding pleasures of his life. On this first journey he went via Luebeck to Hamburg, thence to Brunswick and the Hartz Mountains, Leipzig, Dresden, Bohemia, returning via Berlin, where he struck up a friendship with the German romantic writer Adalbert von Chamisso. He recorded his impressions as he went along and published them as *Travel Silhouettes* on his return. In 1833 he obtained from the King a travelling stipend of about seventy pounds a year for two years, and in April he set out on his second and more ambitious journey, which took him to France, Switzerland, Italy, Austria and Germany. He was given a warm welcome in Paris and introduced to some of the great literary figures of the day.

While in France he wrote *Agnete and the Merman*, a dramatisation of the ancient Danish ballad. Contrary to his fond expectations—Andersen completely lacked the capacity of objective judgment as far as his own work was concerned —it proved a dismal failure.

Italy made a deep impression on him. He spent a considerable time in Rome and visited Naples and Capri. When the time had come to return home (in the summer of 1834) he bemoaned his fate which forced him to live in the cold and unemotional north, where he maintained he was not appreciated. In Rome he had begun his first novel, *The Improvisatore,* which appeared early in 1835 and was an immediate success. The same year also he published a small volume entitled *Fairy Tales as Told to Children*, which among other tales contained *The Tinder Box* and *The Princess and the Pea*. A second booklet followed in 1836 and a third (which consisted of *The Little Mermaid* and *The Emperor's New Clothes*) in 1837. These three booklets made up the first series of his *Tales*. At first their sale was slow, but within a year or two they had found their way into many Danish homes. Andersen himself for many years looked upon his fairy-tales as of small significance, mere casual flowers in his poetic garden in which, so he fancied, he was planting great and wonderful trees with his romances and plays. So, while his fairy-tales were quickly and unobtrusively planting the seeds of his contemporary fame and future immortality, he busied himself with his romances and dramatic productions.

In 1836 he completed his second novel, *O.T.*, and in 1837 the third, *Only a Fiddler*. Both were on the whole well received in Denmark and enthusiastically in Sweden and Germany, where, by this time, he had won for himself a large and admiring public.

Despite his growing success and prestige at home and abroad, Andersen was not able to earn by his writings an income sufficient for his modest needs. The situation was relieved in 1838 when the King granted him an annual pension of 800 kroner (about forty pounds). In later years his earning increased, and towards the end of his life he was moderately well off.

Between 1838 and 1846 he published two further series of *Fairy Tales*. The first volume in the latter series contained *The Ugly Duckling*, which securely established his fame on a world-wide scale. Renewed attempts to gain recognition as a dramatic author led to but ephemeral success with the production of his play *The Mulatto* at the Royal Theatre, Copenhagen (1839), and two one-act plays produced in 1843. Another elaborately staged play, *The Moorish Girl* (1840), was a resounding failure.

In 1840 began Andersen's second great travel period. The railways had made their appearance and Andersen had immediately taken to this new form of travelling with the greatest enthusiasm. He became a pioneer of rail travel, and from 1840 until 1872 he covered nearly the whole of the rapidly expanding European railway network. Among his more memorable journeys were those through Germany, Italy, Greece, Turkey and Austria in 1840–41, to Paris in 1843 and to England in 1847. In England he was given a triumphal reception and formed an abiding friendship with Dickens. He visited Germany almost every year; and in no country (including his own) was he more greatly honoured than in Germany; her kings, reigning dukes and princes vied with each other in showering favours and decorations upon him.

During the first Schleswig-Holstein war (1848–50), when Denmark was cut off from the Continent, he paid a five-month visit to Sweden, a visit described by him in his book *In Sweden* (1851). In 1857 he visited England for the second time and was the guest of Dickens; in 1862 came his grand tour through Spain described in the most famous of his travel books, *In Spain*, 1863. Further journeys to Holland, France and Portugal followed in the years 1866–70.

From about 1848 onwards Andersen devoted himself almost entirely to his fairy-tales, and from 1849 he regularly wrote fairy-tale plays for the Copenhagen stage. Between 1852 and 1862 he published nine volumes of fresh tales of a more didactic kind than his previous ones; further volumes followed in 1865–66 and a last series in 1871–72.

In 1867 Andersen received the freedom of his native city Odense and saw the gipsy's prophecy that Odense would one day be illuminated in his honour come true. The poor cobbler's son had become one of Denmark's most famous writers and perhaps her most honoured and beloved citizen.

Andersen fell romantically in love on more than one occasion and liked to be surrounded by admiring and solicitous ladies; however, he was unable to face the responsibilities of married life and of a permanent domicile; up to almost the last years of his life he had no establishment of his own. When not travelling he lived in furnished rooms or hotels, in later years more and more frequently as a guest at the country seats of the aristocracy.

In 1872, during a trip abroad, his health began to fail. He returned home and spent the following years mostly in retirement in the country, except for a short visit to Norway. He died on August 4th, 1875.

H. de R.

CONTENTS

INTRODUCTION

Sir Arthur Mee summed up the difference between the fairy-stories of Hans Christian Andersen and those of the Brothers Grimm and others by saying that unlike those of Grimm "most of his (Andersen's) wonderful stories were told to him not by peasant folk but by the fairies of his own brain." The fairies of his brain. They spoke to him and he listened. One is reminded of that incorrigible opener of cages, Mr. Gillie, James Bridie's schoolmaster in the play of that name, who mystified and embarrassed poor Mr. Gibb, douce minister of the gospel, by telling him that the "artists are listening to something unguarded and private." "Listening," he said, "to the very mind of God." In their different spheres the two utterances say much the same thing. They try to account for the creative spirit, and they are agreed that its source is beyond the human. The fairy-tales of Hans Andersen are a pure product of this spirit: brief little poetic creations that are the finest flowering of the imagination. Indeed, in his own land he was called "the long poet." But it was many years before he himself perceived their true source and value, or understood that the voice of inspiration is a still, small voice which comes unbidden and stays away when sought. From the time when he set out from Odense for Copenhagen to make his fortune, with all the hope and confidence of untried youth in his heart and only thirty-seven shillings in his pocket, he had a vision of how he was to become famous; a vision different from, but not more splendid than, that which was actually fulfilled. He wished at first to choose his own path. He thought he could sing and act and dance; but he failed to express his real genius through any of these arts. He meant to write novels, epics and plays. He did; but we do not read them now. When his friend Örsted, on reading one of these novels, *The Improvisatore*, and some of the earlier tales which came out about the same time, wrote to him, "*The*

15

Improvisatore may make you famous, but the children's tales will make you immortal," Andersen did not believe him. It was not until his life was nearly over that he ceased to be annoyed when he was referred to as the children's poet. His constant aim was to become the poet of older folk. "Children alone," he said, "cannot represent me."

Örsted was right, however, and it was the children's tales, which at first he regarded as mere trifles, that won him both his remarkable contemporary reputation and his deserved immortality. When we have made every allowance for the lionising that went on in the nineteenth century, Andersen's reception, which he had won through years of hardship, must be regarded as extraordinary. No wonder he believed wonders could happen. They happened to him. Kings and queens showered favours on him; he was received by the great and the gifted in every country of Europe. There is a story that when he visited Scotland he left his cane behind him. It was sent on to him from place to place and caught up with him before he sailed from England. It was addressed simply, "The Danish Poet, Hans Christian Andersen." Everybody knew about him. The *Tales* opened all doors to him, and in the end he came to recognise them for what they were—the unique expression of his vision of life coloured by the light of his own unique experience.

Nearly all children love the *Tales*, yet it is a question whether they do not appeal even more to grown-ups. Or, to put it otherwise, the latter may enjoy a two-fold pleasure from them: spontaneous delight in them as tales, a delight the child may share, and an artistic delight in their perfection of form. For although the fairies of his mind may have whispered the stories, it was Hans Andersen, the conscious artist, who took endless pains with each until, as he himself said, he was satisfied that it contained nothing a child would not understand. He cast out all difficult or pedantic expressions, all abstractions, and substituted for them the simple, the direct and the concrete. In seeking this simplicity he succeeded in doing what every artist is haunted by the desire to do—to turn the material of his art into pure form. We should remember that Andersen intended his stories to be told or read aloud, and that, in a sense, they are incomplete unless this condition is fulfilled. In the same way a song is perfected only when it is sung. It was this intention that governed his choice of word and phrase. He writes as he might speak to a child, and we can watch him rivet the attention with his very first words: "Listen! We are beginning our story! When we arrive at the end of it we shall, it is to be hoped, know more than we do now. There was once a magician! a wicked magician!! a most wicked magician!!!" And with that final double superlative, accompanied by who knows what expression of face or inflection of the voice, the spell is completely cast. "There came a soldier marching along the highroad—right, left! right, left!" "In China, as you well know, the Emperor is Chinese, and all around him are Chinese also." "Surely you know what a microscope is!" "Let us now go to Switzerland," and so on. And, no less important, he knows when to stop, namely, when he has said what he has to say. It is this natural and sincere restraint which makes his stories seem completely artless.

It is not possible to separate Andersen's art from his experience. When he was old, he said that the tales had lain all his life "like seeds in the mind, needing only a current, a ray of sun, a drop of distilled wormwood, to burst into flower." Some of the traditional ones, "fairy tales that used to please me when I was little," as he calls them, he learned from his grandmother and from the attendants in the asylum where his grandfather was lodged; the simple old man, who was the model for the old woodcarver in *Holger the Dane,* as his grandmother was for all the good grandmothers throughout the *Tales.* Such traditional tales are *The Tinder Box*, the first to be written, *The Flying Trunk*, *The Wild Swans* and *The Garden of Paradise*, and the humorous *The Swineherd* and *The Real Princess.* True to their origin in folk-tale, these have a more robust, less delicate quality than those which were the product of Andersen's own imagination. Little personal incidents, too, and objects and even phrases weave themselves into the perfect patterns of many of the tales: the brand-new boots which monopolised Hans Christian's thoughts at his first Communion, transformed into the red shoes that were poor

Karen's doom in *The Red Shoes*; his mother's flower-boxes with their few kitchen herbs, which are compensatingly planted in *The Snow Queen* with a little rose-tree and scarlet-runners that formed a flowery arch across the street. *The Snow Queen* is full of the happier memories of that early childhood, just as *The Ugly Duckling* reflects its sombre side. Andersen was less than fortunate in the affairs of the heart, but it was a "ray of sun" surely as well as a "drop of distilled worm-wood" that brought to flower the exquisite *The Little Mermaid*, which he wrote in sadness for his own lost happiness when his friend Edward Collin married; or *The Nightingale*, which was his tribute to the Swedish singer Jenny Lind.

In a deeper sense too than the incidental, the *Tales* express, or rather interpret, Andersen's experience. A poet's success in creating a visionary world of his own which is acceptable to the reader is one of the real tests of his quality. Andersen's toy world is one of the most acceptable of these visionary worlds, for although it contains all the poetic wonder that is the essential of the nursery tale, it is at the same time completely natural. Even its wonder is coloured by its creator's feelings for those who, like himself, have known poverty and hardship. It is to them that the wonderful things happen, to the Kays and the Gerdas and ordinary folk rather than to kings and princes, the rich or the great. At the centre of the most delicate web woven by his fancy there is reality as he sees it. The little match girl dreams her dreams by the flickering light of her last three matches, but all the same she dies of cold and hunger. In the poignantly beautiful *Story of a Mother*, the Mother, likewise, must give her child to Death. There is no easy absolution for Karen of *The Red Shoes*. The constant tin soldier is melted to a hard lump even if his remains prettily take the shape of a little tin heart. Little Tuk has small reward for his good deed and his neglected lessons, save his wonderful dream and the assurance that the angels remember. Andersen has no interest in finding happy endings that do not belong to his stories any more than to life as he sees it.

It is probably because he never falsifies the elemental truths and emotions that we accept as completely natural the rest of his world: his inventions and the lovely extravagance of his fancies. They have a truth of the imagination that transcends the truth of fact. It seems quite right and fitting that china shepherdesses and chimney sweeps, tin soldiers, tops, balls and darning-needles should share the speech and feelings of human folk; that birds and trees and flowers should be endowed with the same life. The little Mermaid, stepping so painfully in a world for which nature never intended her, could not be more real to us, yet the realm from which she came is in Andersen's description of a beautiful siren-land of the most remote intangibility; and the trolls who hold their grotesque revels in Elfin Mount are quite homely, credible beings, no more difficult to believe in than many of Dickens' creations. Indeed, Hans Andersen has often been compared with Dickens, whom he greatly admired, "dear, noble Charles Dickens," as he called him, and whom he visited more than once in England. Certain traits are common to both, notably their compassion for the poor, the sentiment and pathos that predominate in their work, and some aspects of their humour, particularly the grotesque.

Andersen himself set great store by the humour in his tales. It was one means by which he could reach his double audience of children and adults, writing a simple story for the former with overtones of satire for the latter, in which he has a fling at the snobbery, self-righteousness and pretentiousness that wounded him in the past. But even in his satiric humour there is no real bitterness; for Andersen had a true sweetness and simplicity of spirit that could not harbour rancour for long. His touch is feather-light. "Was not this a lady of real delicacy?" he asks of the princess who was able to feel the three little peas through twenty mattresses and twenty feather-beds. And elsewhere, as in the gay impertinence of *The False Collar*, it bubbles up from the same creative fount as fed his lyric fancy. It is Andersen's shield against the sentimentality to which he might so easily have fallen a victim.

These stories are unique in the literature of the fairy-tale. Some, like the Brothers Grimm, have collected the real fairy-tales—or folk-tales—in their exact form as they have been handed down through generations of story-tellers; survivals of the imaginations of primitive humanity. Others, like

Perrault and Madame D'Aulnoy, have given them an artificial and courtly dress to conform to the prevailing fashion. But Andersen has taken or invented to suit his needs, following no law but the law of his art. When he liked, he could, as we have seen, tell the folk-tales with wonderful verve, but his best works are his own creations. And in all that great variety of the beautiful, the bizarre, the comic, humorous, pathetic, moral, melancholy or tragic, the best of all perhaps are *The Forsaken Mermaid*, which moved him more deeply than any of the others; and that sad and wise analysis of the twofold nature of man, Andersen's *Dr. Jekyll and Mr. Hyde* which he calls *The Shadow*.

MARGARET W. J. JEFFREY

THE GARDEN OF PARADISE

THERE was once a young Prince; no one had so many and such beautiful books as he had. He could read in them the history of all the events which have ever happened in the world, and also see them represented in splendid pictures. He could gain from his books all the information he wanted about any country, or people whatsoever.

But there was not in them a word of what he most desired to know, viz., where the Garden of Paradise was to be found.

When the Prince was a very little boy, just beginning to go to school, his grandmother told him that every flower in the Garden of Paradise tasted like the sweetest of cakes, and the stem like the choicest of wines. On one plant there grew history, on another geography, on a third the German language. Whoever ate the flower immediately knew his lesson; the more he ate, the more he learned of history, geography, or German.

At that time the young Prince believed all this. But by and by, when he had grown bigger and wiser, and had learned more, he saw plainly that what constituted the beauty of the Garden of Paradise must be something quite different.

"Oh! why did Eve touch the Tree of Knowledge? Why did Adam eat of the forbidden fruit? Had I been in their place, it would never have happened. Sin would never have entered the world!"

So said he then, and when he was seventeen, he still said the same. The Garden of Paradise occupied all his thoughts.

One day he went into the wood; he went alone, for to wander thus was his chief delight.

The evening approached, the clouds gathered, the rain poured down, as if all the sky was nothing but a vast flood-gate; it was as dark as we might suppose it to be at night-time in the deepest of wells. The Prince now slipped among the wet grass, now stumbled over bare rocks, which projected from the stony ground. Everything was dripping with water; the poor Prince had not a dry thread on his skin. He was obliged to creep over great blocks of stone, where the water trickled down from the moss.

His strength was just failing him, when he heard a strange rustling, and saw before him a large lighted cavern. A fire was burning in the centre, at which a stag might have been roasted whole, and, indeed, this was the case; a very fine stag, with his branching antlers, was placed on the spit, and was slowly turned between the stems of two fir-trees. An aged woman, but tall and strong as if she were a man in disguise, sat by the fire, throwing upon it one piece of wood after another. "Come nearer," said she; "sit down by the fire and dry your clothes."

"There is a terrible draught here," said the Prince, as he sat down on the ground.

"It will be still worse when my sons come home," answered the woman. "You are now in the Cavern of the Winds; my sons are the four Winds. Do you understand me?"

"Where are your sons?" asked the Prince.

"There is no use in answering stupid questions," said the woman; "my sons do as they please—play at ball with the clouds up there!" and then she pointed to the blue sky above.

"Indeed!" said the Prince; "you speak in rather a harsh manner, and altogether do not seem so gentle as the women I am accustomed to see around me."

"Yes; they have nothing else to do! I must be harsh if I am to control my boys; however, I can control them, although they have stiff necks. Do you see those four sacks hanging by the wall? They have as much respect for them, as you used to have for the rod behind the looking-glass. I puff them together, I tell you, and then they must get into the sacks; we use no ceremony; there they sit, and do not come out till it pleases me. But here comes one of them!"

It was the North Wind: he brought icy coldness with him; large hailstones danced on the ground, and flakes of snow flew around him. He was dressed in a jacket and trousers of bearskin, a cap of sealskin hung over his ears; long icicles hung from his beard, and one hailstone after another fell from under the collar of his jacket.

"Do not go immediately to the fire," said the Prince; "you may perhaps get your face and hands frost-bitten."

"Frost-bitten!" repeated the North Wind, and he laughed aloud; "frost is my greatest delight! But what spindle-shanked boy are you? How did you get into the Cavern of the Winds?"

"He is my guest," said the old woman, "and if you are not content with this explanation, you shall go into the sack! Now you know my mind."

This was quite sufficient; and now the North Wind related whence he came, and how he had spent the last month.

"I come from the Arctic Ocean," said he; "I have been on the Bear's Island, along with the Russian whalers. I sat by the helm, and slept when they sailed from the North Cape; and, if now and then I awoke for a short time, the stormy petrel would fly about my legs. It is a merry bird; he suddenly claps his wings, then holds them immovably stretched out and soars aloft."

"Do not make your story so long!" said the mother. "And so you came to the Bear's Island?"

"That is a glorious place! the ground seems made on purpose for dancing—flat as a plate. It is composed of half-melted snow overgrown with moss; sharp stones, and the skeletons of whalers and polar bears are strewed over it, looking like the arms and legs of giants, covered with musty green; you would fancy the sun had never shone on them.

"I blew a little into the clouds, in order that the people might be able to see the shed, built from a wreck, and covered with the skin of whales, the fleshy side, all green and red, turned outwards. A living polar bear sat growling on the roof. I walked on the shore, peeped into the birds' nests, looked at the poor naked young ones, who were crying, with their beaks wide open: I blew into their thousand little throats, and they learned to be quiet. The sea-horses, with their swine-like heads, and teeth an ell long, rolled like gigantic worms beneath the waters."

"My son can relate his adventures very pleasantly," said the mother; "my mouth waters when I listen to him."

"And now the fishery began; the harpoon was thrust into the breast of the sea-horse, and a stream of blood shot up like a fountain, and streamed over the ice. Then I remembered my part of the sport; I made my ships, the rock-like ice mountains, surround the boats. Oh! how all the crew whistled and shouted; but I whistled still louder. They were obliged to unload all the dead whales, and to throw them, with their trunks and cordage, out upon the ice. I shook snowflakes over them, and drove them to taste sea-water southwards. They will never come again to Bear's Island!"

"Then you have done mischief!" said the mother of the Winds.

"What good I have done, others may relate," said he; "but here comes my brother of the West. I love him the best of all; he smells of the sea, and has a right healthy coldness about him."

"Can that be the delicate Zephyr?" asked the Prince.

"Yes, it is Zephyr certainly," said the old woman; "but delicate he is no longer. In days of yore he was a gallant youth; but those times have long passed away."

The West Wind looked like a wild man, but he had on a sort of padded hat, that he might not be hurt. In his hand he held a club of mahogany wood, hewn in the American forests; it could have been hewn nowhere else.

"Whence come you?" said the mother.

"From those forest wastes," said he, "where the thorny lianas weave hedges between the trees, where the water snake reposes in the damp grass, and men are apparently useless."

"What did you there?"

"I looked at the deep river, marked how it hurled itself from the rocks, and flew like dust towards the clouds, that it might give birth to the rainbow. I saw a buffalo swim down the river—the stream carried him away; a flock of wild geese were swimming also—they flew away when the water fell down the precipice; but the buffalo must have plunged with it—that pleased me, and I then raised such a storm that the primeval old trees fell to the ground with a crash, broken to splinters."

"And have you done nothing else?" said the old woman.

"I have cut capers in the Savannahs; I have ridden wild horses, and shaken cocoanut-trees—ah, yes, I have such stories to tell! But we must not tell all we know, that you know well, my old mother!" And he kissed his mother so roughly that she almost fell. He was a wild fellow.

Now came the South Wind in his turban, and floating Bedouin mantle.

"It is very cold here," said he, as he threw wood upon the fire; "one may see that the North Wind has arrived before me."

"It is so hot that a polar bear might be roasted here," said the North Wind.

"Thou art thyself a polar bear," said the South Wind.

"Do you wish, both of you, to go into the sack?" asked the old woman. "Sit down on yonder stone, and tell me where you have been."

"In Africa, mother," answered he. "I have been hunting lions in the land of the Kaffirs, along with the Hottentots. Such beautiful grass grows on those plains, green as olives! The gnu danced there, and the ostrich ran races with me; but I am swifter than he.

"I came to the yellow sands of the desert; there one might fancy oneself at the bottom of the sea. I met with a caravan; they had just killed their last camel, in hopes of getting water to drink; but they did not find much. The sun was burning over their heads, the sands roasting beneath their feet. There seemed no end to the desert. I rolled myself up in the fine, loose sand, and threw it up into the form of an immense pillar; a famous dance it had!

"You should have seen how puzzled the dromedary looked, and how the merchant drew his caftan over his head. He threw himself down before me as he was accustomed to do before Allah. There they are all buried; a pyramid of sand stands over them: if I should one day blow it away, the sun will bleach their bones; and travellers will see that human beings have passed that way before them; otherwise they would hardly believe it."

"Then you have only done evil!" said the mother. "March into the sack!" and before he was aware of it, the South Wind was seized, and confined in the sack, which rolled about on the floor until the mother sat down on it; and then he was obliged to be still.

"These are desperately wild fellows," said the Prince.

"Yes, truly," answered she; "but they must obey. Here is the fourth."

This was the East Wind, who was dressed like a man.

"So you come from that corner of the world," said the mother. "I thought you had been to the Garden of Paradise?"

"I shall fly there to-morrow," said the East Wind; "it is a hundred years to-morrow since I was there. I now come from China, where I danced round the porcelain tower, so that all the bells began to ring. In the street below, the officers were being flogged till the bamboo canes broke upon their shoulders; and there were people, from the first to the ninth rank, who cried out, 'Thanks, thanks, my fatherly bene-factor!' But they did not mean what they said; and I clinked the bells and sang, 'Tsing, tsang, tsu!'"

"Thou art a wild youth," said the mother; "it is well that thou goest to-morrow to the Garden of Paradise, as thy visits there always contribute to thy improvement. Remember to drink plentifully from the source of wisdom, and bring me a little flask filled with it."

"I will do so," said the East Wind. "But why hast thou put my brother of the south into the sack? Let him come out; I want him to tell me all about the bird called the phoenix. The Princess in the Garden of Paradise, when I visit her once in a hundred years, always asks me about that bird. Open the sack, my ever sweetest mother, and I will give thee two cups full of tea, as fresh and green as when I plucked it."

"Well, then, for the sake of the tea, and because thou art my darling, I will open the sack." She did so, and the South Wind crept forth; but he looked very much cast down be-cause the stranger Prince had seen his disgrace.

"Here is a palm leaf for the Princess," said the South Wind; "it was given to me by the old phoenix—the only one in the world. He has scribbled on it, with his beak, the history of his whole life; the Princess can read it herself.

"I saw the phoenix set fire to his own nest; I saw him as he sat within it, and was consumed like a Hindoo wife. How the dry branches crackled, and how pleasant was the odour that arose from the burning nest! At last everything was consumed by the flames, and the old phoenix was in ashes. But his egg lay glowing in the fire, it burst with a loud noise, and the young one flew out. He is now king over all the birds, and the only phoenix in the world. He has bitten a hole in the leaf I gave you; that is his greeting to the Princess."

"Well, now let us have something to eat," said the mother of the Winds; and accordingly they all sat down to partake of the roasted stag. The Prince sat next to the East Wind, and they soon became good friends.

"Only tell me this," began the Prince; "what Princess is that I heard so much about; and where is the Garden of Paradise?"

"Ha, ha!" said the East Wind, "do you want to go there? Well, then, fly with me to-morrow; but I must tell you that no human being has been there since Adam and Eve's time. You know the Scripture history, I suppose?"

"Of course," said the Prince.

"Well, when they were driven out of it, the Garden of Paradise sank under the earth; but it still retained its warm sunshine, its balmy air, and all its beauty. The queen of the fairies makes it her abode; and there also is the Island of Bliss, where death never comes, and where life is so beautiful! If you seat yourself on my back to-morrow, I will take you there; I think that may be allowed. But do not talk any longer now, for I wish to sleep."

And accordingly they all went to sleep. The Prince awoke early in the morning, and was not a little astonished to find himself already far above the clouds. He was sitting on the back of the East Wind, who kept tight hold of him, and they flew so high that woods and meadows, rivers and seas, appeared like a large illuminated map.

"Good-morning!" said the East Wind; "you may as well sleep a little longer, for there is not much to be seen on the flat surface beneath us, unless you can find amusement in counting churches; they stand like little bits of chalk on the green board there below." What he called the green board, were fields and meadows.

"It was uncivil to depart, without taking leave of your mother and brothers," said the Prince.

"That may be excused, as you were asleep," said the East Wind. And now, they flew even faster than before; how fast, might be seen by the tops of the trees, whose branches and leaves rustled as they passed them; and by the seas and lakes, for as they crossed them the waves rose higher, and large ships bowed low like swans in the water.

In the evening, when it became dark, the large towns had a most curious appearance. Lights were burning here and there; it was just like watching the sparks on a burnt piece of paper, as they vanish one after another, till at last, as children say, out goes the sexton and his family.

The Prince clapped his hands, but the East Wind begged him to be quiet and to hold fast, as otherwise he might fall, and remain suspended from the top of a church-steeple.

The eagle flew swiftly over the dark woods, but the East Wind flew still more swiftly; the Cossack galloped over the desert on his little horse, but the Prince rode in a very different manner.

"Now can you see the Himalaya Mountains," said the East Wind; "they are the highest in Asia: we shall soon come to the Garden of Paradise." So they turned more towards the south, and soon inhaled the fragrance of spices and flowers. Figs and pomegranates were growing wild; red and white grapes hung from the vines. Here they descended, and stretched themselves on the soft grass, while the flowers nodded to the Wind, as if they wished to say, "Welcome, welcome!"

"Are we now in the Garden of Paradise?" asked the Prince.

"No, not yet," said the East Wind, "but we shall soon be there. Do you see yonder rock, and the large cave, in front of which the vine branches hang like large green curtains? We must go through it. Wrap your cloak around you; the sun burns here; but take a step farther, and you will find it as cold as ice. The bird which is flying past the cave has one wing warm as summer, and the other as cold as winter."

"So that is the way to the Garden of Paradise," said the Prince.

VERNON SOPER

They went into the cave. Oh, how freezing it was there! But this did not last long; the East Wind spread out his wings; they shone like the purest flames. Oh, what a cavern! large blocks of stone, from which water was trickling, hung in the strangest forms above them. The cave was now so narrow that they were obliged to creep along on their hands and feet, and now again high and broad as the free air without. It looked like a subterranean chapel, with mute organ-pipes and petrified organ.

"Surely we are going through the path of Death to the Garden of Paradise," said the Prince. But the East Wind answered not a syllable, and pointed to where the loveliest blue light was beaming to meet them. The rocks above them became more and more like mists, and at last were as clear and bright as a white cloud in the moonlight. They now breathed the softest, balmiest air—fresh as among the mountains, fragrant as among the roses of the valley.

Here flowed a river, as clear as the atmosphere itself. Gold and silver fish swam in it; purple eels, which emitted blue sparks at every motion, were playing beneath the surface; and the broad leaves of the water-lily shone with all the colours of the rainbow. The flower itself was like a glowing orange-coloured flame, receiving sustenance from the water, as a lamp from oil. A bridge of marble, shining like glassy pearl, cunningly and delicately carved, led over the water to the Island of Bliss, where bloomed the Garden of Paradise.

The East Wind took the Prince in his arms and bore him over. The flowers and leaves sang the sweetest songs about his childhood, in soft, wavy tones, such as no human voice could imitate.

Whether they were palm-trees or gigantic water-plants that grew here the Prince knew not, but he had never before seen trees so large and full of sap; and hanging about them in long wreaths were the most singular creepers, such as are seen, painted in gold or bright colours, on the margins of old missals, or winding about initial letters. There were the strangest compounds of birds, flowers, and scrolls.

Close to them, in the grass, stood a flock of peacocks, with their bright tails spread out—yes, indeed, they were peacocks

—but no, when the Prince touched them, he found they were not birds but plants. They were large plantain-leaves, that sparkled like the splendid tails of peacocks.

Lions and tigers sprang like cats over green and fragrant hedges, as the flowers of the olive; and both lions and tigers were tame. The timid wood-turtle, her plumage bright as the loveliest pearl, flapped her wings against the lion's mane; and the shy antelope stood by, and nodded his head as if he wished to play too.

And now came the Fairy of Paradise. Her garments shone like the sun, and her countenance was as gentle as that of a happy mother rejoicing over her child. She was very young and very beautiful; the fairest of maidens followed her, each having a star sparkling in her hair. The East Wind gave her the leaf of the phoenix, and her eyes beamed with joy.

She took the Prince by the hand, and led him into her palace, the walls of which resembled in colours those of a splendid tulip-petal held towards the sun; the dome was formed by one single bright flower, whose cup appeared the deeper the longer you looked into it.

The Prince stepped to the window and looked through one of the panes; he saw the Tree of Knowledge, with the Serpent, and Adam and Eve, standing by its side. "Were they not driven out?" asked he; and the Fairy smiled, and explained to him, that Time had stamped its image upon every pane, though not such images as we are accustomed to see; nay, rather, there was life itself; the leaves of the trees moved; men came and went, as in a mirror.

He looked through another pane, and there saw Jacob's dream, the ladder rose to Heaven, and angels with their large wings hovered up and down. Yes, everything that had happened in the world lived and moved in these panes of glass. Time only could have made such cunning pictures.

The Fairy smiled, and led the Prince into a high, spacious hall, whose walls seemed covered with transparent paintings, each countenance more lovely than the last. They were millions of blessed spirits, who smiled and sang; the uppermost of them so little, so very little, even more diminutive than the smallest rosebud, marked on paper with one touch.

And in the midst of the hall stood a large tree with luxuriant branches; golden apples, of different sizes, hung like oranges among the green leaves. This was the Tree of Knowledge, the fruit of which Adam and Eve had eaten. From every leaf there dropped a bright red drop of dew; it seemed as if the tree wept tears of blood.

"Let us get into the boat," said the Fairy; "we shall find it so refreshing. The boat is rocked on the swelling waves, without stirring from its place; but all the countries in the world will appear to glide past us."

And it was strange to see all the coast moving: first came the high, snow-covered Alps, with their clouds and dark fir-trees; the horn's deep melancholy tones were heard, whilst the herdsman was singing merrily in the valley below.

Then the banyan-trees let their long hanging branches fall into the boat; coal-black swans glided along the water, and the strangest-looking animals and flowers were to be seen on the shore: it was New Holland which succeeded the high, blue Alps.

And now came the hymns of priests, the dance of savages, accompanied by the noise of drums, and of the wooden tuba. Egypt's cloud-aspiring pyramids, overthrown pillars, and sphinxes sailed by.

The northern lights beamed over the icy mountains of the north; they were fireworks such as no mortal could imitate. The Prince was so happy! He saw a hundred times more than we have related here.

"And may I stay here always?" asked he.

"That depends upon thyself," answered the Fairy. "If thou dost not, like Adam, allow thyself to be led to do what is forbidden, thou mayest stay here always."

"I will not touch the apple on the Tree of Knowledge," said the Prince; "there are a thousand fruits here quite as beautiful!"

"Examine thyself: if thou art not strong enough, return with the East Wind who brought thee; he is just going to fly back, and will not return for a hundred years. The time will pass away here as if it were only a hundred hours; but it is a long time for temptation and sin.

"Every evening when I leave thee, I must invite thee to 'Come with me!' I must beckon to thee, but—beware of attending to my call; come not with me, for every step will but increase the temptation. Thou wilt come into the hall where the Tree of Knowledge stands; I shall sleep among its fragrant hanging branches; thou wilt bend over me, and if thou touchest me, Paradise will sink beneath the earth, and be lost to thee. The sharp wind of the desert will whistle around; the cold rain will drip from thy hair; sorrow and care will be thy inheritance."

"I will stay here," said the Prince. And the East Wind kissed his forehead, and said, "Be strong, and we shall see each other again after a hundred years. Farewell, farewell!" And the East Wind spread out his great wings; they shone like lightning in harvest-time, or the northern lights in winter. Farewell, farewell, resounded from the trees and flowers. Storks and pelicans, like a long streaming ribbon, flew after him, accompanying him to the boundary of the garden.

"Now we will begin our dances," said the Fairy, "and when the sun is sinking, while I am dancing with thee, thou wilt see me beckon, thou wilt hear me say, 'Come with me'; but do not follow. For a hundred years I must repeat this call to thee every evening; and every day thy strength will increase, till at last thou wilt not even think of following. This evening will be the first time—I have warned thee!"

The Fairy then led him into a large hall of white transparent lilies; their yellow stamens formed little golden harps, sending forth clear sweet tones resembling those of the flute.

And the sun was setting; the whole sky was like pure gold; and the lilies shone amid the purple gleam, like the loveliest roses. The Prince saw the background of the hall opening, where stood the Tree of Knowledge in a splendour which dazzled his eyes; a song floated over him, sweet and gentle as his mother's voice. It seemed as if she said, "My child; my dear, dear child!"

Then the Fairy beckoned gracefully, saying, "Come with me, come with me!" and he rushed to her, forgetting his promise, even on the first evening.

The fragrance, the spicy fragrance around, became

stronger; the harps sounded more sweetly; and it seemed as if the millions of smiling heads, in the hall where the Tree was growing, nodded and sang, "Let us know everything? Man is lord of the earth!" And they were no longer tears of blood that dropped from the leaves of the Tree of Knowledge; they were red sparkling stars—so it appeared to him.

"Come with me, come with me!" thus spoke those trembling tones; and the Fairy bent the boughs asunder, and in another moment was concealed within them.

"I have not yet sinned," said the Prince, "neither will I;" and he flung aside the boughs where she was sleeping—beautiful as only the Fairy of the Garden of Paradise could be. She smiled as she slept; he bent over her, and saw tears tremble behind her eyelashes. "Weepest thou on my account?" whispered he. "Weep not, loveliest of creatures!" and he kissed the tears from her eyes.

There was a fearful clap of thunder, more loud and deep than had ever been heard; all things rushed together in wild confusion; the charming Fairy vanished; the blooming Paradise sank low, so low! The Prince saw it sink amid the darkness of night; it beamed in the distance like a little glimmering star; a deadly coldness shot through his limbs; his eyes closed, and he lay for some time apparently dead.

The cold rain beat upon his face, the sharp wind blew upon his forehead, when the Prince's consciousness returned.

"What have I done?" said he. "I have sinned like Adam; I have sinned, and Paradise has sunk low, beneath the earth!"

And he opened his eyes and saw the star in the distance—the star which sparkled like his lost Paradise; it was the morning star in Heaven.

He stood upright, and found himself in the wood, near the Cavern of the Winds. The mother of the Winds sat by his side; she looked very angry, and raised her hand.

"Already, on the first evening!" said she. "Truly I expected it. Well, if thou wert my son, thou shouldst go forthwith into the sack."

"He shall go there!" said Death. He was a strong old man, with a scythe in his hand, and with large black wings.

"He shall be laid in the coffin, but not now. I shall mark

him. Suffer him to wander yet a little while upon the earth, and repent of his sin; he may improve, he may grow good. I shall return one day when he least expects it; I shall lay him in the black coffin.

"If his head and heart are still full of sin, he will sink lower than the Garden of Paradise sank; but if he have become good and holy, I shall put the coffin on my head, and fly to the star yonder. The Garden of Paradise blooms there also; he shall enter, and remain in the star, that bright sparkling star, for ever!"

THE STORKS

ON the roof of a house situated at the extremity of a small town, a stork had built his nest. There sat the mother-stork, with her four young ones, who all stretched out their little black bills, which had not yet become red. Not far off, upon the parapet, erect and proud, stood the father-stork; he had drawn one of his legs under him, being weary of standing on two. You might have fancied him carved in wood, he stood so motionless. "It looks so grand," thought he, "for my wife to have a sentinel to keep guard over her nest. People cannot know that I am her husband, they will certainly think that I am commanded to stand here; how well it looks!" and so he remained standing on one leg.

In the street below, a number of children were playing together. When they saw the storks, one of the liveliest amongst them began to sing as much as he could remember of some old rhymes about storks, in which he was soon joined by the others.

"Stork! stork! long-legged stork!
Into thy nest, I prithee, walk;
There sits thy mate,
With her four children so great.
The first we'll hang like a cat,
The second we'll burn,

> The third on a spit we'll turn,
> The fourth drown dead as a rat!"

"Only listen to what the boys are singing," said the little storks; "they say we shall be hanged and burned!"

"Never mind," said the mother, "don't listen to them; they will do you no harm."

But the boys went on singing, and pointed their fingers at the storks: only one little boy, called Peter, said it was a sin to mock and tease animals, and that he would have nothing to do with it.

The mother-stork again tried to comfort her little ones. "Never mind," said she; "see how calmly your father is standing there, and upon one leg only."

"But we are so frightened!" said the young ones, drawing their heads down into the nest.

The next day, when the children were again assembled to play together, and saw the storks, they again began their song.

> "The first we'll hang like a cat,
> The second we'll burn!"

"And are we really to be hanged and burned?" asked the young storks.

"No indeed!" said the mother. "You shall learn to fly: I will teach you myself. Then we can fly over to the meadow, and pay a visit to the frogs. They will bow to us in the water, and say, 'Croak, croak!' and then we shall eat them; will not that be nice?"

"And what then?" asked the little storks.

"Then all the storks in the country will gather together, and the autumn exercise will begin. It is of the greatest importance that you should fly well then; for every one who does not, the general will stab to death with his bill. So you must pay great attention when we begin to drill you, and learn very quickly."

"Then we shall really be killed after all, as the boys said. Oh, listen! they are singing it again."

"Attend to me, and not to them!" said the mother. "After the grand exercise, we shall fly to warm countries far, far away from here, over mountains and forests. We shall fly to Egypt, where are the three-cornered stone houses whose tops reach the clouds; they are called pyramids, and are older than it is possible for storks to imagine. There is a river, too, which overflows its banks so as to make the whole country like a marsh, and we shall go into the marsh and eat frogs."

"Oh!" said the young ones.

"Yes, it is delightful! One does nothing but eat all the day long. And while we are so comfortable, in this country not a single green leaf is left on the trees; and it is so cold that the clouds are frozen, and fall down upon the earth in little white pieces."

She meant snow, but she could not express herself more clearly.

"And will the naughty boys be frozen to pieces too?" asked the young storks.

"No, they will not be frozen to pieces; but they will be nearly as badly off as if they were: they will be obliged to crowd round the fire in their little dark rooms; while you, on the contrary, will be flying about in sunny lands, where there are beautiful flowers and warm sunshine."

Well, time passed away, and the young storks grew so tall that when they stood upright in the nest they could see the country around to a great distance. The father-stork used to bring them every day the nicest little frogs, as well as snails, and all the other stork tit-bits he could find. Oh! it was so droll to see him show them his tricks; he would lay his head upon his tail, make a rattling noise with his bill, and then tell them such charming stories all about the moors.

"Now you must learn to fly!" said the mother one day; and accordingly, all the four young storks were obliged to come out upon the parapet. Oh! how they trembled! And though they balanced themselves on their wings, they were very near falling.

"Only look at me," said the mother. "This is the way you must hold your heads; and in this manner place you feet— one, two! one, two! this will help you to get on." She flew a little way, and the young ones made an awkward spring after her—bounce! down they fell; for their bodies were heavy.

"I will not fly," said one of the young ones, as he crept back into the nest. "I do not want to go into the warm countries!"

"Do you want to be frozen to death during the winter? Shall the boys come and hang, burn, or roast you? Wait a little, I will call them!"

"Oh, no!" said the little stork; and again he began to hop about on the roof like the others. By the third day they could fly pretty well, and so they thought they could also sit and take their ease in the air; but bounce! down they tumbled, and found themselves obliged to make use of their wings. The boys now came into the street, singing their favourite song.

"Stork! stork! long-legged stork!"

"Shall not we fly down and peck out their eyes?" said the young ones.

"No, leave them alone!" said the mother. "Attend to me, that is of much more importance!—one, two, three, now to the right! one, two three, now to the left, round the chimney-pot! That was very well; you managed your wings so neatly last time that I will let you come with me tomorrow to the marsh: several first-rate stork families will be there with their children. Let it be said that mine are the prettiest and best behaved of all; and remember to stand very upright, and to throw out your chest: that looks well, and gives such an air of distinction!"

"But are we not to take revenge upon those rude boys?" asked the young ones.

"Let them screech as much as they please! You will fly among the clouds, you will go to the land of the pyramids, when they must shiver with cold, and have not a single green leaf to look at, nor a single sweet apple to eat!"

"Yes, we shall be revenged!" whispered they, one to another. And then they were drilled again.

Of all the boys in the town, the worst for singing nonsensical verses was always the same one who had begun teasing the storks, a little urchin not more than six years old. The young storks, indeed, fancied him a hundred years old, because he was bigger than either their father or their mother —and what should they know about the ages of children or grown-up human beings!

All their schemes of revenge were aimed at this little boy; he had been the first to tease them, and continued to do so. The young storks were highly excited about it, and the older they grew the less they were inclined to endure persecution. Their mother, in order to pacify them, at last promised that they should be revenged, but not until the last day of their stay in this place.

"We must first see how you behave yourselves at the grand exercise; if then you should fly badly, and the general should thrust his beak into your breast, the boys will, in some measure, be proved in the right. Let me see how well you will behave!"

"Yes, that you shall!" said the young ones. And now they really took great pains, practised every day, and at last flew so lightly and prettily that it was a pleasure to see them.

Well, now came the autumn. All the storks assembled, in order to fly together to warm countries for the winter. What a practising there was! Away they went over woods and fields, towns and villages, merely to see how well they could fly, for they had a long journey before them. The young storks distinguished themselves so honourably that they were pronounced "worthy of frogs and serpents." This was the highest character they could obtain; now they were allowed to eat frogs and serpents, and accordingly they did eat them.

"Now we will have our revenge!" said they.

"Very well!" said the mother; "I have been thinking what will be the best. I know where the pool is, in which all the little human children lie until the storks come and take them to their parents: the pretty little things sleep and dream so pleasantly as they will never dream again. All parents like to have a little child, and all children like to have a little brother or sister. We will fly to the pool and fetch one for each of the boys who has not sung that wicked song, nor made a jest of the storks; and the other naughty children shall have none."

"But he who first sang those naughty rhymes! that great

ugly fellow! what shall we do to him?" cried the young storks.

"In the pool there lies a little child who has dreamed away his life; we will take it for him, and he will weep because he has only a little dead brother. But as to the good boy who said it was a sin to mock and tease animals, surely you have not forgotten him? We will bring him two little ones, a brother and a sister. And as this little boy's name is Peter, you too, shall for the future be called 'Peter'!"

And it came to pass just as the mother said, and all the storks were called "Peter," and are still so called to this very day.

THE UGLY DUCKLING

IT was beautiful in the country—it was summertime—the wheat was yellow, the oats were green, the hay was stacked up in the green meadows, and the stork paraded about on his long red legs discoursing in Egyptian, which language he had learned from his mother. The fields and meadows were skirted by thick woods, and a deep lake lay in the midst of the woods.

Yes, it was indeed beautiful in the country! The sunshine fell warm on an old mansion, surrounded by deep canals, and from the walls down to the water's edge there grow large burdock-leaves, so high that children could stand upright among them without being perceived.

This place was as wild and unfrequented as the thickest part of the wood, and a duck had chosen to make her nest there. She was sitting on her eggs; but the pleasure she had felt at first was now almost gone, because she had been there so long, and had so few visitors, for the other ducks preferred swimming on the canals to sitting among the burdock-leaves gossiping with her.

At last the eggs cracked one after another, "Tchick, tchick!" All the eggs were alive, and one little head after another appeared. "Quack, quack," said the duck, and all got up as well as they could; they peeped about from under the green leaves, and as green is good for the eyes, their mother let them look as long as they pleased.

"How large the world is!" said the little ones, for they found their present situation very different from the former one, while they were in the eggshells.

"Do you imagine this to be the whole of the world?" said the mother. "It extends far beyond the other side of the garden, to the pastor's field; but I have never been there. Are you all here?" And then she got up. "No, I have not got you all; the largest egg is still here. How long will this last? I am so weary of it!" and then she sat down again.

"Well, and how are you getting on?" asked an old duck, who had come to pay her a visit.

"This one egg keeps me so long," said the mother, "it will not break; but you should see the others! They are the prettiest little ducklings I have seen in all my days; they are all like their father—the good-for-nothing fellow! He has not been to visit me once."

"Let me see the egg that will not break," said the old duck; "depend upon it, it is a turkey's egg. I was cheated in the same way once myself, and I had such trouble with the young ones; for they were afraid of the water, and I could not get them there. I called and scolded, but it was all of no use. But let me see the egg—ah yes! to be sure, that is a turkey's egg. Leave it, and teach the other little ones to swim."

"I will sit on it a little longer," said the duck. "I have been sitting so long, that I may as well spend the harvest here."

"It is no business of mine," said the old duck, and away she waddled.

The great egg burst at last, "Tchick, tchick," said the little one, and out it tumbled—but oh! how large and ugly it was! The duck looked at it, "That is a great, strong creature," said she, "none of the others are at all like it; can it be a young turkey-cock? Well, we shall soon find out; it must go into the water, though I push it in myself."

The next day there was delightful weather, and the sun shone warmly upon all the green leaves when mother-duck with her family went down to the canal; plump she went into the water. "Quack, quack," cried she, and one duckling after another jumped in. The water closed over their heads, but all came up again, and swam together in the pleasantest manner; their legs moved without effort. All were there, even the ugly grey one.

"No! it is not a turkey," said the old duck; "only see how prettily it moves its legs, how upright it holds itself; it is my own child! It is also really very pretty when one looks more closely at it; quack, quack, now come with me; I will take you into the world, introduce you in the duck-yard; but keep close to me, or some one may tread on you, and beware of the cat."

So they came into the duck-yard. There was a horrid noise; two families were quarrelling about the remains of an eel, which in the end was secured by the cat.

"See, my children, such is the way of the world," said the mother-duck, wiping her beak, for she too was fond of roasted eels. "Now, use your legs," said she, "keep together, and bow to the old duck you see yonder. She is the most distinguished of all the fowls present, and is of Spanish blood, which accounts for her dignified appearance and manners. And look, she has a red rag on her leg; that is considered extremely handsome, and is the greatest distinction a duck can have. Don't turn your feet inwards; a well-educated duckling always keeps his legs far apart, like his father and mother, just so—look! Now bow your necks, and say 'Quack!'"

And they did as they were told. But the other ducks who were in the yard looked at them and said aloud, "Only see, now we have another brood, as if there were not enough of us already; and fie! how ugly that one is, we will not endure it;" and immediately one of the ducks flew at him, and bit him in the neck.

"Leave him alone," said the mother, "he is doing no one any harm."

"Yes, but he is so large, and so strange-looking, and therefore he shall be teased."

"Those are fine children that our good mother has," said the old duck with the red rag on her leg. "All are pretty except one, and that has not turned out well; I almost wish it could be hatched over again."

"That cannot be, please your highness," said the mother. "Certainly he is not handsome, but he is a very good child, and swims as well as the others, indeed rather better. I think he will grow like the others all in good time, and perhaps will look smaller. He stayed so long in the egg-shell, that is the cause of the difference"; and she scratched the duckling's neck, and stroked his whole body. "Besides," added she, "he is a drake; I think he will be very strong, therefore it does not matter so much, as he will fight his way through."

"The other ducks are very pretty," said the old duck. "Pray make yourselves at home, and if you find an eel's head you can bring it to me."

And accordingly they made themselves at home.

But the poor little duckling who had come last out of its egg-shell, and who was so ugly, was bitten, pecked, and teased by both ducks and hens. "It is so large," said they all. And the turkey-cock who had come into the world with spurs on, and therefore fancied he was an emperor, puffed himself up like a ship in full sail, and marched up to the duckling quite red with passion. The poor little thing scarcely knew what to do; he was quite distressed, because he was so ugly, and because he was the jest of the poultry-yard.

So passed the first day, and afterwards matters grew worse and worse; the poor duckling was scorned by all. Even his brothers and sisters behaved unkindly, and were constantly saying, "I wish the cat would catch thee, thou nasty creature!" The mother said, "Ah, if thou wert only far away!" The ducks bit him, the hens pecked him, and the girl who fed the poultry kicked him.

He ran over the hedge; the little birds in the bushes were terrified. "That is because I am so ugly," thought the duckling, shutting his eyes, while he ran on. At last he came to a wide moor, where lived some wild ducks; here he lay the whole night, so tired and so comfortless.

In the morning the wild ducks flew up and perceived their new companion. "Pray, who are you?" asked they; and our little duckling turned himself in all directions, and greeted them as politely as possible.

"You are really very ugly," said the wild ducks, "however that does not matter to us, provided you do not marry into our families." Poor thing! he had never thought of marrying; he only begged leave to lie among the reeds, and drink the water of the moor.

There he lay for two whole days; on the third day there came two wild geese, or rather ganders, who had not been long out of their egg-shells, which accounts for their impertinence.

"Hark ye," said they, "you are so ugly that we like you infinitely well. Will you come with us, and be a bird of passage? On another moor, not far from this, are some dear, sweet, wild geese, as lovely creatures as have ever said 'hiss, hiss.' You are truly in the way to make your fortune, ugly as you are."

Bang! a gun went off all at once, and both wild geese were stretched dead among the reeds, and the water became red with blood;—bang! a gun went off again, whole flocks of wild geese flew up from among the reeds, and another report followed.

There was a grand hunting party; the hunters lay in ambush all around; some were even sitting in the trees, whose huge branches stretched far over the moor. The blue smoke rose through the thick trees like a mist, and was dispersed as it fell over the water; the hounds splashed about in the mud, the reeds and rushes bent in all directions. How frightened the poor little duck was! He turned his head, thinking to hide it under his wings; and in a moment a most formidable-looking dog stood close to him, his tongue hanging out of his mouth, his eyes sparkling fearfully. He opened wide his jaws at the sight of our duckling, showed him his sharp white teeth, and, splash, splash! he was gone—gone without hurting him.

"Well! let me be thankful," sighed he, "I am so ugly that even the dog will not eat me."

And now he lay still, though the shooting continued among the reeds, shot following shot.

The noise did not cease till late in the day, and even then

VERNON SOPER

the poor little thing dared not stir; he waited several hours before he looked around him, and then hastened away from the moor as fast as he could. He ran over fields and meadows, though the wind was so high that he had some difficulty in proceeding.

Towards evening he reached a wretched little hut—so wretched that it knew not on which side to fall, and therefore remained standing. The wind blew violently, so that our poor little duckling was obliged to support himself on his tail in order to stand against it; but it became worse and worse. He then remarked that the door had lost one of its hinges, and hung so much awry that he could creep through the crevice into the room—which he did.

In this room lived an old woman, with her tom-cat and her hen; and the cat, whom she called her little son, knew how to set up his back and purr; indeed he could even emit sparks when stroked the wrong way. The hen had very short legs, and was therefore called "Cuckoo Shortlegs"; she laid very good eggs, and the old woman loved her as her own child.

The next morning the new guest was perceived; the cat began to mew, and the hen to cackle.

"What is the matter?" asked the old woman, looking round; however, her eyes were not good, and so she took the young duckling to be a fat duck who had lost her way. "This is a capital catch," said she.

"I shall now have duck's eggs, if it be not a drake; we must try."

And so the duckling was put to the proof for three weeks, but no eggs made their appearance.

Now the cat was the master of the house and the hen was the mistress, and they used always to say, "We and the world," for they imagined themselves to be not only the half of the world, but also by far the better half. The duckling thought it was possible to be of a different opinion, but that the hen would not allow.

"Can you lay eggs?" asked she.

"No."

"Well, then, hold your tongue."

And the cat said, "Can you set up your back? can you purr?"

"No."

"Well, then, you should have no opinion when reasonable persons are speaking."

So the duckling sat alone in a corner, and was in a very bad humour; however, he happened to think of the fresh air and bright sunshine, and these thoughts gave him such a strong desire to swim again that he could not help telling it to the hen.

"What ails you?" said the hen. "You have nothing to do, and, therefore, brood over these fancies; either lay eggs, or purr, then you will forget them."

"But it is so delicious to swim," said the duckling; "so delicious when the waters close over your head, and you plunge to the bottom."

"Well, that is a queer sort of a pleasure," said the hen; "I think you must be crazy. Not to speak of myself, ask the cat— he is the most sensible animal I know—whether he would like to swim or to plunge to the bottom of the water. Ask our mistress, the old woman—there is no one in the world wiser than she—do you think she would take pleasure in swimming and in the waters closing over her head?"

"You do not understand me," said the duckling.

"What! we do not understand you! So you think yourself wiser than the cat and the old woman, not to speak of myself. Do not fancy any such thing, child, but be thankful for all the kindness that has been shown you. Are you not lodged in a warm room, and have you not the advantage of society from which you can learn something? But you are a simpleton, and it is wearisome to have anything to do with you. Believe me, I wish you well. I tell you unpleasant truths, but it is thus that real friendship is shown. Come, for once give yourself the trouble to learn to purr, or to lay eggs."

"I think I will go out into the wide world again," said the duckling.

"Well, go," answered the hen.

So the duckling went. He swam on the surface of the water, he plunged beneath, but all animals passed him by, on account of his ugliness. And the autumn came, the leaves turned yellow and brown, the wind caught them and danced them about; the air was very cold, the clouds were heavy with hail or snow, and the raven sat on the hedge and croaked. The poor duckling was certainly not very comfortable!

One evening, just as the sun was setting with unusual brilliancy, a flock of large beautiful birds rose from out of the brushwood; the duckling had never seen anything so beautiful before; their plumage was of a dazzling white, and they had long slender necks. They were swans; they uttered a singular cry, spread out their long, splendid wings, and flew away from these cold regions to warmer countries across the open sea. They flew so high, so very high! and the little ugly duckling's feelings were so strange; he turned round and round in the water like a mill-wheel, strained his neck to look after them, and sent forth such a loud and strange cry that it almost frightened himself.

Ah! he could not forget them, those noble birds! those happy birds! When he could see them no longer, he plunged to the bottom of the water, and when he rose again was almost beside himself. The duckling knew not what the birds were called, knew not whither they were flying, yet he loved them as he had never before loved anything. He envied them not; it would never have occurred to him to wish such beauty for himself; he would have been quite contented if the ducks in the duck-yard had only endured his company—the poor ugly animal.

And the winter was so cold, so cold! The duckling was obliged to swim round and round in the water, to keep it from freezing; but every night the opening in which he swam became smaller and smaller. It froze so that the crust of ice crackled; the duckling was obliged to make good use of his legs to prevent the water from freezing entirely; at last, wearied out, he lay stiff and cold in the ice.

Early in the morning there passed by a peasant who saw him, broke the ice in pieces with his wooden shoe, and brought him home to his wife.

He now revived; the children would have played with him, but our duckling thought they wished to tease him, and in his terror jumped into the milk-pail, so that the milk was spilled about the room. The good woman screamed and clapped her hands; he flew thence into the pan where the butter was kept, and thence into the meal-barrel, and out again, and then how strange he looked!

The woman screamed, and struck at him with the tongs; the children ran races with each other trying to catch him, and laughed and screamed likewise. It was well for him that the door stood open; he jumped out among the bushes into the new-fallen snow, and lay there as in a dream.

But it would be too melancholy to relate all the trouble and misery that he was obliged to suffer during the severity of the winter. He was lying on a moor among the reeds, when the sun began to shine warmly again; the larks sang, and beautiful spring had returned.

And once more he shook his wings. They were stronger than formerly, and bore him forwards quickly; and before he was well aware of it he was in a large garden where the apple-trees stood in full bloom, where the syringas sent forth their fragrance and hung their long green branches down into the winding canal! Oh! everything was so lovely, so full of the freshness of spring! And out of the thicket came three beautiful white swans. They displayed their feathers so proudly, and swam so lightly, so lightly! The duckling knew the glorious creatures, and was seized with a strange melancholy.

"I will fly to them, those kingly birds!" said he. "They will kill me, because I, ugly as I am, have presumed to approach them; but it matters not, better to be killed by them than to be bitten by the ducks, pecked by the hens, kicked by the girl who feeds the poultry, and to have so much to suffer during the winter!" He flew into the water, and swam towards the beautiful creatures; they saw him and shot forward to meet him. "Only kill me," said the poor animal, and he bowed his head low, expecting death. But what did he see in the water? He saw beneath him his own form, no longer that of a plump, ugly grey bird—it was that of a swan.

It matters not to have been born in a duck-yard if one has been hatched from a swan's egg.

The good creature felt himself really elevated by all the

troubles and adversities he had experienced. He could now rightly estimate his own happiness, and the larger swans swam round him, and stroked him with their beaks.

Some little children were running about in the garden; they threw grain and bread into the water, and the youngest exclaimed, "There is a new one!" The others also cried out, "Yes, a new swan has come!" and they clapped their hands and danced around. They ran to their father and mother, bread and cake were thrown into the water, and every one said, "The new one is the best, so young, and so beautiful!" and the old swans bowed before him.

The young swan felt quite ashamed, and hid his head under his wings; he scarcely knew what to do, he was all too happy, but still not proud—for a good heart is never proud.

He remembered how he had been persecuted and scorned, and he now heard every one say he was the most beautiful of all beautiful birds. The syringas bent down their branches towards him low into the water, and the sun shone warmly and brightly. He shook his feathers, stretched his slender neck, and in the joy of his heart said, "How little did I dream of so much happiness when I was the ugly despised duckling!"

THE CONSTANT TIN SOLDIER

THERE were once five-and-twenty tin soldiers, all brothers, for they had all been made out of one old tin spoon. They carried muskets in their arms, and held themselves very upright, and their uniforms were red and blue—very gay indeed.

The first word they heard in this world, when the lid was taken off the box in which they lay, was "Tin soldiers!" It was a little boy who made this exclamation, clapping his hands at the same time. They had been given to him because it was his birthday, and he now set them out on the table.

The soldiers resembled each other to a hair—one only was rather different from the rest; he had but one leg, for he had been made last, when there was not quite enough tin left.

However, he stood as firmly upon his one leg as the others did upon their two; and this identical tin soldier it is whose fortunes seem to us worthy of record.

On the table where the tin soldiers were set out were several other playthings, but the most charming of them all was a pretty pasteboard castle. Through its little windows one could look into the rooms. In front of the castle stood some tiny trees, clustering round a little mirror intended to represent a lake, and waxen swans swam in the lake and were reflected on its surface.

All this was very pretty, but prettiest of all was a little damsel standing in the open doorway of the castle; she, too, was cut out of pasteboard, but she had on a frock of the clearest muslin, a little sky-blue ribbon was flung across her shoulders like a scarf, and in the midst of this scarf was set a bright gold wing. The little lady stretched out both her arms, for she was a dancer, and raised one of her legs so high in the air that the tin soldier could not find it, and fancied that she had, like him, only one leg.

"That would be just the wife for me," thought he, "but then, she is of rather too high rank; she lives in a castle. I have only a box; and besides, there are all our five-and-twenty men in it; it is no place for her.

"However, there will be no harm in my making acquaintance with her," and so he stationed himself behind a snuff-box that stood on the table; from this place he had a full view of the delicate little lady, who still remained standing on one leg, yet without losing her balance.

When evening came, all the other tin soldiers were put away into the box, and the people of the house went to bed. The playthings now began to play in their turn; they pretended to visit, to fight battles, and give balls. The tin soldiers rattled in the box, for they wanted to play too, but the lid would not come off. The nut-crackers cut capers, and the slate-pencil played at commerce on the slate; there was such a racket that the canary bird woke up, and began to talk too, but he always talked in verse.

The only two who did not move from their places were the tin soldier and the little dancer; she constantly remained in her graceful position, standing on the point of her foot, with out-stretched arms; and, as for him, he stood just as firmly on his one leg, never for one moment turning his eyes away from her.

Twelve o'clock struck. Crash! Open sprang the lid of the snuff-box, but there was no snuff inside it; no, out jumped a little black conjurer, in fact it was a Jack-in-the-box. "Tin soldier!" said the conjurer, "wilt thou keep thine eyes to thyself?"

But the tin soldier pretended not to hear.

"Well, only wait till to-morrow!" quoth the conjurer.

When the morrow had come, and the children were out of bed, the tin soldier was placed on the window-ledge, and, whether the conjurer or the wind occasioned it, all at once the window flew open, and out fell the tin soldier, head foremost from the third story to the ground.

A dreadful fall was that! His one leg turned over and over in the air, and at last he rested, poised on his soldier's cap, with his bayonet between the paving stones.

The maid-servant and the little boy immediately came down to look for him; but, although they very nearly trod on him, they could not see him. If the tin soldier had but called out, "Here I am!" they might easily have found him; but he thought it would not be becoming for him to cry out, as he was in uniform.

It now began to rain; every drop fell heavier than the last; there was a regular shower. When it was over two boys came by. "Look!" said one, "here is a tin soldier; he shall have a sail for once in his life."

So they made a boat out of an old newspaper, put the tin soldier into it, and away he sailed down the gutter, both the boys running along by the side and clapping their hands. The paper boat rocked to and fro, and every now and then veered round so quickly that the tin soldier became quite giddy; still he moved not a muscle, looked straight before him, and held his bayonet tightly clasped.

All at once the boat sailed under a long gutter-board; he found it as dark here as at home in his own box.

"Where shall I get to next?" thought he. "Yes, to be sure,

it is all that conjurer's doing! Ah, if the little maiden were but sailing with me in the boat I would not care for its being twice as dark!"

Just then a great water-rat that lived under the gutter-board darted out.

"Have you a passport?" asked the rat. "Where is your passport?"

But the tin soldier was silent, and held his weapon with a still firmer grasp. The boat sailed on, and the rat followed. Oh! how furiously he showed his teeth, and cried out to sticks and straws, "Stop him, stop him! he has not paid the toll; he has not shown his passport!"

But the stream grew stronger and stronger. The tin soldier could already catch a glimpse of the bright daylight before the boat came from under the tunnel, but at the same time he heard a roaring noise, at which the boldest heart might well have trembled.

Only fancy! where the tunnel ended the water of the gutter fell perpendicularly into a great canal; this was as dangerous for the tin soldier as sailing down a mighty waterfall would be for us.

He was now so close that he could no longer stand upright; the boat darted forwards; the poor tin soldier held himself as stiff and immovable as possible; no one could accuse him of having even blinked. The boat spun round and round three, nay, four times, and was filled with water to the brim; it must sink. The tin soldier stood up to his neck in water; deeper and deeper sank the boat, softer and softer grew the paper. The water went over the soldier's head, and he thought of the pretty little dancer whom he should never see again, and these words rang in his ears:

> "Wild adventure, mortal danger
> Be thy portion, valiant stranger!"

The paper now tore asunder, the tin soldier fell through the rent; but, in the same moment, he was swallowed up by a large fish. Oh, how dark it was, worse even than under the gutter-board, and so narrow too! But the tin soldier's resolution was as constant as ever; there he lay, at full length, shouldering his arms.

The fish turned and twisted about, and made the strangest movements. At last he became quite still; a flash of lightning, as it were, darted through him. The daylight shone brightly, and someone exclaimed, "Tin soldier!" The fish had been caught, taken to the market, sold, and brought home into the kitchen, where the servant girl was cutting him up with a large knife.

She seized the tin soldier by the middle with two of her fingers, and took him into the parlour, where every one was eager to see the wonderful man who had travelled in the maw of a fish; however, our little warrior was by no means proud. They set him on the table, and there—no, how could anything so extraordinary happen in this world?—the tin soldier was in the very same room in which he had been before.

He saw the same children, the same playthings stood on the table, among them the beautiful castle with the pretty little dancing maiden, who was still standing upon one leg, while she held the other high in the air; she, too, was constant. It quite affected the tin soldier; he could have found it in his heart to weep tin tears, but such weakness would have been unbecoming in a soldier. He looked at her and she looked at him, but neither spoke a word.

And now one of the little boys took the soldier and threw him without ceremony into the stove. He did not give any reason for so doing, but no doubt, the conjurer in the snuff-box must have had a hand in it.

The tin soldier now stood in a blaze of red light; he felt extremely hot. Whether this heat was the result of the actual fire or of the flames of love within him, he knew not. He had entirely lost his colour. Whether this change had happened during his travels, or were the effect of strong emotion, I know not. He looked upon the little damsel, she looked upon him, and he felt that he was melting; but, constant as ever, he still stood shouldering his arms.

A door opened, the wind seized the dancer, and, like a sylph, she flew straightway into the stove to the tin soldier; they both flamed up into a blaze, and were gone. The soldier was melted to a hard lump, and then the maid took out the ashes the next day she found his remains in the shape of a little tin heart; of the dancer there remained only the gold wing, and that was burned black as coal.

THE SHEPHERDESS AND THE CHIMNEY-SWEEPER

HAVE you seen an old-fashioned oaken-wood cabinet, quite black with age and covered with varnish and arving-work?

Just such a piece of furniture, an old heirloom that had been the property of its present mistress's great-grandmother, once stood in a parlour. It was carved from top to bottom—roses, tulips, and little stags' heads with long branching antlers, peering forth from the curious scrolls and foliage surrounding them. Moreover, in the centre panel of the cabinet was carved the full-length figure of a man, who seemed to be perpetually grinning, perhaps at himself, for in truth he was a most ridiculous figure; he had crooked legs, small horns on his forehead, and a long beard.

The children of the house used to call him "the crooked-legged Field-Marshal-Major-General-Corporal-Sergeant," for this was a long hard name, and not many figures, whether carved in wood or in stone, could boast of such a title.

There he stood, his eyes always fixed upon the table under the pier-glass, for on this table stood a pretty little porcelain shepherdess, her mantle gathered gracefully round her, and fastened with a red rose; her shoes and hat were gilt; her hand held a crook. Oh, she was charming!

Close by her stood a little chimney-sweeper, likewise of porcelain. He was as clean and neat as any of the other figures; indeed, the manufacturer might just as well have made a prince as a chimney-sweeper of him, for though elsewhere black as coal, his face was fresh and rosy as a girl's, which was certainly a mistake; it ought to have been black. His ladder in his hand, there he kept his station, close by the little shepherdess. They had been placed together from the first, had always remained on the same spot, and had thus plighted their troth to each other; they suited each other so well; they were both young people, both of the same kind of porcelain, both alike fragile and delicate.

Not far off stood a figure three times as large as the others. It was an old Chinese mandarin who could nod his head; he too was of porcelain, and declared that he was grandfather to the little shepherdess. He could not prove his assertion; however, he insisted that he had authority over her, and so, when the crooked-legged Field-Marshal-Major-General-Corporal-Sergeant made proposals to the little shepherdess, he nodded his head in token of his consent.

"Now you will have a husband," said the old mandarin to her, "a husband who, I verily believe, is of mahogany wood; you will be the wife of a Field-Marshal-Major-General-Corporal-Sergeant, of a man who has a whole cabinet full of silver-plate, besides a store of no one knows what in the secret drawers!"

"I will not go into that dismal cabinet!" declared the little shepherdess. "I have heard say that eleven porcelain ladies are already imprisoned there."

"Then you shall be the twelfth, and you will be in good company!" rejoined the mandarin. "This very night, when the old cabinet creaks, your nuptials shall be celebrated, as sure as I am a Chinese mandarin!"

Whereupon he nodded his head and fell asleep.

But the little shepherdess wept, and turned to the beloved of her heart, the porcelain chimney-sweeper.

"I believe I must ask you," said she, "to go out with me into the wide world, for here we cannot stay."

"I will do everything you wish," replied the little chimney-sweeper; "let us go at once. I think I can support you by my profession."

"If you could but get off the table!" sighed she. "I shall never be happy till we are away, out in the wide world."

And he comforted her, and showed her how to set her little foot on the carved edges and gilded foliage twining round the leg of the table, till at last they reached the floor. But turning to look at the old cabinet, they saw everything in a grand commotion; all the carved stags putting their little heads farther out, raising their antlers, and moving their throats, whilst the crooked-legged Field-Marshal-Major-General-Corporal-Sergeant sprang up, and shouted out to the old Chinese mandarin, "Look, they are eloping! they are eloping!" They were not a little frightened, and quickly jumped into an open drawer for protection.

In this drawer there were three or four incomplete packs of cards, and also a little puppet-theatre; a play was being performed, and all the queens, whether of diamonds, hearts, clubs, or spades, sat in the front row fanning themselves with the flowers they held in their hands. Behind them stood the knaves, showing that they had each two heads, one above and one below, as most cards have. The play was about two persons who were crossed in love, and the shepherdess wept over it, for it was just like her own history.

"I cannot bear this!" said she. "Let us leave the drawer." But when they had again reached the floor, on looking up at the table, they saw that the old Chinese mandarin had awakened, and was rocking his whole body to and fro with rage.

"Oh, the old mandarin is coming!" cried the little shepherdess, and down she fell on her porcelain knees in the greatest distress.

"A sudden thought has struck me," said the chimney-sweeper. "Suppose we creep into the large pot-pourri vase that stands in the corner; there we can rest upon roses and lavender, and throw salt in his eyes if he comes near us."

"That will not do at all," said she; "besides I know that the old mandarin was once betrothed to the pot-pourri vase, and no doubt there is still some slight friendship existing between them. No, there is no help for it, we must wander forth together into the wide world."

"Hast thou indeed the courage to go with me into the wide world?" asked the chimney-sweeper. "Hast thou considered how large it is, and that we may never return home again?"

"I have," replied she.

And the chimney-sweeper looked keenly at her, and then

said, "My path leads through the chimney! Hast thou, indeed, the courage to creep with me through the stove, through the flues and the tunnel? Well do I know the way! We shall mount up so high that they cannot come near us, and at the top there is a cavern, that leads into the wide world."

And he led her to the door of the stove.

"Oh, how black it looks!" sighed she; however, she went on with him, through the flues and through the tunnel, where it was dark, pitch dark.

"Now we are in the chimney," said he; "and look, what a lovely star shines above us!"

And there was actually a star in the sky, shining right down upon them, as if to show them the way. And they crawled and crept—a fearful path was theirs—so high, so very high! But he guided and supported her, and showed her the best places whereon to plant her tiny porcelain feet, till they reached the edge of the chimney, where they sat down to rest, for they were very tired, and, indeed, not without reason.

Heaven with all its stars was above them, and the town with all its roofs lay beneath them; the wide, wide world surrounded them. The poor shepherdess had never imagined all this; she leaned her little head on her chimney-sweeper's arm, and wept so vehemently that the gilding broke off from her waistband.

"This is too much," exclaimed she. "This can I not endure! The world is all too large! Oh, that I were once more upon the little table under the pier-glass! I shall never be happy till I am there again. I have followed thee out into the wide world; surely thou canst follow me home again, if thou lovest me!"

And the chimney-sweeper talked very sensibly to her, reminding her of the old Chinese mandarin and the crooked-legged Field-Marshal-Major-General-Corporal-Sergeant. But she wept so bitterly, and kissed her little chimney-sweeper so fondly, that at last he could not but yield to her request, unreasonable as it was.

So with great difficulty they crawled down the chimney, crept through the flues and the tunnel, and at length found themselves once more in the dark stove; but they still lurked behind the door, listening, before they would venture to return into the room.

Everything was quite still, and they peeped out. Alas! on the ground lay the old Chinese mandarin. In attempting to follow the runaways, he had fallen down off the table and had broken into three pieces; his head lay shaking in a corner. The crooked-legged Field-Marshal-Major-General-Corporal-Sergeant stood where he had always stood, thinking over what had happened.

"Oh, how shocking!" exclaimed the little shepherdess, "old grandfather is broken in pieces, and we are the cause! I shall never survive it!" and she wrung her delicate hands.

"He can be put together again," replied the chimney-sweeper. "He can very easily be put together; only be not so impatient! If they glue his back together, and put a strong rivet in his neck, then he will be as good as new again, and he will be able to say plenty of unpleasant things to us."

"Do you really think so?" asked she. And then they climbed up the table to the place where they had stood before.

"See how far we have been!" observed the chimney-sweeper; "we might have spared ourselves all the trouble."

"If we could but have old grandfather put together!" said the shepherdess. "Will it cost very much?"

And he was put together; the family had his back glued and his neck riveted; and he was as good as new, but could no longer nod his head.

"You have certainly grown very proud since you broke in pieces!" remarked the crooked-legged Field-Marshal-Major-General-Corporal-Sergeant; "but I must say, for my part, I do not see that there is anything to be proud of. Am I to have her or am I not? Just answer me that?"

And the chimney-sweeper and the little shepherdess looked imploringly at the old mandarin. They were so afraid lest he should nod his head, but nod he could not; and it was disagreeable to him to tell a stranger that he had a rivet in his neck. So the young porcelain people always remained together; they blessed the grandfather's rivet, and loved each other till they broke in pieces.

THE WILD SWANS

FAR hence, in a country whither the Swallows fly in our winter-time, there dwelt a King who had eleven sons, and one daughter, the beautiful Elise. The eleven brothers went to school with stars on their breasts, and swords by their sides; they wrote on golden tablets with diamond pens, and could read either with a book or without one; in short, it was easy to perceive that they were princes. Their sister Elise used to sit upon a little glass stool, and had a picture-book which had cost the half of a kingdom. Oh, the children were so happy! But happy they were not to remain always.

Their father, the King, married a very wicked Queen, who was not at all kind to the poor children; they found this out on the first day after the marriage, when there was a grand gala at the palace; for when the children played at receiving company, instead of giving them as many cakes and sweet-meats as they liked, the Queen gave them only some sand in a little dish, and told them to imagine that was something nice.

The week after, she sent the little Elise to be brought up by some peasants in the country, and it was not long before she told the King so many falsehoods about the poor Princes that he would have nothing more to do with them.

"Away, out into the world, and take care of yourselves," said the wicked Queen; "fly away in the form of great speechless birds." But she could not make their transformation so disagreeable as she wished—the Princes were changed into eleven white swans. Sending forth a strange cry, they flew out of the palace windows, over the park and over the wood.

It was still early in the morning when they passed by the place where Elise lay sleeping in the peasant's cottage; they flew several times round the roof, stretched their long necks, and flapped their wings, but no one either heard or saw them; they were forced to fly away, up to the clouds, and into the wide world; so on they went to the forest, which extended as far as the seashore.

The poor little Elise stood in the peasant's cottage amusing herself with a green leaf, for she had no other plaything. She pricked a hole in the leaf and peeped through it at the sun, and then she fancied she saw her brothers' bright eyes, and whenever the warm sunbeams shone full upon her cheeks she thought of her brothers' kisses.

One day passed exactly like the other. When the wind blew through the thick hedge of rose-trees, in front of the house, she would whisper to the roses, "Who is more beautiful than you?" but the roses would shake their heads and say, "Elise." And when the peasant's wife sat on Sundays at the door of her cottage reading her hymn-book, the wind would rustle in the leaves and say to the book, "Who is more pious than thou?"—"Elise," replied the hymn-book. And what the roses and the hymn-book said was no more than the truth.

Elise, who was now fifteen years old, was sent for to return home; but when the Queen saw how beautiful she was, she hated her the more, and would willingly have transformed her like her brothers into a wild swan; but she dared not do so, because the King wished to see his daughter.

So the next morning the Queen went into a bath which was made of marble, and fitted up with soft pillows and the gayest carpets; she took three toads, kissed them, and said to one, "Settle thou upon Elise's head, that she may become dull and sleepy like thee."—"Settle thou upon her forehead," said she to another, "and let her become ugly like thee, so that her father may not know her again."—And "Do thou place thyself upon her bosom," whispered she to the third, "that her heart may become corrupt and evil, a torment to herself."

She then put the toads into the clear water, which was immediately tinted with a green colour, and, having called Elise, took off her clothes and made her get into the bath—one toad settled among her hair, another on her forehead, and the third upon her bosom; but Elise seemed not at all aware of it. She rose up, and three poppies were seen swimming on the water.

Had not the animals been poisonous and kissed by a witch, they would have been changed into roses whilst they remained on Elise's head and heart—she was too good for magic to have any power over her. When the Queen perceived this, she rubbed walnut juice all over the maiden's skin, so that it became quite swarthy, smeared a nasty salve over her lovely face, and entangled her long thick hair. It was impossible to recognise the beautiful Elise after this.

When her father saw her, he was shocked, and said she could not be his daughter; no one would have anything to do with her but the mastiff and the swallows; but they, poor things, could not say anything in her favour.

Poor Elise wept, and thought of her eleven brothers, not one of whom she saw at the palace. In great distress she stole away and wandered the whole day over fields and moors, till she reached the forest. She knew not where to go, but she was so sad, and longed so much to see her brothers, who had been driven out into the world, that she determined to seek and find them.

She had not been long in the forest when night came on, and she lost her way amid the darkness. So she lay down on the soft moss, said her evening prayer, and leaned her head against the trunk of a tree. It was still in the forest, the air was mild, and from the grass and mould around gleamed the green light of many hundred glow-worms; and when Elise lightly touched one of the branches hanging over her, bright insects fell down upon her like falling stars.

All the night long she dreamed of her brothers. They were all children again, played together, wrote with diamond pens upon golden tablets, and looked at the pictures in the beautiful book which had cost half of a kingdom.

But they did not, as formerly, make straight strokes and pothooks upon the tablets; no, they wrote of the bold actions they had performed, and the strange adventures they had encountered, and in the picture-book everything seemed alive. The birds sang, men and women stepped from the book and talked to Elise and her brothers. However, when she turned over the leaves, they jumped back into their places, so that the pictures did not get confused together.

When Elise awoke the sun was already high in the heavens. She could not see it certainly, for the tall trees of the forest entwined their thick-leaved branches closely together, and, as the sunbeams played upon them, they looked like a golden veil waving to and fro. The air was fragrant, and the birds perched upon Elise's shoulders. She heard the noise of water; there were several springs forming a pool, with the prettiest pebbles at the bottom; bushes were growing thickly round. But the deer had trodden a broad path through them, and by this path Elise went down to the water's edge. The water was so clear that, had not the boughs and bushes around been moved by the wind, you might have fancied they were painted upon the smooth surface, so distinctly was each little leaf mirrored upon it.

As soon as Elise saw her face reflected in the water, she was quite startled, so brown and ugly did it look; however, when she wetted her little hand, and rubbed her brow and eyes, the white skin again appeared. So Elise took off her clothes, stepped into the fresh water, and in the whole world there was not a king's daughter more beautiful than she then appeared.

After she dressed herself, and braided her long hair, she went to the bubbling spring, drank out of the hollow of her hand, and then wandered farther into the forest. She did not know where she was going, but she thought of her brothers, and of the good God who, she felt, would never forsake her. He it was who made the wild crab-trees grow in order to feed the hungry, and who showed her a tree whose boughs bent under the weight of their fruit. She made her noonday meal under its shade, propped up the boughs, and then walked on amid the dark twilight of the forest.

It was so still that she could hear her own footsteps, and the rustling of each little withered leaf that was crushed beneath her feet. Not a bird was to be seen; not a single sunbeam penetrated through the thick foliage; and the tall stems of the trees stood so close together that, when she looked straight before her, she seemed encircled by trelliswork. Oh! there was a loneliness in this forest such as Elise had never known before.

And the night was so dark! Not a single glow-worm sent forth its light. Sad at heart she lay down to sleep, and then it seemed to her as if the boughs above her opened, and she saw an Angel looking down with gentle aspect, and a thousand little cherubs all around him. When she awoke in the morning she could not tell whether this was a dream, or whether she had really been so watched.

She walked on and met an old woman with a basket full of berries; the old woman gave her some of them, and Elise asked if she had seen eleven princes ride through the wood.

"No," said the old woman, "but I saw yesterday eleven Swans with golden crowns on their heads swim down the brook near this place."

And she led Elise to a precipice, the base of which was washed by a brook; the trees on each side stretched their long leafy branches towards each other, and where they could not unite, the roots had disengaged themselves from the earth and hung over the water.

Elise bade the old woman farewell, and wandered by the side of the stream till she came to the place where it reached the open sea.

The beautiful sea lay stretched out before the maiden's eyes, but not a ship, not a boat was to be seen; how was she to go on? She observed the little stones on the shore, all of which the waves had washed into a round form; glass, iron, stone, everything that lay scattered there, had been moulded into shape, and yet the water which had done this was much softer than Elise's delicate little hand. "It rolls on unweariedly," said she, "and subdues what is so hard; I will be no less unwearied! Thank you for the lesson you have given me, ye bright rolling waves; some day, my heart tells me, you shall carry me to my dear brothers!"

There lay upon the wet sea-grass eleven white swan-feathers; Elise collected them together; drops of water hung about them, whether dew or tears she could not tell. She was quite alone on the seashore, but she did not care for that; the sea presented an eternal variety to her, more indeed in a few hours than the gentle inland waters would have offered in a whole year.

When a black cloud passed over the sky, it seemed as if the sea were saying, "I too can look dark"; and then the wind would blow and the waves fling out their white foam. But when the clouds shone with a bright red tint, and the winds were asleep, the sea also became like a rose-leaf in hue. It was now green, now white; but as it reposed peacefully, a slight breeze on the shore caused the water to heave gently like the bosom of a sleeping child.

At sunset Elise saw eleven Wild Swans with golden crowns on their heads flying towards the land; they flew one behind another, looking like a streaming white ribbon. Elise climbed the precipice, and concealed herself behind a bush; the swans settled close to her, and flapped their long white wings.

As the sun sank beneath the water, the swans also vanished, and in their place stood eleven handsome princes, the brothers of Elise. She uttered a loud cry, for although they were very much altered, Elise knew them to be her brothers. She ran into their arms, called them by their names—and how happy were *they* to see and recognise their sister, who was now grown so tall and so beautiful! They laughed and wept, and soon told each other how wickedly their stepmother had treated them.

"We," said the eldest of the brothers, "fly or swim as long as the sun is above the horizon, but, when it sinks below, we appear again in our human form. We are therefore obliged to look out for a safe resting-place, for, if at sunset we were flying among the clouds, we should fall down as soon as we resumed our own form. We do not dwell here. A land quite as beautiful as this lies on the opposite side of the sea, but it is far off. To reach it, we have to cross the deep waters, and there is no island midway on which we may rest at night; one little solitary rock rises from the waves, and upon it we find only just room to stand side by side.

"There we spend the night in our human form, and when the sea is rough we are sprinkled by its foam; but we are thankful for this resting-place, for without it we should never be able to visit our dear native country. Only once in the year is this visit to the home of our fathers permitted. We require two of the longest days for our flight, and can remain here only eleven days, during which time we fly over the large forest whence we can see the palace in which we were born, where our father dwells, and the tower of the church in which our mother was buried.

"Here even the trees and bushes seemed of kin to us; here the wild horses still race over the plains, as in the days of our childhood; here the charcoal burner still sings the same old tunes to which we used to dance in our youth; here we are still drawn, and here we have found thee, thou dear little sister! We have yet two days longer to stay here; then we must fly over the sea to a land beautiful indeed, but not our fatherland. How shall we take thee with us? We have neither ship nor boat!"

"How shall I be able to release you?" said the sister. And so they went on talking the whole of the night. They slumbered only a few hours.

Elise was awakened by the rustling of swans' wings which were fluttering above her. Her brothers were again transformed, and for some time flew around in large circles. At last they flew far, far away; one of them remained behind; it was the youngest, and he laid his head in her lap and she stroked his white wings. They remained the whole day together. Towards evening the others came back, and when the sun set they stood again on the firm ground in their natural form.

"To-morrow we shall fly away, and may not return for a year, but we cannot leave thee; hast thou courage to accompany us? My arm is strong enough to bear thee through the forest; shall we not have strength enough in our wings to carry thee over the sea?"

"Yes, take me with you," said Elise. They spent the whole night in weaving a mat of the pliant willow bark and the tough rushes, and their mat was thick and strong. Elise lay down upon it, and when the sun rose, and the brothers were again transformed into wild swans, they seized the mat with their beaks and flew up high among the clouds with their dear sister, who was still sleeping. The sunbeams shone full upon her face; so one of the swans flew over her head, and shaded her with his broad wings.

They were already far from land when Elise woke; she thought she was still dreaming, so strange did it appear to her to be travelling through the air, and over the sea. By her side lay a cluster of pretty berries, and a handful of delicious roots. Her youngest brother had laid them there; and she thanked him with a smile, for she knew him as the swan who flew over her head and shaded her with his wings.

They flew so high that the first ship they saw beneath them seemed like a white seagull hovering over the water. Elise saw behind her a large cloud, which looked like a mountain, and on it she saw the shadows of herself and the eleven swans. It formed a picture more splendid than any she had ever yet seen. Soon, however, the sun rose higher, the cloud remained far behind, and then the floating shadowy picture disappeared.

The whole day they continued to fly with a whizzing noise, somewhat like an arrow; but yet they went slower than usual —they had their sister to carry. A heavy tempest gathered as the evening approached; Elise anxiously watched the sun. It was setting; still the solitary rock could not be seen; it appeared to her that the swans plied their wings with increasing vigour.

Alas! it would be her fault if her brothers did not arrive at the place in time! they would become human beings when the sun set, and if this happened before they reached the rocks, they must fall into the sea and be drowned. She prayed to God most fervently; still no rock was to be seen; the black clouds drew nearer, violent gusts of wind announced the approach of a tempest, the clouds rested upon a huge wave which rolled quickly forwards, and one flash of lightning rapidly succeeded another.

The sun was now on the rim of the sea. Elise's heart beat violently; the swans shot downwards so swiftly that she thought she must fall. But again they began to hover; the sun was half sunk beneath the water, and at that moment she saw the little rock below her; it looked like a seal's head when he raises it just above the water. And the sun was sinking fast—it seemed scarcely larger than a star—her foot touched the hard ground, and the sun vanished like the last spark on a burnt piece of paper.

Arm in arm stood her brothers around her; there was only just room for her and them—the sea beat tempestuously against the rock, flinging over them a shower of foam. The sky seemed in a blaze, with the fast succeeding flashes of fire that lightened it, and peal after peal rolled on the thunder, but sister and brothers kept firm hold of each other's hands. They sang a psalm, and their psalm gave them comfort and courage.

By daybreak the air was pure and still, and, as soon as the sun rose, the swans flew away with Elise from the rock. The waves rose higher and higher, and when they looked from the clouds down upon the blackish-green sea, covered with white foam, they might have fancied that millions of swans were swimming on its surface.

As day advanced, Elise saw floating in the air before her a land of mountains with glaciers, and in the centre, a palace a mile in length, with splendid colonnades, surrounded by palm-trees and gorgeous-looking flowers as large as mill-wheels. She asked if this was the country to which they were flying, but the swans shook their heads, for what she saw was the beautiful airy castle of the fairy Morgana, where no human being was admitted. Whilst Elise still bent her eyes upon it, mountains, trees, and castle all disappeared, and in their place stood twelve churches with high towers and pointed windows—she fancied she heard the organ play, but it was only the murmur of the sea. She was now close to these churches, but behold! they changed into a large fleet sailing under them; she looked down and saw it was only a sea-mist passing rapidly over the water. An endless variety floated before her eyes, till at last the land to which she was going appeared in sight. Beautiful blue mountains, cedar woods, towns, and castles rose to view. Long before sunset Elise sat down among the mountains, in front of a large cavern; delicate young creepers grew thickly around, so that it appeared covered with gay embroidered carpets.

"Now we shall see what thou wilt dream of to-night!" said her youngest brother, as he showed her the sleeping-chamber destined for her.

"Oh, that I could dream how you might be freed from the spell!" said she; and this thought filled her mind. She prayed for God's help, nay, even in her dreams she continued praying, and it appeared to her that she was flying up high in the air towards the castle of the fairy Morgana. The fairy came forward to meet her, radiant and beautiful, and yet she fancied she resembled the old woman who had given her berries in the forest, and told her of the swans with golden crowns.

"Thou *canst* free thy brothers," said she; "but hast thou courage and patience enough? The water is indeed softer than thy delicate hands, and yet can mould the hard stones to its will, but then it cannot feel the pain which thy tender fingers will feel; it has no heart and cannot suffer the anxiety and grief which thou must suffer. Dost thou see these stinging-nettles which I have in my hand? There are many of the same kind growing round the cave where thou art sleeping; only those that grow there or on the graves in the churchyard are of use, remember that!

"Thou must pluck them, although they will sting thy hand, thou must trample on the nettles with thy feet, and get yarn from them, and with this yarn thou must weave eleven shirts with long sleeves; throw them over the eleven wild swans and the spell is broken. But mark this: from the moment that thou beginnest thy work till it is completed, even should it take thee years, thou must not speak a word; the first syllable that escapes thy lips will fall like a dagger into the hearts of thy brothers; on thy tongue depends their life. Mark well all this!"

And at the same moment the fairy touched Elise's hands with a nettle, which made them burn like fire, and Elise awoke. It was broad daylight, and close to her lay a nettle like the one she had seen in her dream. She fell upon her knees, thanked God, and then went out of the cave in order to begin her work. She plucked with her own delicate hands the stinging-nettles; they burned large blisters on her hands and arms, but she bore the pain willingly in the hope of releasing her dear brothers. She trampled on the nettles with her naked feet, and spun the green yarn.

At sunset came her brothers. Elise's silence quite frightened them; they thought it must be the effect of some fresh spell of their wicked stepmother. But when they saw her blistered hands, they found out what their sister was doing for their sakes. The youngest brother wept, and, when his tears fell upon her hands, Elise felt no more pain, and the blisters disappeared.

The whole night she spent in her work, for she could not rest till she had released her brothers. All the following day she sat in her solitude, for the swans had flown away; but never had time passed so quickly. One shirt was ready; she now began the second.

Suddenly a hunting horn resounded among the mountains. Elise was frightened. The noise came nearer, she heard the hounds barking; in great terror she fled into the cave, bound up the nettles which she had gathered and combed into a bundle, and sat down upon it.

In the same moment a large dog sprang out from the bushes. Two others immediately followed, they barked loudly, ran away, and then returned. It was not long before the hunters stood in front of the cave; the handsomest among them was the King of that country; he stepped up to Elise. Never had he seen a lovelier maiden.

"How camest thou here, thou beautiful child?" said he.

Elise shook her head; she dared not speak, for a word might have cost her the life of her brothers, and she hid her hands under her apron lest the King should see how she was suffering.

"Come with me," said he, "thou must not stay here! If thou art good as thou art beautiful, I will dress thee in velvet and silk, I will put a gold crown upon thy head, and thou shalt dwell in my palace!" So he lifted her upon his horse, while she wept and wrung her hands; but the King said, "I only desire thy happiness! thou shalt thank me for this some day!" and away he rode over mountains and valleys, holding her on his horse in front, whilst the other hunters followed.

When the sun set, the King's magnificent capital with its churches and domes lay before them, and the King led Elise into the palace, where, in a marble hall, fountains were playing, and the walls and ceilings displayed the most beautiful paintings. But Elise cared not for all this splendour; she wept and mourned in silence, even whilst some female attendants dressed her in royal robes, wove costly pearls in her hair. and drew soft gloves over her blistered hands.

And now she was full dressed, and, as she stood in her splendid attire, her beauty was so dazzling that the courtiers all bowed low before her; and the King chose her for his bride, although the Archbishop shook his head, and whispered that the "beautiful lady of the wood must certainly be a witch, who had blinded their eyes, and infatuated the King's heart."

But the King did not listen; he ordered that music should be played. A sumptuous banquet was served up, and the loveliest maidens danced round the bride; she was led through fragrant gardens into magnificent halls, but not a smile was seen to play upon her lips, or beam from her eyes. The King then opened a small room next her sleeping apartment; it was adorned with costly green tapestry, and exactly resembled the cave in which she had been found; upon the ground lay the bundle of yarn which she had spun from the nettles, and by the wall hung the shirt she had completed. One of the hunters had brought all this, thinking there must be something wonderful in it.

"Here thou mayst dream of thy former home," said the King; "here is the work which employed thee; amidst all thy present splendour it may sometimes give thee pleasure to fancy thyself there again."

When Elise saw what was so dear to her heart, she smiled, and the blood returned to her cheeks; she thought her brothers might still be freed, and she kissed the King's hand. He pressed her to his heart, and ordered the bells of all the churches in the city to be rung, to announce the celebration of their wedding. The beautiful dumb maiden of the wood was to become Queen of the land.

The Archbishop whispered evil words in the King's ear, but they made no impression upon him; the marriage was solemnised, and the Archbishop himself was obliged to put the crown upon her head. In his rage he pressed the narrow rim so firmly on her forehead that it hurt her; but a heavier weight—sorrow for her brothers—lay upon her heart, and she did not feel bodily pain.

She was still silent, a single word would have killed her brothers; her eyes, however, beamed with love to the King, so good and handsome, who had done so much to make her happy.

She became more warmly attached to him every day. Oh! how much she wished she might confide to him all her sorrows. But she was forced to remain silent; she could not speak until her work was completed. To this end she stole away every night, and went into the little room that was fitted up in imitation of the cave; there she worked at her shirts, but by the time she had begun the seventh, all her yarn was spent.

She knew that the nettles she needed grew in the church-yard, but she must gather them herself; how was she to get them?

"Oh, what is the pain in my fingers compared to the anguish my heart suffers!" thought she. "I must venture to the churchyard; the Good God will protect me!"

Fearful, as though she were about to do something wrong, one moonlight night, she crept down to the garden, and through the long avenues into the lonely road leading to the churchyard. She saw sitting on one of the broadest tomb-stones a number of ugly old witches. They took off their ragged clothes as if they were going to bathe, and digging with their long lean fingers into the fresh grass, drew up the dead bodies and devoured the flesh.

Elise was obliged to pass close by them, and the witches fixed their wicked eyes upon her; but she repeated her prayer, gathered the stinging-nettles, and took them back with her into the palace. One person only had seen her; it was the Archbishop, who was awake when others slept. Now he was convinced that all was not right about the Queen: she must be a witch, who had, through her enchantments, infatuated the King and all the people.

In the Confessional he told the King what he had seen, and what he feared; and, when the words came from his lips, the images of the saints shook their heads, as though they would say, "It is untrue; Elise is innocent!" But the Archbishop ex-plained the omen otherwise; he thought it was a testimony against her that the holy images shook their heads at hearing of her sin.

Two large tears rolled down the King's cheeks; he returned home in doubt; he pretended to sleep at night, though sleep never visited him; and he noticed that Elise rose from her bed every night, and every time he followed her secretly and saw her enter her little room.

His countenance became darker every day; Elise perceived it, though she knew not the cause. She was much pained, and besides, what did she not suffer in her heart for her brothers! Her bitter tears ran down on the royal velvet and purple; they looked like bright diamonds, and all who saw the magnificence that surrounded her wished themselves in her place.

She had now nearly finished her work, only one shirt was wanting; unfortunately, yarn was wanting also; she had not a single nettle left. Once more, only this one time, she must go to the churchyard and gather a few handfuls. She shuddered when she thought of the solitary walk and of the horrid witches, but her resolution was as firm as her trust in God.

Elise went, the King and Archbishop followed her; they saw her disappear at the churchyard door, and, when they came nearer, they saw the witches sitting on the tombstones as Elise had seen them, and the King turned away, for he believed her whose head had rested on his bosom that very evening to be amongst them. "Let the people judge her!" said he. And the people condemned her to be burned.

She was now dragged from the King's apartments into a dark damp prison, where the wind whistled through the grated window. Instead of velvet and silk, they gave her the bundle of nettles she had gathered; on that she must lay her head, and the shirts she had woven must serve her as mattress and counterpane. But they could not have given her anything she valued so much; and she continued her work, at the same time praying earnestly to her God. The boys sang scandalous songs about her in front of her prison; not a soul comforted her with one word of love.

Towards evening she heard the rustling of swans' wings at the grating. It was the youngest of her brothers who had at last found his sister, and she sobbed aloud for joy, although she knew that the coming night would probably be the last of her life; but then her work was almost finished, and her brother was near.

The Archbishop came in order to spend the last hour with her; he had promised the King he would; but she shook her head, and entreated him with her eyes and gestures to go. This night she must finish her work, or all she had suffered— her pain, her anxiety, her sleepless nights—would be in vain. The Archbishop went away with many angry words, but the unfortunate Elise knew herself to be innocent, and went on with her work.

Little mice ran busily about and dragged the nettles to her feet wishing to help her; and the thrush perched on the iron bars of the window, and sang all night as merrily as he could, that Elise might not lose courage.

It was still twilight, just one hour before sunrise, when the eleven brothers stood before the palace gates, requesting an audience with the King. But it could not be, they were told; it was still night, the King was asleep, and they dared not wake him. They entreated, they threatened; the guard came up, and the King himself at last stepped out to ask what was the matter. At that moment the sun rose, the brothers could be seen no longer, and eleven white swans flew away over the palace.

The people poured forth from the gates of the city; they wished to see the witch burned. One wretched horse drew the cart in which Elise was placed, a coarse frock of sackcloth had been put on her, her beautiful long hair hung loosely over her shoulders, her cheeks were of a deadly paleness, her lips moved gently, and her fingers wove the green yarn. Even on her way to her cruel death she did not give up her work; the ten shirts lay at her feet, and she was now labouring to complete the eleventh. The rabble insulted her.

"Look at the witch, how she mutters! She has not a hymn-book in her hand; no, there she sits with her accursed hocus-pocus. Tear it from her; tear it into a thousand pieces!"

And they all crowded about her, and were on the point of snatching away the shirts, when eleven white swans came flying towards the cart; they settled all round her, and flapped their wings. The crowd gave way in terror.

"It is a sign from Heaven! She is certainly innocent!" whispered some; they dared not say so aloud.

The Sheriff now seized her by the hand; in a moment she threw the eleven shirts over the swans, and eleven handsome princes appeared in their place. The youngest had, however, only one arm, and a wing instead of the other, for one sleeve was deficient in his shirt—it had not been quite finished.

"Now I may speak," said she: "I am innocent!"

And the people who had seen what had happened bowed before her as before a saint. She, however, sank lifeless in her brothers' arms; suspense, fear, and grief had quite exhausted her.

"Yes, she is innocent," said her eldest brother, and he now related their wonderful history. Whilst he spoke a fragrance as delicious as though it came from millions of roses diffused itself around, for every piece of wood in the funeral pile had taken root and sent forth branches. A hedge of blooming red roses surrounded Elise, and above all the others blossomed a flower of dazzling white colour, bright as a star. The King plucked it and laid it on Elise's bosom, whereupon she awoke from her trance with peace and joy in her heart.

And all the church-bells began to ring of their own accord; and birds flew to the spot in swarms; and there was a festive procession back to the palace, such as no king has ever seen equalled.

THE NIGHTINGALE

IN China, as you well know, the Emperor is Chinese, and all around him are Chinese also. Now what I am about to tell happened many years ago, but on that very account it is the more important that you should hear the story now, before it is forgotten.

The Emperor's palace was the most magnificent palace in the world; it was made entirely of fine porcelain, exceedingly costly; but, at the same time, so brittle that it was dangerous even to touch it.

The choicest flowers were to be seen in the garden; and to the most splendid of all these little silver bells were fastened, in order that their tinkling might prevent any one from passing by without noticing them. Yes! everything in the Emperor's garden was well arranged; and the garden extended so far that even the gardener did not know the end of it. Whoever walked beyond it, however, came to a beautiful wood, with very high trees; and beyond that, to the sea.

The wood went down to the sea, which was very deep and blue: large ships could sail close under the branches; and among the branches dwelt a nightingale who sang so sweetly that even the poor fisherman, who had so much else to do, when he came out at night-time to cast his nets, would stand still and listen to her song. "Oh, how pretty that is!" he would say—but then he was obliged to mind his work, and forget the bird. Yet the following night, if again the nightingale sang, and the fisherman came out, again he would say, "Oh, how pretty that is!"

Travellers came from all parts of the world to the Emperor's city; and they admired the city, the palace, and the garden; but, if they heard the nightingale, they all said, "This is the best." And they talked about her after they went home, and learned men wrote books about the city, the palace, and the garden. Nor did they forget the nightingale: she was extolled above everything else; and poets wrote the most beautiful verses about the nightingale of the wood near the sea.

These books went round the world, and one of them at last reached the Emperor. He was sitting in his golden arm-chair; he read and read, and nodded his head every moment; for these splendid descriptions of the city, the palace, and the garden, pleased him greatly. "But the nightingale is the best of all," was written in the book.

"What in the world is this?" said the Emperor. "The nightingale! I do not know it at all! Can there be such a bird in my empire, in my garden even, without my having even heard of it? Truly, one may learn something from books."

So he called his Cavalier, or gentleman-in-waiting. Now this was so grand a person that no one of inferior rank might speak to him; and if one did venture to ask him a question, his only answer was "Psha!" which has no particular meaning.

"There is said to be a very remarkable bird here, called the nightingale," said the Emperor; "her song, they say, is worth more than anything else in all my dominions. Why has no one ever told me of her?"

"I have never before heard her mentioned," said the Cavalier; "she has never been presented at court."

"I wish her to come and sing before me this evening," said the Emperor. "The whole world knows what I have, and I do not know it myself?"

"I have never before heard her mentioned," said the Cavalier; "but I will seek her, I will find her."

But where was she to be found? The Cavalier ran up one flight of steps, down another, through halls, and through passages; not one of all whom he met had ever heard of the nightingale. And the Cavalier returned to the Emperor, and said, "It must certainly be an invention of the man who wrote the book. Your Imperial Majesty must not believe all that is written in books; much in them is pure invention, and there is what is called the Black Art."

"But the book in which I have read it," said the Emperor, "was sent me by the high and mighty Emperor of Japan, and therefore it cannot be untrue. I wish to hear the nightingale; she must be here this evening, and if she do not come, after supper the whole court shall be flogged."

"Tsing-pe!" said the Cavalier; and again he ran upstairs, and downstairs, through halls, and through passages, and half the court ran with him; for not one would have relished the flogging. Many were the questions asked respecting the wonderful nightingale whom the whole world talked of, and about whom no one at court knew anything.

At last they met a poor little girl in the kitchen who said, "Oh, yes! the nightingale! I know her very well. Oh, how she can sing! Every evening I carry the fragments left at table to my poor sick mother. She lives by the seashore; and when I am coming back, and stay to rest a little in the wood, I hear the nightingale sing; it makes the tears come into my eyes! It is just as if my mother kissed me."

"Little kitchen-maid," said the Cavalier, "I will procure for you a sure appointment in the kitchen, together with permission to see His Majesty the Emperor dine, if you will conduct us to the nightingale, for she is expected at court this evening."

So they went together to the wood where the nightingale was accustomed to sing; and half the court went with them. Whilst on their way, a cow began to low.

"Oh," said the court pages, "now we have her! It is certainly an extraordinary voice for so small an animal; surely I have heard it somewhere before."

"No, those are cows you hear lowing," said the little kitchen-maid; "we are still far from the place."

The frogs were now croaking in the pond.

"That is famous!" said the chief court-preacher. "Now I hear her; it sounds just like little church-bells."

"No, those are frogs," said the little kitchen-maid, "but now I think we shall soon hear her."

Then began the nightingale to sing.

"There she is!" said the little girl. "Listen! listen! There she sits;" and she pointed to a little grey bird up in the branches.

"Is it possible?" said the Cavalier. "I should not have thought it. How simple she looks! she must certainly have changed colour at the sight of so many distinguished personages."

"Little nightingale!" called out the kitchen-maid; "our gracious Emperor wishes you to sing something to him."

"With the greatest pleasure," said the nightingale, and she sang in such a manner that it was delightful to hear her.

"It sounds like glass bells," said the Cavalier. "And look at her little throat, how it moves! It is singular that we should never have heard her before; she will have great success at court."

"Shall I sing again to the Emperor?" asked the nightingale, for she thought the Emperor was among them.

"Most excellent nightingale!" said the Cavalier, "I have the honour to invite you to a court festival, which is to take place this evening, when His Imperial Majesty will be enchanted with your delightful song."

"My song would sound far better among the green trees," said the nightingale; however, she followed willingly when she heard that the Emperor wished it.

There was a regular decorating and polishing at the palace; the walls and the floors, which were all of porcelain, glittered with a thousand gold lamps; the loveliest flowers, with the merriest tinkling bells, were placed in the passages: there was a running to and fro, which made all the bells ring, so that one could not hear his own words.

In the midst of the grand hall where the Emperor sat a golden perch was erected, on which the nightingale was to sit. The whole court was present, and the little kitchen-maid received permission to stand behind the door, for she had now actually the rank and title of "Maid of the Kitchen." All were dressed out in the finest clothes; and all eyes were fixed upon the little grey bird, to whom the Emperor nodded as a signal for her to begin.

And the nightingale sang so sweetly that tears came into the Emperor's eyes, tears rolled down his cheeks; and the nightingale sang more sweetly still, and touched the hearts of all who heard her. And the Emperor was so merry that he said, "The nightingale should have his golden slippers, and wear them round her neck." But the nightingale thanked him, and said she was already sufficiently rewarded.

"I have seen tears in the Emperor's eyes, and that is the greatest reward I can have. The tears of an Emperor have a particular value. Heaven knows I am sufficiently rewarded." And then she sang again with her sweet, lovely voice.

"It is the most amiable coquetry ever known," said the ladies present; and they put water into their mouths, and tried to move their throats as she did, when they spoke: they thought to become nightingales also. Indeed, even the footmen and chambermaids declared that they were quite contented; which was a great thing to say, for of all people they are the most difficult to satisfy.

Yes, indeed! the nightingale's success was complete. She was now to remain at court, to have her own cage; with leave to fly out twice in the day, and once in the night. Twelve attendants were allotted her, and were to hold a silken band,

VERNON SOPER

fastened round her foot; and they kept good hold: but there was no pleasure in excursions made in this manner.

All the city was talking of the wonderful bird; and when two persons met, one would say only "night," and the other "gale," and then they sighed, and understood each other perfectly. Indeed, eleven of the children of the citizens were named after the nightingale, but none of them had her tones in their throats.

One day a large parcel arrived for the Emperor, on which was written "Nightingale."

"Here we have another new book about our far-famed bird," said the Emperor. But it was not a book; it was a little piece of mechanism lying in a box—an artificial nightingale, which was intended to look like the living one, but which was covered all over with diamonds, rubies, and sapphires. When this artificial bird had been wound up, it could sing one of the tunes that the real nightingale sang; and its tail, all glittering with silver and gold, went up and down all the time. A little band was fastened round its neck, on which was written, "The nightingale of the Emperor of China is poor compared with the nightingale of the Emperor of Japan."

"That is famous!" said every one; and he who had brought the bird obtained the title of "Chief Imperial Nightingale Bringer."

"Now they shall sing together; we will have a duet."

And so they must sing together; but it did not succeed, for the real nightingale sang in her own way, and the artificial bird produced its tones by wheels. "It is not his fault," said the artist; "he keeps exact time and quite according to method."

So the artificial bird must now sing alone: he was quite as successful as the real nightingale; and then he was so much prettier to look at; his plumage sparkled like jewels.

Three-and-thirty times he sang one and the same tune, and yet he was not weary; every one would willingly have heard him again. However, the Emperor now wished the real nightingale should sing something—but where was she? No one had remarked that she had flown out of the open window —flown away to her own green wood.

"What is the meaning of this?" said the Emperor; and all the courtiers abused the nightingale, and called her a most un-grateful creature. "We have the best bird at all events," said they; and for the four-and-thirtieth time they heard the same tune, but still they did not quite know it, because it was so difficult. The artist praised the bird very highly; indeed, he declared it was superior to the real nightingale, not only in its exterior, all sparkling with diamonds, but also internally.

"For see, my noble lords, His Imperial Majesty especially, with the real nightingale one could never reckon on what was coming: but everything is settled with the artificial bird; he will sing in this one way, and no other. This can be proved; he can be taken to pieces, and the works can be shown—where the wheels lie, how they move, and how one follows from another."

"That is just what I think," said everybody; and the artist received permission to show the bird to the people on the following Sunday. "They too should hear him sing," the Emperor said.

So they heard him, and were as well pleased as if they had all been drinking tea—for it is tea that makes Chinese merry; and they all said, "Oh!" and raised their forefingers, and nodded their heads. But the fisherman, who had heard the real nightingale, said, "It sounds very pretty, almost like the real bird; but yet there is something wanting, I do not know what."

The real nightingale was, however, banished from the empire.

The artificial bird had his place on a silk cushion close to the Emperor's bed; all the presents he received, gold and precious stones, lay around him. He had obtained the rank and title of "High Imperial Dessert Singer," and therefore his place was number one on the left side; for the Emperor thought that the side where the heart was situated must be the most honourable—and the heart is situated on the left side of an Emperor, as well as with other folks.

And the artist wrote five-and-twenty volumes about the artificial bird, with the longest and most difficult words that are to be found in the Chinese language. So, of course, all said they had read and understood them, otherwise they would have been stupid, and perhaps would have been flogged.

Thus it went on for a year. The Emperor, the court, and all the Chinese knew every note of the artificial bird's song by heart; but that was the very reason they enjoyed it so much, they could now sing with him. The little boys in the street sang "zizizi, cluck, cluck, cluck!" and the Emperor himself sang too—yes, indeed, that was charming!

But one evening, when the bird was in full voice, and the Emperor lay in bed—and listened, there was suddenly a noise —"bang"—inside the bird, then something sprang— "fur-r-r-r"; all the wheels were running about, and the music stopped.

The Emperor jumped quickly out of bed, and had his chief physician called; but of what use could he be?

Then a clockmaker was sent for, and, at last, after a great deal of discussion and consultation, the bird was in some measure put to rights again. But the clockmaker said he must be spared much singing, for the pegs were almost worn out, and it was impossible to renew them, at least so that the music should be correct.

There was great lamentation, for now the artificial bird was allowed to sing only once a year, and even then there were difficulties. However, the artist made a short speech full of his long words, and said the bird was as good as ever: so then, of course, it was as good as ever.

When five years had passed away, a great trouble befell the whole empire, for in their hearts the people thought highly of their Emperor; and now he was ill, and it was reported that he could not live. A new Emperor had already been chosen, and the people stood in the street, outside the palace, and asked the Cavalier how the Emperor was?

"Psha!" said he, and shook his head.

Cold and pale lay the Emperor in his magnificent bed; all the court believed him to be already dead, and every one had hastened away to greet the new Emperor; the men ran out for a little gossip on the subject, and the maids were having a grand coffee-party.

The floors of all the rooms and passages were covered with

cloth, in order that not a step should be heard— it was everywhere so still! so still! But the Emperor was not yet dead; stiff
and pale he lay in his splendid bed, with the long velvet curtains, and heavy gold tassels. A window was opened above,
and the moon shone down on the Emperor and the artificial
bird.

The poor Emperor could scarcely breathe; it appeared to
him as if something was sitting on his chest; he opened his
eyes and saw that it was Death, who had put on the Emperor's
crown, and with one hand held the golden scimitar, with the
other the splendid imperial banner. From under the folds of
the thick velvet hangings the strangest-looking heads were seen
peering forth; some with an expression absolutely hideous,
and others with an extremely gentle and lovely aspect. They
were the bad and good deeds of the Emperor, which were
now all fixing their eyes upon him, whilst Death sat on his
heart.

"Dost thou know this?" they whispered one after another.
"Dost thou remember that?" And they began reproaching
him in such a manner that the sweat broke out upon his
forehead.

"I have never known anything like it," said the Emperor.
"Music, music, the great Chinese drum!" cried he. "Let me
not hear what they are saying."

They went on, however; and Death, quite in the Chinese
fashion, nodded his head to every word.

"Music, music!" cried the Emperor. "Thou dear little
artificial bird! sing, I pray thee, sing! I have given thee gold
and precious stones; I have even hung my golden slippers
round thy neck. Sing, I pray thee, sing!"

But the bird was silent; there was no one there to wind him
up, and he could not sing without this. Death continued to
stare at the Emperor with his great hollow eyes, and everywhere it was still, fearfully still!

All at once the sweetest song was heard from the window;
it was the little living nightingale, who was sitting on a branch
outside. She had heard of her Emperor's severe illness, and
was come to sing to him of comfort and hope. As she sang,
the spectral forms became paler and paler, the blood flowed

more and more quickly through the Emperor's feeble members, and even Death listened, and said, "Go on, little nightingale, go on."

"Wilt thou give me the splendid gold scimitar? Wilt thou give me the gay banner, and the Emperor's crown?"

And Death gave up all these treasures for a song; and the nightingale sang on. She sang of the quiet churchyard, where white roses blossom, where the lilac sends forth its fragrance, and the fresh grass is bedewed with the tears of the sorrowing friends of the departed. Then Death was seized with a longing after his garden, and, like a cold white shadow, flew out at the window.

"Thanks, thanks," said the Emperor, "thou heavenly little bird, I know thee well. I have banished thee from my realm, and thou hast sung away those evil faces from my bed, and death from my heart; how shall I reward thee?"

"Thou hast already rewarded me," said the nightingale; "I have seen tears in thine eyes, as when I sang to thee for the first time. Those I shall never forget; they are jewels which do so much good to a minstrel's heart! But sleep now, and wake fresh and healthy; I will sing thee to sleep."

And she sang, and the Emperor fell into a sweet sleep. Oh, how soft and kindly was that sleep!

The sun shone in at the window when he awoke, strong and healthy. Not one of his servants had returned, for they all believed him dead; but the nightingale still sat and sang.

"Thou shalt always stay with me," said the Emperor; "thou shalt sing only when it pleases thee; and the artificial bird I will break into a thousand pieces."

"Do not so," said the nightingale; "truly he has done what he could; take care of him. I cannot stay in the palace; but let me come when I like: I will sit on the branches close to the window, in the evening, and sing to thee, that thou mayst become happy and thoughtful.

"I will sing to thee of the joyful and the sorrowing; I will sing to thee of all that is good or bad, which is concealed from thee. The little minstrel flies afar to the fisherman's hut, to the peasant's cottage, to all who are far distant from thee and thy court. I love thy heart more than thy crown, and yet the crown has an odour of something holy about it. I will come; I will sing: but thou must promise me one thing."

"Everything," said the Emperor. And now he stood in his imperial splendour, which he had put on himself, and held the scimitar, so heavy with gold, to his heart.

"One thing I beg of thee: let no one know that thou hast a little bird, who tells thee everything; then all will go on well." And the nightingale flew away.

The attendants came in to look at their dead Emperor, and lo! as there they stood, the Emperor said, "Good-morning!"

THE LITTLE MERMAID

Far out in the wide sea—where the water is blue as the loveliest cornflower, and clear as the purest crystal; where it is so deep that very many church-towers must be heaped one upon another, in order to reach from the lowest depth to the surface above—dwell the Merpeople.

Now you must not imagine that there is nothing but sand below the water: no, indeed, far from it! Trees and plants of wondrous beauty grow there, whose stems and leaves are so light that they are waved to and fro by the slightest motion of the water, almost as if they were living beings. Fishes, great and small, glide in and out among the branches, just as birds fly about among our trees.

Where the water is deepest, stands the palace of the Mer-king. The walls of this palace are of coral, and the high, pointed windows are of amber; the roof, however, is composed of mussel-shells, which, as the billows pass over them, are continually opening and shutting. This looks exceedingly pretty, especially as each of these mussel-shells contains a number of bright, glittering pearls, any one of which would be a costly ornament in the diadem of a king in the upper world.

The Mer-king had been for years a widower; his old mother managed the household affairs for him. She was, on the whole, a sensible sort of a lady, although extremely proud

of her high birth and station; on which account she wore
twelve oysters on her tail, whilst the other inhabitants of the
sea were allowed only six. In every other respect she merited
unlimited praise, especially for the affection she showed to the
six little princesses, her granddaughters. These were all very
beautiful children: the youngest was, however, the most
lovely; her skin was as soft and delicate as a rose-leaf, her
eyes were of as deep a blue as the sea; but, like all other mermaids, she had no feet, and her body ended in a tail like that
of a fish.

The whole day long the children used to play in the
spacious apartments of the palace, where beautiful flowers
grew out of the walls on all sides around them. When the
great amber windows were opened, fishes would swim into
these apartments as swallows fly into our rooms: but the
fishes were bolder than the swallows; they swam straight up
to the little princesses, ate from their hands, and allowed
themselves to be caressed.

In front of the palace there was a large garden full of fiery
red and dark blue trees, whose fruit glittered like gold, and
whose flowers resembled a bright, burning sun. The sand that
formed the soil of the garden was of a bright blue colour,
something like flames of sulphur; and a strangely beautiful
blue was spread over the whole, so that one might have
fancied oneself raised very high in the air, with the sky at
once above and below—certainly not at the bottom of the
sea. When the waters were quite still, the sun might be seen
looking like a purple flower, out of whose cup streamed forth
the light of the world.

Each of the little princesses had her own plot in the garden,
where she might plant and sow at her pleasure. One chose hers
to be made in the shape of a whale; another preferred the
figure of a mermaid; but the youngest had hers quite round
like the sun, and planted in it only those flowers that were red,
as the sun seemed to her. She was certainly a singular child,
very quiet and thoughtful. Whilst her sisters were adorning
themselves with all sort of gay things that came out of a ship
which had been wrecked, she asked for nothing but a beautiful
white marble statue of a boy, which had been found in it. She

put the statue in her garden, and planted a red weeping-willow by its side.

The tree grew up quickly, and let its long boughs fall upon the bright blue ground, where ever-moving shadows played in violet hues, as if boughs and root were embracing.

Nothing pleased the little princess more than to hear about the world of human beings living above the sea. She made her old grandmother tell her everything she knew about ships, towns, men and land animals, and was particularly pleased when she heard that the flowers of the upper world had a pleasant fragrance—for the flowers of the sea are scentless—and that the woods were green, and the fishes fluttering among the branches were of various colours, and that they could sing with a loud clear voice. The old lady meant birds, but she called them fishes, because her grandchildren, having never seen a bird, would not otherwise have understood her.

"When you have attained your fifteenth year," added she, "you will be permitted to rise to the surface of the sea; you will then sit by moonlight in the clefts of the rocks, see the ships sail by, and learn to distinguish towns and men."

The next year the eldest of the sisters reached this happy age, but the others—alas! The second sister was a year younger than the eldest, the third a year younger than the second, and so on; the youngest had still five whole years to wait till that joyful time should come, when she also might rise to the surface of the water and see what was going on in the upper world. However, the eldest promised to tell the others of everything she might see, when the first day of her being of age arrived; for the grandmother gave them but little information, and there was so much that they wished to hear.

But none of all the sisters longed so keenly for the day when she should be released from childish restraint as the youngest—she who had longest to wait, and was so quiet and thoughtful. Many a night she stood by the open window, looking up through the clear blue water, whilst the fishes were leaping and playing around her. She could see the sun and the moon; their light was pale, but they appeared larger than they do to those who live in the upper world. If a shadow passed over them, she knew it must be either a whale, or a

ship sailing by full of human beings, who, indeed, little
thought that, far beneath them, a little mermaiden was
passionately stretching forth her white hands towards their
ship's keel.

The day had now arrived when the eldest princess had
attained her fifteenth year, and was therefore allowed to rise
up to the surface of the sea.

When she returned she had a thousand things to relate. Her
chief pleasure had been to sit upon a sandbank in the moonlight, looking at the large town which lay on the coast, where
lights were beaming like stars, and where music was playing.
She had heard the distant noise of men and carriages; she had
seen the high church-towers, had listened to the ringing of
the bells; and, just because she could not go there, she longed
the more after all these things.

How attentively did her youngest sister listen to her words!
And when she next stood at night-time by her open window,
gazing upward through the blue waters, she thought so
intensely of the great noisy city that she fancied she could
hear the church-bells ringing.

Next year the second sister received permission to swim
wherever she pleased. She rose to the surface of the sea, just
when the sun was setting; and this sight so delighted her that
she declared it to be more beautiful than anything else she had
seen above the waters.

"The whole sky seemed tinged with gold," said she, "and
it is impossible for me to describe to you the beauty of the
clouds: now red, now violet, they glided over me. But still
more swiftly flew over the water a flock of white swans, just
where the sun was descending; I looked after them, but the
sun disappeared, and the bright rosy light of the surface of the
sea and on the edges of the clouds was gradually extinguished."

It was now time for the third sister to visit the upper world.
She was the boldest of the six, and ventured up a river. On its
shore she saw green hills covered with woods and vineyards,
from among which arose houses and castles; she heard the
birds singing, and the sun shone with so much power that she
was continually obliged to plunge below, in order to cool her
burning face. In a little bay she met with a number of children

who were bathing and jumping about; she would have joined in their gambols, but the children fled back to the land in great terror, and a little black animal barked at her in such a manner that she herself was frightened at last, and swam back to the sea. She could not, however, forget the green woods, and the hills, and the pretty children, who, although they had no fins, were swimming about in the river so fearlessly.

The fourth sister was not so bold; she remained in the open sea, and said, on her return home, she thought nothing could be more beautiful. She had seen ships sailing by, so far off that they looked like sea-gulls; she had watched the merry dolphins gambolling in the water, and the enormous whales, sending up into the air a thousand sparkling fountains.

The year after, the fifth sister attained her fifteenth year. Her birthday happened at a different season to that of her sister; it was winter, the sea was of a green colour, and immense icebergs were floating on its surface. These, she said, looked like pearls; they were, however, much larger than the church-towers in the land of human beings. She sat down upon one of these pearls, and let the wind play with her long hair; but then all the ships hoisted their sails in terror, and escaped as quickly as possible.

In the evening the sky was covered with sails; and whilst the great mountains of ice alternately sank and rose again, and beamed with a reddish glow, flashes of lightning burst forth from the clouds, and the thunder rolled on, peal after peal. The sails of all the ships were instantly furled, and horror and affright reigned on board, but the princess sat still on the ice-berg, looking unconcernedly at the blue zigzag of the flashes.

The first time that either of these sisters rose out of the sea, she was quite enchanted at the sight of so many new and beautiful objects; but the novelty was soon over and it was not long ere their own home appeared more attractive than the upper world, for there only did they find everything agreeable.

Many an evening would the five sisters rise hand in hand from the depths of the ocean. Their voices were far sweeter than any human voice, and when a storm was coming on they would swim in front of the ships and sing—oh! how sweetly did they sing! describing the happiness of those who lived at the bottom of the sea, and entreating the sailors not to be afraid, but to come down to them.

The mariners, however, did not understand their words; they fancied the song was only the whistling of the wind, and thus they lost the hidden glories of the sea: for if their ships were wrecked all on board were drowned, and none but dead men ever entered the Mer-king's palace.

Whilst the sisters were swimming at evening time, the youngest would remain, motionless and alone, in her father's palace, looking up after them. She would have wept, but mermaids cannot weep, and therefore, when they are troubled, suffer infinitely more than human beings do.

"Oh! if I were but fifteen," sighed she, "I know that I should love the upper world and its inhabitants so much."

At last the time she had so longed for arrived.

"Well, now it is your turn," said the grandmother; "come here that I may adorn you like your sisters." And she wound around her hair a wreath of white lilies, whose every petal was the half of a pearl, and then commanded eight large oysters to fasten themselves to the princess's tail, in token of her high rank.

"But that is so very uncomfortable!" said the little princess.

"One must not mind slight inconveniences when one wishes to look well," said the old lady.

The princess would have given up all this splendour, and exchanged her heavy crown for the red flowers of her garden, which were so much more becoming to her, but she dared not do so. "Farewell," said she; and she rose from the sea, light as a flake of foam.

When, for the first time in her life, she appeared on the surface of the water, the sun had just sunk below the horizon, the clouds were beaming with bright golden and rosy hues, the evening star was shining in the pale western sky, the air was mild and refreshing, and the sea as smooth as a looking-glass.

A large ship with three masts lay on the still waters; only one sail was unfurled, but not a breath was stirring, and the sailors were quietly seated on the cordage and ladders of the vessel. Music and song resounded from the deck, and after it grew dark hundreds of lamps, all on a sudden, burst forth into light, whilst innumerable flags were fluttering overhead.

The little mermaid swam close up to the captain's cabin, and every now and then, when the ship was raised by the motion of the water, she could look through the clear window-panes. She saw within many richly-dressed men; the handsomest among them was a young prince with large black eyes. He could not certainly be more than sixteen years old, and it was in honour of his birthday that a grand festival was being celebrated. The crew were dancing on the deck, and when the young prince appeared among them a hundred rockets were sent up into the air, turning night into day, and so terrifying the little mermaid that for some minutes she plunged beneath the water.

However, she soon raised her little head again, and then it seemed as if all the stars were falling down upon her. Such a fiery shower she had never even seen before; never had she heard that men possessed such wonderful powers. Large suns revolved around her, bright fishes swam in the air, and everything was reflected perfectly on the clear surface of the sea. It was so light in the ship that everything could be seen distinctly. Oh! how happy the young prince was! He shook hands with the sailors, laughed and jested with them, whilst sweet notes of music mingled with the silence of night.

It was now late, but the little mermaid could not tear herself away from the ship and the handsome young prince. She remained looking through the cabin window, rocked to and fro by the waves. There was a foaming in the depths, and the ship began to move on faster; the sails were spread, the waves rose high, thick clouds gathered over the sky, and the noise of distant thunder was heard.

The sailors perceived that a storm was coming on; so they again furled the sails. The great vessel was tossed about on the stormy ocean like a light boat, and the waves rose to an immense height, towering over the ship, which alternately sank beneath and rose above them.

To the little mermaid this seemed most delightful, but the ship's crew thought very differently. The vessel cracked, the stout masts bent under the violence of the billows, the waters rushed in. For a minute the ship tottered to and fro; then the mainmast broke, as if it had been a reed; the ship turned over, and was filled with water. The little mermaid now saw that the crew was in danger, for she herself was forced to beware of the beams and splinters torn from the vessel, and floating about on the waves.

But at the same time it became pitch dark, so that she could not distinguish anything. Presently, however, a dreadful flash of lightning disclosed to her the whole of the wreck. Her eyes sought the young prince—the same instant the ship sank to the bottom. At first she was delighted, thinking that the prince must now come to her abode; but she soon remembered that man cannot live in water, and therefore if the prince ever entered her palace it would be as a corpse.

"Die! no, he must not die!" She swam through the fragments with which the water was strewn, regardless of the danger she was incurring, and at last found the prince all but exhausted, and with great difficulty keeping his head above water. He had already closed his eyes, and must surely have been drowned, had not the little mermaid come to his rescue. She seized hold of him and kept him above water, and the current bore them on together.

Towards morning the storm was hushed; no trace, however, remained of the ship. The sun rose like fire out of the sea; his beams seemed to restore colour to the prince's cheeks, but his eyes were still closed.

The mermaid kissed his high forehead, and stroked his wet hair away from his face. He looked like the marble statue in her garden. She kissed him again, and wished most fervently that he might recover.

She now saw the dry land with its mountains glittering with snow. A green wood extended along the coast, and at the entrance of the wood stood a chapel or convent—she could not be sure which. Citron and lemon trees grew in the garden adjoining it, an avenue of tall palm-trees led up to the door. The sea here formed a little bay, in which the water was quite smooth but very deep, and under the cliffs there were dry, firm sands. Hither swam the little mermaid with the prince seemingly dead; she laid him upon the warm sand, and took care to place his head high, and turn his face to the sun.

The bells began to ring in the large white building which stood before her, and a number of young girls came out to walk in the garden. The mermaid went away from the shore, hid herself behind some stones, covered her head with foam, so that her little face could not be seen, and watched the prince.

It was not long before one of the young girls approached. She seemed quite frightened at finding the prince in this state, apparently dead. Soon, however, she recovered herself, and ran back to call her sisters. The little mermaid saw that the prince revived, and that all around smiled kindly and joyfully upon him. For her however, he looked not; he knew not that it was she who had saved him: and when the prince was taken into the house, she felt so sad that she immediately plunged beneath the water, and returned to her father's palace.

If she had before been quiet and thoughtful, she now grew still more so. Her sisters asked her what she had seen in the upper world, but she made no answer.

Many an evening she rose to the place where she had left the prince. She saw the snow melt on the mountains, the fruit ripen in the garden, but the prince she never saw; so she always returned sorrowfully to her home in the deep. Her only pleasure was to sit in her little garden gazing on the beautiful statue so like the prince. She cared no longer for her flowers; they grew up in wild luxuriance, covered the steps, and entwined their long stems and tendrils among the boughs of the trees, so that her whole garden became a bower.

At last, being unable to conceal her sorrow any longer, she revealed the secret to one of her sisters, who told it to the other princesses, and they to some of their friends. Among them was a young mermaid who recollected the prince, having been an eye-witness herself to the festivities in the ship; she knew also in what country the prince lived, and the name of its king.

"Come, little sister!" said the princesses; and embracing her, they rose together, arm-in-arm, out of the water, just in front of the prince's palace.

This palace was built of bright yellow stones, a flight of white marble steps led from it down to the sea. A gilded cupola crowned the building, and white marble figures, which might almost have been taken for real men and women, were placed among the pillars surrounding it. Through the clear glass of the high windows one might look into grand apartments hung with silken curtains, the walls adorned with magnificent paintings. It was a real treat to the little royal mermaids to behold so splendid an abode; they gazed through the windows of one of the largest rooms, and in the centre saw a fountain playing, whose waters sprang up to the glittering cupola above, through which the sunbeams fell dancing on the water, and brightening the pretty plants which grew around it.

The little mermaid now knew where her beloved prince dwelt, and henceforth she went there almost every evening. She often approached nearer the land than her sisters had ventured, and even swam up the narrow channel that flowed under the marble balcony. Here, on a bright moonlight night, she would watch the young prince, who believed himself alone.

Sometimes she saw him sailing on the water in a gaily-painted boat with many-coloured flags waving above. She would then hide among the green reeds which grew on the banks, listening to his voice; and if any one in the boat heard the rustling of her long silver veil, which was caught now and then by the light breeze, they only fancied it was a swan flapping his wings.

Many a night, when the fishermen were casting their nets by the beacon's light, she heard them talking of the prince, and telling the noble deeds he had performed. She was then so happy, thinking how she had saved his life when struggling with the waves, and remembering how his head had rested on her bosom, and how she had kissed him when he knew nothing of it, and could never even dream of such a thing.

Human beings became more and more dear to her every day; she wished that she were one of them. Their world seemed to her much larger than that of the Merpeople; they could fly over the ocean in their ships, as well as climb to the summits of those high mountains that rose above the clouds; and their wooded domains extended much farther than a mermaid's eye could see.

There were many things that she wished to hear explained, but her sisters could not give her any satisfactory answer. She was again obliged to have recourse to the old queen-mother, who knew a great deal about the upper world, which she used to call "the country above the sea."

"Do men when they are not drowned live for ever?" she asked one day. "Do they not die as we do, who live at the bottom of the sea?"

"Yes," was the grandmother's reply; "they must die like us, and their life is much shorter than ours. We live to the age of three hundred years, but when we die, we become foam on the sea, and are not allowed even to share a grave among those that are dear to us. We have no immortal souls; we can never live again, and are like the grass which, when cut down, is withered for ever. Human beings, on the contrary, have souls that continue to live when their bodies become dust; and as we rise out of the water to admire the homes of man, they ascend to glorious unknown dwellings in the skies which we are not permitted to see."

"Why have *we* not souls?" asked the little mermaid. "I would willingly give up my three hundred years to be a human being for only one day, thus to become entitled to that heavenly world above."

"You must not think of that," answered her grandmother; "it is much better as it is: we live longer and are far happier than human beings."

"So I must die, and be dashed like foam over the sea, never to rise again and hear the gentle murmur of the ocean—never again see the beautiful flowers and the bright sun! Tell me, dear grandmother, are there no means by which I may obtain an immortal soul?"

"No!" replied the old lady. "It is true that if thou couldst so win the affections of a human being as to become dearer to him than either father or mother; if he loved thee with all his heart, and promised whilst the priest joined his hands with thine to be always faithful to thee; then his soul would flow into thine, and thou wouldst then become partaker of human bliss. But that can never be! For what in our eyes is the most beautiful part of our body—the tail—the inhabitants of the earth think hideous—they cannot bear it. To appear handsome to them, the body must have two clumsy props which they call legs."

The little mermaid sighed and looked mournfully at the scaly part of her form, otherwise so fair and delicate.

"We are happy," added the old lady; "we shall jump and swim about merrily for three hundred years—that is a long time—and afterwards we shall repose peacefully in death. This evening we have a court ball."

The ball which the queen-mother spoke of was far more splendid than any that earth has ever seen. The walls of the saloon were of crystal, very thick, but yet very clear. Hundreds of large mussel-shells were planted along them in rows; some of these shells were rose-coloured, some green as grass, but all sent forth a bright light, which illuminated the whole apartment. They also shone through the glassy walls so as to light up the waters around for a great space, and made the scales of the fishes—great and small, crimson and purple, silver and gold-coloured—appear more brilliant than ever.

Through the centre of the saloon flowed a bright, clear stream, on the surface of which danced mermen and mermaids to the melody of their own sweet voices—voices far sweeter than those of the dwellers upon earth. The little princess sang more harmoniously than any other, and they clapped their hands and applauded her.

She was pleased at this, for she knew well that there was neither on earth nor in the sea a more beautiful voice than hers. But her thoughts soon returned to the world above her: she could not forget the handsome prince; she could not control her sorrow at not having an immortal soul. She stole away from her father's palace, and whilst all was joy within she sat alone, lost in thought, in her little neglected garden.

On a sudden she heard the tones of horns resounding over the water far away in the distance, and she said to herself, "Now he is going out to hunt—he whom I love more than my father and my mother, with whom my thoughts are constantly occupied, and to whom I would so willingly trust the happiness of my life! All! all will I risk to win him—and an immortal soul. Whilst my sisters are still dancing in the palace, I will go to the enchantress whom I have hitherto feared so much, but who is, nevertheless, the only person who can advise and help me."

So the little mermaid left the garden, and went to the foaming whirlpool beyond which dwelt the enchantress. She had never been this way before—neither flowers nor sea-grass bloomed along her path. She had to traverse an expanse of bare grey sand till she reached the whirlpool, whose waters were eddying and whizzing like mill-wheels, tearing everything they could seize along with them into the abyss below. She was obliged to make her way through this horrible place, in order to arrive at the territory of the enchantress. Then she had to pass through a boiling, slimy bog, which the enchantress called her turf-moor: her house stood in a wood beyond this, and a strange abode it was.

All the trees and bushes around were polypi, looking like hundred-headed serpents shooting up out of the ground; their branches were long slimy arms with fingers of worms, every member, from the root to the uttermost tip, ceaselessly moving and extending on all sides. Whatever they seized they fastened upon so that it could not loosen itself from their grasp.

The little mermaid stood still for a minute looking at this horrible wood; her heart beat with fear, and she would certainly have returned without attaining her object had she not remembered the prince—and immortality. The thought gave her new courage. She bound up her long waving hair, that the polypi might not catch hold of it, crossed her delicate arms over her bosom, and, swifter than a fish can glide through the water, she passed these unseemly trees, which stretched their eager arms after her in vain.

She could not, however, help seeing that every polypus had something in his grasp, held as firmly by a thousand little arms as if enclosed by iron bands. The whitened skeletons of a number of human beings who had been drowned in the sea, and had sunk into the abyss, grinned horribly from the arms of these polypi; helms, chests, skeletons of land animals were also held in their embrace. Among other things might be seen even a little mermaid whom they had seized and strangled! What a fearful sight for the unfortunate princess!

But she got safely through this wood of horrors, and then arrived at a slimy place, where huge, fat snails were crawling about, and in the midst of this place stood a house built of the bones of unfortunate people who had been shipwrecked. Here sat the witch caressing a toad in the same manner as some persons would a pet bird. The ugly fat snails she called her chickens, and she permitted them to crawl about her.

"I know well what you would ask of me," said she to the little princess. "Your wish is foolish enough, but it shall be fulfilled, though its accomplishment is sure to bring misfortune on you, my fairest princess. You wish to get rid of your tail, and to have instead two stilts like those of human beings, in order that a young prince may fall in love with you, and that you may obtain an immortal soul. Is it not so?"

While the witch spoke these words, she laughed so violently that her pet toad and snails fell from her lap.

"You come just at the right time," continued she; "had you come after sunset, it would not have been in my power to have helped you before another year. I will prepare for you a drink with which you must swim to land; you must sit down upon the shore and swallow it and then your tail will fall and shrink up to the things which men call legs. This transformation will, however, be very painful; you will feel as though a sharp knife passed through your body. All who look on you after you have been thus changed will say that you are the loveliest child of earth they have ever seen; you will retain your graceful movements, and no dancer will move so lightly: but every step you take will cause you pain all but unbearable—it will seem to you as if you were walking on the sharp edges of swords—and your blood will flow. Can you endure all this suffering? If so, I will grant your request."

"Yes, I will," answered the princess, with a faltering voice; for she remembered her dear prince, and the immortal soul which her suffering might win.

"Only consider," said the witch, "that you can never again become a mermaid, when once you have received a human form. You may never return to your sisters, and your father's palace; and unless you shall win the prince's love to such a degree that he shall leave father and mother for you, that you shall be mixed up with all his thoughts and wishes, and unless the priest join your hands, so that you become man and wife, you will never obtain the immortality you seek. The morrow of the day on which he is united to another, will see your death; your heart will break with sorrow, and you will be changed to foam on the sea."

"Still I will venture!" said the little mermaid, pale and trembling as a dying person.

"Besides all this, I must be paid, and it is no slight thing that I require for my trouble. Thou hast the sweetest voice of all the dwellers in the sea, and thou thinkest by its means to charm the prince; this voice, however, I demand as my recompense. The best thing thou possessest I require in exchange for my magic drink; for I shall be obliged to sacrifice my own blood, in order to give it the sharpness of a two-edged sword."

"But if you take my voice from me," said the princess, "what have I left with which to charm the prince?"

"Thy graceful form," replied the witch; "thy modest gait, and speaking eyes. With such as these, it will be easy to infatuate a vain human heart. Well now! hast thou lost courage? Put out thy little tongue, that I may cut it off, and take it for myself, in return for my magic drink."

"Be it so!" said the princess, and the witch took up the cauldron, in order to mix her potion. "Cleanliness is a good thing," remarked she, as she began to rub the cauldron with a handful of toads and snails. She then scratched her bosom, and let the black blood trickle down into the cauldron, every moment throwing in new ingredients. The smoke from the mixture assumed such horrible forms, as would fill beholders with terror, and a moaning and groaning proceeded from it, which might be compared to the weeping of crocodiles. The magic drink at length became clear and transparent as pure water: it was ready.

"Here it is!" said the witch to the princess, cutting out her tongue at the same moment. The poor little mermaid was now dumb: she could neither sing nor speak. "If the polypi should attempt to seize you, as you pass through my little grove," said the witch, "you have only to sprinkle some of this magic drink over them, and their arms will burst into a thousand pieces."

But the princess had no need of this counsel, for the polypi drew hastily back as soon as they perceived the bright phial, that glittered in her hand like a star; thus she passed safely through the formidable wood, over the moor and across the foaming mill-stream.

She now looked once again at her father's palace; the lamps in the saloon were out, and all the family were asleep. She would not go in, for she could not speak if she did; she was about to leave her home for ever; her heart was ready to break with sorrow at the thought. She stole into the garden, plucked a flower from the bed of each of her sisters as a remembrance, kissed her hand again and again, and then rose through the dark blue waters to the world above.

The sun had not yet risen when she arrived at the prince's dwelling, and ascended those well-known marble steps. The moon still shone in the sky when the little mermaid drank of the wonderful liquid contained in her phial. She felt it run through her like a sharp knife, and she fell down in a swoon. When the sun rose she awoke, and felt a burning pain in all her limbs; but—she saw standing close to her the object of her love, the handsome young prince, whose coal-black eyes were fixed inquiringly upon her. Full of shame, she cast down her own and perceived, instead of the long fish-like tail she had hitherto borne, two slender legs; but she was quite naked, and tried in vain to cover herself with her long, thick hair.

The prince asked who she was, and how she had got there; and she, in reply, smiled and gazed upon him with her bright blue eyes, for alas! she could not speak. He then led her by the hand into the palace. She found that the witch had told her true; she felt as though she was walking on the edges of sharp swords, but she bore the pain willingly. On she passed, light as a zephyr, and all who saw her wondered at her light, graceful movements.

When she entered the palace, rich clothes of muslin and silk were brought to her; she was lovelier than all who dwelt there, but she could neither speak nor sing. Some female slaves, gaily dressed in silk and gold brocade, sang before the prince and his royal parents; and one of them distinguished herself by her clear, sweet voice, which the prince applauded by clapping his hands. This made the little mermaid very sad, for she knew that she used to sing far better than the young slave. "Alas!" thought she, "if he did but know that, for his sake, I have given away my voice for ever."

The slaves began to dance; our lovely little mermaiden then arose, stretched out her delicate white arms, and hovered gracefully about the room. Every motion displayed more and more the perfect symmetry and elegance of her figure; and the expression which beamed in her speaking eyes touched the hearts of the spectators far more than the song of the slaves.

All present were enchanted, but especially the young prince, who called her his dear little foundling. And she danced again and again, although every step cost her excessive pain. The prince then said she should always be with him; and accordingly a sleeping-place was prepared for her on velvet cushions in the ante-room of his own apartment.

The prince caused a suit of male apparel to be made for her, in order that she might accompany him in his rides; so together they traversed the fragrant woods, where green boughs brushed against their shoulders, and the birds sang merrily among the fresh leaves. With him she climbed up steep mountains, and although her tender feet bled, so as to be remarked by the attendants, she only smiled, and followed her dear prince to the heights, whence they could see the clouds chasing each other beneath them, like a flock of birds migrating to other countries.

During the night she would, when all in the palace were at rest, walk down the marble steps, in order to cool her feet in the deep waters; she would then think of those beloved ones who dwelt in the lower world.

One night, as she was thus bathing her feet, her sisters swam together to the spot, arm-in-arm and singing, but alas! so mournfully! She beckoned to them, and they immediately recognised her, and told her how great was the mourning in her father's house for her loss. From this time the sisters visited her every night; and once they brought with them the old grandmother, who had not seen the upper world for a great many years; they likewise brought their father, the Mer-king, with his crown on his head: but these two old people did not venture near enough to land to be able to speak to her.

The little mermaiden became dearer and dearer to the prince every day; but he only looked upon her as a sweet, gentle child, and the thought of making her his wife never entered his head. And yet his wife she must be, ere she could receive an immortal soul; his wife she must be or she would change into foam, and be driven restlessly over the billows of the sea!

"Dost thou not love me above all others?" her eyes seemed to ask, as he pressed her fondly in his arms, and kissed her lovely brow.

"Yes," the prince would say; "thou art dearer to me than any other, for no one is as good as thou art! Thou lovest me so much; and thou art so like a young maiden whom I have seen but once, and may never see again. I was on board a ship which was wrecked by a sudden tempest; the waves threw me on the shore near a holy temple, where a number of young girls are occupied constantly with religious services. The youngest of them found me on the shore, and saved my life. I saw her only once, but her image is vividly impressed upon my memory, and her alone can I love. But she belongs to the holy temple; and thou who resemblest her so much has been given to me for consolation: never will we be parted!"

"Alas! he does not know that it was I who saved his life," thought the little mermaiden, sighing deeply. "I bore him over the wild waves into the wooded bay where the holy temple stood; I sat behind the rocks, waiting till some one should come. I saw the pretty maidens approach, whom he loves more than me"—and again she heaved a deep sigh, for she could not weep. "He said that the young girl belongs to the holy temple; she never comes out into the world: so they cannot meet each other again. And I am always with him, see him daily; I will love him, and devote my whole life to him."

"So the prince is going to be married to the beautiful daughter of the neighbouring king," said the courtiers, "that is why he is having that splendid ship fitted out. It is announced that he wishes to travel, but in reality he goes to see the princess; a numerous retinue will accompany him." The little mermaiden smiled at these and similar conjectures, for she knew the prince's intentions better than any one else.

"I must go," he said to her; "I must see the beautiful princess: my parents require me to do so; but they will not compel me to marry her, and bring her home as my bride. And it is quite impossible for me to love her, for she cannot be so like the beautiful girl in the temple as thou art; and if I were obliged to choose, I should prefer thee, my little silent foundling, with the speaking eyes." And he kissed her rosy lips, played with her locks, and folded her in his arms, whereupon arose in her heart a sweet vision of human happiness and immortal bliss.

"Thou art not afraid of the sea, art thou, my sweet, silent child?" asked he tenderly, as they stood together in the splendid ship which was to take them to the country of the neighbouring king. And then he told her of the storms that sometimes stir the waters; of the strange fishes that inhabit the deep, and of the wonderful things seen by divers. But she smiled at his words, for she knew better than any child of earth what went on in the depths of the ocean.

At night-time, when the moon shone brightly, and when all on board were fast asleep, she sat and looked down into the sea. It seemed to her, as she gazed through the foamy track made by the ship's keel, that she saw her father's palace, and her grandmother's silver crown. She then saw her sisters rise out of the water, looking sorrowful and stretching out their hands towards her. She nodded to them, smiled, and would have explained that everything was going on quite according to her wishes; but just then the cabin-boy approached, upon which the sisters plunged beneath the water so suddenly that the boy thought what he had seen on the waves was nothing but foam.

The next morning the ship entered the harbour of the king's capital. Bells were rung, trumpets sounded, and soldiers marched in procession through the city, with waving banners, and glittering bayonets. Every day witnessed some new entertainments; balls and parties followed each other. The princess, however, was not yet in the town; she had been sent to a distant convent for education, and had there been taught the practice of all royal virtues. At last she arrived at the palace.

The little mermaid had been anxious to see this wonderful princess; and she was now obliged to confess that she had never before seen so beautiful a creature.

The skin of the princess was so white and delicate that the veins might be seen through it, and her dark eyes sparkled beneath a pair of finely-formed eyebrows.

"It is herself!" exclaimed the prince, when they met; "it is she who saved my life, when I lay like a corpse on the sea-shore!" and he pressed his blushing bride to his beating heart. —"Oh, I am all too happy!" said he to his dumb foundling. "What I never dared to hope for has come to pass. Thou must rejoice in my happiness, for thou lovest me more than all others who surround me."

And the little mermaid kissed his hand in silent sorrow; it seemed to her as if her heart was breaking already, although the morrow of his marriage day, which must of necessity see her death, had not yet dawned.

Again the church-bells rang, whilst heralds rode through the streets of the capital, to announce the approaching bridal. Odorous flames burned in silver candlesticks on all the altars; the priests swung their golden censers; and bride and bridegroom joined hands while the holy words that united them were spoken.

The little mermaid, clad in silk and cloth of gold, stood behind the princess, and held the train of the bridal dress. But her ear heard nothing of the solemn music; her eye saw not the holy ceremony: she remembered her approaching end;

she remembered that she had lost both this world and the next.

That very same evening, bride and bridegroom went on board the ship. Cannon were fired, flags waved with the breeze, and in the centre of the deck stood a magnificent pavilion of purple and cloth of gold, fitted up with the richest and softest couches. Here the princely pair were to spend the night. A favourable wind swelled the sails, and the ship glided lightly over the blue waters.

As soon as it was dark, coloured lamps were hung out, and dancing began on the deck. The little mermaid was thus reminded of what she had seen the first time she rose to the upper world. The spectacle that now presented itself was equally splendid—and she was obliged to join in the dance, hovering lightly as a bird over the ship boards. All applauded her, for never had she danced with more enchanting grace. Her little feet suffered extremely, but she no longer felt the pain; the anguish her heart suffered was much greater.

It was the last evening she might see him, for whose sake she had forsaken her home and all her family, had given away her beautiful voice, and suffered daily the most violent pain—all without his having the least suspicion of it. It was the last evening that she might breathe the same atmosphere in which he, the beloved one, lived; the last evening when she might behold the deep blue sea, and the starry heavens. An eternal night, in which she might neither think nor dream, awaited her. And all was joy in the ship; and she, her heart filled with thoughts of death and annihilation, smiled and danced with the others, till past midnight. Then the prince kissed his lovely bride, and arm-in-arm they entered the magnificent tent prepared for their repose.

All was now still; the steersman alone stood at the ship's helm. The little mermaid leaned her white arms on the gallery, and looked towards the east watching for the dawn; she well knew that the first sunbeam would witness her death. She saw her sisters rise out of the sea; their features were deadly pale, and their long hair no more fluttered over their shoulders— it had all been cut off.

"We have given it to the witch," said they, "to induce her

to help thee, so that thou mayest not die. She has given to us a penknife: here it is! Before the sun rises, thou must plunge it into the prince's heart, and when his warm blood trickles down upon thy feet they will again be changed to a fish-like tail. Thou wilt once more become a mermaid, and wilt live thy full three hundred years, ere thou changest to foam on the sea. But hasten! either he or thou must die before sunrise.

"Our aged mother mourns for thee so much, her grey hair has fallen off through sorrow, as ours fell before the scissors of the witch. Kill the prince, and come down to us! Hasten! hasten! dost thou not see the red streaks on the eastern sky, announcing the near approach of the sun? A few minutes more and he rises and then all will be over with thee."

At these words they sighed deeply and vanished.

The little mermaid drew aside the purple curtains of the pavilion, where lay the bride and bridegroom; bending over them, she kissed the prince's forehead, and then glancing at the sky, she saw that the dawning light became every moment brighter. The prince's lips murmured the name of his bride—he was dreaming of her, and her only, whilst the fatal penknife trembled in the hand of the unhappy mermaid.

All at once she threw far out into the sea that instrument of death; the waves rose like bright blazing flames around, and the water where it fell seemed tinged with blood. With eyes fast becoming dim and fixed, she looked once more at her beloved prince, then plunged from the ship into the sea, and felt her body slowly but surely dissolving into foam.

The sun rose from his watery bed; his beams fell so softly and warmly upon her that our little mermaid was scarcely sensible of dying. She still saw the glorious sun, and over her head hovered a thousand beautiful transparent forms; she could still distinguish the white sails of the ship, and the bright red clouds in the sky. The voices of those airy creatures above her had a melody so sweet and soothing that a human ear would be as little able to catch the sounds as her eye was capable of distinguishing their forms; they hovered around her without wings, borne by their own lightness through the air. The little mermaid at last saw that she had a body as transparent as theirs; and felt herself raised gradually from the foam of the sea to higher regions.

"Where are they taking me?" asked she, and her words sounded just like the voices of those heavenly beings.

"Speak you to the daughters of air?" was the answer. "The mermaid has no immortal soul, and can only acquire that heavenly gift by winning the love of one of the sons of men; her immortality depends upon union with man.

"Neither do the daughters of air possess immortal souls, but they can acquire them by their own good deeds. We fly to hot countries, where the children of earth are sinking under sultry pestilential breezes; our fresh cooling breath revives them. We diffuse ourselves through the atmosphere; we perfume it with the delicious fragrance of flowers; and thus spread delight and health over the earth. By doing good in this manner for three hundred years we win immortality, and receive a share of the eternal bliss of human beings. And thou, poor little mermaid! who, followed the impulse of thine own heart, hast done and suffered so much—thou art now raised to the airy world of spirits, that by performing deeds of kindness for three hundred years, thou mayst acquire an immortal soul."

The little mermaid stretched out her transparent arms to the sun; and, for the first time in her life, tears moistened her eyes.

And now again all were awake and rejoicing in the ship. She saw the prince, with his pretty bride; they had missed her; they looked sorrowfully down on the foamy waters, as if they knew she had plunged into the sea. Unseen she kissed the bridegroom's forehead, smiled upon him, and then, with the rest of the children of air, soared high above the rosy cloud which was sailing so peacefully over the ship.

"After three hundred years we shall fly in the kingdom of Heaven!"

"We may arrive there even sooner," whispered one of her sisters. "We fly invisibly through the dwellings of men where there are children; and whenever we find a good child, who gives pleasure to his parents and deserves their love, the good God shortens our time of probation.

"No child is aware that we are flitting about his room; and that whenever joy draws from us a smile, a year is struck out of our three hundred. But when we see a rude, naughty child, we weep bitter tears of sorrow, and every tear we shed adds a day to our time of probation."

LITTLE IDA'S FLOWERS

"MY flowers are quite faded," said little Ida. "Only yesterday evening they were so pretty, and now they are all drooping! What can be the reason of it?" asked she of the student who was sitting on the sofa, and who was a great favourite with her, because he used to tell her stories, and cut out all sorts of pretty things for her in paper—such as hearts with little ladies dancing in them, flowers, high castles with open doors, etc. "Why do these flowers look so deplorable?" asked she again, showing him a bouquet of faded flowers.

"Do you not know?" replied the student. "Your flowers went to a ball last night, and are tired; that is why they all hang their heads."

"Surely flowers cannot dance!" exclaimed little Ida.

"Of course they can dance! When it is dark, and we have all gone to bed, they jump about as merrily as possible. They have a ball almost every night."

"May children go to the ball, too?" asked Ida.

"Yes," said the student; "daisies and lilies of the valley."

"And where do the prettiest flowers dance?"

"Have you never been in the large garden in front of the King's beautiful summer palace—the garden so full of flowers? Surely you remember the swans that come swimming up to you, when you throw them crumbs of bread? There you may imagine they have splendid balls."

"I was there yesterday with my mother," said Ida; "but there were no leaves on the trees, neither did I see a single flower. What could have become of them? There were so many in the summertime!"

"They are now at the palace," answered the student. "As

soon as the King leaves his summer residence, and returns with all his court to the town, the flowers likewise hasten out of the garden and into the palace, where they enjoy themselves famously. Oh, if you could but see them!

"The two loveliest roses sit on the throne, and act King and Queen. The red cocks-combs then arrange themselves in rows before them, bowing very low, they are the gentlemen of the bed-chamber. After that the prettiest among the flowers come in, and open the ball. The blue violets represent midshipmen, and begin dancing with the hyacinths and crocuses, who take the part of young ladies. The tulips and the tall orange-lilies are old dowagers, whose business it is to see that everything goes on with perfect propriety."

"But," asked the astonished little Ida, "may the flowers give their ball in the King's palace?"

"No one knows anything about it," replied the student. "Perhaps once during the night the old chamberlain may come in, with his great bunch of keys, to see that all is right; but as soon as the flowers hear the clanking of the keys they are quite still, and hide themselves behind the long silk window curtains. 'I smell flowers here,' says the old chamberlain; but he is not able to find them."

"That is very funny," said Ida, clapping her little hands; "but could not I see the flowers?"

"To be sure you can see them!" returned the student. "You have only to peep in at the window next time you go to the palace. I did so to-day, and saw a long yellow lily lying on the sofa. That was a court lady."

"Can the flowers in the Botanic Gardens go there too? Can they go so far?" asked Ida.

"Certainly, for flowers can fly if they wish. The pretty red and yellow butterflies, which look so much like flowers, are, in fact, nothing else. They jump from their stalks, move their petals, as if they were little wings, and fly about. As a reward for always behaving themselves well, they are allowed, instead of sitting quietly on their stalks, to flutter hither and thither all day long, till wings actually grow out of their petals. You have often seen it yourself.

"For the rest, it may be that the flowers in the Botanic

Gardens have not heard what merry-making goes on every night at the palace. But I assure you, if, next time you go into the garden, you whisper to one of the flowers that a ball is to be given at night at Friedricksburg, the news will be repeated from flower to flower, and there they will all fly to a certainty. Then, should the professor come into the garden, and find all his flowers gone, he will not be able to imagine what is become of them."

"Indeed!" said Ida, rather vexed at the student's strange words. "And, pray how can the flowers repeat to each other what I say to them? I am sure that flowers cannot speak."

"No, they cannot speak; you are right there," returned the student; 'but they make themselves understood by means of pantomime. Have you never seen them move to and fro at the least breath of air? They can understand each other this way as well as we can by talking."

"And does the professor understand their pantomime?" asked Ida.

"Oh, certainly! One morning he came into the garden, and observed that a tall nettle was conversing in pantomime with a pretty red carnation. 'Thou art so beautiful,' said he to the carnation; 'and I love thee so much!' But the professor could not allow such things; so he gave a rap at the nettle's leaves, which are his fingers, and in doing so he stung himself, and since then has never dared to touch a nettle."

"Ah, ah!" laughed little Ida; "that was very foolish."

"What do you mean by this?" here interrupted the tedious counsellor, who had come on a visit; "putting such things into children's heads."

He could not endure the student, and always used to scold when he saw him cutting out pasteboard figures—as, for instance, a man on the gallows holding a heart in his hand, which was meant for a heart-stealer; or an old witch, riding on a broomstick, and carrying her husband on the tip of her nose. He used always to say then as now: "What do you mean by putting such things into children's heads? It is all non-sensical rubbish."

However, little Ida thought what the student told her about the flowers was very strange, and she could not help thinking of it. She was now sure that her flowers hung their heads because they were tired with dancing so much the night before; so she took them to the pretty little table, where her playthings were arranged. Her doll lay sleeping in the cradle, but Ida said to her, "You must get up, Sophy, and be content to sleep to-night in the table-drawer, for the poor flowers are ill, and must sleep in your bed; perhaps they will be well again by to-morrow." She then took the doll out of the bed; but the good lady looked vexed at having to give up her cradle to the flowers.

Ida then laid the faded flowers in her doll's bed, drew the covering over them, and told them to lie quite still, whilst she made some tea for them to drink, in order that they might be well again the next day. And she drew the curtains round the bed, so that the sun might not dazzle their eyes.

All the evening she thought of nothing but the student's words; and just before she went to bed, she ran up to the window where her mother's tulips and hyacinths stood behind the blinds, and whispered to them, "I know very well that you are going to a ball to-night." But the flowers moved not a leaf, and seemed not to have heard her.

After she was in bed, she thought for a long time how delightful it must be to see the flowers dancing in the palace, and said to herself, "I wonder whether my flowers have been there?" but before she could settle the point she fell asleep.

During the night she awoke; she had been dreaming of the student and the flowers, and of the counsellor who told her that they were making game of her. All was still in the room; the night lamp was burning on the table; and her father and mother were both asleep.

"I wonder whether my flowers are still lying in Sophy's bed?" said she. "I should very much like to know." She raised herself a little, looked towards the door, which stood half open; she saw that the flowers and all her playthings were just as she had left them. She listened, and it seemed to her as if someone must be playing on the piano; but the tones were lower and sweeter than she had ever heard before. "Now my flowers must certainly be dancing," said she.

"Oh, how I should like to see them?" but she dared not get

up for fear of waking her father and mother. "If they would only come in here?" Still the flowers did not come; and the piano sounded so sweetly. At last she could restrain herself no longer, she must see the dancing; so she crept lightly out of bed, and stole towards the door of the room. Oh, what wonderful things she saw then!

The night lamp was burning no longer. However, it was quite light in the room, for the moon shone brightly through the windows on the floor. All the hyacinths and tulips stood there in two rows, whilst their empty pots might still be seen in front of the windows; they performed figures, and took hold of each other by the leaves. At the piano sat a large yellow lily, which Ida fancied she must have seen before, for she remembered the student's saying that this flower was exceedingly like Miss Laura, and how every one had laughed at his remark.

Now she herself agreed that the lily did resemble this young lady, for she had exactly her way of playing, bowing her long yellow face, now to one side, now to the other, and nodding her head to mark the time.

A tall blue crocus now stepped forward, sprang upon the table, on which lay Ida's playthings, went straight up to the bed, and drew back the curtains. There lay the sick flowers; but they rose immediately, and greeted the other flowers, who invited them to dance with them. The sick flowers got up, appeared quite well again, and danced as merrily as the rest.

Suddenly a heavy noise as of something falling from the table was heard. Ida cast a glance that way, and saw that it was the rod which she had found on her bed on the morning of Shrove Tuesday, and which was desirous of ranking itself among the flowers. It was certainly a very pretty rod, for a wax doll was fixed on the top, wearing a hat, as broad-brimmed as the counsellor's, with a blue and red ribbon tied round. She hopped upon her three red stilts in the middle of the flowers, and stamped the floor merrily with her feet: she was dancing the Mazurka, which the flowers could not dance, they were so light-footed.

All at once the wax doll on the rod swelled out to a giant, tall and broad, and exclaimed in a loud voice, "What do you mean by putting such things into children's heads? It is all nonsensical rubbish!"

And now the doll looked as much like the counsellor in his broad-brimmed hat as one drop of water resembles another; her countenance looked as yellow and peevish as his; the paper flowers on the rod, however, pinched her thin legs, and she shrunk up to her original size.

The little Ida thought this scene so droll that she could not help laughing; the company, however, did not notice it, for the rod continued to stamp about, till at last the doll-counsellor was obliged to dance too, whether she would or no, and make herself now thin, now thick, now tall, now short, till at last the flowers interceded for her, and the rod then left her in peace.

A loud knocking was now heard from the drawer in which lay Ida's doll. It was Sophy who made the noise. She put her head out of the drawer, and asked in great astonishment, "Is there a ball here? Why has no one told me of it?"

"Will you dance with me?" asked the nut-crackers.

"Certainly; you are a very fit person to dance with me!" said Sophy, turning her back to him. She then sat down on the table, expecting that one of the flowers would come and ask her to dance; but no one came. She coughed—"Hem! hem!" Still no one came. Meantime the nut-crackers danced by himself, and his steps were not at all badly made.

As no flowers came forward to ask Sophy to dance, all at once she let herself fall down upon the floor, which excited a general commotion, so that all the flowers ran up to ask her whether she had hurt herself; but she had received no injury. The flowers, however, were all very polite, especially Ida's flowers, who took the opportunity of thanking her for the comfortable bed in which they had slept so quietly, and then seized her hands to dance with her, whilst all the other flowers stood in a circle round them. Sophy was now quite happy, and begged Ida's flowers to make use of her bed again after the ball, as she did not at all mind sleeping one night in the table-drawer.

But the flowers said, "We owe you many thanks for your kindness, but we shall not live long enough to need it, as we shall be dead by to-morrow. But ask the little Ida to bury us in the garden near her canary-bird; then we shall grow again next summer, and be even more beautiful than we have been this year."

"No, you must not die!" replied Sophy warmly, as she kissed the flowers. Just then the door was suddenly opened and a number of flowers danced into the room. Ida could not imagine where these flowers came from, unless from the King's garden. First of all entered two beautiful roses wearing golden crowns; then followed stocks and pinks, bowing to the company on all sides.

They had also a band of music with them; great poppies and peonies blew upon the shells of peas till they were quite red in the face, whilst blue and white campanulas rang a merry peal of bells. These were followed by an immense number of different flowers, all dancing—violets, daisies, lilies of the valley, narcissuses, and others, who all moved so gracefully that it was delightful to see them.

At last these happy flowers wished one another "good-night"; so little Ida once more crept into bed, to dream of all the beautiful things she had seen.

The next morning, as soon as she was up and dressed, she went to her little table to see if her flowers were there. She drew aside the bed-curtains—yes! there lay the flowers, but they were to-day much more faded than yesterday; Sophy, too, was lying in the drawer, but she looked uncommonly sleepy.

"Can you not remember what you have to say to me?" asked little Ida of her; but Sophy made a most stupid face, and answered not a syllable. "You are not at all good!" said she, "and yet all the flowers let you dance with them." She then chose out from her playthings a little pasteboard box with birds painted on it, and therein she placed the faded flowers. "That shall be your coffin," said she; "and when my Norwegian cousins come to see me, they shall go with me to bury you in the garden, so that next summer you may bloom again, and be still more beautiful than you have been this year."

The two Norwegian cousins of whom she spoke were two

lively boys, called Jonas and Esben. Their father had given them two new cross-bows, which they brought with them to show to Ida. She then told them of the poor flowers that were dead, and were to be buried in the garden. The two boys walked in front with their bows slung across their shoulders, and little Ida followed carrying the dead flowers in their pretty coffin. A grave was dug for them in the garden, Ida kissed the flowers once more, then laid the box down in the hollow, and Jonas and Esben shot arrows over the grave with their cross-bows, for they had neither guns nor cannon.

THE DAISY

LISTEN to my story!

In the country, close by the roadside, there stands a summer-house—you must certainly have seen it. In front is a little garden full of flowers, enclosed by white palings with green knobs; and on the bank outside the palings there grew, amidst the freshest of grass, a little daisy. The sun shone as brightly and warmly upon the daisy as upon the splendid large flowers within the garden, and therefore it grew hourly; so that one morning it stood fully open with its delicate white gleaming leaves, which, like rays, surrounded the little yellow sun in their centre.

It never occurred to the little flower that no one saw her, hidden as she was among the grass. She was quite contented; she turned towards the warm sun, looked at it, and listened to the lark who was singing in the air.

The daisy was as happy as if it were the day of some high festival; and yet it was only Monday. The children were at school; and, whilst they sat upon their forms and learned their lessons, the little flower upon her green stalk learned from the warm sun, and everything around her, how good God is.

Meanwhile, the little lark expressed clearly and beautifully all she felt in silence! And the flower looked up with a sort of reverence to the happy bird who could fly and sing; it did not distress her that she could not do the same. "I can see and listen," thought she; "the sun shines on me, and the wind kisses me. Oh! how richly am I blessed."

There stood within the palings several grand, stiff-looking flowers; the less fragrance they had, the more airs they gave themselves. The peonies puffed themselves out in order to make themselves larger than the roses. The tulips had the gayest colours of all; they were perfectly aware of it, and held themselves as straight as a candle, that they might be the better seen.

They took no notice at all of the little flower outside the palings; but she looked all the more upon them, thinking, "How rich and beautiful they are! Yes, that noble bird will surely fly down and visit them. How happy am I, who live so near them and see their beauty!"

Just at that moment, "quirrevit!" the lark did fly down; but he came not to the peonies or the tulips; no, he flew down to the poor little daisy in the grass, who was almost frightened from pure joy, and knew not what to think, she was so surprised. The little bird hopped about and sang, "Oh, how soft is this grass! and what a sweet little flower blooms here, with its golden heart, and silver garment!" For the yellow centre of the daisy looked just like gold, and the little petals around gleamed silver white.

How happy the little daisy was! No one can imagine how happy. The bird kissed her with his beak, sang to her, and then flew up again into the blue sky. It was a full quarter of an hour before the flower recovered herself. Half ashamed, and yet completely happy, she looked at the flowers in the garden; they must certainly be aware of the honour and happiness that had been conferred upon her; they must know how delighted she was.

But the tulips held themselves twice as stiff as before, and their faces grew quite red with anger. As to the peonies, they were so thick-headed—it was, indeed, well that they could not speak, or the little daisy would have heard something not very pleasant. The poor little flower could see well that they were in an ill humour, and she was much vexed at it.

Soon after a girl came into the garden with a knife sharp and bright; she went up to the tulips and cut off one after another. "Oh! that is horrible," sighed the daisy; "it is now all over with them."

The girl then went away with the tulips.

How glad was the daisy that she grew in the grass outside the palings, and was a despised little flower! She felt really thankful; and when the sun set, she folded her leaves, went to sleep, and dreamed all night of the sun and the beautiful bird.

The next morning, when our little flower, fresh and cheerful, again spread out all her white leaves in the bright sunshine and clear blue air, she heard the voice of the bird; but he sang so mournfully.

Alas! the poor lark had good reason for sorrow; he had been caught, and put into a cage close by the open window. He sang of the joys of a free and unrestrained flight; he sang of the young green corn in the fields, and of the pleasure of being borne up by his wings in the open air. The poor bird was certainly very unhappy; he sat a prisoner in his narrow cage!

The little daisy would so willingly have helped him, but how could she? Ah, that she knew not; she quite forgot how beautiful all around her was, how warmly the sun shone, how pretty and white her leaves were. Alas! she could only think of the imprisoned bird—for whom it was not in her power to do anything.

All at once two little boys came out of the garden; one of them had a knife in his hand, as large and as sharp as that with which the girl had cut the tulips. They went up straight to the little daisy, who could not imagine what they wanted.

"Here we can cut a nice piece of turf for the lark," said one of the boys; and he began to cut deep all round the daisy, leaving her in the centre.

"Tear out the flower," said the other boy; and the little daisy trembled all over for fear; for she knew that if she were torn out she would die, and she wished so much to live, as she was to be put into the cage with the imprisoned lark.

"No, leave it alone!" said the first, "it looks so pretty;" and so it was left alone, and was put into the lark's cage.

But the poor bird loudly lamented the loss of its freedom, and beat its wings against the iron bars of its cage; and the little flower could not speak, could not say a single word of comfort to him, much as she wished to do so. Thus passed the whole morning.

"There is no water here!" said the imprisoned lark; "they have all gone out and forgotten me; not a drop of water to drink! My throat is dry and burning! there is fire and ice within me; and the air is so heavy! Alas! I must die; I must leave the warm sunshine, the fresh green trees, and all the beautiful things which God has created."

And then he pierced his beak into the cool grass, in order to refresh himself a little; and his eye fell upon the daisy, and the bird bowed to her, and said, "Thou too wilt wither here, thou poor little flower! They had given me thee, and the piece of green around thee, instead of the whole world which I possessed before! Every little blade of grass is to be to me a green tree, thy every white petal a fragrant flower! Alas! thou only remindest me of what I have lost."

"Oh, that I could comfort him!" thought the daisy; but she could not move. Yet the fragrance which came from her delicate blossom was stronger than is usual with this flower; the bird noticed it, and although, panting with thirst, he tore the green blades in very anguish, he did not touch the flower.

It was evening, and yet no one came to bring the poor bird a drop of water; he stretched out his slender wings, and shook them convulsively. His song was a mournful "pipi"; his little head bent towards the flowers; and the bird's heart broke from thirst and desire. The flower could not now, as on the preceding evening, fold together her leaves and sleep; she bent down sad and sick to the ground.

The boys did not come till the next morning; and when they saw the bird was dead they wept bitterly. They dug a pretty grave, which they adorned with flower petals; the bird's corpse was put into a pretty red box—royally was the poor bird buried! While he lived and sang they forgot him, left him suffering in his cage, and now he was highly honoured and bitterly bewailed.

But the piece of turf with the daisy in it was thrown out into the street: no one thought of her who had felt most for the little bird, and who had so much wished to comfort him.

THE BUCKWHEAT

IF, after a tempest, you chance to walk through a field where buckwheat is growing, you may observe that it is burned as black as though a flame of fire had passed over it; and, should you ask the reason, the peasant will tell you, "The lightning has done it."

But how is it that the lightning has done it? I will tell you what the sparrow told me; and the sparrow heard the story from an old willow-tree, which grew, and still grows, close to a field of buckwheat.

This willow-tree is tall and highly respectable, but at the same time old and wrinkled. Its trunk has been riven asunder from top to bottom; grass and brambles grow out of the gap; the tree bends forward, and the branches hang down almost to the ground, looking like long green hair.

There were different kinds of corn growing in the fields around the willow—rye, wheat, and oats—the beautiful oats, whose ears, when they are ripe, look like a number of little yellow canary-birds, sitting upon one branch. The corn-ears were richly blessed; and the fuller they were, the lower they bowed their heads in pious humility.

But there was also a field of buckwheat, lying just in front of the old willow-tree; the buckwheat bowed not like the rest of the corn; he stood stiff and proud.

"I am quite as rich as the wheat," said he; "and besides, I am so much more handsome. My flowers are as beautiful as the blossoms of the apple-tree; it is delightful to look at me and my companions. Do you know anything more beautiful than we are, you old willow-tree?"

And the willow-tree bent his head, as much as to say, "Yes, indeed I do!" But the buckwheat was puffed up with pride, and said, "The stupid tree! he is so old that grass is growing out of his body."

Now came a dreadful storm; all the flowers of the field folded their leaves, or bent their heads, whilst it passed over them; the buckwheat, however, in his pride still stood erect.

"Bow thy heads as we do!" said the flowers.

"I have no need," said the buckwheat.

"Bow thy head as we do," said the corn. "The angel of storms comes flying hitherward; he has wings which reach from the clouds to the earth; he will strike thee down before thou hast time to plead for mercy!"

"No, I will not bow!" said the buckwheat.

"Close thy flowers, and fold thy leaves," said the old willow-tree; "look not into the flash, when the cloud breaks. Even men dare not do that; for in the flash, one looks into God's Heaven, and that sight can dazzle even human eyes. What, then, would it prove to mere vegetables like us, if we should dare to do so—we, who are so inferior to men?"

"So inferior, indeed!" said the buckwheat. "Now then, I *will* look right into God's Heaven." And in his pride and haughtiness, he did gaze upon the lightning without shrinking. Such was the flash that it seemed as if the whole world was in flames.

When the tempest was over, flowers and corn, greatly refreshed by the rain, once more breathed pure air; but the buckwheat had been burned as black as coal by the lightning; it stood on the field a dead, useless plant.

The old willow-tree waved its branches to and fro in the wind; and large drops of water fell from the green leaves, as though the tree wept. And the sparrows asked, "Why weepest thou? It is so beautiful here! See how the sun shines; how the clouds pass over the clear sky; how sweet is the fragrance of the flowers! Why, then, weepest thou, old willow-tree?"

And the willow-tree told of the buckwheat's pride and haughtiness; and of the punishment which followed. I, who relate this story, heard it from the sparrows—they told it to me one evening, when I asked them for a tale.

THE DUSTMAN

There is no one in the whole world who knows so many stories as the Dustman. Oh! his are delightful stories.

In the evening, when children are sitting quietly at table, or on their little stools, he takes off his shoes, comes softly upstairs, opens the doorway gently, and all on a sudden throws dust into the children's eyes. He then glides behind them, and breathes lightly, very lightly upon their necks, and their heads become, oh, so heavy! But it does them no harm, for the Dustman means it kindly; he only wants the children to be quiet, and they are most quiet when they are in bed. They must be quiet, in order that he may tell them his stories.

When the children are asleep, the Dustman sits down upon the bed; he is gaily dressed, and his coat is of silk; but of what colour it is impossible to say, for it seems now green, now red, now blue, according to the light. Under each arm he holds an umbrella; one, which has pictures painted on it, he holds over good children: it makes them have the most delightful dreams all night long. The other, which has nothing on it, he holds over naughty children, so that they sleep heavily, and awake in the morning without having dreamed at all.

Now let us hear what stories the Dustman told to a little boy, of the name of Hialmar, to whom he came every evening for a whole week through. There are seven stories altogether, for the week has seven days.

Monday

"Listen to me," said the Dustman, as soon as he had got Hialmar into bed. "Now I will decorate your room;" and all at once, as he was speaking, the flowers in the flower-pots grew up into large trees, whose long branches reached to the ceiling, and along the walls, so that the room looked like a beautiful arbour. All these branches were full of flowers, and every flower was more beautiful even than the rose, and had such a pleasant smell.

Moreover, could you have tasted them, you would have found them sweeter than preserves. And fruit, which shone like gold, hung from the trees; also dumplings full of currants: never was the like seen before. But, at the same time, a loud wailing was heard in the table-drawer, where Hialmar's school-books were kept.

"What is the matter?" said the Dustman, going up to the table, and taking out the drawer. There lay the slate, on which the figures were pressing and squeezing together, because a wrong figure had got into the sum. The pencil hopped and skipped about like a little dog; he wanted to help the sum, but he could not.

And a little farther off lay Hialmar's copy-book. A complaining and moaning came thence also, which was quite unpleasant to hear: at the beginning of every line on each page, there stood a large letter with a little letter by its side. This was the copy; and after them stood other letters intended to look like the copy. Hialmar had written these; but they seemed to have fallen over the lines, upon which they ought to have stood.

"Look, this is the way you must hold yourselves," said the copy; "look, slanting just so, and turning round with a jerk."

"Oh! we would do so willingly," said Hialmar's letters; "but we cannot, we are so badly made."

"Then you shall have some of the children's powders," said the Dustman.

"Oh, no!" cried they, and stood so straight that it was a pleasure to see them.

"Well, I cannot tell you any more stories now," said the Dustman; "I must drill these letters—right, left, right, left!" So he drilled the letters till they looked as straight and perfect as only the letters in a copy can be. However, after the Dustman had gone away, and when Hialmar looked at them the next morning, they were as miserable and badly formed as before.

Tuesday

As soon as Hialmar was in bed, the Dustman touched, with his little magic wand, all the pieces of furniture in the room; whereupon they all began to talk. They all talked about themselves, except the spittoon, who stood quite still, and was much vexed at their being so vain—all talking about themselves, without ever thinking of him who stood so modestly in the corner, and suffered himself to be spat upon.

Over the wardrobe there hung a large picture in a gilt frame; it was a landscape. There you might see tall trees, flowers blossoming in the grass, and a river that wound round the wood, passing many a grand old castle on its way to the sea.

The Dustman touched the picture with his magic wand, and immediately the birds began to sing, the boughs of the trees waved to and fro, and the clouds actually flew; one could see their shadows move over the landscape.

The Dustman then lifted little Hialmar up to the frame, and Hialmar put his legs into the picture. There he stood amid the tall grass. He ran to the water's edge, and sat down in a little boat, painted red and white, with sails glittering like silver; six swans, with golden wreaths round their necks, and bright blue stars upon their heads, drew the boat along, near a green wood, where the trees were telling stories about robbers and witches, and the flowers were talking of the pretty little fairies, and what the butterflies had said to them.

Beautiful fishes, with scales like gold and silver, swam behind the boat, every now and then leaping up, so that the water was splashed over Hialmar's head; birds red and blue, great and small, flew after him in two long rows; the gnats danced, and the cockchafers said "Boom, boom!" They all wished to accompany Hialmar, and every one of them had a story to tell.

A pleasant voyage was that! The woods were now thick and gloomy, now like beautiful gardens beaming with flowers and sunshine. Large palaces built of glass or marble rose from among the trees; young princesses stood in the balconies— they were all little girls whom Hialmar knew well, and with whom he had often played. They stretched out their hands to him, each holding a pretty little image made of sugar, such as are in confectioners' shops. Hialmar seized the end of one of these little images as he sailed by, and a princess kept hold of the other; so each got half—the princess the smaller, Hialmar the larger.

At every castle little princes were keeping guard; they shouldered their golden scimitars, and showered down raisins and tin soldiers—these were true princes. Hialmar sailed sometimes through woods, sometimes through large halls, or the middle of a town. Among others he passed through the town where his nurse lived, she who had brought him up from his infancy, and who loved him so much. She nodded and beckoned to him as he passed by, and sang the pretty verses she had herself composed and sent to him.

> 'How many, many hours I think on thee,
>   My own dear Hialmar, still my pride and joy!
> How have I hung delighted over thee,
>   Kissing thy rosy cheeks, my darling boy!
>
> "Thy first low accents it was mine to hear,
>   To-day my farewell words to thee shall fly.
> Oh! may the Lord thy shield be ever near,
>   And fit thee for a mansion in the sky!"

And all the birds sang with her, the flowers danced upon their stalks, and the old trees nodded their heads whilst the Dustman told stories to them also.

Wednesday

Oh, how the rain was pouring down! Hialmar could hear it even in his sleep; and when the Dustman opened the window the water came in upon the ledge; there was quite a lake in front of the house, and on it a splendid ship.

"Will you sail with me, little Hialmar?" said the Dustman. "If you will, you shall visit foreign lands to-night, and be here again by the morning."

And now Hialmar, dressed in his Sunday clothes, was in the ship; the weather immediately cleared up, and they floated down the street, cruised round the church, and were soon sailing upon the wide sea. They quickly lost sight of land, and could see only a number of storks, who had all come from Hialmar's country, and were going to a warmer one.

The storks were flying one after another, and were already very far from land, when one of them was so weary that his wings could scarcely bear him up any longer; he was last in the train, and was soon far behind the others. He sank lower and lower, with his wings outspread; he still endeavoured to move them, but it was all in vain; his wings touched the ship's cordage; he slid down the sail, and—bounce! there he stood on the deck.

So the cabin-boy put him into the place where the hens, ducks, and turkeys were kept; the poor stork stood amongst them quite confounded.

"Only look, what a foolish fellow!" said all the hens. And the turkey-cock made himself as big as he could, and asked him who he was; and the ducks waddled backwards and pushed each other—"Quack, quack!"

The stork then told them about his warm Africa, about the pyramids, and about the ostrich, who races through the desert like a wild horse. But the ducks did not understand him, and again pushed each other, saying, "Do we not all agree in thinking him very stupid?"

"Yes, indeed he is stupid!" said the turkey-cock, and began to gobble.

So the stork was silent, and thought of his Africa.

"You have really very pretty slender legs!" said the turkey-cock. "What did they cost you per yard?"

"Quack, quack, quack," all the ducks began to titter; but the stork seemed not to have heard the question.

"You might just as well have laughed with them," said the turkey-cock to him, "for it was a capital joke! But perhaps it was not high enough for you? Ah! ah! he has very grand ideas; let us go on amusing ourselves." And then he gobbled, the hens cackled, and the ducks quacked; they made a horrid noise with their amusements.

But Hialmar went to the hen-house, opened the door and called the stork, who immediately jumped on deck. He had now rested himself sufficiently; and bowed his head to Hialmar, as if to thank him. He then spread his wings and flew away—whilst the hens cackled, the ducks quacked, and the turkey-cock turned red as fire.

"To-morrow we will have you all made into soup!" said Hialmar; then he awoke, and found himself in his own little bed. A strange journey had the Dustman taken him that night!

Thursday

"I'll tell you what!" said the Dustman—"do not be afraid, and you shall see a little mouse!" and he held out his hand, with the pretty little animal in it. "She is come to invite you to a wedding: there are two little mice here, who intend, this very night, to enter into matrimony. They live under the floor of the dining-room; theirs must be such a pretty house."

"But how can I get through the little hole?" asked Hialmar.

"Let me take care of that," said the Dustman. "I will make you very little!" And he touched Hialmar with his magic wand, and he became smaller and smaller, till at last he was no larger than his own fingers. "Now you can borrow the tin soldier's clothes; I think they will just fit you; and it looks so grand to wear uniform when you are in company."

"Ah, yes!" said Hialmar, and in another moment he was dressed like the prettiest little tin soldier.

"Will you have the goodness to sit down in your mother's thimble?" said the little mouse. "In that case, I shall feel honoured by drawing you along."

"What! will you really take so much trouble?" said Hialmar; and away they went to the mouse's wedding.

They first came to a long passage under the floor, which was high enough for the thimble to be drawn along through it, and was lighted up with toadstools throughout.

"Is there not a pleasant smell here?" said the mouse who was drawing the thimble. "The whole passage is covered with rind of bacon; there is nothing more delightful!"

They now entered the bridal apartment: the lady mice stood on the right-hand side, whispering together, seemingly very merry; on the left side stood the gentlemen mice, who were all stroking their whiskers with their paws. In the middle of the room, the bride and bridegroom were seen standing in the scooped-out rind of a cheese; and kissing each other incessantly before the eyes of all present. They were already betrothed, and were to be married immediately.

Strangers were arriving every moment; the mice almost trod each other to death; and the bridal pair had placed themselves just in the centre of the doorway, so that one could get neither out nor in. The whole room was, like the passage, covered with the rind of bacon; this was all the entertainment given. For dessert, however, a pea was exhibited, in which a little mouse, belonging to the family, had bitten the initials of the married couple. Was not this an exquisite idea?

All the mice agreed that the wedding had been extremely genteel, and the conversation delightful.

So now Hialmar returned home; he had certainly been in most distinguished company; but still, he felt as though he had rather lowered himself, by becoming so small, and wearing the uniform of a tin soldier.

Friday

"It is wonderful what a number of old people there are, always wanting to have me with them," said the Dustman; "especially those who have done anything wicked."

"'Dear, good Dustman,' they say to me, 'we cannot sleep a wink all night; we lie awake, and see all our bad deeds sitting on the edge of the bed, like little ugly goblins, and sprinkling hot water over us. If you would but come and drive them away, so that we could have a little sleep;' and then they sigh so deeply, 'we will be sure to pay you well. Good-night, Dustman, the money is lying at the window.'— But I do not come for money," said the Dustman.

"What are we to do to-night?" asked Hialmar.

"Why, I do not know whether you would like to go again to a wedding? The one of which I am now speaking is quite of another kind from yesterday's. Your sister's great doll, that looks like a man, and is called Herman, is going to marry the doll Bertha; besides which, it is a birthday, so they will doubtless receive a great many presents."

"Oh, yes! I know that already," said Hialmar; "whenever the dolls want new clothes, my sister calls it either their birthday or their wedding-day. They must certainly have been married a hundred times already."

"Yes, but to-night they will be married for the hundred and first time; and when it has come to that number, they can never be married again. So this time the wedding will be splendid! only look!"

And Hialmar looked upon the table, where stood the little doll's house; the windows were lighted up, and tin soldiers presented arms at the door. The bride and bridegroom were sitting on the ground, and leaning against the leg of the table; they seemed very thoughtful; there was, perhaps, good reason for being so. But the Dustman had, meanwhile, put on his grandmother's black gown, and married them. When the ceremony was over, all the furniture in the room began singing the following pretty song, which had been written by the lead pencil—

"Waft, gentle breeze, our kind farewell
 To the tiny house where the bridefolks dwell,
 With their skin of kid-leather fitting so well;
 They are straight and upright as a tailor's ell.
 Hurrah, hurrah for beau and belle!
 Let echo repeat our kind farewell."

And now presents were brought to them; all eatables, however, they declined accepting: love was enough for them to live upon.

"Shall we go into the country, or make a tour in some foreign land?" asked the bridegroom. So the swallow, who had travelled a good deal, and the old hen, who had hatched five broods of chickens, were consulted. And the swallow spoke of those beautiful, warm countries where bunches of grapes, large and heavy, hang on the vines; where the air is so balmy, and the mountains of various hues such as are never known here.

"But then they have not our green cabbages!" said the hen. "One summer, I and all my chickens lived in the country; there was a gravel-pit in which we might go and scrape about; besides, we had access to a garden, full of green cabbages. Oh, how green they were! I cannot imagine anything more beautiful!"

"But one head of cabbage looks exactly like another," said the swallow; "and then we so often have wet weather here!"

"One gets accustomed to that," said the hen.

"But it is so cold, it freezes!"

"That is good for the cabbages," said the hen; "besides which, it can be warm sometimes. Did we not, four years ago, have a summer which lasted five weeks? It was so hot that one could hardly breathe. Then, too, we have not all the poisonous animals which they have in foreign countries; and we are free from robbers.

"He is a blockhead who does not think our country the most beautiful of all! He does not deserve to live here!" and at these words, tears rolled down the hen's cheeks. "I too have travelled; I have been twelve miles in a coop. There is no pleasure at all in travelling."

"Yes, the hen is a sensible animal!" said the doll Bertha. "I do not wish to travel over the mountains; one is always going up and down! No, we will go to the gravel-pit, and walk in the garden, among the cabbages."

And so it was settled.

Saturday

"Now may I have some stories?" asked little Hialmar, as soon as the Dustman had put him to sleep.

"We shall have no time for them this evening," said the Dustman, spreading his picture umbrella over him. "Look at these Chinese!" The umbrella resembled a large Chinese plate, with blue trees, and pointed bricks; little Chinese men and women stood nodding their heads among them.

"By to-morrow morning all the world must be put in

order," said the Dustman; "it is a festival day—it is Sunday. I must go to the church-tower, to see whether the little spirits of the church are rubbing the bells, so as to make them ring merrily. I must away to the fields, to see that the winds are sweeping the dust off the grass and leaves.

"I must take down the stars, in order to brighten them. I put them into my apron, but first they must be numbered; and the holes in which they sit, up in the sky, must be numbered also, that every one may return to his proper place; else they would not sit firmly, and we should have too many falling stars, one coming down after another."

"Listen to me, Mr. Dustman," said an old portrait, which hung by the wall, near where Hialmar was sleeping. "Do you know that I am Hialmar's great-grandfather? I am much obliged to you for telling the boy stories; but you must not puzzle him. Stars cannot be taken down and brightened; they are bodies like our earth."

"Many thanks, old great-grandfather!" said the Dustman, "many thanks. Thou art certainly very old, but I am older still! I am an old heathen; the Greeks and Romans called me the God of Dreams. I have been in families of the greatest distinction, and I go there still! I know how to deal with great and small! Now it is thy turn; say what thou pleasest!"

"So one is no longer allowed to speak one's mind!" muttered the old portrait.

And presently Hialmar awoke.

Sunday

"Good-evening!" said the Dustman; and Hialmar nodded his head to him, and jumped up to turn his great-grandfather's portrait to the wall, in order that he might not interrupt them, as yesterday.

"Now you shall tell me stories, about the five green peas who all lived in one pod; and about the cock courting the hen; and about the darning-needle who wished to be fashionable, and fancied herself a fine needle."

"One may have too much of a good thing!" said the Dustman. "I would rather show you something else; I will show you my brother. He never comes more than once to any one; and whomsoever he visits, he takes on his horse, and tells him a story. He knows only two stories—the one unspeakably delightful, such as no one in the world can imagine; the other so dreadful, so horrible—it is not to be described."

And the Dustman lifted little Hialmar up to the window, saying, "There is my brother, the other Dustman, he is also called Death! You see he is not so frightful as he is represented in picture-books, where he seems to be all bones. No, he wears clothes embroidered with silver; it is the gayest of uniforms! a mantle of black velvet flies over his horse, behind him. See how he gallops!"

And Hialmar saw the other Dustman ride on, and take old and young with him on his horse; some he placed in front, and others behind; but he always asked first, what sort of a journal they had to show.

"Good!" they all replied. "Yes, but let me see it," said he. So they were obliged to show it to him; and all those who had "Very Good" written in it, were put in front of the horse, and heard the story that was so delightful. But those who had "Pretty Good" or "Bad" inscribed in their journal, were obliged to get up behind and listen to the horrible story. They trembled and wept; they tried to jump down from the horse's back but that they could not do, for they were as firmly fixed on as if they had grown there.

"Death is a most beautiful Dustman," said Hialmar. "I am not afraid of him."

"That you should not be," said the Dustman; "only take care to have a good journal to show."

"Ah, this is very instructive," muttered the great-grand-father's portrait. "It is always of use to give one's opinion." He was now satisfied.

These are the stories of the Dustman; perhaps he may tell you more this very evening.

THE RED SHOES

THERE was once a little girl, very pretty and delicate, but so poor that in summer-time she always went barefoot, and in winter wore large wooden shoes, so that her little ankles grew quite red and sore.

In the village dwelt the shoemaker's mother. She sat down one day and made out of some old pieces of red cloth a pair of little shoes; they were clumsy enough, certainly, but they fitted the little girl tolerably well, and she gave them to her. The little girl's name was Karen.

It was the day of her mother's funeral when the red shoes were given to Karen; they were not at all suitable for mourning, but she had no others, and in them she walked with bare legs behind the miserable straw bier.

Just then a large old carriage rolled by, in it sat a large old lady, who looked at the little girl and pitied her, and said to the priest, "Give me the little girl and I will take care of her."

And Karen thought it was all for the sake of the red shoes that the old lady had taken this fancy to her; but the old lady said they were frightful, and they were burned. And Karen was dressed very neatly, and she was taught to read and to work; and people told her she was pretty. But the mirror said, "Thou art more than pretty, thou art beautiful!"

It happened one day that the Queen travelled through that part of the country with her little daughter, the Princess; and all the people, Karen amongst them, crowded in front of the palace, whilst the little Princess stood, dressed in white at a window, for every one to see her. She wore neither train nor gold crown; but on her feet were pretty red morocco shoes—much prettier ones, indeed, than those the shoemaker's mother had made for little Karen. Nothing in the world could be compared to these red shoes!

Karen was now old enough to be confirmed; she was to have both new frock and new shoes. The rich shoemaker in the town took the measure of her little foot. Large glass cases full of neat shoes and shining boots were fixed round the room; however, the old lady's sight was not very good, and, naturally enough, she had not so much pleasure in looking at them as Karen had. Amongst the shoes was a pair of red ones, just like those worn by the Princess. How gay they were! And the shoemaker said they had been made for a count's daughter, but had not quite fitted her.

"They are of polished leather," said the old lady; "see how they shine!"

"Yes, they shine beautifully!" exclaimed Karen. And, as the shoes fitted her, they were bought; but the old lady did not know that they were red, for she would never have suffered Karen to go to confirmation in red shoes. But Karen did so.

Everybody looked at her feet, and, as she walked up the nave to the chancel, it seemed to her that even the antique sculptured figures on the monuments, with their stiff ruffs, and long black robes, fixed their eyes on her red shoes. Of them only she thought when the Bishop laid his hand on her head, when he spoke of Holy Baptism, of her covenant with God, and how that she must now be a full-grown Christian. The organ sent forth its deep, solemn tones, the children's sweet voices mingled with those of the choristers, but still Karen only thought of her red shoes.

That afternoon, when the old lady was told that Karen had worn red shoes at her confirmation, she was very much vexed; and told Karen that they were quite unsuitable; and that, henceforward, whenever she went to church, she must wear black shoes, were they ever so old.

Next Sunday was the communion day. Karen looked first at the red shoes, then at the black ones, then at the red again— and—put them on.

It was beautiful sunshiny weather; Karen and the old lady walked to church through the cornfields; the path was very dusty.

At the church door stood an old soldier; he was leaning on crutches, and had a marvellously long beard, not white, but reddish-hued; and he bowed almost to the earth, and asked the old lady if he might wipe the dust off her shoes. And

Karen put out her little foot also. "Oh, what pretty dancing-shoes!" quoth the old soldier; "take care, and mind you do not let them slip off when you dance;" and he passed his hands over them.

The old lady gave the soldier a halfpenny, and then went with Karen into church.

And every one looked at Karen's red shoes, and all the carved figures, too, bent their gaze upon them; and when Karen knelt before the altar, the red shoes still floated before her eyes; she thought of them, and of them only; and she forgot to join in the hymn of praise—she forgot to repeat "Our Father."

At last all the people came out of church, and the old lady got into her carriage. Karen was just lifting her foot to follow her, when the old soldier standing in the porch exclaimed, "Only look, what pretty dancing-shoes!"

And Karen could not help it; she felt she must make a few of her dancing steps; and after she had once begun, her feet continued to move, just as if the shoes had received power over them; she danced round the churchyard, she could not stop. The coachman was obliged to run after her; he took hold of her and lifted her into the carriage, but the feet still continued to dance, so as to kick the good old lady most cruelly. At last the shoes were taken off, and the feet had rest.

And now the shoes were put away in a cupboard, but Karen could not help going to look at them every now and then.

The old lady lay ill in bed; the doctor said she could not live very much longer. She certainly needed careful nursing, and who should be her nurse and constant attendant but Karen?

But there was to be a grand ball in the town, and Karen was invited; she looked at the old lady who was almost dying—she looked at the red shoes—she put them on, there could be no harm in doing that, at least; she went to the ball, and began to dance.

But when she wanted to move to the right, the shoes bore her to the left; and, when she would dance up the room, the shoes danced down the room, danced down the stairs, through the streets, and through the gates of the town. Dance

VERNON SOPER

she did, and dance she must, straight out into the dark world.

Something all at once shone through the trees. She thought at first it must be the moon's bright face, shining blood-red through the night mists; but no, it was the old soldier with the red beard. He sat there, nodding at her, and repeating, "Only look what pretty dancing-shoes!"

She was very much frightened, and tried to throw off her red shoes, but could not unclasp them. She hastily tore off her stockings, but the shoes she could not get rid of—they had, it seemed, grown on to her feet. Dance she did, and dance she must, over field and meadow, in rain and in sunshine, by night and by day.

By night! that was most horrible! She danced into the lonely churchyard, but the dead there danced not; they were at rest. She would fain have sat down on the poor man's grave, where the bitter tansy grew, but for her there was neither rest nor respite. She danced past the open church door; there she saw an angel, clad in long white robes, and with wings that reached from his shoulders to the earth; his countenance was grave and stern, and in his hand he held a broad glittering sword.

"Dance thou shalt," said he; "dance on, in thy red shoes, till thou art pale and cold, and thy skin shrinks and crumples up like a skeleton's! Dance thou shalt still, from door to door, and wherever proud, vain children live thou shalt knock, so that they may hear thee and fear! Dance shalt thou, dance on——"

"Mercy!" cried Karen; but she heard not the angel's answer, for the shoes carried her through the gate into the fields, along highways and byways, and still she must dance.

One morning she danced past a door she knew well; she heard psalm-singing from within, and presently a coffin, strewn with flowers, was borne out. Then Karen knew that the good old lady was dead; and she felt herself a thing forsaken by all mankind, and accursed by the Angel of God.

Dance she did, and dance she must, even through the dark night; the shoes bore her continually over thorns and briers, till her limbs were torn and bleeding. Away she danced over the heath to a little solitary house; she knew that the headsman dwelt there, and she tapped with her fingers against the panes, crying,—"Come out! come out! I cannot come in to you, I am dancing."

And the headsman replied, "Surely thou knowest not who I am. I cut off the heads of wicked men, and my axe is very sharp and keen."

"Cut not off my head!" said Karen; "for then I could not live to repent of my sin; but cut off my feet with the red shoes."

And then she confessed to him all her sin, and the headsman cut off her feet with the red shoes on them; but even after this the shoes still danced away with those little feet over the fields, and into the deep forests.

And the headsman made her a pair of wooden feet, and hewed down some boughs to serve her as crutches; and he taught her the psalm which is always repeated by criminals; and she kissed the hand that had guided the axe, and went her way over the heath.

"Now I have certainly suffered quite enough through the red shoes," thought Karen; "I will go to church and let people see me once more!" and she went as fast as she could to the church-porch; but, as she approached it, the red shoes danced before her, and she was frightened and turned her back.

All that week through she endured the keenest anguish, and shed many bitter tears. However, when Sunday came, she said to herself, "Well, I must have suffered and striven enough by this time; I dare say I am quite as good as many of those who are holding their heads so high in church."

So she took courage and went there; but she had not passed the churchyard gate before she saw the red shoes again dancing before her, and in great terror she again turned back, and more deeply than ever bewailed her sin.

She then went to the pastor's house, and begged that some employment might be given her, promising to work diligently and do all she could. She did not wish for any wages, she said: she only wanted a roof to shelter her, and to dwell with good people. And the pastor's wife had pity on her, and took her into her service. And Karen was grateful and industrious.

Every evening she sat silently listening to the pastor while he read the Holy Scriptures aloud. All the children loved her; but when she heard them talk about dress and finery, and about being as beautiful as a queen, she would sorrowfully shake her head.

Again Sunday came; all the pastor's household went to church, and they asked her if she would not go too, but she sighed and looked, with tears in her eyes, upon her crutches.

When they were all gone, she went into her own little, lowly chamber—it was but just large enough to contain a bed and chair—and there she sat down with her psalm-book in her hand; and while she was meekly and devoutly reading in it, the wind wafted the tones of the organ from the church into her room, and she lifted up her face to heaven and prayed, with tears, "O God, help me!"

Then the sun shone brightly, so brightly—and behold! close before her stood the white-robed Angel of God, the same whom she had seen on that night of horror at the church-porch, but his hand wielded not now, as then, a sharp, threatening sword. He held a lovely green bough full of roses.

With this he touched the ceiling, which immediately rose to a great height, a bright gold star spangling in the spot where the Angel's green bough had touched it. And he touched the walls, upon which the room widened, and Karen saw the organ, the old monuments, and the congregation all sitting in their richly-carved seats, and singing from their psalm-books.

For the church had come home to the poor girl in her narrow chamber, or rather the chamber had grown, as it were, into the church; she sat with the rest of the pastor's household, and, when the psalm was ended, they looked up and nodded to her, saying, "Thou didst well to come, Karen!"

"This is mercy!" said she.

And the organ played again, and the children's voices in the choir mingled so sweetly and plaintively with it. The bright sunbeams streamed warmly through the windows upon Karen's seat. Her heart was so full of sunshine, of peace and gladness, that it broke; her soul flew upon a sunbeam to her Father in heaven, where not a look of reproach awaited her, not a word was breathed of the red shoes.

THE TOP AND THE BALL

A TOP and a ball were lying close together in a drawer, among other playthings.

Thus said the top to the ball—

"Why should we not become bride and bridegroom, since we are thrown so much together?"

But the ball, who was made of morocco leather, and fancied herself a very fashionable young lady, would not hear of such a proposal.

The next day, the little boy to whom the playthings belonged came to the drawer; he painted the top red and yellow, and drove a brass nail through the middle of it; it was glorious after that to see the top spin round.

"Look at me now!" said he to the ball; "what do you say to me now? Why should not we become man and wife? We suit each other so well; you can jump, and I can spin; it would not be easy to find a couple happier than we should be."

"Do you think so?" said the ball; "perhaps you do not know that my father and mother were morocco slippers, and that I have cork in my body."

"Yes; but I am made of mahogany," said the top; "the Burgomaster manufactured me with his own hands; for he has a lathe of his own, and took great pleasure in turning me."

"Can I trust you in this?" said the ball.

"May I never be whipped again if I lie," said the top.

"You don't talk amiss," said the ball; "but I am not at liberty, I am as good as betrothed to a young swallow. Whenever I fly up in the air, he puts his head out of his nest and says, 'Will you marry me?' I have said yes to him in my heart, and that is almost the same as a betrothal. But one thing I promise you, I will never forget you!"

"That will be of great use!" said the top; and no more was then said on the subject.

Next day the ball was taken out. The top saw it fly like a bird into the air, so high that it could be seen no longer; it came back again, but every time it touched the ground it sprang higher than before.

Either love, or the cork she had in her body, must have been the cause of this.

The ninth time she did not return; the boy sought and sought, but she was gone.

"I know well where she is," sighed the top; "she is in the swallow's nest, celebrating her wedding." The more the top thought of it, the more amiable did the ball appear to him; that she could not be his only made his love the more vehement. Another had been preferred to him; he could not forget that! And the top spinned and hummed; but was always thinking of the dear ball, who in his imagination grew more and more amiable. Thus passed several years, and there was constant love!

The top was no longer young. However, he was one day gilded all over; never before had he looked so handsome. He was now a gilt top, and spun most bravely, humming all the time: yes, that was famous! But all at once he sprang too high, and was gone! They sought and sought, even in the cellar; he was nowhere to be found.

Where was he?

He had jumped into a barrel full of all sorts of rubbish—cabbage-stalks, sweepings, dust, etc., which had fallen in from the gutter.

"Alas! here I lie, my gay gilding will soon be spoiled; and what sort of trumpery can I have fallen in with?" And he peeped at a long cabbage-stalk which lay fearfully near him, and at a strange round thing somewhat like an apple. But it was not an apple, it was an old ball, which had lain several years in the gutter, and was quite soaked through with water.

"Thank goodness! At last I see an equal, with whom I may speak," said the ball, looking fixedly at the gilt top. "I am made of real morocco, sewed together by a young lady's hands, and I have cork in my body; but I shall never again be noticed by any one! I was on the point of marriage with the swallow when I fell into the gutter, and there I have lain five years, and am now wet through. Only think what a wearisome time it is for a young lady to be in such a situation!"

But the top answered not a word; he thought on his long-lamented companion; and the more he heard the more certain he became that it was she herself.

The servant-maid now came, and was going to turn the barrel over. "Hurrah!" exclaimed she, "there is the gilt top."

And the top was brought back to the play-room; it was used and admired as before: but nothing more was heard of the ball, nor did the top ever even speak of his former love for her; such a feeling must have passed away. How could it be otherwise, when he found that she had lain five years in the gutter, and that she was so much altered he scarcely knew her again when he met her in the barrel among rubbish?

THE FIR-TREE

FAR away in the deep forest there once grew a pretty Fir-Tree. The situation was delightful; the sun shone full upon him, the breeze played freely around him, and in the neighbourhood grew many companion fir-trees, some older, some younger.

But the little Fir-Tree was not happy. He was always longing to be tall; he thought not of the warm sun and the fresh air; he cared not for the merry, prattling peasant children who came to the forest to look for strawberries and raspberries. Unless indeed, sometimes, when having filled their pitchers, or threaded the bright berries on a straw, they would sit down near the little Fir-Tree, and say, "What a pretty little tree this is;" and then the Fir-Tree would feel very much vexed.

Year by year he grew, and sent forth a long green shoot every year! For you may always tell how many years a fir-tree has lived by counting the number of joints in its stem.

"Oh, that I was as tall as the others are," sighed the little Tree; "then I should spread out my branches so far, and my crown should look out over the wide world around! The birds would build their nests among my branches; and when the wind blew I should bend my head so grandly, just as the others do!"

He had no pleasure in the sunshine, in the song of the birds, or in the red clouds that sailed over him every morning and evening.

In the winter-time, when the ground was covered with the white glistening snow, there was a hare that would come continually scampering about, and jumping right over the little Tree's head, and that was most provoking!

However, two winters passed away, and by the third the Tree was so tall that the hare was obliged to run round it. "Oh! to grow, to grow, to become tall and old, that is the only thing in the world worth living for," so thought the Tree.

The wood-cutters came in the autumn and felled some among the largest of the trees. This happened every year; and our young fir, who was by this time a tolerable height, shuddered when he saw those grand, magnificent trees fall with a tremendous crash crackling to the earth. Their boughs were then all cut off; terribly naked and lanky and long did the stem look after this; they could hardly be recognised. They were laid one upon another in wagons, and horses drew them away, far, far away from the forest.

Where could they be going? What might be their fortunes?

So next spring, when the swallows and the storks had returned from abroad, the Tree asked them, saying, "Know you not whither they are taken? Have you not met them?"

The swallows knew nothing about the matter, but the stork looked thoughtful for a moment. Then he nodded his head, and said, "Yes, I believe I have seen them! As I was flying from Egypt to this place I met several ships; those ships had splendid masts. I have little doubt that they were the trees that you speak of; they smelled like fir-wood. I may congratulate you, for they sailed gloriously, quite gloriously!"

"Oh, that I too were tall enough to sail upon the sea! Tell me what it is, this sea! and what it looks like."

"Thank you, it would take too long, a great deal!" said the stork, and away he stalked.

"Rejoice in thy youth!" said the sunbeams; "rejoice in thy luxuriant youth, in the fresh life that is within thee!"

And the wind kissed the Tree, and the dew wept tears over him, but the Fir-Tree understood them not.

When Christmas approached, many quite young trees were felled—trees which were some of them not so tall or of just the same height as the young restless Fir-Tree, who was always longing to be away. These young trees were always chosen from the most beautiful; their branches were not cut off; they were laid in a wagon, and horses drew them away, far, far away from the forest.

"Where are they going?" asked the Fir-Tree. "They are not much larger than I am, indeed one of them was much less. Why do they keep all their branches? Where can they be gone?"

"We know! we know!" twittered the sparrows. "We peeped in through the windows of the town below! We know where they are gone. Oh, you cannot think what honour and glory they receive! We looked through the window-panes and saw them planted in a warm room, and decked out with such beautiful things—gilded apples sweetmeats, playthings, and hundreds of bright candles!"

"And then?" asked the Fir-Tree, trembling in every bough—"and then—what happened then?"

"Oh, we saw no more. That was beautiful—beautiful beyond compare!"

"Is this glorious lot destined to be mine?" cried the Fir-Tree with delight. "This is far better than sailing over the sea. How I long for the time! Oh, that Christmas were come! I am now tall and full of branches, like the others which last year were carried away. Oh, that I were even now in the wagon! that I were in the warm room, honoured and adorned! Then—yes, then, something still better must happen, else why should they take the trouble to decorate me? It must be that something still greater, still more splendid, must happen—but what? Oh, I suffer, I suffer with longing! I know not what it is that I feel."

"Rejoice in our love," said the air and the sunshine. "Rejoice in thy youth and thy freedom!"

But rejoice he never would. He grew and grew, in winter as in summer; he stood there clothed in green, dark green foliage. The people that saw him said, "That is a beautiful tree!" and, next Christmas, he was the first that was felled.

The axe struck sharply through the wood; the Tree fell to the earth with a heavy groan. He suffered an agony, a faintness that he had never expected; he quite forgot to think of his good fortune, he felt such sorrow at being compelled to leave his home—the place whence he had sprung. He knew that he should never see again those dear old comrades, or the little bushes and flowers that had flourished under his shadow—perhaps not even the birds. Neither did he find the journey by any means pleasant.

The Tree first came to himself when, in the courtyard to which he was first taken with the other trees, he heard a man say, "This is a splendid one; the very thing we want!"

Then came two smartly-dressed servants, and carried the Fir-Tree into a large and handsome saloon. Pictures hung on the walls, and on the mantelpiece stood large Chinese vases with lions on the lids. There were rocking-chairs, silken sofas, tables covered with picture-books, and toys that had cost a hundred times a hundred rix dollars—at least, so said the children.

And the Fir-Tree was planted in a large cask filled with sand, but one one could know it was a cask, for it was hung with green cloth, and placed upon a carpet woven of many gay colours. Oh, how the Tree trembled! What was to happen next?

A young lady, assisted by the servants, now began to adorn him. Upon some branches they hung little nets cut out of coloured paper, every net filled with sugar plums; from others gilded apples and walnuts were suspended, looking just as if they had grown there, and more than a hundred little wax tapers, red, blue, and white, were placed here and there among the boughs. Dolls that looked almost like men and women—the Tree had never seen such things before—seemed dancing to and fro among the leaves, and highest, on the summit, was fastened a large star of gold tinsel; this was indeed splendid—splendid beyond compare.

"This evening," they said—"this evening it will be lighted up."

"Would that it were evening," thought the Tree. "Would that the lights were kindled, for then—what will happen then? Will the trees come out of the forest to see me? Will the sparrows fly here and look in through the window-panes? Shall I stand here adorned both winter and summer?"

He thought much of it; he thought till he had barkache with longing—and barkaches with trees are as bad as head-aches with us.

The candles were lighted. Oh, what a blaze of splendour! The Tree trembled in all its branches so that one of them caught fire. "Oh, dear!" cried the young lady, and it was extinguished in great haste.

So the Tree dared not tremble again; he was so fearful of losing something of his splendour, he felt almost bewildered in the midst of all this glory and brightness. And now, all of a sudden, both folding doors were flung open, and a troop of children rushed in as if they had a mind to jump over him; the older people followed more quietly; the little ones stood quite silent, but only for a moment. Then their jubilee burst forth afresh, they shouted till the walls re-echoed; they danced round the Tree; one present after another was torn down.

"What are they doing?" thought the Tree; "what will happen now?" And the candles burned down to the branches; so they were extinguished, and the children were given leave to plunder the tree. Oh! they rushed upon him in such riot that the boughs all crackled; had not his summit been festooned with the gold star to the ceiling, he would have been overturned.

The children danced and played about with their beautiful playthings. No one thought any more of the Tree except the old nurse, who came and peered among the boughs, but it was only to see whether, perchance, a fig or an apple had not been left among them.

"A story! a story!" cried the children, pulling a short, thick man towards the Tree. He sat down, saying, "It is pleasant to sit under the shade of green boughs; besides, the Tree may be benefited by hearing my story: but I shall only tell you one.

Would you like to hear about Ivedy Avedy, or about Humpty Dumpty, who fell downstairs, and yet came to the throne and won the Princess?"

"Ivedy Avedy!" cried some; "Humpty Dumpty!" cried others: there was a famous uproar. The Fir-Tree alone was silent, thinking to himself. "Ought I to make a noise as they do? or ought I to do nothing at all?" He most certainly was one of the company, and had done all that had been required of him.

And the short thick man told the story of Humpty Dumpty, who fell downstairs, and yet came to the throne and won the Princess. And the children clapped their hands and called out for another; they wanted to hear the story of Ivedy Avedy also, but they did not get it.

The Fir-Tree stood, meanwhile, silent and thoughtful; the birds in the forest had never related anything like this. "Humpty Dumpty fell downstairs, and yet was raised to the throne and won the Princess! Yes, yes, strange things come to pass in the world!" thought the Fir-Tree, who believed it must all be true, because such a pleasant man had related it. "Ah, ah! who knows but I may fall downstairs and win a Princess?"

And he rejoiced in the expectation of being next day again decked out with candles and playthings, gold and fruit. "To-morrow I will not tremble," thought he. "I will rejoice in my magnificence. To-morrow I shall again hear the story of Humpty Dumpty, and perhaps that about Ivedy Avedy likewise." And the Tree mused thereon all night.

In the morning the maids came in.

"Now begins my state anew!" thought the Tree. But they dragged him out of the room, up the stairs, and into an attic chamber, and there thrust him into a dark corner where not a ray of light could penetrate.

"What can be the meaning of this?" thought the Tree. "What am I to do here? What shall I hear in this place?" And he leaned against the wall, and thought and thought. And plenty of time he had for thinking it over, for day after day, and night after night passed away, and yet no one ever came into the room.

At last somebody did come in, but it was only to push into the corner some old trunks. The Tree was now entirely hidden from sight, and apparently entirely forgotten.

"It is now winter," thought the Tree. "The ground is hard and covered with snow; they cannot plant me now; so I am to stay here in shelter till the spring. Men are so clever and prudent! I only wish it were not so dark and dreadfully lonely —not even a little hare! Oh, how pleasant it was in the forest, when the snow lay on the ground, and the hare scampered about—yes, even when he jumped over my head, though I did not like it then. It is so terribly lonely here."

"Squeak! squeak!" cried a little mouse, just then gliding forward. Another followed; they snuffed about the Fir-Tree, and then slipped in and out among the branches. "It is horribly cold!" said the little mice. "Otherwise it is very comfortable here. Don't you think so, you old Fir-Tree?"

"I am not old," said the Fir-Tree; "there are many who are much older than I am."

"How came you here?" asked the mice; "and what do you know?" They were uncommonly curious. "Tell us about the most delightful place on earth? Have you ever been there? Have you been into the store-room, where cheeses lie on the shelves, and bacon hangs from the ceiling; where one can dance over tallow-candles; where one goes in thin and comes out fat?"

"I know nothing about that," said the Tree, "but I know the forest, where the sun shines and where the birds sing!" and then he spoke of his youth and its pleasures. The little mice had never heard anything like it before; they listened attentively, and said, "Well, to be sure, how much you have seen! How happy you have been!"

"Happy!" repeated the Fir-Tree, in surprise; and he thought a moment over all that he had been saying. "Yes, on the whole those were pleasant times!" He then told them about the Christmas Eve when he had been decked out with cakes and candles.

"Oh," cried the little mice, "how happy you have been, you old Fir-Tree!"

"I am not old at all!" returned the Fir; "it is only this

winter that I have left the forest; I am just in the prime of life!'

"How well you can talk!" said the little mice. And the next night they came again and brought with them four other little mice, who wanted also to hear the Tree's history, and the more the Tree spoke of his youth in the forest, the more vividly he remembered it, and said, "Yes, those were pleasant times! but they may come again, they may come again! Humpty Dumpty fell downstairs, and yet, for all that he won the Princess; perhaps I too may win a princess!" Then the Fir-Tree thought of a pretty little delicate birch-tree that grew in the forest— a real princess; a very lovely princess was she to the Fir-Tree.

"Who is this Humpty Dumpty?" asked the little mice. Then he related the tale; he could remember every word of it perfectly: and the little mice were ready to jump to the top of the Tree for joy. The night following several more mice came, and on Sunday came also two rats; they, however, declared that the story was not at all amusing, which much vexed the little mice, who, after hearing their opinion, could not like it so well either.

"Do you know only that one story?" asked the rats.

"Only that one!" answered the Tree. "I heard it on the happiest evening of my life, though I did not then know how happy I was."

"It is a miserable story! Do you know none about pork and tallow? No storeroom story?"

"No," said the Tree.

"Well, then, we have heard enough of it!" returned the rats; and they went their ways.

The little mice, too, never came again. The Tree sighed, "It was pleasant when they sat round me, those busy little mice, listening to my words. Now that too is all past! However, I shall have pleasure in remembering it when I am taken from this place."

But when would that be? One morning, people came and routed out the lumber-room; the trunks were taken away, the Tree too was dragged out of the corner; they threw him carelessly on the floor, but one of the servants picked him up and carried him downstairs. Once more he beheld the light of day.

"Now life begins again!" thought the Tree. He felt the fresh air, the warm sunbeams—he was out in the court. All happened so quickly that the Tree quite forgot to look at himself—there was so much to look at all around. The court joined a garden, everything was so fresh and blooming, the roses clustered so bright and so fragrant round the trellis-work, the lime trees were in full blossom, and the swallows flew backwards and forwards, twittering, "Quirri-virrivit, my beloved is come!" but it was not the Fir-Tree whom they meant.

"I shall live! I shall live!" He was filled with delightful hope; he tried to spread out his branches; but alas! they were all dried up and yellow. He was thrown down upon a heap of weeds and nettles. The star of gold tinsel that had been left fixed on his crown now sparkled brightly in the sunshine. Some merry children were playing in the court, the same who at Christmas-time had danced round the Tree. One of the youngest now perceived the gold star, and ran to tear it off.

"Look at it, still fastened to the ugly old Christmas Tree!" cried he, trampling upon the boughs till they broke under his boots.

And the Tree looked on all the flowers of the garden, now blooming in the freshness of their beauty; he looked upon himself and he wished from his heart that he had been left to wither alone in the dark corner of the lumber-room. He called to mind his happy forest-life, the merry Christmas Eve, and the little mice who had listened so eagerly when he related the story of Humpty Dumpty.

"Past, all past!" said the poor Tree. "Had I but been happy, as I might have been! Past, all past!"

And the servant came and broke the Tree into small pieces, heaped them up and set fire to them. And the Tree groaned deeply, and every groan sounded like a little shot; the children all ran up to the place and jumped about in front of the blaze, looking into it and crying, "Piff! piff!" But at each of those heavy groans the Fir-Tree thought of a bright summer day, or a starry winter night in the forest, of

Christmas Eve, or of Humpty Dumpty, the only story that he knew and could relate. And at last the Tree was burned.

The boys played about in the court; on the bosom of the youngest sparkled the gold star that the Tree had worn on the happiest evening of his life; but that was past, and the Tree was past, and the story also, past! past! for all stories must come to an end, some time or other.

THE LITTLE MATCH-GIRL

I T was dreadfully cold; it was snowing fast, and almost dark; the evening—the last evening of the old year—was drawing in. But, cold and dark as it was, a poor little girl, with bare head and feet, was still wandering about the streets.

When she left her home she had slippers on, but they were much too large for her—indeed, properly, they belonged to her mother—and had dropped off her feet while she was running very fast across the road, to get out of the way of two carriages. One of the slippers was not to be found; the other had been snatched up by a little boy, who ran off with it, thinking it might serve him as a doll's cradle.

So the little girl now walked on, her bare feet red and blue with the cold. She carried a small bundle of matches in her hand, and a good many more in her tattered apron. No one had bought any of them the livelong day—no one had given her a single penny. Trembling with cold and hunger she crept on, the picture of sorrow—poor little child!

The snow-flakes fell on her long fair hair, which curled in such pretty ringlets over her shoulders; but she did not think of her own beauty, or of the cold. Lights were glimmering through every window, and the savour of roast goose reached her from several houses; it was New Year's Eve, and it was of this that she thought.

In a corner formed by two houses, one of which projected beyond the other, she sat down, drawing her little feet close under her, but in vain—she could not warm them. She dared not go home; she had sold no matches, earned not a single

penny, and perhaps her father would beat her. Besides, her
home was almost as cold as the street, for it was an attic; and
although the larger of the many chinks in the roof were
stopped up with straw and rags, the wind and snow often
penetrated through.

Her hands were nearly dead with cold; one little match
from her bundle would warm them, perhaps, if she dared
light it. She drew one out, and struck it against the wall.
Bravo! it was a bright, warm flame, and she held her hands
over it. It was quite an illumination for that poor little girl;
nay, call it rather a magic taper, for it seemed to her as if she
were sitting before a large iron stove with brass ornaments,
so beautifully blazed the fire within! The child stretched out
her feet to warm them also. Alas! in an instant the flame had
died away; the stove vanished; the little girl sat cold and
comfortless, with the burnt match in her hand.

A second match was struck against the wall; it kindled and
blazed, and, wherever its light fell, the wall became transparent as a veil; the little girl could see into the room within.
She saw the table spread with a snow-like damask cloth, on
which were ranged shining china dishes. The roast goose
stuffed with apples and dried plums stood at one end, smoking
hot, and—which was pleasantest of all to see—the goose, with
knife and fork still in her breast, jumped down from the dish,
and waddled along the floor right up to the poor child.

The match was burned out, and only the thick, hard wall
was beside her.

She kindled a third match. Again up shot the flame; and
now she was sitting under a most beautiful Christmas-tree,
far larger, and far more prettily decked out than one she had
seen last Christmas Eve through the glass doors of the rich
merchant's house. Hundreds of wax-tapers lighted up the
green branches, and tiny painted figures, such as she had seen
in the shop windows, looked down from the tree upon her.

The child stretched out her hands towards them in delight,
and in that moment the light of the match was quenched;
still, however, the Christmas candles burned higher and
higher. She beheld them beaming like stars in heaven; one of
them fell, the light streaming behind it like a long, fiery tail.

"Now some one is dying," said the little girl softly; for she had been told by her old grandmother—the only person who had ever been kind to her, and who was now dead—that whenever a star falls an immortal spirit returns to the God who gave it. She struck yet another match against the wall; it flamed up, and, surrounded by its light, that same dear grandmother appeared before her, gentle and loving as always, but bright and happy, as she had never looked during her lifetime.

"Grandmother!" exclaimed the child. "Oh, take me with you; I know thou wilt leave me as soon as the match goes out; thou wilt vanish like the warm fire in the stove, like the splendid New Year's feast, like the beautiful large Christmas-tree;" and she hastily lighted all the remaining matches in the bundle lest her grandmother should disappear.

And the matches burned with such a blaze of splendour, that noonday could scarcely have been brighter. Never had the good old grandmother looked so tall and stately, so beautiful and kind; she took the little girl in her arms, and they both flew together. Joyfully and gloriously they flew—higher and higher, till they were in that place where neither cold, nor hunger, nor pain is ever known. They were in Paradise.

But in the cold morning hour, crouching in the corner of the wall, the poor little girl was found—her cheeks glowing, her lips smiling—frozen to death on the last night of the Old Year. The New Year's sun shone on the lifeless child; motionless she sat there with the matches in her lap, one bundle of them quite burned out.

"She has been trying to warm herself, poor thing!" the people said; but no one knew of the sweet visions she had beheld, or how gloriously she and her grandmother were celebrating their New Year's festival.

THE HAPPY FAMILY

THE largest green leaves that you can find in the country are the burdock-leaves. If a little girl takes one of them and holds it in front of the skirt of her frock, it serves her as an apron; and if she place it on her head, it is almost as good a shelter against rain as an umbrella—so very large are these leaves.

Never is one burdock-leaf found growing alone; wherever one grows, a whole colony of them grow also; they are sociable leaves and beautiful, too, but all their beauty is food for the snails.

Those large white snails of which the grand folks used, in olden time, to make fricassees, dined off burdock-leaves, and greedily ate them, saying all the while, "Hum, how nice, how exquisite!"

They thought the food delicious; they lived upon burdock-leaves, and for their sakes, they imagined, burdock-leaves had been sown.

Now there was an old-fashioned manor-house; snails were no longer cooked and eaten there, for not only had the custom died away, but the last owners of the house had also died, and no one lived in it at all. But burdock-leaves grew near this house, and they had not died away; they still grew and thrived and multiplied, and as there was no one to weed them up, they spread over all the paths and all the beds till the garden at last became a perfect wilderness of burdock-leaves.

Here and there, indeed, might still be seen a solitary apple or plum tree. Otherwise no one could possibly have guessed that this place had ever been a garden; on all sides you saw burdock-leaves—nothing but burdock-leaves. And among them dwelt two old snails, the last of their race.

Even they themselves could not tell how old they were, but they could remember perfectly that their family had once been very numerous, that they belonged to a colony from a foreign land, and that for them and theirs the whole grove had been planted. Beyond the burdock-grove they had never been, but they knew that there was another place in the world called the manor-house, and that there snails were cooked, and then became black, and were laid upon silver dishes.

But what happened afterwards they could not divine. Nor could they at all imagine how they would feel when cooked and laid on silver dishes; but that it was very delightful, and a very great honour and distinction, of that they were certain. Neither the cockchafer, the toad, or the earthworm, all of whom they had questioned on the subject, could give them any correct information, for not one of these had ever been cooked or laid in a silver dish. No creatures in the world were held in such high honour as these old white snails, they were quite sure of that. The burdock-wood had grown up solely on their account, and the manor-house stood beyond merely that they might some day be taken there, cooked and laid on silver dishes.

They now lived a very lonely and yet a very happy life, and as they had no children of their own, they had taken a liking to a little common snail, and brought it up as their own child. Unfortunately, this little snail, being of a different species, could not grow larger, so as to become like its foster-parents; however, old mother snail insisted that she could perceive he was growing fast, and she begged father snail, since he could not see it as she did, to touch the little snail's house and feel it. And old father snail felt the house, and acknowledged that the mother was in the right.

One day there came a heavy shower of rain. "Only listen, what a drum-drum-drumming there is on the burdock-leaves!" remarked father snail.

"It is the drops that make that drumming," rejoined the mother snail. "Look, now they are running straight down the stalk; you will see it quite wet presently. I am glad we have our own good house, and the little one, too, he is safe in his. Certainly, it cannot be denied that more is done for us than for all other creatures put together; it is easily seen that we are of the first importance in the world. We have houses provided for us from our birth, and the burdock-wood is planted for our sakes! I should rather like to know, though, how far it extends, and what is beyond it!"

"There is nothing beyond it!" quoth father snail. "And if there were any other places, what would it signify? No place can be better than this; we have nothing to wish for."

"I cannot say that for my part," replied mother snail. "I own I should like to go up to the manor-house, and there be cooked and laid in a silver dish. All our forefathers went there, and only think what an honour it must be!"

"Most probably the manor-house has fallen to pieces," said father snail, "or else the burdock-grove has grown over it, so that the human beings cannot now get out to fetch us. However, there is no need to be in such haste, but you are always in such a violent hurry about everything, and the little one too, he begins to take after you. Why, he has crept all up the stalk in less than three days; it makes my head turn quite dizzy to look at him!"

"Don't scold him," said mother snail, "he crawls so cleverly! We shall have great pride and pleasure in him, and what else have we old folk got to live for? But there is one thing we ought to think of now; how are we to get him a wife? Don't you think that far out in the burdock-grove there may perhaps be a few more of our family left?"

"Black snails, no doubt, there are in plenty," replied the other; "black snails without houses, but they are so low, so vulgar! I'll tell you what we can do; we can commission the ants to look about for us. They are always running backwards and forwards, as if all the business in the world had to be done by them; they must certainly be able to find a wife for our little snail."

"To be sure, we know where is the loveliest little creature imaginable!" exclaimed five or six ants, who were passing by just then. "But perhaps she may not choose to listen to the proposal, for she is a Queen."

"What does that matter?" returned the two old snails. "Has she a house? That is much more to the purpose."

"A house!" repeated the ants; "she has a palace! the most magnificent ant-palace, with seven hundred passages."

"Oh, thank you," said mother snail; "if you fancy our son

is going to live in an ant-hill you are very much mistaken,
that's all. If you have no better proposal to make than that,
we can give the commission to the white gnats; they flutter
about in rain and in sunshine; they know every corner of the
burdock-grove quite intimately."

"Ah, yes, we know the wife for him!" declared the gnats
on being appealed to. "A hundred human paces off there sits,
on a gooseberry bush, a little snail with a house; she lives so
solitary, poor thing, like a hermit, and she is quite old enough
to marry. It is only the distance of a hundred human
paces."

"Well, then, let her come to him," said the old snails; "that
will be most fitting; he has a burdock-grove, she has only a
gooseberry bush."

And so the gnats fluttered away to make the offer to little
Miss Snail. Eight days passed before she made her appearance;
so much the better; that showed she came of the right breed.

And now the bridal solemnities were held. Six glow-worms
shone as brightly as they could; otherwise, the whole affair
passed off very quietly, for neither of the two old snails could
endure merriment and rioting. Indeed, father snail was too
much moved to be able to say a word; but mother snail made
a most beautiful and affecting speech, giving to the two young
people the whole burdock-grove for their inheritance, and
declaring, as she always had declared, that it was the best, if
not the only place in the world. Moreover, she promised that,
if they lived together peaceably and honestly, and multiplied
in the grove, they and their children should at last be taken to
the manor-house, there to be cooked till they were black, and
then be laid on silver dishes.

And after this speech was ended, the two old snails crept
back into their houses, and never came out again; there they
slept. And the young snails reigned in the burdock-wood in
their stead, and had a numerous posterity.

But they never had the good fortune to be cooked, or to
be put in silver dishes, and so they decided that the manor-
house must have fallen to pieces, and that all the human beings
in the world must be dead. No one ever contradicted them in
this opinion, and therefore it must needs be true. And, for

their sakes, the raindrops beat upon the burdock-leaves and made drum music; and, for their sakes, the sun shone on the burdock-leaves, giving them a bright green colour; and they were very happy, and the whole snail family were very happy.

THE SNOW QUEEN

PART THE FIRST

Which treats of the Mirror and its Fragments

LISTEN! We are beginning our story! When we arrive at the end of it we shall, it is to be hoped, know more than we do now. There was once a magician! a wicked magician!! a most wicked magician!!! Great was his delight at having constructed a mirror possessing this peculiarity—that everything good and beautiful, when reflected in it, shrank up almost to nothing, whilst those things that were ugly and useless were magnified, and made to appear ten times worse than before.

The loveliest landscapes reflected in this mirror looked like boiled spinach; and the handsomest persons appeared ugly, or as if standing upon their heads; their features being so distorted that their friends could never have recognised them. Moreover, if one of them had a freckle, he might be sure that it would seem to spread over the nose and mouth; and if a good or pious thought glanced across his mind a wrinkle was seen in the mirror.

All this the magician thought highly entertaining, and he chuckled with delight at his own clever invention. Those who frequented the school of magic where he taught spread abroad the fame of this wonderful mirror, and declared that by its means the world and its inhabitants might be seen now for the first time as they really are.

They carried the mirror from place to place, till at last there was no country or person that had not been misrepresented in it. Its admirers now must needs fly up to the sky with it, to see if they could not carry on their sport even there. But the higher they flew the more wrinkled did the mirror become; they could scarcely hold it together. They flew on and on, higher and higher, till at last the mirror trembled so fearfully that it escaped from their hands, and fell to the earth, breaking into millions, billions, and trillions of pieces.

And then it caused far greater unhappiness than before, for fragments of it, scarcely so large as a grain of sand, would be flying about in the air, and sometimes get into people's eyes, causing them to view everything the wrong way, or to have eyes only for what was perverted and corrupt; each little fragment having retained the peculiar properties of the entire mirror. Some people were so unfortunate as to receive a little splinter into their hearts—that was terrible! The heart became cold and hard, like a lump of ice. Some pieces were large enough to be used as window-panes, but it was of no use to look at one's friends through such panes as those. Other fragments were made into spectacles, and then what trouble people had with setting and re-setting them!

The wicked magician was greatly amused with all this, and he laughed till his sides ached.

There are still some little splinters of this mischievous mirror flying about in the air. We shall hear more about them very soon.

PART THE SECOND

A Little Boy and a Little Girl

IN a large town, where there are so many houses and inhabitants that there is not room enough for all the people to have a little garden of their own, and where many are obliged to content themselves with keeping a few plants in pots, there dwelt two poor children, whose garden was somewhat larger than a flower-pot.

They were not brother and sister, but they loved each other as much as if they had been, and their parents lived in two attics exactly opposite. The roof of one neighbour's house nearly joined the other—the gutter ran along between—and there was in each roof a little window, so that you could stride across the gutter from one window to the other.

The parents of each child had a large wooden box in which grew herbs for kitchen use, and they had placed these boxes upon the gutter, so near that they almost touched each other. A beautiful little rose-tree grew in each box, scarlet runners entwined their long shoots over the windows, and, uniting with the branches of the rose-trees, formed a flowery arch across the street. The boxes were very high, and the children knew that they might not climb over them, but they often obtained leave to sit on their little stools, under the rose-tree, and thus they passed many a delightful hour.

But when winter came there was an end to these pleasures. The windows were often frozen over, and then they heated halfpence on the stove, held the warm copper against frozen pane, and thus made a little round peep-hole, behind which would sparkle a bright gentle eye—one from each window. The little boy was called Kay, the little girl's name was Gerda. In summer-time they could get out of window and jump over to each other; but in winter there were stairs to run down, and stairs to run up, and sometimes the wind roared, and snow fell out-of-doors.

"Those are the white bees swarming there!" said the old grandmother.

"Have they a Queen bee?" asked the little boy; for he knew that the real bees have one.

"They have," said the grandmother. "She flies yonder where they swarm so thickly; she is the largest of them, and never remains upon the earth, but flies up again into the black cloud. Sometimes on a winter's night she flies through the streets of the town, and breathes with her frosty breath upon the windows, and then they are covered with strange and beautiful forms like trees and flowers."

"Yes. I have seen them!" said both the children—they knew that this was true.

"Can the Snow Queen come in here?" asked the little girl.

"If she does come in," said the boy, "I will put her on the warm stove, and then she will melt."

And the grandmother stroked her hair and told him some stories.

That same evening, after little Kay had gone home, and was half undressed, he crept upon the chair by the window and peeped through the little round hole. Just then a few snow-flakes fell outside, and one, the largest of them, remained lying on the edge of one of the flower-pots.

The snow-flake appeared to grow larger and larger, and at last took the form of a lady dressed in the finest white crape, that seemed composed of millions of star-like particles. She was exquisitely fair and delicate, but entirely of ice—glittering, dazzling ice; her eyes gleamed like two bright stars, but there was no rest or repose in them.

She nodded at the window, and beckoned with her hand. The little boy was frightened and jumped down from the chair; he then fancied he saw a large bird fly past the window.

There was a clear frost next day, and soon afterwards came spring; the trees and flowers budded, the swallows built their nests, the windows were opened, and the little children sat once more in their little garden upon the gutter that ran along the roofs of the houses.

The roses blossomed beautifully that summer, and the little girl had learned a hymn in which there was something about roses; it reminded her of her own. So she sang it to the little boy, and he sang it with her.

> Our roses bloom and fade away,
> Our Infant Lord abides alway;
> May we be blessed His face to see,
> And ever little children be!

And the little ones held each other by the hand, kissed the roses, and looked up into the blue sky, talking away all the time. What glorious summer days were those! How delightful it was to sit under those rose-trees, which seemed as if they never intended to leave off blossoming! One day Kay and Gerda were sitting looking at their picture-book full of birds and animals, when suddenly—the clock on the old church tower was just striking five—Kay exclaimed, "Oh, dear! what was that shooting pain in my heart? and now again, something has certainly got into my eye!"

The little girl turned and looked at him. He winked his eyes; no, there was nothing to be seen.

"I believe it is gone," said he; but gone it was not. It was one of those glass splinters from the Magic Mirror, the wicked glass which made everything great and good reflected in it to appear little and hateful, and which magnified everything ugly and mean. Poor Kay had also received a splinter in his heart; it would now become hard and cold like a lump of ice. He felt the pain no longer, but the splinter was there. "Why do you cry?" asked he; "you look so ugly when you cry! there is nothing the matter with me.—Fie!" exclaimed he again, "this rose has an insect in it, and just look at this! After all, they are ugly roses, and it is an ugly box they grow in!" Then he kicked the box, and tore off the roses.

"Oh, Kay, what are you doing?" cried the little girl; but, when he saw how it grieved her, he tore off another rose, and jumped down through his own window, away from his once dear little Gerda.

Ever afterwards when she brought forward the picture-book, he called it a baby's book; and when her grandmother told stories he interrupted her with a "but," and sometimes, whenever he could manage it, he would get behind her, put on her spectacles, and speak just as she did; he did this in a very droll manner, and so people laughed at him.

Very soon he could mimic everybody in the street. All that was singular and awkward about them Kay could imitate, and his neighbours said, "What a remarkable head that boy has!" But no, it was the glass splinter which had fallen into his eye, the glass splinter which had pierced into his heart—it was these which made him regardless whose feelings he wounded, and even made him tease the little Gerda who loved him so fondly.

His games were now quite different from what they used to be; they were so rational! One winter's day when it was snowing, he came out with a large burning-glass in his hand, and, holding up the skirts of his blue coat, let the snow-flakes fall upon them. "Now look through the glass, Gerda!" said he, returning to the house. Every snow-flake seemed much larger, and resembled a splendid flower, or a star with ten points; they were quite beautiful. "See, how curious!" said Kay, "these are far more interesting than real flowers—there is not a single blemish in them; they would be quite perfect if only they did not melt."

Soon after this Kay came in again, with thick gloves on his hands, and his sledge slung across his back. He called out to Gerda, "I have got leave to drive on the great square where the other boys play!" and away he went.

The boldest boys in the square used to fasten their sledges firmly to the wagons of the country people, and thus drive a good way along with them; this they thought particularly pleasant. While they were in the midst of their play, a large sledge painted white passed by; in it sat a person wrapped in a rough white fur, and wearing a rough white cap. When the sledge had driven twice round the square, Kay bound to it his little sledge, and was carried on with it. On they went, faster and faster, into the next street.

The person who drove the large sledge turned round and nodded kindly to Kay, just as if they had been old acquaintances; and every time Kay was going to loose his little sledge, turned and nodded again, as if to signify that he must stay: so Kay sat still, and they passed through the gates of the town.

Then the snow began to fall so thickly that the little boy could not see his own hand, but he was still carried on. He tried hastily to unloose the cords and free himself from the large sledge, but it was of no use; his little carriage could not be unfastened, and glided on swift as the wind. Then he cried out as loud as he could, but no one heard him—the snow fell and the sledge flew. Every now and then it made a spring as if driving over hedges and ditches. He was very much frightened; he would have repeated "Our Father," but he could remember nothing but the multiplication table.

The snow-flakes seemed larger and larger, and at last they looked like great white fowls. All at once they fell aside, the large sledge stopped, and the person who drove it rose from the seat. He saw that the cap and coat were entirely of snow; that it was a lady, tall and slender, and dazzlingly white—it was the Snow Queen!

"We have driven fast," said she, "but no one likes to be frozen; creep under my bear-skin;" and she seated him in the sledge by her side, and spread her cloak around him. He felt as if he were sinking into a drift of snow.

"Are you still cold?" asked she; and then she kissed his brow. Oh! her kiss was colder than ice. It went to his heart, although that was half frozen already; he thought he should die. It was, however, only for a moment; directly afterwards he was quite well, and no longer felt the intense cold around.

"My sledge! do not forget my sledge!" He thought first of that—it was fastened to one of the white fowls, which flew behind with it on his back. The Snow Queen kissed Kay again, and he entirely forgot little Gerda, her grandmother, and all at home.

"Now you must have no more kisses!" said she, "else I should kiss thee to death."

Kay looked at her, she was so beautiful; a more intelligent, more lovely countenance he could not imagine. She no longer appeared to him to be ice, cold ice, as at the time when she sat outside the window and beckoned to him; in his eyes she was perfect; he felt no fear. He told her how well he could reckon in his head, even fractions; that he knew the number of square miles of every country, and the number of the inhabitants contained in different towns.

She smiled, and then it occurred to him that, after all, he did not yet know so very much. He looked up into the wide, wide space, and she flew with him high up into the black cloud while the storm was raging; it seemed now to Kay as if it were singing songs of olden time.

They flew over woods and over lakes, over sea and over land; beneath them the cold wind whistled, the wolves howled, the snow glittered, and the black crow flew cawing over the plain; while above them shone the moon, clear and tranquil.

Thus did Kay spend the long, long winter night; all day he slept at the feet of the Snow Queen.

Part the Third

The Enchanted Flower Garden

But how fared it with little Gerda when Kay never returned?
Where could he be? No one knew, no one could give any
account of him. The boys said that they had seen him fasten
his sledge to another larger and very handsome one which had
driven into the street, and thence through the gates of the
town.

No one knew where he was, and many were the tears that
were shed. Little Gerda wept much and long, for the boys
said he must be dead—he must have been drowned in the
river that flowed not far from the town. Oh, how long and
dismal the winter days were now! At last came the spring,
with its warm sunshine.

"Alas, Kay is dead and gone," said little Gerda.

"That I do not believe," said the sunshine.

"He is dead and gone," said she to the swallows.

"That we do not believe," returned they; and at last little
Gerda herself did not believe it.

"I will put on my new red shoes," said she one morning;
"those which Kay has never seen; and then I will go down to
the river and ask after him."

It was quite early. She kissed her old grandmother, who
was still sleeping, put on her red shoes, and went alone
through the gates of the town towards the river.

"Is it true," said she, "that thou hast taken my little play-
fellow away? I will give thee my red shoes if thou wilt restore
him to me!"

And the wavelets of the river flowed towards her in a manner which she fancied was unusual; she fancied that they
intended to accept her offer. So she took off her red shoes—
though she prized them more than anything else she possessed
—and threw them into the stream; but they fell near the shore,
and the little waves bore them back to her, as though they
would not take from her what she most prized, seeing they
had not got little Kay. However, she thought she had not
thrown the shoes far enough; so she stepped into a little boat
which lay among the reeds by the shore, and standing at the

farthest end of it, threw them thence into the water. The boat was not fastened, and her movements in it caused it to glide away from the shore. She saw this, and hastened to get out; but, by the time she reached the other end of the boat, it was more than a yard distant from the land; she could not escape, and the boat glided on.

Little Gerda was much frightened and began to cry, but no one besides the sparrows heard her, and they could not carry her back to the land. However, they flew along the banks, and sang, as if to comfort her, "Here we are, here we are!" The boat followed the stream. Little Gerda sat in it quite still; her red shoes floated behind her, but they could not overtake the boat, which glided along faster than they did.

Beautiful were the shores of that river; lovely flowers, stately old trees, and bright green hills dotted with sheep and cows, were seen in abundance, but not a single human being.

"Perhaps the river may bear me to my dear Kay," thought Gerda, and then she became more cheerful, and amused herself for hours with looking at the lovely country around her. At last she glided past a large cherry garden, in which stood a little cottage with thatched roof and curious red and blue windows. Two wooden soldiers stood at the door, who presented arms when they saw the little vessel approach.

Gerda called to them, thinking that they were alive; but they, naturally enough, made no answer. She came close up to them, for the stream drifted the boat to the land.

Gerda called still louder, and an old lady came out of the house, leaning on a crutch; she wore a large hat, with beautiful flowers painted on it.

"Poor little child!" said the old woman, "the mighty flowing river has indeed borne thee a long, long way;" and she walked right into the water, seized the boat with her crutch, drew it to land, and took out the little girl.

Gerda was glad to be on dry land again, although she was a little afraid of the strange old lady.

"Come and tell me who thou art, and how thou camest hither," said she.

And Gerda told her all, and the old lady shook her head, and said, "Hem! hem!" And when Gerda asked if she had seen little Kay, the lady said that he had not arrived there yet, but that he would be sure to come soon, and that in the meantime Gerda must not be sad. She might stay with her, might eat her cherries, and look at her flowers, which were prettier than any picture-book, and could each tell her a story.

She then took Gerda by the hand; they went together into the cottage, and the old lady shut the door.

The windows were very high, and the panes were of different coloured glass—red, blue, and yellow—so that when the bright daylight streamed through them various and beautiful were the hues reflected into the room.

Upon a table in the middle was a plate of fine cherries, and of these Gerda was allowed to eat as many as she liked. And while she was eating them, the old dame combed her hair with a golden comb, and the bright flaxen ringlets fell on each side of her pretty, gentle face, which looked as round and as fresh as a rose.

"I have long wished for such a dear little girl," said the old lady. "We shall see if we cannot live happily together." And, as she combed little Gerda's hair, the child thought less and less of her foster-brother Kay, for the old lady was an enchantress. She did not, however, follow magic for the sake of mischief, but merely for her own amusement.

Now she wished very much to keep little Gerda, to live with her; so, fearing that if Gerda saw her roses, she would be reminded of her own flowers and of little Kay, and that then she might run away, she went out into the garden, and held her crutch out over all her rose-bushes. At once, although they were full of leaves and blossoms, they sank into the black earth, and no one would have guessed that such plants had ever grown there.

Then she led Gerda into this flower garden. Oh, how beautiful and how fragrant it was! Flowers of all seasons and all climes grew there in fullness of beauty—certainly no picture-book could be compared with it.

Gerda jumped with delight, and played among the flowers till the sun set behind the tall cherry-trees. Then a pretty little bed, with crimson silk cushions, stuffed with blue violet leaves, was prepared for her, and here she slept so sweetly, and had such dreams as a queen might have on her marriage eve.

The next day she again played among the flowers in the warm sunshine, and many more days were spent in the same manner. Gerda knew every flower in the garden, but, numerous as they were, it seemed to her that one was wanting —she could not tell which.

She was sitting, one day, looking at her hostess's hat, which had flowers painted on it, and, behold, the loveliest among them was a rose! The old lady had entirely forgotten the painted rose on her hat, when she made the real roses to disappear from her garden and sink into the ground.—This is often the case when things are done hastily.

"What!" cried Gerda, "are there no roses in the garden?" And she ran from one bed to another, sought and sought again, but no rose was to be found. She sat down and wept, and it so chanced that her tears fell on a spot where a rose-tree had formerly stood, and as soon as her warm tears had moistened the earth, the bush shot up anew, as fresh and as blooming as it was before it had sunk into the ground. Gerda threw her arms around it, kissed the blossoms, and immediately recalled to memory the beautiful roses at home, and her little play-fellow Kay.

"Oh, how could I stay here so long!" exclaimed the little maiden. "I left my home to seek for Kay. Do you know where he is?" she asked of the roses; "think you that he is dead?"

"Dead he is not," said the roses. "We have been down in the earth; the dead are there, but not Kay."

"I thank you," said little Gerda; and she went to the other flowers, bent low over their cups, and asked, "Know you not where little Kay is?"

But every flower stood in the sunshine dreaming its own little tale. They related their stories to Gerda, but none of them knew anything of Kay.

"And what think you?" said the tiger-lily.

"Listen to the drums beating, boom! boom! They have but two notes—always boom! boom! Listen to the dirge the women are singing! Listen to the chorus of priests! Clothed in her long red robes stands the Hindoo wife of the funeral pile, the flames blaze around her and her dead husband, but the Hindoo wife thinks not of the dead. She thinks only of the living, and the anguish which consumes her spirit is keener than the fire which will soon turn her body to ashes. Can the flame of the heart expire amid the flames of the funeral pile?"

"I do not understand that at all," said little Gerda.

"That is my tale!" said the tiger-lily.

"What says the convolvulus?"

"Hanging over a narrow mountain causeway, behold an ancient baronial castle. Thick evergreens grow amongst the time-stained walls, their leafy branches entwine about the balcony, and there stands a beautiful maiden. She bends over the balustrades and fixes her eyes with eager hopes on the road winding beneath. The rose hangs not fresher and lovelier on its stem than she; the apple-blossom, which the wind threatens every moment to tear from its branch, is not more fragile and trembling. Listen to the rustling of her silken robe! Listen to her half-whispered words, 'He comes not yet!'"

"Is it Kay you mean?" asked little Gerda.

"I do but tell you my tale—my dream," replied the convolvulus.

"What says the little snowdrop?"

"Between two trees hangs a swing. Two pretty little maidens, their dress as white as snow, and with long green ribbons fluttering from their hats, sit and swing themselves in it. Their brother stands up in the swing; he has thrown his arms round the ropes to keep himself steady, for in one hand he holds a little cup, in the other a pipe made of clay; he is blowing soap bubbles. The swing moves and the bubbles fly upwards with bright, ever-changing colours; the last hovers on the edge of the pipe, and moves with the wind. The swing is still in motion, and the little black dog, almost as light as the soap bubbles, rises on his hind feet, and tries to get into the swing also. Away goes the swing; the dog falls, is out of temper, and barks; he is laughed at, and the bubbles burst. A swinging board, a frothy, fleeting image is my song."

"What you describe may be all very pretty, but you speak mournfully, and there is nothing about Kay.

"What say the hyacinths?"

"There were three fair sisters; transparent and delicate they were. The kirtle of the one was red, that of the second blue, of the third pure white. Hand in hand they danced in the moonlight beside the quiet lake; they were not fairies, but daughters of men. Sweet was the fragrance when the maidens vanished into the wood; the fragrance grew stronger. Three biers, on which lay the fair sisters, glided out from the depths of the wood, and floated upon the lake; the glow-worms flew shining around like little hovering lamps. Sleep the dancing maidens, or are they dead? The odour from the flowers tells us they are corpses, the evening bells peal out their dirge."

"You make me quite sad," said little Gerda. "Your fragrance is so strong I cannot help thinking of the dead maidens. Alas! and is little Kay dead? The roses have been under the earth, and they say no!"

"Ding dong! ding dong!" rang the hyacinth bells. "We toll not for little Kay—we know him not! We do but sing our own song, the only one we know!"

And Gerda went to the buttercup, which shone so brightly from among her smooth green leaves.

"Thou art like a little bright sun," said Gerda; "tell me, if thou canst, where I may find my play-fellow."

And the buttercup glittered brightly, and looked at Gerda. What song could the buttercup sing? Neither was hers about Kay.

"One bright spring morning, the sun shone warmly upon a little courtyard, the bright beams streamed down the white walls of a neighbouring house, and close by grew the first yellow flower of spring, glittering like gold in the warm sunshine. An old grandmother sat without in her arm-chair, her granddaughter, a pretty, lowly maiden, had just returned home from a short visit; she kissed her grandmother; there was gold, pure gold, in that loving kiss—

"Gold was the flower!
Gold the fresh, bright, morning hour!"

"That is my little story," said the buttercup.

"My poor old grandmother!" sighed Gerda; "yes, she must be sighing for me, just as she wished for little Kay. But I shall soon go home again, and take Kay with me. It is of no use to ask the flowers about him; they know only their own song; they can give me no information."

And she folded her little frock round her, that she might run the faster; but, in jumping over the narcissus, it caught her foot, as if wishing to stop her: so she turned and looked at the tall yellow flower, "Have you any news to give me?" She bent over the narcissus, waiting for an answer.

And what said the narcissus?

"I can look at myself! I can see myself! Oh, how sweet is my fragrance!" Up in the little attic-chamber stands a little dancer. She rests sometimes on one leg, sometimes on two. She has trampled the whole world under her feet; she is nothing but an illusion. She pours water from a teapot under a piece of cloth she holds in her hand—it is her bodice; cleanliness is a fine thing! Her white dress hangs on the hook; that has also been washed by the water from the teapot, and dried on the roof of the house. She puts it on, and wraps a saffron-coloured handkerchief round her neck; it makes the dress look all the whiter. With one leg extended, there she stands, as though on a stalk. "I can look at myself, I see myself!"

"I don't care if you do," said Gerda. "You need not have told me that!" and away she ran to the end of the garden.

The gate was closed, but she pressed upon the rusty lock till it broke. The gate sprang open, and little Gerda, with bare feet, ran out into the wide world. Three times she looked back, but there was no one following her; she ran till she could run no longer, and then sat down to rest upon a large stone. Casting a glance around, she saw that the summer was past, that it was now late in the autumn. Of course, she had not remarked this in the enchanted garden, where there were sunshine and flowers all the year round.

"How long I must have stayed there!" said little Gerda. "So, it is now autumn! Well, then, there is no time to lose!" and she rose to pursue her way.

Oh, how sore and weary were her little feet! and all around looked cold and barren. The long willow-leaves had already turned yellow, and the dew trickled down from them like water. The leaves fell off the trees, one by one; the sloe alone bore fruit, and its berries were sharp and bitter. Cold, and grey, and sad seemed the world to her that day.

PART THE FOURTH

The Prince and the Princess

GERDA was again obliged to stop and take rest. Suddenly a large raven hopped upon the snow in front of her, saying, "Caw! Caw!—Good-day! Good-day!" He sat for some time on the withered branch of a tree just opposite, eyeing the little maiden, and wagging his head; and he now came forward to make acquaintance, and to ask her whither she was going all alone.

That word "alone" Gerda understood right well—she felt how sad a meaning it has. She told the raven the history of her life and fortunes, and asked if he had seen Kay.

And the raven nodded his head, half doubtfully, and said.

"That is possible—possible."

"Do you think so?" exclaimed the little girl; and she kissed the raven so vehemently that it is a wonder she did not squeeze him to death.

"More moderately—moderately!" said the raven. "I think I know. I think it may be little Kay; but he has certainly forsaken thee for the princess."

"Dwells he with a princess?" asked Gerda.

"Listen to me," said the raven; "but it is so difficult to speak your language! Do you understand Ravenish? If so, I can tell you much better."

"No! I have never learned Ravenish," said Gerda, "but my grandmother knew it, and Magpie-language also. Oh, how I wish I had learned it!"

"Never mind," said the raven, "I will relate my story in the best manner I can, though bad will be the best;" and he told all he knew.

"In the kingdom in which we are now sitting there dwells a princess—a very clever princess. All the newspapers in the world she has read, and forgotten them again, so clever is she. It is not long since she ascended the throne—which I have heard is not quite so agreeable a situation as one would fancy —and immediately after she began to sing a new song, the burden of which was this, 'Why should I not marry me?' 'There is some sense in this song!' said she; and she determined she would marry, but at the same time declared that the man whom she would choose must be able to answer sensibly whenever people spoke to him, and must be good for something else besides merely looking grand and stately.

"The ladies of the court were then all drummed together, in order to be informed of her intentions, at which they were highly delighted, and one exclaimed, 'That is just what I wish'; and another, that she had lately been thinking of the very same thing. Believe me," continued the raven, "every word I say is true, for I have a tame beloved one who hops at pleasure about the palace, and she has told me all this."

Of course, the beloved one was also a raven, for birds of a feather flock together.

"Proclamations, adorned with borders of hearts, were immediately issued, in which, after giving the style and titles of the princess, it was set forth that every well-favoured youth was free to go to the palace and talk with the princess, and that whoever should speak in such wise as showed that he felt himself at home, there would be the one the princess would choose for her husband.

"Yes, indeed," continued the raven, "you may believe me; all this is as true as that I sit here. The people all crowded to the palace; there was famous pressing and squeezing; but it was all of no use, either the first or the second day. The young men could speak well enough while they were outside the palace gates, but, when they entered, and saw the royal guard in silver uniform, and the lackeys on the staircase in gold, and the spacious saloon all lighted up, they were quite confounded.

"They stood before the throne where the princess sat, and when she spoke to them they could only repeat the last word

she had uttered, which, you know, it was not particularly
interesting for her to hear over again. It was just as though
they had been struck dumb the moment they entered the
palace, for as soon as they got out they could talk fast enough.
There was a regular procession constantly moving from the
gates of the town to the gates of the palace.

"I was there, and saw it with my own eyes," said the raven.
"They grew both hungry and thirsty whilst waiting at the
palace, but no one could get even so much as a glass of water;
to be sure, some of them, wiser than the rest, had brought
with them slices of bread-and-butter, but none would give
any to his neighbour, for he thought to himself, 'Let him
look hungry, and the princess will be sure not to choose him.'"

"But Kay, little Kay, when did he come?" asked Gerda.
"Was he among the crowd?"

"Presently, presently; we have just come to him. On the
third day arrived a youth with neither horse nor carriage;
gaily he marched up to the palace; his eyes sparkled like
yours; he had long, beautiful hair, but was very meanly clad."

"That was Kay!" exclaimed Gerda. "Oh, then I have
found him," and she clapped her hands with delight.

"He carried a knapsack on his back," said the raven.

"No, not a knapsack," said Gerda, "a sledge, for he had a
sledge with him when he left home."

"It is possible," rejoined the raven. "I did not look very
closely, but this I heard from my beloved, that when he
entered the palace gates and saw the royal guard in silver, and
the lackeys in gold upon the staircase, he did not seem in the
least confused, but nodded pleasantly and said to them, 'It
must be very tedious standing out here, I prefer going in.'

"The halls glistened with light; cabinet councillors and
high officers were walking about barefooted and carrying
golden keys. It was just a place to make a man solemn and
silent; and the youth's boots creaked horribly, yet he was not
at all afraid."

"That most certainly was Kay!" said Gerda. "I know he
had new boots; I have heard them creak in my grandmother's
room."

"Indeed, they did creak," said the raven; "but he went

merrily up to the princess, who was sitting upon a pearl as large as a spinning-wheel, while all the ladies of the court, with the maids-of-honour and their hand-maidens, ranged in order, stood on one side, and all the gentlemen-in-waiting with their gentlemen, and their gentlemen's gentlemen, who also kept pages, stood ranged in order on the other side, and the nearer they were to the door the prouder they looked. The gentlemen's page, who always wears slippers, one dare hardly look at, so proudly he stands at the door."

"That must be dreadful!" said little Gerda. "And has Kay really won the princess?"

"Had I not been a raven I should have won her myself, notwithstanding my being betrothed. The young man spoke as well as I speak when I converse in Ravenish; that I have heard from my tame beloved. He was handsome and lively. 'I do not come to woo you,' he said, 'I have only come to hear the wisdom of the princess;' and he liked her much, and she liked him in return."

"Yes, to be sure, that was Kay," said Gerda; "he was so clever, he could reckon in his head, even fractions! Oh, will you not take me into the palace?"

"Ah! that is easily said," replied the raven, "but how is it to be done? I will talk it over with my tame beloved; she will advise us what to do, for I must tell you that such a little girl as you are will never gain permission to enter publicly."

"Yes, I shall!" cried Gerda. "When Kay knows that I am here, he will immediately come out and fetch me."

"Wait for me at the trellis yonder," said the raven. He wagged his head and away he flew.

The raven did not return till late in the evening.

"Caw, caw," he said. "My tame beloved greets you kindly, and sends you a piece of bread which she took from the kitchen; there is plenty of bread there, and you must certainly be hungry. It is not possible for you to enter the palace, for you have bare feet; the royal guard in silver uniform, and the lackeys in gold, would never permit it: but do not weep, you shall go there. My beloved knows a little back staircase leading to the sleeping apartments, and she knows also where to find the key."

And they went into the garden, down the grand avenue, where the leaves dropped upon them as they passed along, and, when the lights in the palace one by one had all been put out, the raven took Gerda to a back-door which stood half open.

Oh, how Gerda's heart beat with fear and expectation! It was just as if she was about to do something wrong, although she only wanted to know whether Kay was really there—yes, it must be he, she remembered so well his bright eyes and long hair. She would see if his smile were the same as it used to be when they sat together under the rose-trees. He would be so glad to see her, to hear how far she had come for his sake, how all at home mourned his absence. Her heart trembled with fear and joy.

They went up the staircase. A small lamp placed on a cabinet gave a glimmering light. On the floor stood the tame raven, who first turned her head on all sides, and then looked at Gerda, who made her curtsey, as her grandmother had taught her.

"My betrothed has told me much about you, my good young maiden," said the tame raven; "your adventures, too, are extremely interesting! If you will take the lamp, I will show you the way. We are going straight on, we shall not meet any one now."

"It seems to me as if some one were behind us," said Gerda; and, in fact, there was a rushing sound as of something passing. Strange-looking shadows flitted rapidly along the wall—horses with long, slender legs and fluttering manes, huntsmen, knights, and ladies.

"These are only dreams!" said the raven; "they come to amuse the great personages here at night; you will have a better opportunity of looking at them when you are in bed. I hope that, when you arrive at honours and dignities, you will show a grateful heart."

"Do not talk of that!" said the wood-raven.

They now entered the first saloon; its walls were covered with rose-coloured satin, embroidered with gold flowers. The Dreams rustled past them, but with such rapidity that Gerda could not see them. The apartments through which they passed vied with each other in splendour; and at last they reached the sleeping-hall.

In the centre of this room stood a pillar of gold resembling the stem of a large palm-tree, whose leaves of glass, costly glass, formed the ceiling; and near the door there hung from the tree, on thick golden stalks, two beds in the form of lilies. The one was white, and on it reposed the princess; the other was red, and here must Gerda seek her play-fellow, Kay.

She bent aside one of the red leaves and saw a brown neck. Oh, it must be Kay! She called him aloud by his name; held the lamp close to him. The Dreams again rushed by—he awoke, turned his head, and behold! it was not Kay.

The Prince resembled him only about the throat; he was, however, young and handsome; and the princess looked out from the white lily petals, and asked what was the matter. Then little Gerda wept and told her whole story, and what the ravens had done for her.

"Poor child!" said the prince and princess; and they praised the ravens, and said they were not at all angry with them. Such liberties must never be taken again in their palace, but this time they should be rewarded.

"Would you like to fly away free to the woods?" asked the princess, addressing the ravens—"or to have the appointment secured to you as court-ravens with the perquisites belonging to the kitchen, such as crumbs and leavings?"

And both the ravens bowed low and chose the appointment at court, for they thought of old age, and said it would be so comfortable to be well provided for in their declining years. Then the prince arose, and gave Gerda his bed to sleep in; and she folded her little hands, thinking, "How kind both men and animals are to me!"

She closed her eyes and slept soundly and sweetly, and all the Dreams flitted about her: they looked like angels from heaven, and seemed to be drawing a sledge on which Kay sat. He nodded to her, but this was only fancy, for as soon as she awoke all the beautiful visions had vanished.

The next day she was dressed from head to foot in silk and velvet. She was invited to stay at the palace and enjoy all sorts of pleasures; but she begged only for a little carriage and a horse, and a pair of little boots—all she wished was to go out again into the wide world to seek Kay.

They gave her the boots, and a muff besides, she was dressed so prettily. And as soon as she was ready there drove up to the door a new carriage of pure gold, with the arms of the prince and princess glittering upon it like a star; the coachman, the footman, and outriders, all wearing gold crowns. The prince and princess themselves helped her into the carriage and wished her success.

The wood-raven, who was now married, accompanied her the first three miles; he sat by her side, for riding backwards was a thing he could not bear. The other raven stood at the door flapping her wings; she did not go with them on account of a headache she had felt ever since she had received her appointment—a consequence of eating too much. The carriage was well provided with sugar-plums, fruit, and gingerbread nuts.

"Farewell! farewell!" cried the prince and princess. Little Gerda wept, and the raven wept out of sympathy. But his farewell was a far sorer trial; he flew up to the branch of a tree and flapped his black wings at the carriage till it was out of sight.

Part the Fifth

The Little Robber-Maiden

They drove through the dark, dark forest; the carriage shone like a torch. Unfortunately its brightness attracted the eyes of the robbers who dwelt in the forest shades; they could not bear it.

"That is gold! gold!" they cried. Forward they rushed, seized the horses, stabbed the outriders, coachman, and footmen to death, and dragged little Gerda out of the carriage.

"She is plump; she is pretty; she has been fed on nut-kernels," said the old robber-wife, who had a long bristly beard, and eyebrows hanging like bushes over her eyes. "She is like a little fat lamb; and how smartly she is dressed!" and she drew out her bright, glittering dagger. "Oh, oh!" cried the woman; for at the very moment she had lifted her dagger to stab Gerda, her own wild and wilful daughter jumped upon her back and bit her ear violently. "You naughty child!" said the mother.

"She shall play with me," said the little robber-maiden; "she shall give me her muff and her pretty frock, and sleep with me in my bed!" And then she bit her mother again, till the robber-wife sprang up and shrieked with pain, whilst the robbers all laughed, saying, "Look at her playing with her young one!"

"I will get into the carriage;" and so spoiled and wayward was the little robber-maiden that she always had her own way. So she and Gerda sat together in the carriage, and drove over stock and stone farther and farther into the wood.

The little robber-maiden was about as tall as Gerda, but much stronger; she had broad shoulders, and a very dark skin; her eyes were quite black, and had an expression almost melancholy. She put her arm round Gerda's waist, and said, "She shall not kill thee so long as I love thee! Art thou not a princess?"

"No!" said Gerda; and then she told her all that had happened to her, and how much she loved little Kay.

The robber-maiden looked earnestly in her face, shook her head, and said, "She shall not kill thee, even if I do quarrel with thee; then, indeed, I would rather do it myself!" And she dried Gerda's tears, and put both her hands into the pretty muff that was so soft and warm.

The carriage at last stopped in the middle of the courtyard of the robbers' castle. This castle was half ruined. Crows and ravens flew out of the openings, and some fearfully large bull-dogs, looking as if they could devour a man in a moment, jumped round the carriage; they did not bark, for that was forbidden.

The maidens entered a large smoky hall, where a tremendous fire was blazing in the stone floor. The smoke rose up to the ceiling, seeking a way of escape, for there was no chimney. A large cauldron full of soup was boiling over the fire; while hares and rabbits were roasting on the spit.

"Thou shalt sleep with me and my little pets to-night!"

said the robber-maiden. Then they had some food, and afterwards went to the corner in which lay straw and a piece of carpet. Nearly a hundred pigeons were perched on staves and laths around them; they seemed to be asleep, but were startled when the little maidens approached.

"These all belong to me," said Gerda's companion; and seizing hold of one of the nearest, she held the poor bird by the feet and swung it. "Kiss it," said she, flapping it into Gerda's face. "The rabble from the wood sit up there," continued she, pointing to a number of laths fastened across a hole in the wall. "Those are wood-pigeons; they would fly away if I did not keep them shut up. And here is my old favourite!"

She pulled forward by the horn a reindeer who wore a bright copper ring round his neck, by which he was fastened to a large stone. "We are obliged to chain him up, or he would run away from us: every evening I tickle his neck with my sharp dagger; it makes him fear me so much!" and the robber-maiden drew out a long dagger from a gap in the wall, and passed it over the reindeer's throat. The poor animal struggled and kicked, but the girl laughed, and then she pulled Gerda into bed with her.

"Will you keep the dagger in your hand whilst you sleep?" asked Gerda, looking timidly at the dangerous plaything.

"I always sleep with my dagger by my side," replied the little robber maiden; "one never knows what may happen. But now tell me all over again what you told me before about Kay, and the reason of your coming into the wide world all by yourself."

And Gerda again related her history and the wood-pigeons imprisoned above listened, but the others were fast asleep. The little robber-maiden threw one arm round Gerda's neck, and, holding the dagger with the other, was also soon asleep. One could hear her heavy breathing, but Gerda could not close her eyes throughout the night; she knew not what would become of her, whether she would even be suffered to live. The robbers sat round the fire drinking and singing. Oh, it was a dreadful night for the poor girl!

Then spoke the wood-pigeons, "Coo, coo, coo! we have seen little Kay. A white fowl carried his sledge; he himself was in the Snow Queen's chariot, which passed through the wood whilst we sat in our nest. She breathed upon us young ones as she passed, and all died of her breath excepting us two—coo, coo, coo!"

"What are you saying?" cried Gerda. "Where was the Snow Queen going? Do you know anything about it?"

"She travels most likely to Lapland, where ice and snow abide all the year round. Ask the reindeer bound to the rope there."

"Yes, ice and snow are there all through the year; it is a glorious land!" said the reindeer! "There, free and happy, one can roam through the wide sparkling valleys! There the Snow Queen has her summer-tent; her strong castle is very far off, near the North Pole, on the Island called Spitsbergen."

"Oh, Kay, dear Kay!" sighed Gerda.

"You must lie still," said the robber-maiden, "or I will thrust my dagger into your side."

When morning came Gerda repeated to her what the wood-pigeons had said, and the little robber-maiden looked grave for a moment, then nodded her head, saying, "No matter! no matter! Do you know where Lapland is?" asked she of the reindeer.

"Who should know but me?" returned the animal, his eyes kindling. "There was I born and bred; there have I bounded over the wild icy plains!"

"Listen to me!" said the robber-maiden to Gerda; "you see all our men are gone, my mother is still here and will remain, but towards noon she will drink a little out of the great flask, and after that she will sleep—then I will do something for you!"

And, so saying, she jumped out of bed, sprang upon her mother, pulled her by the beard, and said, "My own dear mam, good-morning!" and the mother caressed her so roughly that she was red and blue all over. However, it was from pure love.

When her mother was fast asleep, the robber-maiden went up to the reindeer and said, "I should have great pleasure in stroking you a few more times with my sharp dagger, for then you look so droll. But never mind; I will unloose your chain and help you to escape, on condition that you run as fast as you can to Lapland, and take this little girl to the castle of the Snow Queen, where her playfellow is. You must have heard her story, for she speaks loud enough, and you know well how to listen."

The reindeer bounded with joy, and the robber-maiden lifted Gerda on his back, taking the precaution to bind her on firmly, as well as to give her a little cushion to sit on. "And here," said she, "are your fur boots, which you will need in that cold country. The muff I must keep myself, as it is too pretty to part with; but you shall not be frozen. Here are my mother's huge gloves; they reach up to the elbow; put them on—now your hands look as clumsy as my old mother's!"

And Gerda shed tears of joy.

"I cannot bear to see you crying!" said the little robber-maiden, "you ought to look glad. See, here are two loaves and a piece of bacon for you, that you may not be hungry on the way." She fastened this provender also on the reindeer's back, opened the door, called away the great dogs, and then, cutting asunder with her dagger the rope which bound the reindeer, shouted to him, "Now then, run! but take good care of the little girl."

And Gerda stretched out her hands to the robber-maiden and bade her farewell; and the reindeer fleeted through the forest, over stock and stone, over desert and heath, over meadow and moor. The wolves howled and the ravens shrieked. "Isch! Isch!" a red light flashed—one might have fancied the sky was sneezing.

"Those are my dear old Northern Lights!" said the reindeer; "look at them, how beautiful they are!" And he ran faster than ever; night and day he ran. The loaves were eaten, and so was the bacon—at last they were in Lapland.

Part the Sixth

The Lapland Woman and the Finland Woman

THEY stopped at a little hut, a wretched hut it was; the roof very nearly touched the ground, and the door was so low that whoever wished to go either in or out was obliged to crawl upon hands and knees. No one was at home except an old Lapland woman, who was busy boiling fish over a lamp filled with train oil.

The reindeer related to her Gerda's whole history, not, however, till after he had made her acquainted with his own, which appeared to him of much more importance. Poor Gerda, meanwhile, was so overpowered by the cold that she could not speak.

"Ah, poor things!" said the Lapland woman, "you have still a long way before you! You have a hundred miles to run before you can arrive in Finland: the Snow Queen dwells there, and burns blue lights every evening. I will write for you a few words on a piece of dried stock-fish—paper I have none —and you may take it with you to the wise Finland woman who lives there; she will advise you better than I can."

So when Gerda had well warmed herself and taken some food, the Lapland woman wrote a few words on a dried stock-fish, bade Gerda take care of it, and bound her once more firmly on the reindeer's back.

Onwards they sped; the wondrous Northern Lights, now of the loveliest, brightest blue colour, shone all through the night, and amidst these splendid illuminations they arrived in Finland, and knocked at the chimney of the wise woman, for door to her house she had none.

It was very hot within—so much so that the wise woman wore scarcely any clothing; she was low in stature, and very dirty. She immediately loosened little Gerda's dress, took off her fur boots and thick gloves, laid a piece of ice on the reindeer's head, and then read what was written on the stock-fish: she read it three times. After the third reading she knew it by heart, and threw the fish into the porridge-pot, for it might make a very excellent supper, and she never wasted anything.

The reindeer then repeated his own story, and when that was finished he told of little Gerda's adventures; and the wise woman twinkled her wise eyes, but spoke not a word.

"Thou art so powerful," continued the reindeer, "that I know thou canst twist all the winds of the world into a

thread, and if the pilot loosen one knot of it he will have a
favourable wind; if he loosen the second it will blow sharp,
and if he loosen the third, so tremendous a storm will arise
that the trees of the forest will be uprooted, and the ship
wrecked. Wilt thou not mix for this little maiden that
wonderful draught which will give her the strength of twelve
men, and thus enable her to overcome the Snow Queen?"

"The strength of twelve men!" repeated the wise woman,
"that would be of much use, to be sure!" and she walked
away, drew forth a large parchment roll from a shelf and
began to read. What strange characters were seen inscribed
on the scroll as the wise woman slowly unrolled it! She read
so intently that the perspiration ran down her forehead.

But the reindeer pleaded so earnestly for little Gerda, and
Gerda's eyes were raised so entreatingly and tearfully, that at
last the wise woman's eyes began to twinkle again out
of sympathy, and she drew the reindeer into a corner,
and putting a fresh piece of ice upon his head, whispered
thus—

"Little Kay is still with the Snow Queen, in whose abode
everything is according to his taste, and therefore he believes
it to be the best place in the world. But that is because he has
a glass splinter in his heart, and a glass splinter in his eye. Until
he has got rid of them he will never feel like a human being,
and the Snow Queen will always maintain her influence
over him."

"But canst thou not give something to little Gerda whereby
she may overcome all these evil influences?"

"I can give her no power so great as that which she already
possesses. Seest thou not how strong she is? Seest thou not that
both men and animals must serve her—a poor girl wandering
barefoot through the world?

"Her power is greater than ours; it proceeds from her
heart, from her being a loving and innocent child. If this
power which she already possesses cannot give her access to
the Snow Queen's palace, and enable her to free Kay's eye and
heart from the glass fragment, we can do nothing for her!
Two miles hence is the Snow Queen's garden; thither thou
canst carry the little maiden. Put her down close by the bush

bearing red berries and half covered with snow: lose no time, and hasten back to this place!"

And the wise woman lifted Gerda on the reindeer's back, and away they went.

"Oh, I have left my boots behind! I have left my gloves behind!" cried little Gerda, when it was too late. The cold was piercing, but the reindeer dared not stop; on he ran until he reached the bush with the red berries. Here he set Gerda down, kissed her, the tears rolling down his cheeks the while, and ran fast back again—which was the best thing he could do. And there stood poor Gerda, without shoes, without gloves, alone in that barren region, that ice-cold Finland.

She ran on as fast as she could, and a whole regiment of snow-flakes came to meet her. They did not fall from the sky, which was cloudless and bright with the Northern Lights; they ran straight along the ground, and the farther Gerda advanced the larger they grew. Gerda then remembered how large and curious the snow-flakes had appeared to her when one day she had looked at them through a burning-glass. These, however, were very much larger; they were living forms; they were, in fact, the Snow Queen's guards. Their shapes were the strangest that could be imagined; some looked like great ugly porcupines, others like snakes rolled into knots, with their heads peering forth, and others like little fat bears with bristling hair. All, however, were alike dazzlingly white—all were living snow-flakes.

Little Gerda began to repeat "Our Father." Meanwhile the cold was so intense that she could see her own breath, which, as it escaped her mouth, ascended into the air like vapour. The cold grew intense, the vapour more dense, and at length it took the forms of little bright angels, which, as they touched the earth, became larger and more distinct.

They wore helmets on their heads, and carried shields and spears in their hands; their number increased so rapidly that, by the time Gerda had finished her prayer, a whole legion stood around her. They thrust with their spears against the horrible snow-flakes, which fell into thousands of pieces, and little Gerda walked on unhurt and undaunted. The angels touched her hands and feet, and then she scarcely felt the cold, and boldly approached the Snow Queen's palace.

But before we accompany her there, let us see what Kay is doing. He is certainly not thinking of little Gerda, least of all can he imagine that she is now standing at the palace gate.

PART THE SEVENTH

The Snow Queen's Palace, and what came to pass there

THE walls of the palace were formed of the driven snow, its doors and windows of the cutting winds. There were above a hundred halls, the largest of them many miles in extent, all illuminated by the Northern Lights, all alike vast, empty, icily cold, and dazzlingly white.

No sounds of mirth ever resounded through these dreary spaces; no cheerful scene refreshed the sight, not even so much as a bear's ball, such as one might imagine sometimes takes place; the tempest forming a band of musicians, and the polar bears standing on their hind paws and exhibiting themselves in the oddest positions. Nor was there ever a card-party, where the cards might be held in the mouth and dealt out by paws; nor even a small select coffee-party for the white young lady foxes.

Vast, empty, and cold were the Snow Queen's halls, and the Northern Lights flashed, now high, now low, in regular movement. In the midst of the empty, endless snow saloon lay a frozen lake; it was broken into a thousand pieces, but these pieces so exactly resembled each other that the breaking of them might well be deemed a work of more than human skill.

The Snow Queen, when at home, always sat in the middle of this lake; she used to say that she was then sitting on the Mirror of Reason, and that hers was the best, indeed the only one, in the world.

Little Kay was quite blue, nay, almost black with cold. But he did not observe it, for the Snow Queen had kissed away the shrinking feeling he used to experience; and his heart was like a lump of ice. He was busied among the sharp icy fragments, laying and joining them together in every possible way, just as people do with what are called Chinese puzzles.

Kay could form the most curious and complete figures— this was the ice-puzzle of reason—and in his eyes these figures were of the utmost importance. He often formed whole words, but there was one word he could never succeed in forming—it was Eternity. The Snow Queen had said to him, "When thou canst put that figure together, thou shalt become thine own master, and I will give thee the whole world, and a new pair of skates besides."

But he could never do it.

"Now I am going to the warm countries," said the Snow Queen. "I shall flit through the air and look into the black cauldrons"—she meant the burning mountains, Etna and Vesuvius. "I shall whiten them a little; that will be good for the citrons and vineyards."

So away flew the Snow Queen, leaving Kay sitting all alone in the large empty hall of ice. He looked at the fragments, and thought and thought till his head ached. He sat so still and so stiff that one might have fancied that he too was frozen.

Cold and cutting blew the winds when little Gerda passed through the palace gates, but she repeated her evening prayer, and they immediately sank to rest. She entered the large, cold, empty hall: she saw Kay, she recognised him, she flew upon his neck, she held him fast, and cried, "Kay! dear, dear Kay! I have found thee at last!"

But he sat still as before, cold, silent, motionless; his un-kindness wounded poor Gerda deeply. Hot and bitter were the tears she shed; they fell upon his breast; they reached his heart; they thawed the ice and dissolved the tiny splinter of glass within it. He looked at her while she sang her hymn—

> Our roses bloom and fade away,
> Our infant Lord abides alway;
> May we be blessed His face to see,
> And ever little children be!

Then Kay burst into tears. He wept till the glass splinter floated in his eye and fell with his tears; he knew his old companion immediately, and exclaimed with joy, "Gerda, my dear little Gerda, where hast thou been all this time? And where have I been?" He looked around him. "How cold it is here! how wide and empty!" and he embraced Gerda, whilst she laughed and wept by turns.

Even the pieces of ice took part in their joy; they danced about merrily, and when they were wearied and lay down they formed of their own accord the mystical letters of which the Snow Queen had said that when Kay could put them together he should be his own master, and that she would give him the whole world, with a new pair of skates besides.

And Gerda kissed his cheeks, which then became fresh and glowing as ever; she kissed his eyes, and they sparkled like her own; she kissed his hands and feet, and he was once more healthy and merry. The Snow Queen might now come home as soon as she liked—it mattered not; Kay's charter of freedom stood written on the mirror in bright icy characters.

They took each other by the hand, and wandered forth out of the palace, talking about the aged grandmother, and the rose-trees on the roof of their houses; and as they walked on, the winds were hushed into a calm, and the sun burst forth in splendour from among the dark storm-clouds.

When they arrived at the bush with the red berries, they found the reindeer standing by awaiting their arrival. He had brought with him another and younger reindeer, whose udders were full, and who gladly gave her warm milk to refresh the young travellers.

The old reindeer and the young hind now carried Kay and Gerda on their backs, first to the little hot room of the wise woman of Finland, where they warmed themselves, and received advice how to proceed in their journey home; and afterwards to the abode of the Lapland woman, who made them some new clothes and provided them with a sledge.

The whole party now went on together till they came to the boundary of the country; but, just where the green leaves began to sprout, the Lapland woman and the two reindeers took their leave. "Farewell! farewell!" said they all.

Then the first little birds they had seen for many a long day began to chirp, and warble their pretty songs; and the trees of the forest burst upon them full of rich and variously-tinted foliage. Suddenly the green boughs parted asunder, and a spirited horse galloped up.

Gerda knew it well, for it was the one which had been harnessed to her gold coach; and on it sat a young girl wearing a bright scarlet cap, and with pistols in the holster before her. It was, indeed, no other than the robber-maiden, who, weary of her home in the forest, was going on her travels, first to the north and afterwards to other parts of the world. She at once recognised Gerda, and Gerda had not forgotten her. Most joyful was their greeting.

"A fine gentleman you are, to be sure, you graceless young truant!" said she to Kay. "I should like to know if you deserved that any one should be running to the end of the world on your account!"

But Gerda stroked her cheeks, and asked after the prince and princess.

"They are gone travelling into foreign countries," replied the robber-maiden.

"And the raven?" asked Gerda.

"Ah! the raven is dead," returned she. "The tame beloved has become a widow; so she hops about with a piece of worsted wound round her leg; she moans most piteously, and chatters more than ever! But tell me now all that has happened to you, and how you managed to pick up your old playfellow."

And Gerda and Kay told their story.

"Snip-snap-snurre-basselurre!" said the robber-maiden. She pressed the hands of both, promised that if ever she passed through their town she would pay them a visit, and then bade them farewell, and rode away out into the wide world.

Kay and Gerda walked on hand in hand, and wherever they went it was spring, beautiful spring, with its bright flowers and green leaves.

They arrived at a large town, the church-bells were ringing merrily, and they immediately recognised the high towers rising into the sky—it was the town wherein they had lived. Joyfully they passed through the streets; joyfully they stopped at the door of Gerda's grandmother; they walked up the stairs and entered the well-known room. The clock said "Tick, tick!" and the hands moved as before.

Only one alteration could they find, and that was in themselves, for they saw that they were now full-grown persons. The rose-trees on the roof blossomed in front of the open window, and there beneath them stood the children's seats.

Kay and Gerda went and sat down upon them, still holding each other by the hands; the cold, hollow splendour of the Snow Queen's palace they had forgotten—it seemed to them only an unpleasant dream.

The grandmother meanwhile sat amid God's bright sunshine, and read from the Bible these words: "Unless ye become as little children, ye shall not enter into the kingdom of heaven."

And Kay and Gerda gazed on each other; they now understood the words of their hymn—

> Our roses bloom and fade away,
> Our infant Lord abides alway;
> May we be blessed His face to see,
> And ever little children be.

There they sat, those two happy ones, grown-up and yet children—children in heart, while all around them glowed bright summer—warm, glorious summer.

HOLGER THE DANE

IN Denmark there is an old castle called Kronborg; it stands close by the sound of Elsinore, where every day large ships —English, Russian, and Prussian—may be seen sailing along. And as they pass the old castle they salute it with their cannon, "Boom!" and the castle answers with its cannon, "Boom!" This is the same as saying "Good-day!" and "Thank you."

No ships sail past during the winter, for then the Sound is covered with ice, and becomes a very broad highway leading from Denmark to Sweden. The Danish and Swedish flags flutter overhead, and Danes and Swedes walk and drive to and fro, meet and say to each other, "Good-day!" "Thank you!" not with the report of cannon, but with a hearty, friendly shake of the hands. They buy wheaten bread and biscuits of each other, because every one fancies foreign bread the best.

But the glory of the scene is still the old Kronborg, and beneath, in those great, dark caverns, which no man can approach, sits Holger the Dane. He is clothed in iron and steel; he rests his head on his sinewy arms; his long beard hangs over the marble table, into which it seems to have grown fast. There he sleeps and dreams, and in his dreams he sees all that is going on up in Denmark.

Every Christmas Eve an angel of God comes to him and tells him that he has dreamed truly, and that he may sleep on, for Denmark is in no danger. But whenever danger shall threaten her, then will Holger the Dane arise in his might, and, as he disengages his beard the marble table will burst in twain. Then he will come forth and fight in such wise that all the countries of the world shall ring with the fame thereof!

All this about Holger the Dane was told one evening by an old grandfather to his little grandson, and the boy was sure that all that his grandfather said must be true.

Now this old man was a carver, one of those whose employment is to carve the beaks of ships, and, as he sat talking to the little boy, he cut out of wood a large figure intended to represent Holger the Dane. There he was with his long beard, standing so proudly erect, holding in one hand his broad battle-sword, and leaning the other on his Danish coat-of-arms.

And the old grandfather told so many stories about different men and women famed in Danish history that at last the little boy began to imagine he must know quite as much as Holger the Dane, for he could only dream about these things. After the child had gone to bed, he still thought over what he had heard, and pressed his chin down into the mattress, fancying that he, too, had a long beard, and that it had grown into the bed.

But the old grandfather still sat at his work, carving the Danish coat-of-arms; and when he had finished it, he looked at the whole figure, and thought over all that he had heard and read, and told that evening to the little boy. Then he nodded his head, and wiped his spectacles, and then put them on again, saying, "Ah, yes, Holger the Dane will certainly not come in my time; but the boy in the bed yonder, he, perchance may see him and stand beside him in the hour of need."

And again the old grandfather nodded his head; and the more he looked at his Holger the Dane the more he felt persuaded that this was a very good figure that he had just made. He could almost fancy it had colour, and that the armour shone like real iron and steel; the hearts on the Danish arms grew redder and redder, and the lions, with their gold crowns, sprang forward fiercely—so it seemed—while he looked at them.

"Surely this is the prettiest coat of arms in the world!" said the old man. "The lions denote strength, and the hearts stand for mildness and love."

He looked on the uppermost lion and thought of King Canute, who subjected proud England to Denmark's throne. He looked at the second lion, and then remembered Waldemar, who gathered the Danish states into one, and vanquished the Vends. He looked at the third lion and thought of Margaret, who united the crowns of Denmark, Sweden, and Norway. He looked at the red hearts, and they seemed to shine brighter than ever; they were changed into moving flames, and his thoughts followed each flame.

The first flame led him into a dark, narrow dungeon, in which sat a captive, a beautiful woman. It was Eleanora Ulfeld, the daughter of Christian the Fourth; the flame settled upon her bosom, and bloomed like a rose above the heart of that noblest and best of all Danish women.

"Yes, that is one heart in Denmark's standard!" quoth the old grandfather.

And his thoughts followed the second flame, and it led him to the sea, where the cannon roared and the ships lay wrapped in smoke; and the flame rested, like the badge of an order of knighthood, upon Hvitfeldt's breast, just when, to save the fleet, he blew up himself and his ship.

And the third flame led him into Greenland's wretched

huts, where stood the priest, Hans Egede, with love in his words and deeds, and the flame shone like a star upon his breast, pointing to the third heart in the Danish standard.

And the old grandfather's thoughts preceded the fourth flame, for he knew well where that hovering torchlight would lead. In the peasant woman's lonely chamber stood Frederick the Sixth, writing his name with chalk on the rafters; the flame flickered about his bosom, flickered in his heart; it was in that peasant's cot that his heart became a heart for Denmark's arms.

And the old grandfather wiped his eyes, for he had known and served King Frederick of the silver-white hair, and kind blue eyes; and he folded his hands and gazed before him in silence. Just then the old man's daughter-in-law came up and reminded him that it was late, and time for him to rest, and that the board was spread for supper.

"But what a beautiful figure you have made, grandfather!" said she. "Holger the Dane, and our old coat-of-arms complete! I fancy I have seen this face before."

"No, that you have not," replied the old man; "but I have seen it and I have tried to cut it in wood just as I remember it. It was on the 2nd of April, when the English fleet lay off the coast, when we showed ourselves to be Danes of the true old breed! I was of Steen Bille's squadron; I stood on deck of the *Denmark*; there was a man by my side, and it really seemed that the cannon balls feared and shunned him! So merrily he sang the fine old battle songs, and fired and fought as if he were more than mortal.

"I can recall his face even now; but whence he came, or whither he went, I knew not; indeed, no one knew. I have often thought it must have been Holger the Dane himself, and that he had swum down from Kronborg to help us in the hour of danger; that was only my fancy perhaps—at any rate, here stands his likeness!"

And the figure cast its huge shadow up the wall, even to the ceiling, and the shadow seemed to move, too, just as if the real living Holger the Dane were actually present in the room; but this might be because the flame of the candle flickered so unsteadily.

And his son's wife kissed the old grandfather and led him to the large arm-chair at the table, where she and her husband, who, of course, was son to the old grandfather, and father to the little boy in bed, sat down to eat their evening meal. And the old grandfather talked the while about the Danish lions and the Danish hearts, and about the strength and gentleness they were meant to typify.

And he showed how there was another kind of strength, quite different from that which lies in the sword; pointing, as he spoke, to the shelf where a few old, well-read, well-worn books were lying, among them Holberg's comedies—those comedies which people take up and read again and again, because they are so charmingly written that all the characters described in them seem as well known to you as persons you have lived with all your life.

"You see, he, too, knew how to carve!" remarked the old man; "he could carve out people's humours and caprices!"

And then the old grandfather nodded at the looking-glass, over which the almanac with the "Round Tower"[1] on its cover was stuck, saying, "Tycho Brahe, again, he was one of those who used the sword, not to cut into human flesh and bone, but to make clear a plain highway among all the stars of heaven!

"And then he, whose father was of my own craft, the old carver's son, he with the white hair and broad shoulders, whom we ourselves have seen, he whose fame is in all countries of the earth! he, to be sure, could sculpture in stone. I can carve only wood. Ah, yes, Holger the Dane comes to us in many different ways, that all the world may hear of Denmark's strength! Now, shall we drink Bertel Thorwaldsen's health?"

But the little boy in bed, all this while, saw distinctly before him the ancient castle of Kronborg, standing alone above the Sound of Elsinore, and the real Holger the Dane sitting in the caverns underground, with his beard growing fast into the marble table, and dreaming of all that happens in the world above him. And Holger the Dane, among other things, dreamed of the narrow, meanly-furnished chamber, wherein

[1] The astronomical tower in Copenhagen.

sat the wood-carver; he heard all that was said there, and bowed his head in his dream, saying—

"Yes, remember me still, good Danish people! Bear me in mind! I will not fail to come in your hour of need!"

And the sun shone brightly on Kronborg's towers, and the wind wafted the notes of the hunter's horn across from the neighbour country. The ships sailed past and saluted the castle, "Boom! boom!" and Kronborg returned in answer, "Boom! boom!" But, loud as their cannon roared, Holger the Dane awaked not yet, for they did but mean "Good-day!" and "Thank you!"

The cannon must mean something very different from that before he will awake; yet awake he will, when there is need, for worth and strength dwell in Holger the Dane!

THE TINDER-BOX

THERE came a soldier marching along the high-road—right, left! right, left! He had his knapsack on his back and a sword by his side, for he had been to the wars, and was now returning home. And on the road he met an old witch, a horrid-looking creature she was; her lower lip hung down almost to her neck.

"Good-evening, soldier!" said she. "What a bright sword, and what a large knapsack you have, my fine fellow! I'll tell you what; you shall have as much money for your own as you can wish!"

"Thanks, old witch!" cried the soldier.

"Do you see yonder large tree?" said the witch, pointing to a tree that stood close by the wayside. "It is quite hollow within. Climb up to the top, and you will find a hole large enough for you to creep through, and thus you will get down into the tree. I will tie a rope round your waist, so that I can pull you up again when you call me."

"But what am I to do down in the tree?" asked the soldier.

"What are you to do?" repeated the witch. "Why, fetch money, to be sure? As soon as you get to the bottom, you will

VERNON SOPER

find yourself in a wide passage; it is quite light, more than a hundred lamps are burning there. Then you will see three doors; you can open them, the keys are in the locks.

"On opening the first door you will enter a room. In the midst of it, on the floor, lies a large chest; a dog is seated on it, his eyes are as large as teacups; but never you mind, don't trouble yourself about him! I will lend you my blue apron; you must spread it out on the floor, then go briskly up to the dog, seize him, and set him down on it; and after that is done, you can open the chest, and take as much money out of it as you please.

"That chest contains none but copper coins; but if you like silver better, you have only to go into the next room; there you will find a dog with eyes as large as mill-wheels, but don't be afraid of him; you have only to set him down on my apron, and then rifle the chest at your leisure.

"But if you would rather have gold than either silver or copper, that is to be had, too, and as much of it as you can carry, if you pass on into the third chamber. The dog that sits on this third money-chest has two eyes, each as large as the round tower. A famous creature he is, as you may fancy; but don't be alarmed, just set him down on my apron, and then he will do you no harm, and you can take as much golden treasure from the chest as you like."

"Not a bad plan that, upon my word!" said the soldier. "But how much of the money am I to give you, old woman? For you'll want your full share of the plunder, I've a notion!"

"Not a penny will I have," returned the witch. "The only thing I want you to bring me is an old tinder-box which my grandmother left there by mistake last time she was down in the tree."

"Well then, give me the rope to tie round my waist, and I'll be gone," said the soldier.

"Here it is," said the witch; "and here is my blue apron."

So the soldier climbed the tree, let himself down through the hole in the trunk, and suddenly found himself in the wide passage, lighted up by many hundred lamps, as the witch had described.

He opened the first door. Bravo! There sat the dog with eyes as large as tea cups, staring at him in utter amazement.

"There's a good creature!" quoth the soldier, as he spread the witch's apron on the floor, and lifted the dog upon it. He then filled his pockets with the copper coins in the chest, shut the lid, put the dog back into his place, and passed on into the second apartment.

Huzza! There sat the dog with eyes as large as mill-wheels.

"You had better really not stare at me so," remarked the soldier, "it will make your eyes weak!" and he set the dog down on the witch's apron.

But when, on raising the lid of the chest, he beheld the vast quantity of silver money it contained, he threw all his pence away in disgust, and hastened to fill his pockets and his knapsack with the pure silver.

And he passed on into the third chamber. Now, indeed, that was terrifying! The dog in this chamber actually had a pair of eyes each as large as the round tower, and they kept rolling round and round in his head like wheels.

"Good-evening!" said the soldier, and he lifted his cap respectfully, for such a monster of a dog as this he had never in his life before seen or heard of. He stood still for a minute or two, looking at him; then, thinking the sooner it was done the better, he took hold of the immense creature, removed him from the chest to the floor, and raised the lid of the chest.

Oh, what a sight of gold was there! Enough to buy not only all Copenhagen, but all the cakes and sugar-plums, all the tin soldiers, whips, and rocking-horses in the world! Yes, he must be satisfied now.

Hastily the soldier threw out all the silver money he had stuffed into his pockets and knapsack, and took gold instead; not only his pockets and knapsack, but his soldier's cap and boots he crammed full of gold—bright gold! heavy gold! He could hardly walk for the weight he carried. He lifted the dog on the chest again, banged the door of the room behind him, and called out through the tree—

"Hallo, you old witch! pull me up again!"

"Have you got the tinder-box?" asked the witch.

"Upon my honour, I'd quite forgotten it!" shouted the

soldier, and back he went to fetch it. The witch then drew him up through the tree, and now he again stood in the high road, his pockets, boots, knapsack, and cap stuffed with gold pieces.

"Just tell me now, what are you going to do with the tinder-box?" inquired the soldier.

"That's no concern of yours," returned the witch. "You've got your money; give me my tinder-box this instant!"

"Well, take your choice," said the soldier. "Either tell me at once what you want with the tinder-box, or I draw my sword, and cut off your head."

"I won't tell you!" screamed the witch.

So the soldier drew his sword and cut off her head. There she lay, but he did not waste time in looking at what he had done. He made haste to knot all his money securely in the witch's blue apron, made a bundle of it, and slung it across his back, put the tinder-box into his pocket, and went straight to the nearest town.

It was a large handsome town—a city, in fact. He walked into the first hotel in the place, called for the best rooms, and ordered the choicest and most expensive dishes for his supper, for he was now a rich man, with plenty of gold to spend.

The servant who cleaned his boots could not help thinking they were disgracefully shabby and worn to belong to such a grand gentleman; however, next day he provided himself with new boots and very gay clothes besides.

Our soldier was now a great man, and the people of the hotel were called in to give him information about all the places of amusement in the city, and about their King, and the beautiful Princess, his daughter.

"I should rather like to see her!" observed the soldier; "just tell me when I can."

"No one can see her at all," was the reply; "she dwells in a great copper palace, with ever so many walls and towers round it. No one but the King may go and visit her there, because it has been foretold that she will marry a common soldier, and our King would not like that at all."

"Shouldn't I like to see her though, just for once," thought the soldier; but it was of no use for him to wish it.

And now he lived such a merry life! He went continually to the theatre, drove out in the Royal Gardens, and gave much money in alms to the poor—to all, in fact, who asked him.

And this was well done in him; to be sure, he knew by past experience how miserable it was not to have a shilling in one's pocket.

He was always gaily dressed, and had such a crowd of friends, who, one and all, declared he was a most capital fellow, a real gentleman; and that pleased our soldier uncommonly.

But, as he was now giving and spending every day, and never received anything in return, his money began to fail him, and at last he had only twopence left, and was forced to remove from the splendid apartments where he had lodged hitherto, and take refuge in a little bit of an attic-chamber, where he had to brush his boots and darn his clothes himself, and where none of his friends ever came to see him, because there were so many stairs to go up, it was quite fatiguing.

It was a very dark evening, and he could not afford to buy himself so much as a rushlight. However, he remembered, all at once, that there were a few matches lying in the tinder-box that the old witch had made him fetch out of the hollow tree.

So he brought out this tinder-box and began to strike a light; but no sooner had he rubbed the flint-stone and made the sparks fly out than the door burst suddenly open, and the dog with eyes as large as tea cups, and which he had seen in the cavern beneath the tree, stood before him and said, "What commands has my master for his slave?"

"Upon my honour, this is a pretty joke!" cried the soldier. "A fine sort of tinder-box this is, if it will really provide me with whatever I want. Fetch me some money this instant!" said he to the dog; upon which the creature vanished, and lo! in half a minute he was back again, holding in his mouth a large bag full of pence.

So now the soldier understood the rare virtue of this charming tinder-box. If he struck the flint only once, the dog that sat on the chest full of copper came to him; if he struck it twice, the dog that watched over the silver answered his summons; and if he struck it three times, he was forthwith attended by the monstrous guardian of the golden treasure.

The soldier could now remove back to his princely apartments; he bought himself an entirely new suit of clothes, and all his friends remembered him again, and loved him as much as ever.

But one evening the thought occurred to him, "How truly ridiculous it is that no one should be allowed to see this Princess! They all say she is so very beautiful; what a shame it is that she should be mewed up in that great copper palace with the towers guarding it round! And I do want so to see her! Where's my tinder-box, by the by?" He struck the flint, and lo! before him stood the dog with eyes as large as tea cups.

"It is rather late, I must own," began the soldier; "but I do want to see the Princess so much, only for one minute, you know!"

And the dog was out of the door, and, before the soldier had time to think of what he should say or do, he was back again with the Princess sitting asleep on his back. A real Princess was this, so beautiful, so enchantingly beautiful! The soldier could not help himself; he knelt down and kissed her hand.

The dog ran back to the palace with the Princess that very minute. However, next morning, while she was at breakfast with the King and Queen, the Princess said that she had had such a strange dream during the past night. She had dreamt that she was riding on a dog, an enormously large dog, and that a soldier had knelt down to her, and kissed her hand.

"A pretty sort of a dream, indeed!" exclaimed the Queen.

And she insisted that one of the old ladies of the court should watch by the Princess's bedside on the following night, in case she should again be disturbed by dreams.

The soldier longed so exceedingly to see the fair Princess of the copper palace again; accordingly, next evening, the dog was summoned to fetch her. So he did, and ran as fast as he could; however, not so fast but that the ancient dame watching at the Princess's couch found time to put on a pair of waterproof boots before running after them.

She saw the dog vanish into a large house; then, thinking to herself, "Now I know what to do," she took out a piece of chalk and made a great white cross on the door. She then went home and betook herself to rest, and the Princess was home almost as soon.

But on his way the dog chanced to observe the white cross on the door of the hotel where the soldier lived; so he immediately took another piece of chalk and set crosses on every door throughout the town. And this was wisely done on his part.

Early in the morning came out the King, the Queen, the old court dame, and all the officers of the royal household, every one of them curious to see where the Princess had been.

"Here it is!" exclaimed the King, as soon as he saw the first street-door with a cross chalked on it.

"My dear, where are your eyes? This is the house," cried the Queen, seeing the second door bear the cross.

"No, this is it surely—why, here's a cross, too!" cried all of them together, on discovering that there were crosses on all the doors. It was evident that their search would be in vain, and they were obliged to give it up.

But the Queen was an exceedingly wise and prudent woman; she was good for something besides sitting in a state carriage, and looking very grand and condescending. She now took her gold scissors, cut a large piece of silk stuff into strips, and sewed these strips together, to make a pretty, neat little bag. This bag she filled with the finest, whitest flour, and with her own hands tied it to the Princess's waist; and, when this was done, again took up her golden scissors and cut a little hole in the bag, just large enough to let the flour drop out gradually all the time the Princess was moving.

That evening the dog came again, took the Princess on his back, and ran away with her to the soldier. Oh, how the soldier loved her, and how he wished he were a prince, that he might have this beautiful Princess for his wife!

The dog never perceived how the flour went drip, drip, dripping all the way from the palace to the soldier's room, and from the soldier's room back to the palace. So next morning the King and Queen could easily discover where their daughter had been carried; and they took the soldier and cast him into prison.

And now he sat in the prison. Oh! how dark it was, and how wearisome, and the turnkey kept coming in to remind him that to-morrow he was to be hanged.

This piece of news was by no means agreeable; and the tinder-box had been left in his lodgings at the hotel. When morning came, he could, through his narrow iron grating, watch the people all hurrying out of the town to see him hanged; he could hear the drums beating, and presently, too, he saw the soldiers marching to the place of execution. What a crowd there was rushing by! Among the rest was a shoe-maker's apprentice in his leathern apron and slippers; he bustled on with such speed that one of his slippers flew off and bounded against the iron staves of the soldier's prison window.

"Stop, stop, little 'prentice!" cried the soldier; "it's of no use for you to be in such a hurry, for none of the fun will begin till I come, but if you'll oblige me by running to my lodgings and fetching me my tinder-box, I'll give you two-pence. But you must run for your life!"

The shoemaker's boy liked the idea of earning twopence; so away he raced after the tinder-box, returned, and gave it to the soldier, and then—ah, yes, now we shall hear what happened then.

Outside the city a gibbet had been erected; round it were marshalled the soldiers with many hundred thousand people —men, women, and children; the King and Queen were seated on magnificent thrones, exactly opposite the judges and the whole assembled council.

Already had the soldier mounted the topmost step of the ladder, already was the executioner on the point of fitting the rope round his neck when, turning to their Majesties, he began to entreat most earnestly that they would suffer a poor criminal's innocent fancy to be gratified before he underwent his punishment. He wished so much, he said, to smoke a pipe of tobacco, and as it was the last pleasure he could enjoy in this world, he hoped it would not be denied him.

The King could not refuse this harmless request, accordingly the soldier took out his tinder-box and struck the flint. Once he struck it, twice he struck it, three times he struck it, and lo! all the three wizard dogs stood before him—the dog with eyes as large as tea cups, the dog with eyes as large as mill wheels, and the dog with eyes each as large as the round tower!

"Now help me, don't let me be hanged!" cried the soldier. And forthwith the three terrible dogs fell upon the judges and councillors, tossing them high into the air, so high that on falling to the ground again they were broken in pieces.

"We will not——" began the King, but the monster dog with eyes as large as the round tower did not wait to hear what his Majesty would not; he seized both him and the Queen, and flung them up into the air after the councillors. And the soldiers were all desperately frightened, and the people shouted out with one voice, "Good soldier, you shall be our King, and the beautiful Princess shall be your wife, and our Queen!"

So the soldier was conducted into the royal carriage, and all the three dogs bounded to and fro in front, little boys whistled upon their fingers, and the guards presented arms.

The Princess was forthwith sent for and made Queen, which she liked much better than living a prisoner in the copper palace. The bridal festivities lasted for eight whole days, and the three wizard dogs sat at the banquet-table, staring about them with their great eyes.

MOTHER ELDER

ONCE there was a little boy who had caught a cold by getting his feet wet; how he had managed it no one could conceive, for the weather was perfectly fine and dry. His mother took off his clothes, put him to bed, and brought in the teapot, intending to make him a cup of good, warm elder-tea.

Just then the pleasant old man who lodged in the uppermost floor of the house came in. He lived quite alone, poor man! He had neither wife nor children of his own, but he loved all his neighbours' children very fondly, and had so many charming stories and fairy tales to tell them, that it was a pleasure to see him among them.

"Now drink your tea, like a good boy," said the mother, "and who knows but you may hear a story."

"Ah, yes, if one could only think of something new!" said the old man, smiling and nodding his head. "But where did the little one get his feet wet?" asked he.

"Where indeed?" said the mother, "that's just what nobody can make out."

"Mayn't I have a story?" asked the boy.

"Yes, if you can tell me exactly how deep the gutter is in the little street yonder, along which you go to school. I want to know that first."

"The water just comes up to the middle of my boot," replied the boy, "but not unless I walk through the deep hole."

"Ah, then, that's where we got our feet wet!" said the old man. "And now, I suppose, you will call upon me for a tale, but really I don't know any more."

"But you can get one ready in a moment," insisted the boy. "Mother says that everything you look at quickly becomes a fairy tale, and that everything you touch you turn into a story."

"Yes, but those stories and fairy tales are not good for much! The right sort come of their own accord; they tap at my forehead, and cry, 'Here we are!'"

"I hope they will soon come and tap," said the little boy; and his mother laughed, put some elder-flowers into the tea-pot, and poured boiling water over them. "Come, now for a story! Tell me one, pray!"

"Yes, if the stories would but come; but they are proud, and will only visit me when it so pleases them. Hush!" cried he, all of a sudden, "here we have it! Keep a good lookout; now it is in the teapot!"

And the little boy looked at the teapot; he saw the lid rise up, and the elder-flowers spring forth, fresh and white. They shot out long, thick branches—even out of the spout they shot forth—spreading on all sides, and growing larger and larger, till at last there stood by the bedside a most charming elderbush, a perfect tree, some of its boughs stretching over the bed and thrusting the curtains aside.

Oh, how full of blossoms was this tree, and how fragrant were those blossoms! In the midst of the tree sat a kind-looking old dame, wearing the strangest dress in the world. It was green like the elder-leaves with a pattern of large white elder-flower clusters spreading all over it. One could not be sure whether it was really a gown, or living green leaves and flowers.

"What is her name?" inquired the little boy.

"Why, those old Greeks and Romans," replied the old man, "used to call her Dryad, but we don't understand those outlandish names. The sailors in the New Booths[1] have a much better name for her; they call her Mother Elder, and that suits her very well. Now listen to me, and keep looking at the pretty elder-tree the while.

"Just such another large tree as that stands among the New Booths; it has grown up in the corner of a miserable little courtyard. Under the shade of this tree there sat, one afternoon, with the glorious sunshine around them, two old people—a very old sailor, and his very old wife.

"They were great-grandparents already, and would soon have to keep their golden wedding-day, but they could not exactly remember on what day it would fall; and Mother Elder sat in the tree above them, looking so pleased, just as she does now. 'Ah, I know which is the golden wedding-day!' said she, but they did not hear her. There they sat talking over old times.

"'Can't you remember,' said the sailor, 'the days when we were little ones, and used to be always running and playing about in this very same yard where we are sitting now, and how we stuck slips in the ground to make a garden?'

"'To be sure I remember it!' replied the old woman. 'We watered the slips every day, but only one of them took root, and that was an elder-slip, and it shot out its green shoots till it grew up to be this large tree that we old folks are now sitting under.'

"'So it did!' said the sailor; 'and in the corner yonder

---

[1] Nyboder (new Booths) is the quarter of Copenhagen inhabited by the seamen.

used to stand a water-pail, where I swam my boats. I carved them out with my own hand—such famous boats they were! But I soon had to sail myself, in rather larger vessels than those, though.'

"'Yes, but first we went to school to be made scholars of,' said his wife; 'and then we were confirmed. We both of us cried, I remember; and in the afternoon we went hand-in-hand up to the Round Tower, and looked out upon the world, out over all Copenhagen and the sea; and then we went to Fredericksberg, where the King and Queen were sailing about the canals in their magnificent barges.'"

"'But those barges were scarcely more like the great ships I sailed in than my poor little boats were; and oh, for how many, many years I was away on those long voyages!'"

"'Yes, and how often I wept for you!' said she. 'I believed you must be dead and gone for ever, lying low down beneath the deep waters. Many a night have I got up to look at the weather-cock, to see if the wind had changed; and change it did, over and over again, but still you did not return.

"'There is one day I shall never forget; it was pouring with rain: the dustmen had come to the house where I was in service. I came down with the dustbox, and remained standing at the door. Oh, what weather it was! and while I stood there, the postman came up and gave me a letter; it was from you.

"'What a journey that letter had made! I tore it open and read it; I laughed and cried by turns, I was so happy. The letter told me you were in the warm countries, where the coffee-trees grow—what charming countries those must be; it told me so many things, and I fancied I could see all that you had described. And the rain still kept pouring down in torrents, and there I stood at the door with the dust-box. Just then somebody came up behind me, and took hold of me——'

"'Yes, indeed; and didn't you give him a good box on the ear! Didn't his ear tingle after it!'

"'But I did not know that it was you. You had arrived as soon as your letter; and you were so handsome!—but that you are still; and you had a large yellow silk handkerchief in your pocket, and a new hat on your head. Oh, what weather it was; the streets were quite flooded.'

"'And then we were married,' said the sailor; 'don't you remember that? And then we had our first little boy, and after him we had Marie, and Niels, and Peter, and Hans Christian.'

"'Ah! and how happy it was that they should all grow up to be good, and honest, and industrious, and to be loved by everybody.'

"'And their children, too—they have little ones now,' added the old sailor. 'Yes, they are fine healthy babies, those great-grandchildren of ours. And so it was, I fancy, just about this time of year that we had our wedding.'

"'Yes, this very day is your golden wedding-day!' said Mother Elder, putting out her head between the two old people; but they fancied she was their neighbour nodding to them. They gave little heed to her, but again looked at each other, and took hold of each other's hand.

"Presently their children and grandchildren came out into the court; they knew well that this was the golden wedding-day, and had come that very morning to congratulate their parents. But the two old people had quite forgotten that, although they could remember so clearly things that had happened half a century ago.

"And the elder-blossoms smelled sweetly; and the sun, which was near setting, shone full into the old couple's faces. A red rosy light he shed over their features; and the youngest of the grandchildren danced round them, shouting with glee that this evening there should be a grand feast, for they were all to have hot potatoes for supper. Mother Elder nodded her head to them from the tree, and shouted 'Hurrah!' as loudly as they did."

"But I don't call that a tale at all," said the little boy in the bed.

"Don't you?" said the kind old story-teller. "Well, suppose we ask Mother Elder what she thinks about it."

"No, you are right, that was not a tale," replied Mother Elder; "but now you shall have one. I will show you how the most charming fairy tales spring out of the commonest incidents of everyday life; were it not so, you know, my pretty elder-bush could hardly have grown out of the tea-pot!"

And then she took the little boy out of bed, pillowing his

head upon her bosom, and the elder-boughs laden with blossoms entwined around them, so that they seemed to be sitting in a thick-leaved, fragrant arbour, and the arbour flew away with them through the air—that was most delightful!

Mother Elder had, all of a sudden, changed into a pretty and graceful young girl; her robe was still of the same fresh-green, white-flowered material that Mother Elder had worn. On her bosom rested a real elder-flower cluster, and a whole garland of elder-flowers was wreathed among her curling flaxen hair. Her eyes were large and blue—it was a delight to behold a creature so lovely! And she and the boy embraced, and immediately they were of the same age: they loved each other, and were unspeakably happy.

Hand in hand they walked out of the arbour, and were now in the pretty flower-garden of their home. On the grass plot they found their father's walking-stick. For the children, it seemed, there was life in this stick: as soon as they got astride it the bright knob of the handle became a fiery neighing head, a long black mane fluttered to and fro in the wind, four long, slender legs shot out. A fine spirited creature was their new steed, and off he galloped with them round the grass plot— hurrah!

"Now we will ride many miles away," said the boy; "let us ride to the dear old manor house we went to last year." And still they rode round and round the grass plot; the little girl, who, as we know, was no other than Mother Elder, crying out all the while, "Now we are in the country. Seest thou not yonder pretty cottage? The elder-tree lowers its branches over it, and the cock is strutting about, and scraping up the ground for the hens. See how proudly he strides! And now we are close to the church; it stands high on the hill, among the great oak-trees, one of which is quite hollow. Now we are at the smithy; the fire is blazing, and the half-naked men are banging away with their hammers, and the sparks are flying about all round. Away, away, to the old manor house!"

And all that the little maiden riding on the stick described flew past them; the boy saw it all, and still they only rode round and round the grass plot. Then the children played in one of the walks, and marked out a tiny garden for themselves in the mould; and the girl took one of the elder-blossoms out of her hair and planted it, and it grew up, just as the elder-sprig grew which was planted among the New Booths by the old sailor and his wife when they were little ones, as has been told already.

And hand in hand the children now went on together, just as the children in the New Booths had done; but not up to the Round Tower or to the gardens of Fredericksberg. No, the little girl threw her arms round the little boy's waist, and then away they flew over all Denmark; and spring deepened into summer, and summer mellowed into autumn, and autumn faded into pale, cold winter: and a thousand pictures were mirrored in the boy's eyes and heart; and still the little girl sang to him, "Never, oh never, forget thou this!"

And wherever they flew, the sweet strong perfume of the elder-tree floated round them; the little boy could distinguish the delicious fragrance of the roses blooming in the gardens he flew past, and the wind wafted to him the fresh odour of the beech-trees; but the elder-perfume far excelled these, he thought, for its blossoms nestled to his fairy-like maiden's heart, and over those blossoms he continually bowed his head while flying.

"How beautiful is spring!" exclaimed the young girl, as they stood together in the beech-wood where the trees had newly burst into fresh loveliness, where the sweet-scented woodruff grew at their feet, the pale-tinted anemones looking so pretty amid its green. "Oh, would it were always spring in the fragrant Danish beech-wood!"

"How beautiful is summer!" said she again, as they passed an ancient baronial castle; its red-stained walls and battlements mirrored in the moat encircling them; swans swimming in the moat, and peering up into the cool shady avenues. A sea of green corn waved to and fro in the fields; tiny red and golden blossoms peeped out of the ditches; and the hedges were wreathed with wild, wantoning hops, and the bell-flowered white bindweed. It was evening; the moon rose large and round; the meadows were odorous with the scent of haystacks. "Never, oh never, forget thou this!"

"How beautiful is autumn!" exclaimed the little maiden; and the vault of heaven seemed to rise higher and to grow more intensely blue, and the woods became flushed with the richest and most varied hues of crimson, green, and yellow. The hounds bounded past in full cry; whole flocks of wild-fowl flew screaming over the cairn-stones, to which luxuriant brambles were clinging; in the far distance lay the deep, blue sea, dotted over with white sails; old women, young maids, and children were assembled in a barn, picking hops into a great cask: the young ones of the party were singing, and the ancient dames were telling old legends of fairies and enchantments. What could be pleasanter than this?

"How beautiful is winter!" declared our young damsel; and behold! the trees stood around them all covered with hoar-frost, like white branching corals they looked; the snow crisped under the children's feet with a noise as if they had creaking new boots on, and falling stars, one after another, shot across the sky. The Christmas-tree was lighted up in the parlour; everybody had had presents given him, and everybody was in good humour; the peasant's cot in the country was merry with the sound of the violin, and the pancakes disappeared fast! Even the poorest child might have reason to echo the words, "How beautiful is winter!"

Yes, truly it was beautiful! and it was our fairy maiden who showed all these fair sights to the little boy, and still the elder-perfume floated round him, when a new picture rose up before his eyes—the red flag with its white cross fluttering in the breeze, the very same flag under which the old mariner in the New Booths had sailed. And the boy felt that he was now grown up to be a youth, and that he must go to seek his fortune in the wide world; far away must he go to the warm countries, where grow the coffee-trees, but at their parting the young maiden took the cluster of elder-blossoms from her bosom, and gave it to him. And he kept it carefully; he kept it between the leaves of his hymn-book; and when he was in foreign lands he never took up the book but it opened upon the place where the flower of memory lay, and the oftener he looked at it the fresher, he fancied, it became. He seemed, while he looked at it, to breathe the sweet air of the Danish beech-groves, to see peeping among the tiny elder-flowerets the pretty maiden with her bright blue eyes, and to hear her low whisper, "How beautiful is Denmark in spring, in summer, in autumn, and in winter!" and a hundred fair visions of the past flitted unbidden across his mind.

Many, very many years passed away, and he was now an old man sitting with his old wife under a flowering tree. They held each other by the hand, just as the old couple in the New Booths had done, and they talked, too, of old times, and of their golden wedding-day. The little maiden, with the blue eyes and elder-blossoms in her hair, sat on the tree above, and nodded her head to them, saying, "To-day is your golden wedding-day!" and then she took two flower clusters out of her hair and kissed them twice: at the first kiss they shone like silver; after the second, like gold; and when she had set them on the two old people's heads each cluster became a gold crown. And thus the two sat there, like a crowned King and Queen, under the fragrant elder-tree; and the old man began to tell his wife the story about Mother Elder, which had been told him when a little boy; and it seemed to them both that a great part of the story was very like their own real history— and they liked that part far the best.

"Yes, so it is!" said the little maiden in the tree. "Some call me Mother Elder, others call me a Dryad, but my proper name is Memory. Here I sit in the tree whilst it grows and grows; I never forget—I remember all things well—I could tell such famous stories. Now let me see if you still have your flower safe."

And the old man opened his hymn-book; there lay the elder-flower, as fresh as though it had but just been laid between the leaves, and Memory nodded her head: and the two old people with their gold crowns sat under the tree, their faces flushed with the red evening sunlight. They closed their eyes, and then—and then—why then there was an end of the tale.

The little boy lay in his bed; he did not rightly know whether he had been dreaming all this, or whether it had been told him. The teapot stood on the table, but no elder-tree was growing out of it; and his friend the old story-teller was just on the point of going out at the door. Whilst the boy was rubbing his eyes he was gone.

"How pleasant that was!" said the little boy. "Mother, I have been to the warm countries."

"Yes, I have no doubt of that!" replied the mother; "after you had drunk two brimful cups of good hot elder-tea, you were likely enough to get into the warm countries!" and she covered him up well for fear he should get chilled. "You have had such a famous sound sleep, while I sat disputing with him as to whether it were a fairy tale, or a real, true history."

"And where is Mother Elder?" asked the boy.

"She is in the teapot," said his mother, "and there she may stay."

LITTLE TUK

A DROLL name, to be sure, is Tuk. However, it was not the little boy's real name: his real name was Carl, but when he was so young he could hardly speak, he used to call himself Tuk; why, it would be difficult to say, for Tuk is not at all like Carl. However, the boy was still called Little Tuk by all who knew him.

Little Tuk had to take care of his sister Gustava, who was smaller even than himself, and he had also to learn his lesson; here were two things to be done, and the difficulty was how to do them both at once.

The poor boy sat with his little sister in his lap, singing to her all the pretty songs he knew, yet every now and then casting a sidelong glance at his geography book, which lay open beside him. By to-morrow morning he must be able not only to repeat without book the names of all the towns in the diocese of Zealand, but to tell about them all that could be told.

At last his mother came home, and took little Gustava. Tuk then ran to the window, and read and read till he had nearly read his eyes out, for it was growing darker every minute, and his mother could not afford to buy candles.

"There goes the old washerwoman home through the street," said the mother, looking out of the window; "she can hardly carry herself, poor thing, and she has the weight of that great heavy pail of water from the pump to bear besides. Jump up, like a good boy, Little Tuk, go and help the poor old creature." And Little Tuk immediately jumped up, and ran to help her.

When he came back, it was quite dark; it was of no use to wish for a candle, he must go to bed. There he lay still thinking of his geography lesson, of the diocese of Zealand, and all that his master had told him. It should have been all read over again by rights, but that he could not do now. His geography book he put under his pillow, for somebody had told him that would help him wonderfully to remember his lesson. However, he had never yet found that this sort of help was at all to be depended upon.

So there he lay, thinking and thinking, till all at once he felt as though someone were gently sealing his eyes and mouth with a kiss. He slept, and yet he slept not, for he seemed to see the old washerwoman's mild eyes fixed upon him, and to hear her say—

"It would be a sin and a shame, Little Tuk, if you were not to know your lesson. You helped me, now I will help you, and then our Lord will help us both."

And then the leaves of the book under Little Tuk's head began to rustle, and to turn over and over.

"Cluck, cluck, cluck!" cried the hen—she came from the town of Kiöge.

"I am a Kiöge hen," said she; and she told Little Tuk how many inhabitants the town contained, and about the battle that had once been fought there, and how it was now a place of no consequence at all.

"Kribbley krabbley, kribbley krabbley!"—and here a great wooden bird bounced down upon the bed; it was the popinjay from the shooting-ground at Prestoe. It declared that there were as many inhabitants in Prestoe as it had nails in its body: it was a proud bird. "Thorwaldsen lived in one corner of Prestoe. Am not I a pretty bird—a merry popinjay?"

And now Little Tuk no longer lay in bed; he was on horseback—on he went, gallop, gallop! A magnificently-clad knight—a knight of the olden time—wearing a bright helmet and a waving plume, held him on his own horse, and on they rode together through the wood to the ancient city of Vordingborg; and it was once again full of life and bustle as in the days of yore.

The high towers of the King's castle rose up against the sky, and bright lights were seen gleaming through the windows. Within were song, and dance, and merriment; King Waldemar was leading out the noble young ladies of his court to tread stately measures with him.

Suddenly the morning dawned, the lamps grew pale, the sun rose, and the outlines of the buildings gradually faded away; one high form after another seemed blotted out of the clear morning sky, till at last one tower alone remained to mark the spot where that royal castle had stood. And the vast city had shrunk up into a poor, mean-looking little town, and the schoolboys came out of school, their books under their arms, and they said, "Two thousand inhabitants"; but that was not true, there were not nearly so many.

And Little Tuk lay in his bed again; he knew not whether he had been dreaming or not. Again there was somebody close by his side.

"Little Tuk, Little Tuk!" cried a voice; it was the voice of a young sailor-boy.

"I come to salute you from Corsöer. Corsöer is a new town —a living town; it has steamships and stage-coaches of its own; once people used to call it a low, vulgar place, but that is an old, worn-out prejudice.

"I dwell by the seaside," says Corsöer; "I have broad high roads and pleasure-gardens; and I have given birth to a poet, a very amusing one, too, which is more than all poets are. I once thought of sending a ship all round the world; I did not send it, but I might just as well have done so—and I dwell so pleasantly, close by the port. The loveliest roses are blossoming round about me!"

And Little Tuk could see the roses; their soft, blushing red petals, and their fresh green leaves gleamed before his eyes, but in a moment the flowers had vanished, and the green leaves spread and thickened; a perfect grove had grown up above the bright waters of the fiord, and above the grove towered the two high-pointed steeples of a glorious old church. From the grass-grown side of the hill gushed forth, as in clear rainbow-hued streams of light, a fountain; a merry, musical voice it had, and close beside it sat a king, wearing a gold crown upon his long dark hair.

This was King Hroar sitting by the fountain, and hard by was the town now called Roeskilde (Hroar's Fountain). And beyond the hill, on a broad highway, advanced all Denmark's kings and queens, all wearing their gold crowns; hand in hand they passed on into the church, and the organ's deep tones mingled with the clear rippling of the fountains. And Little Tuk saw and heard it all.

All at once this scene, too, had vanished! What had become of it? It was just like turning over the leaves of a book. Now he saw an old woman; she was a weeder; she came from Soroe, where grass grows in the very market-place. Her grey linen apron was thrown over her head and back; the apron was wet—it must have been raining.

"Yes, so it has," said she; and then she began to repeat something very funny out of Holberg's comedies; nor were they all she knew—she could recite old ballads about Waldemar and Absalon. But all of a sudden she shrunk up together, and rocked her head just as if she were going to jump.

"Croak," said she, "it is wet—it is wet; it is still as the grave in Soroe!" She had become a frog. "Croak!" and again she was an old woman. "One must dress to suit the weather," says she; "it is wet—it is wet; my town is like a flask—one goes into it through the cork, and through the cork one must get out again. But I have healthy, rosy-cheeked boys at the bottom of the flask; there they learn wisdom—Greek, Greek! Croak, croak, croak!"

Her voice was like frog music, or like the noise one makes in walking through a marsh in great boots: always the same tone, so monotonous, so dull, that Little Tuk fell into a sound sleep, and a very good thing it was for him.

But even in this sleep a dream visited him; his little sister Gustava, with her blue eyes and curling flaxen hair, had, it

VERNON SOPER

seemed, all at once grown up into a beautiful girl; and, though she had no wings, she could fly, and they flew together over all Zealand—over its green woods and blue waters.

"Listen to the cock crowing, Little Tuk! Cock-a-doodle-do!—look at the hens scraping away in the town of Kiöge! There thou shalt have such a famous poultry-yard; thou shalt no longer suffer hunger and want; thou shalt shoot at the popinjay, and reach the mark; thou shalt be a rich and happy man; thy house shall rise as proudly as King Waldemar's castle at Vordingborg, and shall be decked so splendidly with marble statues, like those that Thorwaldsen sculptured at Prestoe. Thy good name shall be borne round the world like the ship which should have gone out from Corsöer, and in the town of Roeskilde thou shalt speak and give counsel, wisely and well, like King Hroar—and then at last, Little Tuk, when thou shalt lie in thy peaceful grave, thou shalt sleep as quietly——"

"As if I lay sleeping in Soroe!" said Little Tuk, and hereupon he awoke. It was bright morning, and he remembered nothing of all his dreams; they were to him as if they had never been.

He jumped out of bed and sought for his book; he knew the names of all the towns in his lesson perfectly well. And the old washerwoman put her head in at the door, and nodded to him, saying,—

"Thanks for yesterday's help, thou dear, sweet child! May the angels bring thy best dream to pass!"

But Little Tuk had forgotten what he had dreamt—it mattered not, though; the angels knew it.

ELFIN MOUNT

Several large lizards were running nimbly in and out among the clefts of an old tree; they could understand each other perfectly well, for they all spoke the lizard's language. "Only hear what a rumbling and grumbling there is in the old Elfin-mount yonder!" observed one lizard. "I have not been able to close my eyes for the last two nights; I might as well have had the toothache for the sleep I have had!"

"There is something in the wind, most certainly!" rejoined the second lizard. "They raise the Mount upon four red pillars till cock-crowing; there is a regular cleaning and dusting going on, and the Elfin-maidens are learning new dances, such a stamping they make in them! There is certainly something in the wind!"

"Yes; I have been talking it over with an earth-worm of my acquaintance," said a third lizard. "The earth-worm has just come from the Mount; he has been grubbing in the ground there for days and nights together, and has overheard a good deal; he can't see at all, poor wretch! but no one can be quicker than he is at feeling and hearing. They are expecting strangers at the Elfin-mount—distinguished strangers, but who they are the earth-worm would not say; most likely he did not know. All the wills-o'-the-wisp are engaged to form a procession of torches—so they call it; and all the silver and gold, of which there is such a store in the Elfin-mount, is being fresh rubbed up, and set out to shine in the moonlight."

"But who can these strangers be?" exclaimed all the lizards with one voice. "What can be in the wind? Only listen! what buzzing and humming!"

Just then the Elfin-mount parted asunder; and an elderly Elfin damsel came tripping out—she was the old Elfin-King's housekeeper, and distantly related to his family, on which account she wore an amber heart on her forehead, but was otherwise plainly dressed. Like all other elves, she was hollow in the back. She was very quick and light-footed; trip—trip—

trip, away she ran, straight into the marsh, to the night-raven. "You are invited to Elfin-mount, for this very evening," said she; "but will you not first do us a very great kindness, and be the bearer of the other invitations? You do not keep house yourself, you know; so you can easily oblige us. We are expecting some very distinguished strangers, Trolds in fact; and his Elfin Majesty intends to welcome them in person."

"Who are to be invited?" inquired the night-raven.

"Why, to the grand ball all the world may come; even men, if they could but talk in their sleep, or do a little bit of anything in our way. But the first banquet must be very select; none but guests of the very highest rank must be present. To say the truth, I and the King have been having a little dispute; for I insist that not even ghosts may be admitted to-night. The Mer-King and his daughters must be invited first; they don't much like coming on land, but I'll promise they shall each have a wet stone, or, perhaps, something better still, to sit on; and then, I think, they cannot possibly refuse us this time. All old Trolds of the first rank we must have; also, the River-Spirit and the Nisses; and, I fancy, we cannot pass over the Death-Horse and Kirkegrim: true, they do not belong to our set, they are too solemn for us, but they are connected with the family, and pay us regular visits."

"Caw!" said the night-raven; and away he flew to bear the invitations.

The Elfin-maidens were still dancing in the Elfin-mount; they danced with long scarfs woven from mist and moonlight, and for those who like that sort of thing it looks pretty enough. The large state-room in the Mount had been regularly cleaned and cleared out; the floor had been washed with moonshine, and the walls rubbed with witches' fat till they shone as tulips do when held up to the light. In the kitchen, frogs were roasting on the spit; while divers other choice dishes, such as mushroom seed, hemlock soup, etc., were prepared or preparing. These were to supply the first courses; rusty nails, bits of coloured glass, and such like dainties, were to come in for the dessert; there was also bright saltpetre wine, and ale brewed in the brewery of the Wise Witch of the Moor.

The old Elfin-King's gold crown had been fresh rubbed with powdered slate-pencil; new curtains had been hung up in all the sleeping-rooms—yes, there was indeed a rare bustle and commotion.

"Now, we must have the rooms scented with cows' hairs and swines' bristles; and then, I think, I shall have done my part!" said the Elfin-King's housekeeper.

"Dear papa," said the youngest of the daughters, "won't you tell me now who these grand visitors are?"

"Well!" replied his Majesty, "I suppose there's no use in keeping it a secret. Let two of my daughters get themselves ready for their wedding day, that's all! Two of them most certainly will be married. The Chief of the Norwegian Trolds, he who dwells in old Dofrefield, and has so many castles of freestone among those rocky fastnesses, besides a gold mine— which is a capital thing, let me tell you—he is coming down here with his two boys, who are both to choose themselves a bride. Such an honest, straightforward, true old Norseman is this mountain chief! so merry and jovial! He and I are old comrades; he came down here years ago to fetch his wife; she is dead now; she was the daughter of the Rock-King at Möen. Oh, how I long to see the old Norseman again! His sons, they say, are rough, unmannerly cubs, but perhaps report may have done them injustice, and at anyrate they are sure to improve in a year or two, when they have sown their wild oats. Let me see how you will polish them up!"

"And how soon are they to be here?" inquired his youngest daughter again.

"That depends on wind and weather!" returned the Elfin-King. "They travel economically; they come at the ship's convenience. I wanted them to pass over by Sweden, but the old man would not hear of that. He does not keep pace with the times, that's the only fault I can find with him."

Just then two wills-o'-the-wisp were seen dancing up in a vast hurry, each trying to get before the other, and to be the first to bring the news.

"They come, they come!" cried both with one voice. "Give me my crown, and let me stand in the moonlight!" said the Elfin-King.

And his seven daughters lifted their long scarfs and bowed low to the earth.

There stood the Trold Chief from the Dofrefield, wearing a crown composed of icicles and polished pine cones; for the rest, he was equipped in a bear-skin cloak and sledge-boots; his sons were clad more slightly, and kept their throats uncovered, by way of showing that they cared nothing about the cold.

"Is that a mount?" asked the youngest of them, pointing to it. "Why, up in Norway we should call it a cave!"

"You foolish boy!" replied his father; "a cave you go into, a mount you go up! Where are your eyes, not to see the difference?"

The only thing that surprised them in this country, they said, was that the people should speak and understand their language.

"Behave yourselves now!" said the old man; "don't let your host fancy you never went into decent company before!"

And now they all entered the Elfin-mount, into the grand saloon, where a really very select party was assembled, although at such short notice that it seemed almost as though some fortunate gust of wind had blown them together. And every possible arrangement had been made for the comfort of each of the guests; the Mer-King's family, for instance, sat at table in large tubs of water, and they declared they felt quite as if they were at home. All behaved with strict good-breeding except the two young northern Trolds, who at last so far forgot themselves as to put their legs on the table.

"Take your legs away from the plates!" said their father; and they obeyed, but not so readily as they might have done. Presently they took some pine cones out of their pockets and began pelting the lady who sat between them, and then, finding their boots incommode them, they took them off, and coolly gave them to this lady to hold. But their father, the old mountain Chief, conducted himself very differently; he talked so delightfully about the proud Norse mountains, and the torrents, white with dancing spray, that dashed foaming down their rocky steeps with a noise loud and hoarse as thunder, yet musical as the full burst of an organ, touched by a master hand; he told of the salmon leaping up from the wild waters while the Neck was playing on his golden; he told of the starlight winter nights when the sledge bells tinkled so merrily, and the youths ran with lighted torches over the icy crust, so glassy and transparent that through it they could see the fishes whirling to and fro in deadly terror beneath their feet; he told of the gallant northern youths and pretty maidens singing songs of old time, and dancing the Hallinge dance— yes, so charmingly he described all this, that you could not but fancy you heard and saw it all. Oh fie, for shame! all of a sudden the mountain Chief turned round upon the elderly Elfin-maiden, and gave her a cousinly salute, and he was not yet connected ever so remotely with the family.

The young Elfin-maidens were now called upon to dance. First they danced simple dances, then stamping dances, and they did both remarkably well. Last came the most difficult of all, the "Dance out of the dance," as it was called. Bravo! how long their legs seemed to grow, and how they whirled and spun about! You could hardly distinguish legs from arms, or arms from legs. Round and round they went, such whirling and twirling, such whirring and whizzing there was that it made the death-horse feel quite dizzy, and at last he grew so unwell that he was obliged to leave the table.

"Hurrah!" cried the mountain Chief, "they know how to use their limbs with a vengeance! but can they do nothing else than dance, stretch out their feet, and spin round like a whirlwind?"

"You shall judge for yourself," replied the Elfin-King; and here he called the eldest of his daughters to him. She was transparent and fair as moonlight; she was, in fact, the most delicate of all the sisters; she put a white wand between her lips and vanished: that was her accomplishment.

But the mountain Chief said he should not at all like his wife to possess such an accomplishment as this, and he did not think his sons would like it either.

The second could walk by the side of herself, just as though she had a shadow, which elves and trolds never have.

The accomplishment of the third sister was of quite another kind: she had learned how to brew good ale from the Wise

8

Witch of the Moor, and she also knew how to lard alder-wood with glow-worms.

"She will make a capital housewife," remarked the old mountain Chief.

And now advanced the fourth Elfin damsel: she carried a large gold harp; and no sooner had she struck the first chord than all the company lifted their left feet—for elves are left-sided—and when she struck the second chord, they were all compelled to do whatever she wished.

"A dangerous lady, indeed!" said the old Trold Chief. Both of his sons now got up and strode out of the mount; they were heartily weary of these accomplishments.

"And what can the next daughter do?" asked the mountain Chief.

"I have learned to love the north," replied she; "and I have resolved never to marry unless I may go to Norway."

But the youngest of the sisters whispered to the old man, "That is only because she has heard an old Norse rhyme, which says that when the end of the world shall come, the Norwegian rocks shall stand firm amid the ruins; she is very afraid of death, and therefore she wants to go to Norway."

"Ho, ho!" cried the mountain Chief; "sits the wind in that quarter? But what can the seventh and last do?"

"The sixth comes before the seventh," said the Elfin-King; for he could count better than to make such a mistake. However, the sixth seemed in no hurry to come forward.

"I can only tell people the truth," said she. "Let no one trouble himself about me, I have enough to do to sew my shroud!"

And now came the seventh and last, and what could she do? Why, she could tell fairy tales, as many as any one could wish to hear.

"Here are my five fingers," said the mountain Chief; "tell me a story for each finger."

And the Elfin-maiden took hold of his wrist, and told her stories, and he laughed till his sides ached; and when she came to the finger that wore a gold ring, as though it knew it might be wanted, the mountain Chief suddenly exclaimed, "Hold fast **what** thou hast, the hand is thine! I will have thee myself to wife!" But the Elfin-maiden said that she had still two more stories to tell, one for the ring-finger, and another for the little finger.

"Keep them for next winter; we'll hear them then," replied the mountain Chief. "And we'll hear about the Loves of the Fir-Tree and the Birch, about the Valkyria's gifts, too, for we all love fairy legends in Norway, and no one there can tell them so charmingly as thou dost. And then we will sit in our rocky halls, whilst the fir-logs are blazing and crackling in the stove, and drink mead out of the golden horns of the old Norse kings; the Neck has taught me a few of his rare old ditties; besides, the Garbo will often come and pay us a visit, and he will sing thee all the sweet songs that the mountain maidens sang in days of yore—that will be most delightful! The salmon in the torrent will spring up and beat himself against the rock walls, but in vain; he will not be able to get in. Oh, thou canst not imagine what a happy, glorious life we lead in that dear old Norway! But where are the boys?"

Where were the boys? Why, they were racing about in the fields and blowing out the poor wills-o'-the-wisp, who were just ranging themselves in the proper order to make a procession of torches.

"What do you mean by making all this riot?" inquired the mountain Chief. "I have been choosing you a mother, now you come and choose yourselves wives from among your aunts."

But his sons said they would rather make speeches and drink toasts, they had not the slightest wish to marry. And accordingly they made speeches, tossed off their glasses and turned them topsy-turvy on the table, to show that they were quite empty; after this they took off their coats, and most unceremoniously lay down on the table and went to sleep. But the old mountain Chief, the while, danced round the hall with his young bride, and exchanged boots with her, because that is not so vulgar as exchanging rings.

"Listen, the cock is crowing!" exclaimed the lady-housekeeper. "We must make haste and shut the window-shutters close, or the sun will scorch our complexions."

And herewith Elfin-mount closed.

But outside, in the cloven trunk, the lizards kept running up and down, and one and all declared, "What a capital fellow that old Norwegian Trold is!" "For my part, I prefer the boys," said the earth-worm; but he, poor wretch, could see nothing either of them or of their father, so his opinion was not worth much.

STORY OF A MOTHER

A MOTHER sat watching her little child; she was so sad, so afraid lest it should die. For the child was very pale; its eyes had closed; its breathing was faint; and every now and then it fetched a deep sigh, and the mother's face grew sadder and sadder as she watched the little, tiny creature.

There was a knock at the door, and a poor old man wrapped up in a great horse-cloth came in. He had need of warm clothing, for it was a cold winter's night; the ground outside the house was covered with ice and snow, and the wind blew keen and cutting into the wanderer's face.

And as the old man was shivering with cold, and the little child seemed just at that moment to have fallen asleep, the mother rose up and fetched some beer in a little pot, placing it inside the stove to warm it for her guest. And the old man sat rocking the cradle; and the mother sat down on a chair beside him, still gazing on her sick child, listening anxiously to its hard breathing, and holding its tiny hand.

"I shall keep him, do you not think so?" she inquired. "God is good; He will not take my darling away from me!"

And the old man—it was Death himself—bowed his head so strangely, you could not tell whether he meant to say Yes or No. And the mother cast down her eyes, and tears streamed over her cheeks. She felt her head growing so heavy; for three whole days and nights she had not closed her eyes, and now she slept, but only for a minute; presently she started up shivering with cold.

"What is this?" she exclaimed, and she looked around her. The old man was gone, and her little child was gone; he had

taken it with him. And yonder, in the corner, the old clock
ticked and ticked; the heavy-laden pendulum swung lower
and lower, till at last it fell on the floor, and then the clock
stood still also.

But the poor bereaved mother rushed out of the house,
and cried for her child.

Outside, amidst the snow, there sat a woman clad in long,
black garments, who said, "Death has been in thy room; I
saw him hurry out of it with thy little child; he strides along
more swiftly than the wind, and never brings back anything
that he has taken away."

"Only tell me which way he has gone!" entreated the
mother. "Tell me the way, and I will find him."

"I know the way," replied the woman in black robes;
"but before I show it thee, thou must sing to me all the songs
thou hast ever sung to thy child. I am Night, and I love these
songs. I have heard thee sing them many a time, and have
counted the tears thou hast shed whilst singing them."

"I will sing them all, every one," said the mother, "but do
not keep me now; let me hasten after Death; let me recover
my child!"

But Night made no reply; there she sat, mute and un-
relenting. Then the mother began to sing, weeping and
wringing her hands the while. Many were the songs she sang,
but many more were the tears she wept! And at last Night
said, "Turn to the right, and go through the dark fir-grove,
for thither did Death wend his way with thy child."

But deep within the grove several roads crossed, and the
poor woman knew not in which direction she should turn.
Here grew a thorn-bush, without leaves or flowers, for it was
winter, and icicles clung to the bare branches.

"Oh! tell me, hast thou not seen Death pass by, bearing
my little child with him?"

"Yes, I have," was the thorn-tree's reply; "but I will not
tell thee which way he has gone, unless thou wilt first warm
me at thy bosom. I am freezing to death in this place: I am
turning into ice."

And she pressed the thorn-bush to her breast so closely as to
melt all the icicles. And the thorns pierced into her flesh, and

the blood flowed in large drops. But the thorn-bush shot forth
fresh leaves, and was crowned with flowers in that same bitter
cold winter's night—so warm is the heart of a sorrowing
mother! And the thorn-bush told her which path she must
take.

And the path brought her on to the shore of a large lake
where neither ship nor boat was to be seen. The lake was not
frozen hard enough to bear her weight, nor shallow enough
to be waded through, and yet she must cross it if she would
recover her child. So she lay down, thinking to drink the lake
dry. That was quite impossible for one human being to do,
but the poor unhappy mother imagined that perchance a
miracle might come to pass.

"No, that will never do!" said the lake. "Rather let us see
if we cannot come to some agreement. I love to collect pearls,
and never have I seen any so bright as thine eyes; if thou wilt
weep them into my bosom, I will bear thee over to the vast
conservatory where Death dwells and tends his trees and
flowers—each one of them a human life."

"Oh, what would I not give to get my child!" cried the
mother. And she wept yet again, and her eyes fell down into
the lake, and became two brilliant pearls. And the lake
received her, and its bosom heaved and swelled, and its current
bore her safely to the opposite shore where stood a wondrous
house many miles in length. It were hard to decide whether
it was really a house and built with hands, or whether it was
not rather a mountain with forests and caverns in its sides. But
the poor mother could not see it at all; she had wept out her
eyes.

"Where shall I find Death that I may ask him to restore to
me my little child?" inquired she.

"He has not yet returned," replied a hoary-haired old
woman who was wandering to and fro in Death's conservatory, which she had been left to guard in his absence. "How
didst thou find thy way here? Who has helped thee?"

"Our Lord has helped me," she answered; "He is merciful,
and thou, too, wilt be merciful. Where shall I find my little
child?"

"I do not know," said the old woman; "and thou, I perceive, canst not see. Many flowers and trees have withered during this night; Death will come very soon to transplant them. Thou must know that every human being has his tree or flower of life, as is appointed for each. They look like common vegetables, but their hearts beat. So be of good cheer; perchance thou mayst be able to distinguish the heart-beat of thy child; but what wilt thou give me if I tell thee what else thou must do?"

"I have nothing to give," said the mourning mother; "but I will go to the end of the world at thy bidding."

"I want nothing from the end of the world," said the old woman; "but thou canst give me thy long black hair. Thou must know well that it is very beautiful; it pleases me exceedingly! And thou canst have my white hair in exchange; even that will be better than none."

"Desirest thou nothing?" returned the mother; "I will give it thee right willingly." And she gave away her beautiful hair, and received instead the thin snow-white locks of the old woman.

And then they entered Death's vast conservatory, where flowers and trees grew in wonderful order and variety. There were delicate hyacinths protected by glasses, and great, healthy peonies. There grew water-plants, some looking quite fresh, some sickly; water-snakes were clinging about them, and black crabs clung fast by the stalks. Here were seen magnificent palm-trees, oaks, and plantains; yonder clustered the humble parsley and fragrant thyme.

Not a tree, not a flower, but had its name, and each corresponded with a human life; the persons whose names they bore lived in all countries and nations on the earth; one in China, another in Greenland, and so forth.

There were some large trees planted in little pots, so that their roots were contracted and the trees themselves ready to break out from the pots; on the other hand, there was many a weakly, tiny herb set in rich mould, with moss laid over its roots, and the utmost care and attention bestowed upon its preservation.

And the grieving mother bent down over all the tiniest plants; in each one she heard the pulse of a human life, and out

of a million others she distinguished the heart-throb of her
child. "There it is!" cried she, stretching her hand over a little
blue crocus-flower which was hanging down on one side,
sickly and feeble.

"Touch not the flower!" said the old woman, "but place
thyself here; and when Death shall come—I expect him every
minute—then suffer him not to tear up the plant, but threaten
to do the same by some of the other flowers—that will terrify
him; for he will have to answer for it to our Lord; no plant
may be rooted up before the Almighty has given permission."

Suddenly an icy cold breath swept through the hall, and the
blind mother felt that Death had arrived.

"How hast thou found the way hither?" asked he. "How
couldst thou arrive here more quickly than I?"

"I am a mother!" was her answer.

And Death extended his long hand towards the tiny, delicate
crocus-flower; but she held her hands clasped firmly round it,
so closely, and yet with such anxious care lest she should touch
one of the petals. Then Death breathed upon her hands, and
she felt that his breath was more chilling than the coldest,
bitterest winter wind; and her hands sank down, numbed
and powerless.

"Against me thou hast no strength!" said Death.

"But our Lord has, and He is merciful," replied she.

"I do but accomplish His will!" said Death. "I am His
gardener. I take up all His plants and trees, one by one, and
transplant them into the glorious garden of Paradise—into the
unknown land. Where that lies, and how they thrive there,
that I dare not tell thee!"

"Oh, give me back my child!" cried the mother; and she
wailed and implored. All at once she seized hold of two pretty
flowers, one with each hand, exclaiming, "I will tear off all
thy flowers, for I am in despair!"

"Touch them not!" commanded Death. "Thou sayest that
thou art very unhappy; and wouldst thou therefore make
another mother as unhappy as thyself?"

"Another mother!" repeated the poor woman, and she
immediately loosed her hold of both the flowers.

"There are thine eyes again," said Death. "I fished them

out of the lake, they glistened so brightly; but I did not know that they were thine. Take them back; they are now even brighter than before: now look down into this deep well. I will tell thee the names of the two flowers which thou wert about to pluck, and thou shalt see pictured in the well their whole future, the entire course of their human lives. Thou shalt see all that thou hast yearned to destroy."

And she gazed into the well; and a lovely sight it was to see how one of these lives became a blessing to the whole world, to see what a sunshine of joy and happiness it diffused around it. And she beheld the life of the other, and there were sin and sorrow, misfortune and utter misery.

"Both are God's will!" said Death.

"Which of them is the flower of unhappiness, and which the blessed and blessing one?" inquired she.

"That I will not tell thee," returned Death; "but this shalt thou learn from me, that one of those two flowers was the flower of thine own child. Thou hast seen the destiny, the future of thine own child!"

Then the mother shrieked out with terror, "Which of the two is my child? Tell me that! Save the innocent child! Release my child from all this misery; rather bear it away—bear it into God's kingdom. Forget my tears; forget my entreaties and all that I have done!"

"I do not understand thee!" said Death. "Wilt thou have thy child back again, or shall I carry him away to that place which thou knowest not?"

And the mother wrung her hands, fell upon her knees, and prayed to the All-wise, All-merciful Father, "Hear me not when I pray for what is not Thy will; Thy will is always best! Hear me not, Lord, hear me not!"

And her head drooped upon her breast.

And Death departed, and bore away her child to the unknown land.

THE EMPEROR'S NEW CLOTHES

MANY years ago there was an Emperor who was so very fond of new clothes that he spent all his money in dress. He did not trouble himself in the least about his soldiers; nor did he care to go either to the theatre or to the chase, except for the opportunities then afforded him of displaying his new clothes. He had a different suit for each hour of the day; and, as of any other king or emperor, one is accustomed to say, "He is sitting in council," it was always said of him. "The Emperor is sitting in his wardrobe."

Time passed away merrily in the large town which was his capital; strangers arrived every day at the court. One day two rogues, calling themselves weavers, made their appearance. They gave out that they knew how to weave stuffs of the most beautiful colours and elaborate patterns; the clothes made from which should have the wonderful property of remaining invisible to every one who was unfit for the office he held, or who was extraordinarily simple in character.

"These must indeed be splendid clothes!" thought the Emperor. "Had I such a suit, I might, at once, find out what men in my realms are unfit for their office, and also be able to distinguish the wise from the foolish! This stuff must be woven for me immediately." And he caused large sums of money to be given to both the weavers, in order that they might begin their work at once.

So the two pretended weavers set up two looms, and affected to work very busily, though in reality they did nothing at all. They asked for the most delicate silk and the purest gold thread; put both into their own knapsacks; and then continued their pretended work at the empty looms until late at night.

"I should like to know how the weavers are getting on with my cloth," said the Emperor to himself, after some little time had elapsed. He was, however, rather embarrassed when he remembered that a simpleton, or one unfit for his office, would be unable to see the manufacture. "To be sure," he

thought, "he had nothing to risk in his own person; but yet, he would prefer sending somebody else, to bring him intelligence about the weavers and their work, before he troubled himself in the affair."

All the people throughout the city had heard of the wonderful property the cloth was to possess; and all were anxious to learn how wise, or how ignorant, their neighbours might prove to be.

"I will send my faithful old minister to the weavers," said the Emperor at last, after some deliberation; "he will be best able to see how the cloth looks; for he is a man of sense, and no one can be more suitable for his office than he is."

So the faithful old minister went into the hall, where the knaves were working with all their might at their empty looms. "What can be the meaning of this?" thought the old man, opening his eyes very wide. "I cannot discover the least bit of thread on the looms!" However, he did not express his thoughts aloud.

The impostors requested him very courteously to be so good as to come nearer their looms; and then asked him whether the design pleased him, and whether the colours were not very beautiful; at the same time pointing to the empty frames. The poor old minister looked and looked, he could not discover anything on the looms, for a very good reason—there was nothing there.

"What!" thought he again, "is it possible that I am a simpleton? I have never thought so myself; and no one must know it now, if I am so. Can it be that I am unfit for my office? No, that must not be said either. I will never confess that I could not see the stuff."

"Well, Sir Minister!" said one of the knaves, still pretending to work, "you do not say whether the stuff pleases you."

"Oh, it is excellent!" replied the old minister, looking at the loom through his spectacles. "This pattern and the colours—yes, I will tell the Emperor without delay how very beautiful I think them."

"We shall be much obliged to you," said the impostors; and then they named the different colours and described the pattern of the pretended stuff. The old minister listened attentively to their words, in order that he might repeat them to the Emperor; and then the knaves asked for more silk and gold, saying that it was necessary to complete what they had begun. However, they put all that was given them into their knapsacks, and continued to work, with as much apparent diligence as before, at their empty looms.

The Emperor now sent another officer of his court to see how the men were getting on, and to ascertain whether the cloth would soon be ready. It was just the same with this gentleman as with the minister; he surveyed the looms on all sides, but could see nothing at all but the empty frames.

"Does not the stuff appear as beautiful to you as it did to my lord the minister?" asked the impostors of the Emperor's second ambassador; at the same time making the same gestures as before, and talking of the design and colours which were not there.

"I certainly am not stupid!" thought the messenger. "It must be that I am not fit for my good, profitable office! That is very odd; however, no one shall know anything about it." And accordingly he praised the stuff he could not see, and declared that he was delighted with both colours and patterns.

"Indeed, please your Imperial Majesty," said he to his sovereign, when he returned, "the cloth which the weavers are preparing is extraordinarily magnificent."

The whole city was talking of the splendid cloth which the Emperor had ordered to be woven at his own expense.

And now the Emperor himself wished to see the costly manufacture whilst it was still on the loom. Accompanied by a select number of officers of the court, among whom were the two honest men who had already admired the cloth, he went to the crafty impostors who, as soon as they were aware of the Emperor's approach, went on working more diligently than ever; although they still did not pass a single thread through the looms.

"Is not the work absolutely magnificent?" said the two officers of the crown, already mentioned. "If your Majesty will only be pleased to look at it! What a splendid design! what glorious colours!" and at the same time they pointed to the empty frames; for they imagined that every one else could see this exquisite piece of workmanship.

"How is this?" said the Emperor to himself. "I can see nothing! this is indeed a terrible affair! Am I a simpleton, or am I unfit to be an Emperor? That would be the worst thing that could happen—Oh! the cloth is charming," said he aloud. "It has my complete approval." And he smiled most graciously, and looked closely at the empty looms; for on no account would he say that he could not see what two of the officers of his court had praised so much.

All his retinue now strained their eyes, hoping to discover something on the looms, but they could see no more than the others. Nevertheless, they all exclaimed, "Oh, how beautiful!" and advised his Majesty to have some new clothes made from this splendid material, for the approaching procession.

"Magnificent! charming! excellent!" resounded on all sides; and every one was uncommonly gay. The Emperor shared in the general satisfaction; and presented the impostors with the riband of an order of knighthood, to be worn in their button-holes, and bestowed on them the title of "Gentlemen Weavers." The rogues sat up the whole of the night before the day on which the procession was to take place, and had six-teen lights burning, so that everyone might see how anxious they were to finish the Emperor's new suit. They pretended to roll the cloth off the looms; cut the air with their scissors; and sewed with needles without any thread in them. "See!" cried they at last, "the Emperor's new clothes are ready!"

And now the Emperor, with all the grandees of his court, came to the weavers; and the rogues raised their arms, as if in the act of holding something up, saying, "Here are your Majesty's trousers! Here is the scarf! Here is the mantle! The whole suit is as light as a cobweb; one might fancy one has nothing at all on, when dressed in it. That, however, is the great virtue of this delicate cloth."

"Yes, indeed!" said all the courtiers, although not one of them could see anything of this exquisite manufacture.

"If your Imperial Majesty will be graciously pleased to take off your clothes, we will fit on the new suit, in front of the looking-glass."

The Emperor was accordingly undressed, and the rogues pretended to array him in his new suit; the Emperor turning round, from side to side, before the looking-glass.

"How splendid his Majesty looks in his new clothes; and how well they fit!" every one cried out. "What a design! What colours! These are indeed royal robes!"

"The canopy which is to be borne over your Majesty in the procession is waiting," announced the chief master of the ceremonies.

"I am quite ready," answered the Emperor. "Do my new clothes fit well?" asked he, turning himself round again before the looking-glass in order that he might appear to be examining his handsome suit.

The lords of the bedchamber, who were to carry his Majesty's train, felt about on the ground, as if they were lifting up the ends of the mantle, and pretended to be carrying something; for they would by no means betray anything like simplicity or unfitness for their office.

So now the Emperor walked under his high canopy in the midst of the procession, through the streets of his capital; and all the people standing by, and those at the windows, cried out, "Oh, how beautiful are our Emperor's new clothes! What a magnificent train there is to the mantle; and how gracefully the scarf hangs.

In short, no one would allow that he could not see these much admired clothes; because, in doing so, he would have declared himself either a simpleton or unfit for his office. Certainly, none of the Emperor's various suits had ever made so great an impression as these invisible ones.

"But the Emperor has nothing on at all!" said a little child. "Listen to the voice of innocence!" exclaimed his father; and what the child had said was whispered from one to another.

"But he has nothing at all on!" at last cried out all the people. The Emperor was vexed, for he knew that the people were right; but he thought the procession must go on now. And the lords of the bedchamber took greater pains than ever to appear holding up a train although, in reality, there was no train to hold.

THE SWINEHERD

THERE was once a poor Prince, who had a kingdom; it was very small, but still quite large enough to marry upon, and he wished to marry.

It was certainly rather cool of him to say to the Emperor's daughter, "Will you have me?" But so he did; for his name was renowned far and wide; and there were a hundred princesses who would have answered "Yes!" and "Thank you kindly." We shall see what this Princess said.

Listen!

It happened that where the Prince's father lay buried there grew a rose-tree—a most beautiful rose-tree, which blossomed only once in every five years, and even then only bore one flower. But that *was* a rose! It smelt so sweet that all cares and sorrows were forgotten by him who inhaled its fragrance.

And, furthermore, the Prince had a nightingale who could sing in such a manner that it seemed as if all sweet melodies dwelt in her little throat. So the Princess was to have the rose and the nightingale; and they were accordingly put into large silver caskets, and sent to her.

The Emperor had them brought into a large hall, where the Princess was playing at "Visiting," with the ladies of the court; and when she saw the casket with the presents she clapped her hands for joy.

"Ah, if it were but a little pussy-cat!" said she; but the rose-tree, with its beautiful rose, came to view.

"Oh, how prettily it is made!" said all the court-ladies.

"It is more than pretty," said the Emperor; "it is charming!"

But the Princess touched it, and was almost ready to cry. "Fie, papa!" said she, "it is not made at all, it is natural!"

"Let us see what is in the other casket, before we get into a bad humour," said the Emperor. So the nightingale came forth, and sang so delightfully that at first no one could say anything ill-humoured of her.

"*Superbe! charmant!*" exclaimed the ladies; for they all used to chatter French, each one worse than her neighbour.

"How much the bird reminds me of the musical box that belonged to our blessed Empress," said an old knight. "Oh, yes! these are the same tones; this is the same style of execution."

"Yes, yes!" said the Emperor, and he wept like a child at the remembrance.

"I will still hope that it is not a real bird," said the Princess.

"Yes, it is a real bird," said those who had brought it.

"Well, then, let the bird fly," said the Princess; and she positively refused to see the Prince.

However, he was not to be discouraged; he daubed his face over brown and black; pulled his cap over his ears, and knocked at the door.

"Good-day to my lord the Emperor!" said he. "Can I have employment at the palace?"

"Why, yes," said the Emperor; "I want some one to take care of the pigs, for we have a great many of them."

So the Prince was appointed "Imperial Swineherd." He had a dirty little room close by the pig-sty, and there he sat the whole day and worked. By the evening, he had made a pretty little kitchen-pot; little bells were hung all round it; and when the pot was boiling, these bells tinkled in the most charming manner, and played the old melody—

> "Ach! du lieber Augustin,
> Alles ist weg, weg, weg!"[1]

But what was still more curious, whoever held his finger in the smoke of the kitchen-pot immediately smelt all the dishes that were cooking on every hearth in the city—and this, you see, was something quite different from the rose.

Now the Princess happened to walk that way; and when she heard the tune she stood quite still, and seemed pleased; for she could play "Lieber Augustin."

It was the only piece she knew; and she played it with one finger.

[1] "Ah! dear Augustine !
All is gone, gone, gone!"

"Why, there is my piece," said the Princess; "that swine-herd must certainly have been well educated! Go in and ask him the price of the instrument."

So one of the court-ladies had to run in; however, she drew on wooden slippers first.

"What will you take for the kitchen-pot?" said the lady.

"I will have ten kisses from the Princess," said the swineherd.

"Yes, indeed!" said the lady.

"I cannot sell it for less," rejoined the swineherd.

"He is an impudent fellow!" said the Princess, and she walked on; but when she had gone a little way, the bells tinkled so prettily—

> "Ach! du lieber Augustin,
> Alles ist weg, weg, weg!"

"Stay," said the Princess. "Ask him if he will have ten kisses from the ladies of my court."

"No, thank you!" said the swineherd; "ten kisses from the Princess, or I keep the kitchen-pot myself."

"That must not be either!" said the Princess; "but do you all stand before me, that no one may see us."

And the court-ladies placed themselves in front of her, and spread out their dresses.

The swineherd got ten kisses, and the Princess—the kitchen-pot.

That was delightful! The pot was boiling the whole evening, and the whole of the following day. They knew perfectly well what was cooking at every fire throughout the city, from the chamberlain's to the cobbler's: the court-ladies danced, and clapped their hands.

"We know who has soup, and who has pancakes for dinner to-day; who has cutlets, and who has eggs. How interesting!"

"Yes, but keep my secret, for I am an Emperor's daughter."

The swineherd—that is to say, the Prince, for no one knew that he was other than an ill-favoured swineherd—did not let a day pass without working at something. He at last constructed a rattle, which, when it was swung round, played all the waltzes and jig tunes which have ever been heard since the creation of the world.

"Ah, that is *superbe*!" said the Princess when she passed by. "I have never heard prettier compositions! Go in and ask him the price of the instrument; but mind, he shall have no more kisses!"

"He will have a hundred kisses from the Princess!" said the lady who had been to ask.

"I think he is not in his right senses!" said the Princess, and walked on; but when she had gone a little way, she stopped again. "One must encourage art," said she. "I am the Emperor's daughter. Tell him he shall, as on yesterday, have ten kisses from me, and may take the rest from the ladies of the court."

"Oh! but we should not like that at all!" said they.

"What are you muttering?" asked the Princess. "If I can kiss him, surely you can! Remember that you owe everything to me." So the ladies were obliged to go to him again.

"A hundred kisses from the Princess!" said he, "or else let every one keep his own."

"Stand round!" said she; and all the ladies stood round her whilst the kissing was going on.

"What can be the reason for such a crowd close by the pig-sty?" said the Emperor, who happened just then to step out on the balcony: he rubbed his eyes and put on his spectacles. "They are the ladies of the court; I must go down and see what they are about!"

So he pulled up his slippers at the heel, for he had trodden them down.

As soon as he had got into the courtyard, he moved very softly; and the ladies were so much engrossed with counting the kisses, that all might go on fairly, that they did not perceive the Emperor. He rose on his tiptoes.

"What is all this?" said he, when he saw what was going on; and he boxed the Princess's ears with his slipper, just as the swineherd was taking the eighty-sixth kiss.

"March out!" said the Emperor, for he was very angry; and both Princess and swineherd were thrust out of the city.

The Princess now stood and wept; the swineherd scolded; and the rain poured down.

"Alas! unhappy creature that I am," said the Princess. "If I had but married the handsome young Prince! Ah, how unfortunate I am!"

And the swineherd went behind a tree, washed the black and brown colour from his face, threw off his dirty clothes, and stepped forth in his princely robes; he looked so noble that the Princess could not help bowing before him.

"I am come to despise thee," said he. "Thou wouldst not have an honourable prince! thou couldst not prize the rose and the nightingale, but thou wast ready to kiss the swineherd for the sake of a trumpery plaything. Thou art rightly served."

He then went back to his own little kingdom, and shut the door of his palace in her face. Now she might well sing—

> "Ach! du lieber Augustin,
> Alles ist weg, weg, weg!"

THE FLAX

THE flax was in full bloom; its pretty blue blossoms were as soft as the wings of a moth, and still more delicate. And the sun shone on the flax-field, and the rain watered it; and that was as good for the flax-flowers as it is for little children to be washed and kissed by their mother. They look so much fresher and prettier afterwards. Thus it was with the flax-flowers.

"People say I am so fine and flourishing," observed the flax, "and that I am growing so charmingly tall; a splendid piece of linen will be got from me. Oh, how happy I am. How can any one be happier? Everything around me is so pleasant, and I shall be of use for something or another. How the sun cheers one up, and how fresh and sweet the rain tastes. I am incomparably happy. I am the happiest vegetable in the world."

"Ah, ah, ah!" jeered the stakes in the hedge; "you don't know the world, not you; but we know it, there are knots in us," and then they cracked so dolefully—

"Snip, snap, snurre,
Bassilurre
And so the song is en—ded—ded—ded."

"No, it is not ended," replied the flax; "the sun shines every morning; the rain does me so much good I can see myself grow; I can feel that I am in blossom. Who so happy as I?"

However, one day people came, took hold of the flax, and pulled it up, root and all. That was exceedingly uncomfortable. And then it was thrown into water as if intended to be drowned, and, after that, put before the fire as if to be roasted. This was most cruel.

"One cannot always have what one wishes," sighed the flax; "it is well to suffer sometimes, it gives one experience."

But matters seemed to get worse and worse. The flax was bruised and broken, hacked and hackled, and at last put on the wheel—snurre rur! snurre rur! It was not possible to keep one's thoughts collected in such a situation as this.

"I have been exceedingly fortunate," thought the flax amid all these tortures. "One ought to be thankful for the happiness one has enjoyed in times past. Thankful, thankful; oh yes," and still the flax said the same when taken to the loom. And there it was made into a large, handsome piece of linen; all the flax of that one field was made into a single piece.

"Well, but this is charming. Never should I have expected it. What unexampled good fortune I have carried through the world with me. What arrant nonsense the stakes in the hedge used to talk with their

'Snip, snap, snurre,
Bassilurre.'

"The song is not ended at all; life is but just beginning. It is a very pleasant thing, too, is life. To be sure, I have suffered, but that is past now, and I have become something through suffering. I am so strong, and yet so soft; so white and so long. This is far better than being a vegetable; even during blossom time nobody attends to one, and only gets water when it is raining.

"Now, I am well taken care of. The girl turns me over every morning, and I have a shower-bath from the water-tub every evening; nay, the parson's wife herself came and looked at me, and said I was the finest piece of linen in the parish. No one can possibly be happier than I am."

The linen was taken into the house, and cut up with scissors. Oh, how it was cut and clipped, how it was pierced and stuck through with needles! That was certainly no pleasure at all. It was at last made up into twelve articles of attire, such articles as are not often mentioned, but which people can hardly do without; there were just twelve of them.

"So this, then, was my destiny. Well, it is very delightful; now I shall be of use in the world, and there is really no pleasure like that of being useful. We are now twelve pieces, but we are still one and the same—we are a dozen. Certainly this is being extremely fortunate."

Years passed away. At last the linen could endure no longer. "All things must pass away some time or another," remarked each piece. "I should like very much to last a little while longer, but one ought not to wish for impossibilities."

And so the linen was rent into shreds and remnants number-less. They believed all was over with them, for they were hacked and mashed and boiled, and they knew not what else; and thus they became beautiful, fine, white paper.

"Now, upon my word, this is a surprise! And a most delightful surprise too!" declared the paper. "Why, now I am finer than ever, and I shall be written upon. I wonder what will be written upon me. Was there ever such famous good fortune as mine?"

And the paper was written upon; the most charming stories in the world were written on it, and they were read aloud; and people declared that these stories were very beautiful and very instructive; that to read them would make mankind both wiser and better. Truly, a great blessing was given to the world in the words written upon that same paper.

"Certainly, this is more than I could ever have dreamt of when I was a little blue flower of the field. How could I then have looked forward to becoming a messenger destined to bring knowledge and pleasure among men? I can hardly understand it even now. Yet so it is, actually.

"And for my own part, I have never done anything, beyond the little that in me lay, to strive to exist, and yet I am carried on from one state of honour and happiness to another; and every time that I think within myself, 'Now, surely, the song is en—ded—ded—ded,' I am converted into something new, something far higher and better.

"Now, I suppose I shall be sent on my travels, shall be sent round the wide world, so that all men may read me. I should think that would be the wisest plan. Formerly I had blue blossoms; now, for every single blossom I have some beautiful thought or pleasant fancy. Who so happy as I?"

But the paper was not sent on its travels; it went to the printer's instead, and there all that was written upon it was printed in a book, nay, in many hundred books; and in this way an infinitely greater number of people received pleasure and profit from it than if the written paper itself had been sent round the world, and perhaps got torn and worn to pieces before it had gone half-way.

"Yes, to be sure, this is much more sensible," thought the paper. "It never occurred to me, though. I am to stay at home and be held in as great honour as if I were an old grandfather. The book was written on me first, the ink flowed in upon me from the pen and formed the words. I shall stay at home while the books go about the world, to and fro; that is much better. How glad I am, how fortunate I am!"

So the paper was rolled up and laid on one side. "It is good to repose after labour," said the paper. "It is quite right to collect oneself, and quietly think over all that dwelleth within one. Now first do I rightly know myself. And to know oneself, I have heard, is the best knowledge, the truest progress. And, come what will, this I am sure of, all will end in progress—always is there progress!"

One day the roll of paper was thrown upon the stove to be burned, it must not be sold to the grocer to wrap round pounds of butter and sugar. And all the children in the house flocked round, they wanted to see the blaze, they wanted to count the multitude of tiny red sparks which seem to dart to and fro among the ashes, dying out, one after another, so quickly. They call them "The children going out of school," and the last spark of all is the schoolmaster. They often fancy he is gone out, but another and another spark flies up unexpectedly, and the schoolmaster always tarries a little behind the rest.

And now all the paper lay heaped up on the stove. "Ugh!" it cried, and all at once it burst into a flame; so high did it rise into the air; never had the flax been able to rear its tiny blue blossom so high, and it shone as never the white linen had shone. All the letters written on it became fiery red in an instant, and all the words and thoughts of the writer were surrounded with a glory.

"Now, then, I go straight up into the sun!" said something within the flames. It was as if a thousand voices at once had spoken thus, and the flame burst through the chimney, and rose high above it; and brighter than the flame, yet invisible to mortal eyes, hovered little tiny beings, as many as there had been blossoms on the flax.

They were lighter and of more subtle essence than even the flame that bore them; and, when that flame had died away, and nothing remained of the paper but the black ashes, they once again danced over them, and, wherever their feet touched the ashes, their footprints—the fiery red sparks— were seen. Thus "The children went out of school, and the schoolmaster came last"; it was a pleasure to see the pretty sight; and the children of the house stood looking at the black ashes and singing—

> "Snip, snap, snurre,
> Bassilurre,
> And now the song is en—ded—ded—ded."

But the tiny invisible beings replied every one, "The song is never ended! That is the best of it! We know that, and therefore none are so happy as we are!"

However, the children could neither hear nor understand the reply, nor would it be well that they should, for children must not know everything.

THE FALSE COLLAR

THERE was once a fine gentleman whose toilet-table displayed nothing but a boot-jack and a comb, but he possessed the most charming false collar in the world, and it is the history of this collar that the following pages would relate. The collar was so old that he began to think of marriage.

It so chanced that one day in the wash he and the garter were thrown together. "Well, upon my honour," quoth the false collar, "never have I seen anything so slender and delicate, so pretty and soft! May I take the liberty of asking your name?"

"Certainly not, and if you do ask, I shall not tell you," replied the garter.

"Where do you live?" inquired the collar.

But the garter was very modest, and seemed to think that this was too impertinent a question.

"Surely you must be a waist-band," said the collar, "a Queen's waist-band, perhaps! I see you are useful as well as ornamental, pretty lady!"

"You must not speak to me," retorted the garter; "I do not think I have given any encouragement to such behaviour."

"Yes, indeed," insisted the false collar; "beauty like yours may encourage one to anything."

"You are not to come so near me," said the garter; "you look as if you belonged to a man."

"I am a fine gentleman!" retorted the false collar proudly, "I have a boot-jack and a comb, all to myself." But this boasting was not true; they belonged to his master, not to himself.

"Don't come so near me, I tell you," repeated the garter; "I am not accustomed to such familiarities."

"So you're a prude, are you?" quoth the discomfited false collar, and just then he was taken out of the wash-tub. He was starched, and next he was hung across a chair in the sunshine, and at last laid upon the ironing-board. And now the hot iron approached him.

"Lady!" cried the false collar; "pretty widow lady, I am growing so warm—I am burning hot! I am becoming quite another creature, the wrinkles are all taken out of me; you will burn a hole in me. Ugh! Pretty widow, suffer me to pay my addresses to you!"

"Stuff!" exclaimed the iron, as she passed haughtily over the collar; for she imagined herself to be a steam engine, and that she was meant, some day or another, to be put on a railroad to draw carriages. "Stuff!" she said again.

The collar was a little unravelled at the edges; so a pair of scissors was brought to clip off the loose threads.

"Oh!" cried the false collar, "surely you must be a ballet-dancer; how cleverly you can throw out your limbs! Never have I seen anything half so charming. I am sure that no human being in the world could do anything at all like it!"

"You need not tell me that, I know it already," replied the scissors.

"You deserve to be a countess," said the false collar.

"Alas! I am only a fine gentleman; to be sure, I have a boot-jack and a comb. Oh, if I had but an earldom!"

"Does he really mean this for courtship?" said the scissors. "I wonder what next!" And forthwith she cut him, for she was very indignant. So he had his third dismissal.

"I can still address the comb. It is quite delightful to see how long you have kept all your teeth, fair lady!" Thus spoke the false collar to the comb. "Have you never thought of betrothing yourself?"

"Why, yes," replied the comb; "if you particularly wish to know, I will tell you a secret. I am engaged to the boot-jack."

"Engaged to the boot-jack?" repeated the false collar in consternation. There was now no one left to whom he could pay his addresses; accordingly he began to despise the fair sex altogether.

A long, long time passed away. At last the collar found himself in a box at the paper-mill. The box harboured a large community of rags and tatters, and this community formed itself into snug coteries, the fine keeping by themselves, and the coarse by themselves, just as it ought to be. Every one of them had a lot to say, but the false collar most of all, for he was a perfect braggadocio.

"I have had so many sweethearts!" declared the false collar, "they would not let me have any peace because I was such a fine gentleman, and so well starched; I had both a boot-jack and a comb, neither of which I ever used. You should have seen me when I lay down, I looked so charming then.

"Never shall I forget my first love; she was a waist-band, so delicate, so soft and pretty; she threw herself into a tub of water, in her despair of winning my love.

"Then there was the widow lady, who grew red with passion because I slighted her; however, I left her to stand and cool at her leisure. Cool she did, no doubt, and black she turned, but that does not matter.

"There was the ballet-dancer, too; she gave me the cut direct. I shall never forget how furious she was. Why, even my own comb was in love with me; she lost all her teeth through care and anxiety.

"Yes, indeed, I have lived to make many experiences of this sort, but I suffer most remorse on account of the garter—I mean the waist-band—who threw herself into the tub of water. I have a great deal on my conscience. I wish I could become pure white paper!"

And white paper the collar became. All the rags were made into white paper, but the false collar was made into this very identical sheet of white paper now before you, gentle reader, the sheet upon which this history is printed. And this was the punishment for his shameless boasting and falsehood.

And it is well that we should all read the story and think over it, that we may beware how we brag and boast as the false collar did; for we can hardly make sure that we may not some unlucky day get into a rag-chest, too, and be made into white paper, and have our whole history, even our most secret thoughts and doings, printed upon us, and thus be obliged to travel about the world and make our misdeeds known everywhere, just like the false collar.

THE FLYING TRUNK

THERE was once a merchant, so rich that he might have paved the whole street where he lived, and an alley besides, with pieces of silver, but this he did not do; he knew another way of using his money, and whenever he laid out a shilling he gained a crown in return. A merchant he lived, and a merchant he died.

All his money then went to his son. But the son lived merrily, and spent all his time in pleasures—went to masquerades every evening, made bank-notes into paper kites, and played at ducks and drakes in the pond with gold pieces instead of stones.

In this manner his money soon vanished, until at last he had only a few pennies left, and his wardrobe was reduced to a pair of slippers and an old dressing-gown. His friends cared no more about him, now that they could no longer walk abroad with him; one of them, however, more good-natured than the rest, sent him an old trunk, with this advice, "Pack up, and be off!" This was all very fine, but he had nothing that he could pack up; so he put himself into the trunk.

It was a droll trunk: when the lock was pressed close it could fly. The merchant's son did press the lock, and lo! up flew the trunk with him through the chimney, high into the clouds, on and on, higher and higher. The lower part cracked, which rather frightened him, for if it had broken in two, a pretty fall he would have had.

However, it descended safely, and he found himself in Turkey. He hid the trunk under a heap of dry leaves in a wood, and walked into the next town. He could do so very well, for among the Turks everybody goes about clad as he was, in dressing-gown and slippers. He met a nurse carrying a little child in her arms. "Hark ye, Turkish nurse," quoth he; "what palace is that with the high windows close by the town?"

"The King's daughter dwells there," replied the nurse. "It

has been told of her that she shall be made very unhappy by a lover, and therefore no one may visit her, except when the King and Queen are with her."

"Thank you," said the merchant's son, and he immediately went back into the wood, sat down in his trunk, flew up to the roof of the palace, and crept through the window into the Princess's apartment.

She was lying asleep on the sofa. She was so beautiful that the merchant's son could not help kneeling down to kiss her hand, whereupon she awoke, and was not a little frightened at the sight of this unexpected visitor. But he told her, however, that he was the Turkish prophet, and had come down from the sky on purpose to woo her, and on hearing this she was well pleased.

So they sat down side by side, and he talked to her about her eyes, how they were beautiful dark-blue seas, and that thoughts and feelings floated like mer-maidens therein; and he spoke of her brow, how it was a fair snowy mountain, with splendid halls and pictures, and many other such like things he told her.

Oh, these were charming stories: and thus he wooed the Princess, and she immediately said "Yes."

"But you must come here on Saturday," said she; "the King and Queen have promised to drink tea with me that evening; they will be so proud and so pleased when they hear that I am to marry the Turkish prophet! And mind you tell them a very pretty story, for they are exceedingly fond of stories. My mother likes them to be very moral and high-class, and my father likes them to be merry, so as to make him laugh."

"Yes, I shall bring no other bridal present than a tale," replied the merchant's son; and here they parted, but not before the Princess had given her lover a sabre all covered with gold. He knew excellently well what use to make of this present.

So he flew away, bought a new dressing-gown, and then sat down in the wood to compose the tale which was to be ready by Saturday, and certainly he found composition not the easiest thing in the world.

At last he was ready, and at last Saturday came.

The King, the Queen, and the whole court were waiting tea for him at the Princess's palace. The suitor was received with much ceremony.

"Will you not tell us a story?" asked the Queen; "a story that is instructive and full of deep meaning."

"But let it make us laugh," said the King.

"With pleasure," replied the merchant's son; and now you must hear his story.

"There was once a bundle of matches, who were all extremely proud of their high descent, for their genealogical tree—that is to say, the tall fir-tree from which each of them was a splinter—had been a tree of great antiquity, and distinguished by his height from all the other trees of the forest. The matches were now lying on the mantelpiece, between a tinder-box and an old iron saucepan, and to these two they often talked about their youth.

"'Ah, when we were upon the green branches,' said they; 'when we really lived upon green branches—that was a happy time! Every morning and evening we had diamond-tea' (that is dew); 'the whole day long we had sunshine, at least whenever the sun shone, and all the little birds used to tell stories to us.

"'It might easily be seen, too, that we were rich, for the other trees were clothed with leaves only during the summer, whereas our family could afford to wear green clothes both summer and winter.

"'But at last came the wood-cutters: then was the great revolution, and our family was dispersed. The paternal trunk obtained a situation as main-mast to a magnificent ship, which could sail round the world if it chose; the boughs were transported to various places, and our vocation was henceforth to kindle lights for low, common people. Now you will understand how it comes to pass that persons of such high descent as we are should be living in a kitchen.'

"'To be sure, mine is a very different history,' remarked the iron saucepan, near which the matches were lying. 'From the moment I came into the world until now, I have been rubbed and scrubbed, and boiled over and over again—oh, how many times! I love to have to do with what is solidly good, and am really of the first importance in this house.

"'My only recreation is to stand clean and bright upon this mantelpiece after dinner, and hold some rational conversation with my companions. However, excepting the water-pail, who now and then goes out into the court, we all of us lead a very quiet domestic life here. Our only newsmonger is the turf-basket, but he talks in such a democratic way about 'government' and the 'people'—why, I assure you, not long ago, there was an old jar standing here who was so much shocked by what he heard said that he fell down from the mantelpiece and broke into a thousand pieces! That turf-basket is a Liberal, that's the fact.'

"'Now, you talk too much,' interrupted the tinder-box; and the steel struck the flint, so that the sparks flew out. 'Why should we not spend a pleasant evening?'

"'Yes, let us settle who is of highest rank among us!' proposed the matches.

"'Oh, no; for my part I would rather not speak of myself,' objected the earthenware pitcher. 'Suppose we have an intellectual entertainment? I will begin; I will relate something of everyday life, such as we have all experienced; one can easily transport oneself into it, and that is so interesting! Near the Baltic, among the Danish beech-groves——'

"'That is a capital beginning!' cried all the plates at once; 'it will certainly be just the sort of story for me!'

"'Yes, there I spent my youth in a very quiet family; the furniture was rubbed, the floors were washed, clean curtains were hung up every fortnight.'

"'How very interesting. What a charming way you have of describing things!' said the hair-broom. 'Any one might guess immediately that it is a lady who is speaking; the tale breathes such a spirit of cleanliness!'

"'Very true; so it does!' exclaimed the water-pail; and in the excess of his delight he gave a little jump, so that some of the water splashed upon the floor.

"And the pitcher went on with her tale, and the end proved as good as the beginning.

"All the plates clattered applause, and the hair-broom took

some green parsley out of the sand-hole and crowned the pitcher, for he knew that this would vex the others; and, thought he, 'If I crown her to-day, she will crown me to-morrow.'

"'Now I will dance,' said the fire-tongs, and accordingly she did dance, and oh! it was wonderful to see how high she threw one of her legs up into the air; the old chair-cover in the corner tore with horror at seeing her. 'Am not I to be crowned too?' asked the tongs; and she was crowned forthwith.

"'These are the vulgar rabble!' thought the matches.

"The tea-urn was now called upon to sing, but she had a cold; she said she could only sing when she was boiling; however, this was all her pride and affectation. The fact was she never cared to sing except when she was standing on the parlour table before company.

"On the window-ledge lay an old quill pen, with which the maids used to write; there was nothing remarkable about her, except that she had been dipped too low in the ink; however, she was proud of that. 'If the tea-urn does not choose to sing,' quoth she, 'she may let it alone; there is a nightingale in the cage hung just outside, he can sing. To be sure, he had never learned the notes; never mind—we will not speak evil of any one this evening!'

"'I think it highly absurd,' observed the tea-kettle, who was the vocalist of the kitchen, and a half-brother of the tea-urn's, 'that a foreign bird should be listened to. Is it patriotic? I appeal to the turf-basket.'

"'I am only vexed,' said the turf-basket; 'I am vexed from my inmost soul that such things are thought of at all. Is it a becoming way of spending the evening? Would it not be much more rational to reform the whole house, and establish a totally new order of things, rather more according to nature? Then every one would get into his right place, and I would undertake to direct the revolution. What say you to it? That would be something worth the doing!'

"'Oh, yes; we will make a grand commotion!' cried they all. Just then the door opened—it was the servant-maid. They all stood perfectly still, not one dared stir; yet there was not a single kitchen-utensil among them all but was thinking about the great things he could have done, and how great was his superiority over the others.

"'Ah, if I had chosen it,' thought each of them, 'what a merry evening we might have had!'

"The maid took the matches and struck a light—oh, how they spluttered and blazed up!

"'Now every one may see,' thought they, 'that we are of highest rank. What a splendid, dazzling light we give—how glorious!' and in another moment they were burned out."

"That is a capital story," said the Queen; "I quite felt myself transported into the kitchen. Yes, thou shalt have our daughter!"

"With all my heart," said the King; "on Monday thou shalt marry our daughter." They said "thou" to him now, since he was so soon to become one of the family.

The wedding was a settled thing; and, on the evening preceding, the whole city was illuminated; cakes, buns, and sugar-plums were thrown out among the people; all the little boys in the streets stood upon tiptoes, shouting "Hurrah!" and whistling through their fingers—it was famous!

"Well, I suppose I ought to do my part, too," thought the merchant's son; so he went and bought sky-rockets, squibs, Catherine-wheels, Roman-candles, and all kinds of fireworks conceivable; put them all into his trunk, and flew up into the air, letting them off as he flew.

Hurrah! what a glorious sky-rocket was that!

All the Turks jumped up to look so hastily that their slippers flew about their ears; such a meteor they had never seen before. Now they might be sure that it was indeed the prophet who was to marry the Princess.

As soon as the merchant's son had returned in his trunk to the wood, he said to himself, "I will now go into the city and hear what people say about me, and what sort of figure I made in the air;" and, certainly, this was a very natural idea.

Oh, what strange accounts were given! Every one whom he accosted had beheld the bright vision in a way peculiar to himself, but all agreed that it was marvellously beautiful.

"I saw the great prophet with my own eyes," declared one; "he had eyes like sparkling stars, and a beard like foaming water."

"He flew enveloped in a mantle of fire," said another, "the prettiest little cherubs were peeping forth from under its folds."

Yes; he heard of many beautiful things, and the morrow was to be his wedding-day.

He now went back to the wood, intending to get into his trunk again, but where was it?

Alas! the trunk was burned. One spark from the fireworks had been left in it, and set it on fire; the trunk now lay in ashes. The poor merchant's son could never fly again—could never again visit his bride.

She sat the livelong day upon the roof of her palace expecting him; she expects him still. He, meantime, goes about the world telling stories, but none of his stories now are so pleasant as that one which he related in the Princess's palace about the Brimstone Matches.

THE DARNING-NEEDLE

THERE was once a darning-needle so fine that she fancied herself a sewing-needle.

"Now take care, and hold me fast!" said the darning-needle to the fingers that took her up. "Don't lose me, pray! If I were to fall down on the floor, you would never be able to find me again, I am so fine!"

"That's more than you can tell!" said the fingers, as they took hold of her.

"See, I come with a train!" said the darning-needle, drawing a long thread, without a single knot in it, after her.

The fingers guided the needle to the cook-maid's slippers; the upper leather was torn, and had to be sewn together.

"This is vulgar work!" said the darning-needle. "I shall never get through; I break—I am breaking!"—and break she did. "Did I not say so?" continued she. "I am too fine!"

"Now she is good for nothing," thought the fingers; however, they must still keep their hold. The cook-maid dropped sealing-wax upon the darning-needle and then stuck her into her neckerchief.

"See, now I am a breast-pin!" said the darning-needle. "I knew well that I should come to honour; when one is something, one always becomes something." And at this she laughed, only inwardly, of course, for nobody has ever seen or heard a darning-needle laugh; there sat she now at her ease, as proud as if she were driving in her carriage, and looking about her on all sides.

"May I take the liberty of asking if you are of gold?" inquired she of the pin that was her neighbour. "You have a pleasing exterior, and a very peculiar head; it is but small, though. You must take care that it grows, for it is not every one that can have sealing-wax dropped upon her!" And the darning-needle drew herself up so proudly that she fell off from the neckerchief into the sink, where the cook was engaged just then in washing-up.

"Not for our travels!" said the darning-needle; "but I hope I shall not go very far." However, she did travel far, very far.

"I am too fine for this world," said she, as at last she sat still in the gutter. "However, I know who I am, and there is always some little pleasure in that."

And so the darning-needle held herself erect, and did not lose her good humour.

All sorts of things sailed past her—splinters of wood, straws, scraps of old newspapers. "See, how they sail along!" said the darning-needle. "They do not know what is sticking under them! It is I. I stick—I sit here. There goes a splinter, he thinks of nothing in the world but himself, splinter as he is. There floats a straw, to see how it turns round and round! Nay, think not so much of thyself, thou mightst easily float against one of the stones. There swims a newspaper—everything in it is forgotten, yet now it spreads itself out! I sit patiently and quietly! I know what I am, and that I shall always be the same!"

One day there chanced to be close by her something that

glittered so charmingly that the darning-needle felt persuaded it must needs be a diamond; it was, in reality, only a splinter of glass, but, delighted with its appearance, the darning-needle addressed it, introducing herself as a breast-pin. "Surely you are a diamond?"

"Why, yes, something of the sort!" was the reply. So now each believed the other to be some very rare and costly trinket, and they both began to complain of the extraordinary haughtiness of the world.

"Yes, I have dwelt in a box belonging to a young lady," said the darning-needle, "and this young lady was a cook-maid; she had five fingers on each hand, and anything so arrogant, so conceited as these five fingers I have never known; and after all, what were they good for? For nothing, but to hold me, to take me out of the box, and lay me in the box!"

"And were they at all bright? Did they shine?" asked the glass splinter.

"Shine!" repeated the darning-needle, "not they, but conceited enough they were notwithstanding! They were five brothers: 'Finger' was the family name; they held themselves so erect, side by side, although they were not all of the same height.

"The first, Thumbkin he was called, was short and thick; he generally stood out of the rank rather before the others; he had only one bend in his back, so that he could only bow once, but he used to say that if he were cut off from a man, that man would no longer be fit for military service.

"Foreman, the second, would put himself forward everywhere, meddled with sweet and with sour, pointed at sun or moon, and he it was who pressed upon the pen whenever the fingers wrote. Middleman was so tall that he could look over the others' heads. Ringman wore a gold belt round his body; and as for Littleman, he did nothing at all, and was proud of that, I suppose. Proud they were, and proud they could be; therefore I took myself off into the gutter!"

"And now we sit together and shine!" quoth the glass splinter.

Just then some more water was poured into the gutter; it

overflowed its boundaries and carried the glass splinter along with it.

"So now he has advanced farther," observed the darning-needle. "I stay here, I am too fine, but such it is my pride to be; it is respectable!" So still she sat there erect, enjoying her own thoughts.

"I could almost believe I was born of a sunbeam, I am so fine; and yet the sunbeams do not seem to seek me out under the water. Alas! I am so fine that even my mother cannot find me. Had I still my old eye which broke, I believe I could weep. I would not, though—it is not refined to weep."

One day some boys were raking about in the gutter, hunting for old nails, pennies, and such like. This was very dirty, certainly, but such was their pleasure.

"Hallo!" cried one, pricking himself with the darning-needle; "there's a fellow for you!"

"Do not call me a fellow; I am a young lady," said the darning-needle, but no one heard it. The sealing-wax had worn off, and she had become quite black. Black, however, makes a person look thin; so she fancied herself finer than ever.

"There sails an egg-shell," said the boys, and they stuck the darning-needle into the shell.

"White walls and a lady in black," said the darning-needle; "that is very striking. Now every one can see me. But I hope I shall not be sea-sick, for then I shall break." Her fear was needless; she was not sea-sick, neither did she break.

"Nothing is so good to prevent sea-sickness as being of steel, and then, too, never to forget that one is a little more than man. Now my trial is over. The finer one is, the more one can endure."

Crash went the egg-shell. A wagon rolled over it. "Ugh, what a pressure!" sighed the darning-needle; "now I shall be sea-sick after all. I shall break—I shall break!"

But she broke not, although the wheel had passed over her. Long did she lie there—and there let her die.

THE REAL PRINCESS

THERE was once a Prince who wished to marry a Princess; but then she must be a real Princess. He travelled all over the world in hopes of finding such a lady; but there was always something wrong. Princesses he found in plenty; but whether they were real Princesses it was impossible for him to decide, for now one thing, now another, seemed to him not quite right about the ladies. At last he returned to his palace quite cast down, because he wished so much to have a real Princess for his wife.

One evening a fearful tempest arose. It thundered and lightened, and the rain poured down from the sky in torrents; besides, it was as dark as pitch. All at once there was heard a violent knocking at the door, and the old King, the Prince's father, went out himself to open it.

It was a Princess who was standing outside the door. What with the rain and the wind, she was in a sad condition. The water trickled down from her hair, and her clothes clung to her body. She said she was a real Princess.

"Ah, we shall soon see that!" thought the old Queen-mother. However, she said not a word of what she was going to do; but went quietly into the bedroom, took all the bed-clothes off the bed, and put three little peas on the bedstead. She then laid twenty mattresses one upon another over the three peas, and put twenty feather beds over the mattresses.

Upon this bed the Princess was to pass the night.

The next morning she was asked how she had slept. "Oh, very badly indeed!" she replied. "I have scarcely closed my eyes the whole night through. I do not know what was in my bed, but I had something hard under me, and am all over black and blue. It has hurt me so much!"

Now it was plain that the lady must be a real Princess, since she had been able to feel the three little peas through the twenty mattresses and twenty feather-beds. None but a real Princess could have had such a delicate sense of feeling.

The Prince accordingly made her his wife; being now convinced that he had found a real Princess. The three peas were, however, put into the cabinet of curiosities, where they are still to be seen, provided they are not lost.

Was not this a lady of real delicacy?

THE DROP OF WATER

SURELY you know what a microscope is—that wonderful glass which makes everything appear a hundred times larger than it really is? If you look through a microscope at a single drop of ditch-water, you will perceive more than a thousand strangely-shaped creatures, such as you never could imagine dwelling in the water.

It looks not unlike a plateful of shrimps, all jumping and crowding upon each other; and so ferocious are these little creatures that they will tear off each other's arms and legs without mercy; and yet they are happy and merry after their fashion.

Now there was once an old man whom all his neighbours called Cribbley Crabbley—a curious name to be sure. He always liked to make the best of everything, and, when he could not manage it otherwise, he tried magic.

So one day he sat with his microscope held up to his eye, looking at a drop of ditch-water. Oh, what a strange sight was that! All the thousand little imps in the water were jumping and springing about, devouring each other, or pulling each other to pieces.

"Upon my word, this is too horrible!" quoth old Cribbley Crabbley; "there must surely be some means of making them live in peace and quiet." And he thought and thought, but still could not hit on the right plan. "I must give them a colour," he said at last; "then I shall be able to see them more distinctly:" and accordingly he let fall into the water a tiny drop of something that looked like red wine, but in reality it was witches' blood; whereupon all the strange little creatures immediately became red all over, not unlike the Red Indians;

the drop of water now seemed a whole townful of naked wild men.

"What have you there?" inquired another old magician, who had no name at all, which made him more remarkable even than Cribbley Crabbley.

"Well, if you can guess what it is," replied Cribbley Crabbley, "I will give it you; but I warn you, you'll not find it out so easily."

And the magician without a name looked through the microscope.

The scene now revealed to his eyes actually resembled a town where all the inhabitants were running about without clothing. It was a horrible sight, but still more horrible was it to see how they kicked and cuffed, struggled and fought, pulled and bit each other.

All those that were lowest must needs strive to get uppermost, and all those that were highest must be thrust down. "Look, look!" they seemed to be crying out, "his leg is longer than mine; pah! off with it. And there is one who has a little lump behind his ear, an innocent little lump enough, but it pains him, and it shall pain him more!" and they hacked at it, and seized hold of him, and devoured him, merely because of this little lump.

Only one of the creatures was quiet and still; it sat by itself, like a little modest damsel, wishing for nothing but peace and rest; but the others would not have it so. They pulled the little damsel forward, cuffed her, cut at her, and ate her.

"This is most uncommonly amusing," remarked the nameless magician.

"Do you think so? Well, but what is it?" asked Cribbley Crabbley. "Can you guess, or can you not? That's the question."

"To be sure I can guess," was the reply of the nameless magician, "easy enough. It is either Copenhagen or some other large city, I don't know which, for they are all alike. It is some large city."

"It is a drop of ditch-water!" said Cribbley Crabbley.

THE SHADOW

IN hot countries the sun's rays burn with a vengeance! People have their complexions dyed a mahogany brown colour, and in the very hottest regions of all are scorched into negroes.

Our story, however, relates not to these very sultry climes, but to one of the moderately hot countries, which was visited, once upon a time, by a learned man from the cold, cold north.

This learned man at first imagined that he might run about as freely as he had been used to do at home; but he was soon undeceived, and, like all other sensible people, he remained in his house all day long, keeping the doors and window-shutters closed, just as if everybody were asleep or away from home. The narrow street of high-built houses where he dwelt was so situated that the sunbeams fell full upon it from dawn of day till evening. It was positively unbearable, and the learned man from the cold country felt as if sitting in a heated oven.

He was a young, as well as a wise man, and the sun injured his health; he became quite thin; his shadow also—for the sun affected that as well as himself—was, during the daytime, considerably smaller than it had used to be. However, at night, after the sun had set, both man and shadow constantly revived.

It was really a pleasure to see the change. As soon as lights were brought into the room the shadow stretched itself up the wall, nay, even as far as the ceiling; it seemed stretching itself to the utmost in order to recover its original size.

The learned man used to go out on the balcony—that was *his* place for stretching—and, when the stars shone forth in the clear balmy atmosphere, he felt a new life breathing through his limbs. Figures of men and women then made their appearance on all the balconies in the street, and in hot countries no single window is without a balcony, for people must have air, even though they are accustomed to be turned to mahogany colour.

Above and below, everything became full of life; butchers and bakers, cobblers and tailors, flitted about the streets; chairs and tables were brought out, and lamps, nay, thousands of lamps, were lighted. One shouted, another sang, some walked, some drove, some rode on asses—klinge-linge, ling, the little bells on their harness tinkled merrily as they passed —little boys let off squibs and crackers, the church-bells pealed, psalms were sung, and many a solemn funeral procession moved along. Yes, the street was then thoroughly alive!

Only in one house—it was that which stood exactly opposite the one in which dwelt the northern student—there was silence, and yet it could not be uninhabited for flowers adorned the balcony. They flourished beautifully amid the sun's burning heat, and flourish they could not unless constantly watered, and watered they could not be without hands. Besides, every evening the balcony window used to open, and, although it was quite dark within, at least in the foremost chamber, from some deeper recess the notes of music were heard, incomparably delicious—at least, so thought our stranger. But this might very possibly be only a fancy, as, according to him, everything in this hot country was incomparably delicious, always excepting the sun.

The stranger's landlord declared that he did not know who occupied the house opposite, no one had ever been seen there, and as for the music, it seemed to him dreadfully tedious. "It is," said he, "just like a person sitting and practising a piece which he cannot play—always the same piece. 'I shall play it at last,' he keeps on saying, but it is plain that he never will, with all his practising."

One night the stranger was sleeping. He slept close to the open window, the curtains were waved aside by the wind, and the opposite balcony was discovered wrapped in a wondrous splendour. All the flowers shone like flames of the loveliest and most varied hues, and amid the flowers stood a tall, graceful maiden, surrounded by a glory which dazzled his eyes—indeed, in his eagerness he opened them so fearfully wide that he awoke.

With one spring he was on the floor, crept softly behind

the curtain, but the lady was gone—the glory which had dazzled his eyes was gone—the flowers no longer shone. They looked exactly as they had been wont to look, the door was half open, and deep from within sounded music soft and plaintive. Surely this was sorcery, for who could be living there?

One evening the stranger was sitting in his balcony; lights were burning in the apartment behind him, and consequently, as was quite natural, his shadow fell upon the opposite wall. There it seemed to sit among the flowers of the balcony, and whenever its master moved, the shadow moved also, as a matter of course.

"I verily believe my shadow is the only thing stirring to be seen over there," said the learned stranger. "See how comfortably it sits among the flowers; the door within is half open; I do wish my shadow would but have the sense to walk in, look about, and then return to tell me what it had seen there. Ah, it might be of great advantage to thee!" continued he jestingly. "Be so kind as to step forward! Well, wilt thou go?" And he nodded to the shadow, and the shadow nodded again in return. "Well then, go, but don't stay!"

And forthwith the stranger arose, and his shadow on the opposite balcony rose also; the stranger then turned round, whereupon the shadow likewise turned round, and any close observer might have seen that the shadow passed through the half-opened door, into the apartment in the opposite house, just as the stranger retired into his own room, closing the long curtains behind him.

Next morning the learned man went out to drink coffee and read the journals. "How is this!" he exclaimed, as he came out into the sunshine; "why, I have no shadow! Then it really did pass over into the opposite house yesterday evening, and has not returned! Now, on my word, this is the most provoking thing ever heard of!"

He was vexed, not so much because his shadow was gone, as because he knew that there was already a story about a man without a shadow which was well known to all the people in his own country, so that now, if he were to tell his story, everybody would call him a plagiarist, and that would not please him at all. So he determined to say nothing about it, and this was certainly a wise resolve.

In the evening he went again into the balcony, first placing the candles so as to be just behind his back, for he knew that a shadow always requires its master to act as its screen. But he could by no means entice it forth; he stretched himself, he contracted himself, but no shadow made its appearance. He said, "Hem, hem!" but that was of no avail either.

All this was vexatious; however, in hot countries everything grows very fast; accordingly, after eight days had elapsed, on going into the sunshine, he observed to his great delight that a new shadow was beginning to spring out from under his feet. The root must have remained there, and in three weeks' time he had once more a very tolerable shadow, which as he was now travelling homewards, increased rapidly in size during the journey, until at last it became so long and so broad that half of it might have sufficed him.

So this same learned man now returned to his cold fatherland, and he wrote books about all that was true, and good, and beautiful in the world. Days passed on—and weeks passed on—and years passed on—many years.

One evening, when he was sitting alone in his room, he heard a low tapping at the door.

"Come in!" he said, but no one came in; so he arose and opened the door. Before him stood a man so thin and meagre that the sight quite startled him. The stranger was, however, exceedingly well dressed, and appeared a person of rank. "With whom have I the honour of speaking?" inquired the scholar.

"Ah, I thought as much!" replied the thin gentleman. "I expected that you would not recognise me. I have gained so much body lately—I have gained both flesh and clothes—I dare say you never thought to see me in such excellent condition. Do you not recollect your old *shadow*? Ah, you must have fancied I never meant to return at all. Things have gone so well with me since I was last with you that I have become quite wealthy! I can easily ransom myself, if it be necessary!"

And with these words he passed his hand over the heavy gold watch-chain which he wore round his neck, and rattled the large bunch of costly seals which hung from it—and oh! how his fingers glittered with the diamonds encircling them! And all this was real!

"No, I cannot recover my senses!" exclaimed the scholar. "What can all this mean?"

"Certainly it is rather extraordinary," said the shadow. "But then you yourself are by no means an ordinary man; and, as you know, I have trod in your steps from childhood. As soon as you thought me capable of going alone, I went my own way in the world. My circumstances are most brilliant; nevertheless, a sort of yearning came over me to see you once more before you die. You must die, you know! Besides, I felt a wish to see this country again, for one cannot help feeling love for one's own fatherland. I know that you have now another shadow; have I to pay you anything for it? Be so kind as to tell me how much?"

"Is it really and truly thyself?" cried the scholar; "this is, indeed, most extraordinary! Never could I have believed that my old shadow would return to me a man!"

"Tell me what I am to pay?" repeated the shadow, "for on no account would I remain in any one's debt."

"How canst thou speak so?" said the scholar. "Why talk about debts? Thou art perfectly free, and I am exceedingly rejoiced to hear of thy good fortune. Come, old friend, sit down and tell me how it has all come to pass, and what thou didst see in that mysterious house just opposite mine in the hot country!"

"Well, I will tell you," said the shadow, sitting down as requested; "but then, you must first promise that you will never let any one in this town, where, perchance, you may meet me again, know that I was once your shadow. I have some thoughts of matrimony; I have the means for supporting more than one family!"

"Have no fear," replied the scholar, "I will not reveal to any one what thou really art. Here is my hand—upon my honour as a gentleman I promise it!"

"And I will speak truly—upon my honour as a shadow!" rejoined the mysterious visitor; of a truth, he could hardly express himself otherwise.

It was, certainly, quite wonderful to see how much of a man he had become. He was dressed completely in black, the finest black cloth, with shining boots, and a hat which could be squeezed together, so as to be only crown and brim—not to speak of things we have already mentioned—gold chain, seals, and diamond rings. Yes, indeed, the shadow was uncommonly well dressed; and, in fact, it was his dress which made him appear so completely a man.

"Well, then, now I will tell you all about it," said the shadow; and he planted his legs, with the shining boots, as firmly as he could upon the arm of the scholar's new shadow, which lay like a poodle at its master's feet. This was done, perhaps, out of pride, but more probably under the idea that he might, perchance, induce it into cleaving to himself for the future. And the recumbent shadow kept its place on the ground, still and motionless, lest it should lose a word; for it was naturally anxious to learn how it might, in its turn, free itself and become its own master.

"Can you guess who proved to be dwelling in the opposite house?" asked the shadow triumphantly. "It was Poesy—most beautiful, most charming Poesy! I was there three weeks, and that is as good as if I had lived there three thousand years, and had read all that was imagined and written during that time. This I declare to you, and it is true; I have seen all, and I know all!"

"Poesy!" cried the scholar; "ah, yes! she often dwells, a hermitess, in the very heart of a bustling city. Poesy! yes. I, too, have seen her, but it was only for one moment, when sleep had charmed my eyes; she stood at the balcony, radiant and glorious as the Northern Lights. Oh, tell me, pray tell me! Thou wert in the balcony, thou didst enter by the door, and then——"

"Why, then I was in the antechamber," said the shadow; "you recollect you used to sit looking across into the antechamber. It was not lighted up; it was in a kind of twilight. But door after door, all open, led through a long suite of rooms and saloons, and in the distance there were lights in plenty, quite an illumination. Indeed, the glare would have killed me had I passed on into the lady's apartment. But I was prudent, I took my time and was patient, as every one should be."

"And what didst thou see?" inquired the scholar.

"I saw everything! and I would tell you all about it, only— it is not pride by any means, but as a free man, and a man of education and science, not to speak of my high position and circumstances—I do wish you would treat me with more respect. Cannot you give up that way of continually *thou*-ing me, and call me *you*?"

"I beg pardon!" said the scholar; "it is an old habit, and, therefore, difficult to cure oneself of. You are quite right, and I will try to remember. But now tell me all you saw."

"All, indeed," returned the shadow; "for I have seen all, and I know all."

"What were the inner chambers like?" again inquired the scholar. "Seemed they like fresh, balm-breathing groves? Seemed they like a holy church? Were those chosen halls like the starry heavens when beheld from a mountain height?"

"Everything beautiful was there!" said the shadow. "I did not exactly go in; I remained in the twilight of the outer room, but that was an excellent position! I saw everything, and I know everything! I have been at Poesy's Court—I have been in the antechamber!"

"But what did you see? Did all the ancient divinities pass through spacious halls? Did not bold heroes and chivalrous knights do battle there as in olden times? Were there not pretty, fairy-like children gambolling together, and telling each other their dreams?"

"I repeat that I was there, and I beg you to understand that I saw everything which was to be seen, and I became a man! Had you gone over, possibly you might have become something more; but thus was it with me. I gained the knowledge of my inmost nature, my properties, and the relationship I bore to Poesy.

"During the time I spent with you, I thought little of these matters. Whenever the sun rose or set, as you know, I became wonderfully tall; indeed, by moonlight I might have been thought more noticeable even than yourself, but I did not then understand my own nature. In that antechamber all was made plain—I became a man—I left the place completely altered.

"You were no longer in the hot country, and I was ashamed to go about as man then. I wanted boots and clothes; in short, all that distinguishes a man, or rather, makes him known to be such.

"I took my way—yes, I think I may trust you with my secret, and you must not put it into a book—I took my way under the cook-maid's cloak. I hid myself in it; she little thought whom she was sheltering. It was evening when I first ventured out; I ran along the street in the moonlight, I stretched myself up along the wall; that is so pleasant and cooling to one's back! I ran up and I ran down, I peeped into rooms through the uppermost, even through the attic windows; I peeped where no one else could peep! I saw what no one else could see!

"After all, this is but a poor miserable affair of a world! I would not be a man but for the imaginary honour of the thing. I saw the most incredible, unheard of things among all ranks and classes.

"I saw," continued the shadow emphatically, "what none must know, but all would so much like to know—*their neighbour's secret evil deeds*. Had I published a new journal, would not people have read it? But, instead of this, I wrote to the individuals themselves, whose private doings I had spied out; and thus I raised wonder and fear in every town I visited.

"They were so afraid of me, and they loved me so much! Professors made me a professor; tailors gave me new clothes —you will observe I am well provided; coiners struck coin for me; and women declared I was so handsome! And thus I became the man you see me. And now, I must bid you farewell. Here is my card; I dwell on the sunny side of the way, and I am always at home in rainy weather."

And the shadow took his departure.

"Strange, certainly, very strange!" said the scholar.

Days and years passed away—the shadow came again.

"How is it with you?" he inquired.

"Alas!" sighed the scholar, "I still write of what is true,

and good, and beautiful, but no one seems to care to hear of such things. I am quite in despair. I suppose I take it to heart too much."

"That I never do," returned the shadow. "I am growing fat, as every one should try to be. Ah, you don't understand the world, and thus you suffer yourself to be disgusted with it. You should travel; I intend to make a tour this summer; suppose you come with me? I should like to have a companion; will you travel with me as my shadow? It would be a great pleasure to me to have you with me, and I will pay your expenses."

"An odd proposal, certainly!" and the scholar smiled at the idea.

"What matter, when it suits both of us? Travelling will do wonders for you. Be my shadow, and you shall have everything you want."

"This is too absurd; you are mad!"

"If I am, all the rest of the world is mad, too, and mad it will be to the end." And with this the shadow went his way.

Meantime, the scholar's affairs grew worse and worse, sorrow and care pursued him, and as for his writing about the true, and the good, and the beautiful—all this was for the multitude about just as much use as it would be to scatter roses at the feet of a cow. At last he became downright ill.

"Actually, you look like a shadow!" said his friends; and a shiver thrilled through the scholar's frame on hearing the words.

"You must go to the baths," said the shadow at his next visit; "there is nothing else for you. I will take you with me for old acquaintance' sake. I will pay the expenses of the journey, and you shall write descriptions and entertain me on the way. I want to go to the baths myself; my beard does not grow quite as it should do, and that is as bad as a disease; for one cannot do without a beard. Now, be reasonable, and accept my offer; we shall travel as comrades."

And so they travelled; the shadow was now the master, and the master was the shadow. They drove, they rode, they walked always together, sometimes side by side, sometimes before or behind one another, according to the position of the sun.

The shadow always took care to secure the place of honour for himself, but for this the scholar cared little; he was really a kind-hearted man, and of mild and placid temper. One day, however, he said to the shadow, "As we are now fellow-travellers, not to speak of having grown up together from childhood, why should we not call each other 'thou'? It sounds so much more affectionate and familiar."

"There is something in what you say," replied the shadow, or rather the master, for such he was to all intents and purposes. "It is kindly and honestly said; I will be no less honest and kind. You, as a man of learning, must know well what strange whims nature is subject to at times.

"Some men there are who cannot endure the smell of brown paper—it makes them quite ill; others shiver all over whenever any one scratches a pane of glass with a nail, and, in like manner, I have a most painful feeling whenever I hear you say 'thou' to me. I feel myself, as it were, pressed to the earth—reduced to my former servile position. You see it is a delicacy of feeling; certainly it is not pride. At any rate I cannot suffer you to say 'thou' to me, but I will willingly call you 'thou,' and thus your wish will be half-fulfilled."

So, henceforth, the shadow called its former master "thou."

"This is rather cool," thought the latter; "I to address him as 'you,' and he to say 'thou' to me." But there was no help for it.

They arrived at one of the spas. Many strangers were there, and amongst them a King's daughter, marvellously beautiful. Her malady consisted in this—that she was too sharp-sighted; so much so as rendered her quite uncomfortable.

She, of course, perceived at once that the newcomer was quite a different sort of person from all the other visitors. "They say," observed she, "that he comes here because his beard will not grow, but I see well the real cause—he cannot cast a shadow."

Her curiosity was excited. Accordingly, one day, meeting him on her walk, she took the opportunity of accosting him. Being a King's daughter, it was not necessary for her to use much ceremony; so she said at once, "Your malady is that you cannot cast a shadow."

'I am delighted to find that your Royal Highness is so much better!" was the shadow's reply. "I am aware that it has been your misfortune to be too keen-sighted; but that disease must be entirely cured, for the fact is, that I have a very unusual shadow! Do you not see the person who always walks close to me?

"Other men have mere common shades for their shadows, but I do not like anything that is common. You may have observed that people often give their servants finer clothes for their liveries than they wear themselves; in like manner, I have allowed my shadow to dress himself up like a man, in fact, as you see, I have even given him a shadow of his own. This has been rather expensive, certainly; but I love to be peculiar."

"Hem!" thought the Princess, "am I actually recovered? There is nothing like these baths; the waters have of late years had powers almost miraculous. But I shall not leave the place at present, for it is only just beginning to grow amusing; this stranger pleases me exceedingly; it is to be hoped that his beard will not grow; for, if it does, I suppose he will go away."

That evening, in the grand assembly room, the King's daughter danced with the shadow. She was very light, but he was still lighter; such a partner she had never had before. She told him what country she came from, and he knew the country. He had been there, though at a time when she was not at home. He had peeped in at both upper and lower windows of the palace; he had seen many curious things, so that he could answer the questions of the Princess and make revelations to her that were positively startling.

Surely, he must be the wisest man living! She was struck with wonder and awe, and by the time they had danced the second dance she was fairly in love with him. Of this the shadow soon became aware; her eyes were continually piercing him through and through. They danced a third time, and she was very near telling him what she thought.

But, very prudently, she restrained herself, remembering

her land and heritage, and the multitude of beings over whom she would reign at some future period.

"He is a wise man," thought she; "that is well! and he dances charmingly, that is well, too; but has he solid acquirements? They are of no less importance. I must try him;" and she began to propound to him various questions, so difficult that she could not have answered them herself; and the shadow made up a very strange face.

"Then you cannot answer me?" said the King's daughter.

"Oh, I have learned all that in the days of my childhood," replied her new acquaintance. "I believe that my shadow, even now standing at the door yonder, could answer you."

"Your shadow? That would be rather remarkable!"

"Mind, I do not say decidedly that he can, but I should think so; he has followed me and listened to all I have said for so many years—yes, really, I should think he could answer you. But your Royal Highness must first permit me to warn you that he especially prides himself upon passing for a man, so that to keep him in good humour—and without that you will get nothing out of him—he must be treated quite as if he were a man."

"Oh, with all my heart!" said the Princess. So she went up to the learned man standing at the door, and began conversing with him about the sun and moon, and different nations, both far and near; and he answered her in such a manner as fully proved his wisdom and learning.

"What a wonderful man must he be who has so wise a shadow!" thought the Princess; "it would be a positive blessing to my kingdom and people if I were to choose him for my consort. And I will do it!"

And they were soon agreed—the King's daughter and the shadow; but no one was to know of their engagement before the Princess returned to her own country.

"No one shall know, not even my shadow!" declared the intended bridegroom; and for this arrangement, no doubt, he had his own reasons.

So they went forthwith to the country of the Princess.

"Listen to me, my good friend!" said the shadow to the scholar. "I have now arrived at the height of happiness and power—I must think of doing something for thee! Thou shalt always live with me at the palace, drive out with me in the royal carriage, and receive an annuity of a hundred thousand rix-dollars; but, in return, thou must suffer every one to call thee a shadow; thou must never tell any one that thou hast been a man. Once every year, when I sit publicly in the balcony in the sunshine, thou must lie meekly at my feet, as every shadow should lie. For know this: I am going to marry the King's daughter; this very evening the nuptials will be celebrated."

"No, this is too bad!" exclaimed the scholar; "this shall never be. It would be deceiving the whole country, not to speak of the King's daughter. I will make everything public —how that I am the man and thou art the shadow—that thou art only dressed like a man!"

"No one will believe you," returned the shadow. "Be reasonable, pray, or I shall call the guard."

"I am going straight to the King's daughter!" cried the scholar.

"But I am going first," said the shadow, "and thou art going to prison."

And to prison he went, for, of course, the guard obeyed him whom they knew their Princess had chosen as her consort.

"Thou tremblest!" observed the Princess, when the shadow entered her apartment; "has anything happened? Thou must not be ill this evening—our bridal evening!"

"I have lived to see the most fearful thing," said the shadow; "you would never believe it; ah! a poor shadow-brain cannot bear much—just imagine it. My shadow has become crazy; he actually believes that he is a man, and that I—only think!—that I am his shadow."

"This is shocking, indeed!" said the Princess; "I hope he is locked up."

"Of course; I am much afraid he will never recover himself."

"Poor shadow! he is truly unfortunate; it would really be a charity to free him from the little life he possesses. And indeed, when I consider how ready people are in these days to take part with the lower classes against the great, it seems to me that the best thing we can do will be to make away with him privately.

"It is a hard case, for he was a faithful servant." And the shadow made as though he sighed.

"You are a noble character!" exclaimed the King's daughter.

That evening the whole city was illuminated; cannon were fired—boom!—and the soldiers presented arms. All this was in honour of the royal wedding. The King's daughter and the shadow went out on the balcony to show themselves, and hear "Hurrah!" shouted again and again.

The scholar heard nothing of all these grand doings, for they had already taken his life.

THE LEAPING MATCH

THE flea, the grasshopper, and the frog once wanted to try which of them could jump highest; so they invited the whole world, and anybody else who liked to come and see the grand sight. Three famous jumpers were they, as was seen by every one when they met together in the room.

"I will give my daughter to him who shall jump highest," said the King; "it would be too bad for you to have the trouble of jumping, and for us to offer you no prize."

The flea was the first to introduce himself; he had such polite manners, and bowed to the company on every side, for he was of noble blood; besides, he was accustomed to the society of man, which had been a great advantage to him.

Next came the grasshopper; he was not quite so slightly and elegantly formed as the flea; however, he knew perfectly well how to conduct himself, and wore a green uniform, which belonged to him by right of birth.

Moreover, he declared himself to have sprung from a very ancient and honourable Egyptian family, and that in his present home he was very highly esteemed, so much so, indeed, that he had been taken out of the field and put into a

card-house three stories high, built on purpose for him, and
all of court-cards, the coloured sides being turned inwards.
As for the doors and windows in his house, they were cut out
of the body of the Queen of Hearts.

"And I can sing so well," added he, "that sixteen parlour-
bred crickets, who have chirped and chirped ever since they
were born, and yet could never get anybody to build them a
card-house, after hearing me, have fretted themselves ten
times thinner than ever, out of sheer envy and vexation!"

Both the flea and the grasshopper knew excellently well
how to make the most of themselves, and each considered
himself quite an equal match for a princess.

The frog said not a word; however, it might be that he
thought the more, and the house-dog, after going snuffing
about him, confessed that the frog must be of a good family.
And the old councillor, who in vain received three orders to
hold his tongue, declared that the frog must be gifted with
the spirit of prophecy, for that one could read on his back
whether there was to be a severe or a mild winter, which, to
be sure, is more than can be read on the back of the man who
writes the weather almanac.

"Ah, I say nothing for the present!" remarked the old
King, "but I observe everything, and form my own private
opinion thereupon."

And now the match began. The flea jumped so high that
no one could see what had become of him, and so they
insisted that he had not jumped at all, which was disgraceful,
after he had made such a fuss!

The grasshopper only jumped half as high, but he jumped
right into the King's face, and the King declared he was quite
disgusted by his rudeness.

The frog stood still as if lost in thought; at last people
fancied he did not intend to jump at all.

"I'm afraid he is ill!" said the dog; and he went snuffing at
him again, when lo! all at once he made a little sidelong jump
into the lap of the Princess, who was sitting on a low stool
close by.

Then spoke the King: "There is nothing higher than my
daughter, therefore, he who jumps up to her jumps highest;

but only a person of good understanding would ever have thought of that, and thus the frog has shown us that he has understanding. He has brains in his head, that he has!"

And thus the frog won the Princess.

"I jumped highest for all that!" exclaimed the flea. "But it's all the same to me; let her have the stiff-legged, slimy creature, if she like him! I jumped highest, but I am too light and airy for this stupid world; the people can neither see me nor catch me; dullness and heaviness win the day with them!"

And so the flea went into foreign service, where, it is said, he was killed.

And the grasshopper sat on a green bank, meditating on the world and its goings on, and at length he repeated the flea's last words—"Yes, dullness and heaviness win the day! dullness and heaviness win the day!"

And then he again began singing his own peculiar melancholy song, and it is from him that we have learned this history; and yet, my friend, though you read it here in a printed book, it may not be perfectly true.

THE ICE MAIDEN

1. *Little Rudy*

LET us now go to Switzerland, and wander through the glorious land of mountains, where the forests cling to the steep walls of rock.

Let us mount up to the dazzling snow-fields, and then descend into the green valleys, through which rivers and brooks are hurrying on as if they could not reach the sea quickly enough.

The sun shines hotly down upon the deep valley, and glares upon the heavy masses of snow, so that they harden in the course of centuries into gleaming blocks of ice, or form themselves into falling avalanches, or become piled up into glaciers.

Two such glaciers lie in the broad, rocky gorges under the Schreckhorn and the Wetterhorn, by the mountain town of

Grindelwald: they are wonderful to behold, and in the summer-time many strangers come from all parts of the world to see them.

On both sides of the road that leads uphill stand wooden houses. Each has its potato patch; as they all must have, for there are many little mouths to fill in those cottages. The little ones peep forth everywhere, and gather round the traveller, whether he be on foot or in a carriage. All the children here carry on a trade—offer carved houses for sale, models of those that are built here in the mountains. In rain or in sunshine, there they are, trying to sell their wares.

About twenty years ago, a little boy might often be seen standing there, anxious to carry on his trade, though always standing a short distance away from the rest. His earnest look, together with the fact of his being such a little fellow, often attracted the notice of strangers; so that he was very frequently beckoned forward, and a great part of his stock was bought, without himself knowing why the strangers should thus favour him.

A couple of miles away, in the mountains, lived his grandfather, who carved the pretty little houses; and in the old man's room stood a wooden cupboard filled with the kind of things that delight children's eyes—carved toys in abundance, nut-crackers, knives and forks, boxes adorned with carved leaves and with leaping chamois. But the boy looked with greater longing at an old rifle that hung from the beam under the ceiling, for his grandfather had promised him that it should be his one day.

Young as the boy was, he had to keep the goats; and if being able to climb with his flock makes a good goatherd, then Rudy was certainly a good one, for he even climbed higher than the goats could mount.

He never played with the other children, and only met them when his grandfather sent him down the mountain to deal in carved toys; and this was a business Rudy did not exactly like. He would rather clamber about alone among the mountains, or sit beside his grandfather hearing the old man tell stories of the old times, or of the people in the neighbouring town of Meiningen, his birthplace.

He had others also who taught him something, and these were four-footed companions. There was a great dog, whose name was Ajola, and who had belonged to Rudy's father; and a Tom Cat was there too: this Tom Cat was a real crony of Rudy's, for it was Pussy who had taught him to climb.

"Come with me out on the roof," the cat had said, quite plainly, to Rudy; for, you see, children who cannot talk yet, can understand the language of fowls and ducks; and cats and dogs speak to them as plainly as father and mother can do. But that is only when the children are very little. "Come out with me on to the roof," was perhaps the first thing the cat said that Rudy understood.

"What people say about falling down is all fancy: one does not fall down if one is not afraid. Just you come, and put one of your paws thus and the other thus. Feel your way with your fore-paws. You must have eyes in your head and nimble paws; and if there is a hole, jump over, and then hold tight, as I do."

And Rudy did so too; and was often found seated on the top of the roof by the cat; and afterwards he sat with him in the tree-tops, and at last was even seen seated on the window-sills, whither Puss could not come.

Small as he was, he had been a traveller, and for such a little fellow had made no mean journey. He was born over in the canton of Wallis, and had been carried across the high mountains to his present dwelling. He had also been in the Grindelwald, at the great glacier; but that was a sad story.

His mother had met her death there; and there, said grand-father, little Rudy had lost his childlike cheerfulness. When the boy was not a year old, his mother had written to say that he laughed more than he cried, but from the time when he sat in the ice cleft, another spirit came upon him. His grand-father seldom talked of it, but they knew the story through the whole mountain region.

Rudy's father had been a postilion. The great dog that lay in grandfather's room had always followed him in his journeys over the Simplon down to the Lake of Geneva. In the valley of the Rhone, in the Canton of Wallis, lived some relatives of Rudy on the father's side. His uncle was a first-rate chamois hunter and a well-known guide.

Rudy was only a year old when he lost his father, and the mother now longed to return with her child to her relatives in the Overland of Berne. Her father lived a few miles from Grindelwald; he was a wood-carver, and earned enough to live on. Thus, in the month of June, carrying her child, and accompanied by two chamois hunters, she set out on her journey home, across the Gemmi towards Grindelwald.

They had gone the greater part of the way, had crossed the high ridge as far as the snow-field, and had already caught sight of her native valley, with all the well-known wooden houses, and had only one great glacier to cross. The snow had fallen freshly, and hidden a cleft which did not indeed reach to the deep ground where the water gushed but was still more than six feet deep.

The young mother, with her child in her arms, stumbled, slipped over the edge, and vanished. More than an hour passed before ropes and poles could be brought up from the nearest house for the purpose of giving help, and after much trouble what appeared to be two corpses were brought forth from the icy cleft.

Every means was tried; and the child, but not the mother, was brought back to life; and thus the old grandfather had a daughter's son brought into his house, an orphan, the boy who had laughed more than he cried. It seemed, however, that a great change had taken place in him, and this change must have been wrought in the glacier cleft, in the cold, wondrous ice world, in which, according to the Swiss peasants, the souls of the wicked are shut up until the last day.

The glacier lies stretched out, a foaming body of water stiffened into ice, and, as it were, pressed together into green blocks, one huge lump piled upon another. From beneath it the rushing stream of melted ice and snow thunders down into the valley, and deep caverns and great clefts extend below. It is a wondrous glass palace, and within dwells the Ice Maiden, the Glacier Queen. She, the death-dealing, the crushing one, is partly a child of air, partly the mighty ruler of the river.

"To crush and to hold, mine is the power!" she says. "They

have stolen a beautiful boy from me—a boy whom I have kissed, but not kissed to death. He is again among men: he keeps the goats on the mountains, and climbs upwards, ever higher, far away from the others, but not from me. He is mine, and I will have him!" And she commanded the spirit called Giddiness to seize upon Rudy.

"Yes, but to seize *him*," said Giddiness, "is more than I can do. The cat, that wretched creature, has taught him her tricks. That child has a particular power which thrusts me away; I am not able to seize him, when he hangs by a bough over the abyss. How gladly would I tickle the soles of his feet, or thrust him head over heels into the air! But I am not able to do it."

"We shall manage to do it," said the Ice Maiden. "Thou or I—I shall do it—I!"

"No, no!" sounded a voice around her, like the echo of the church-bells among the mountains; but it was a song; it was the melting chorus of other spirits of nature—of good, affectionate spirits—the Daughters of the Sunshine.

"You shall not catch him—you shall not have him," they said.

"I have caught them larger and stronger than he," said the Ice Maiden.

2. The Journey to the New Home

RUDY was now eight years old. His uncle, who dwelt beyond the mountains in the Rhone Valley, wished that the boy should come to him to learn something and get on in the world; the grandfather saw this was right, and let the lad go.

Accordingly Rudy said good-bye. There were others besides his grandfather to whom he had to say farewell; and foremost came Ajola, the old dog.

"Your father was the postilion and I was the post-dog," said Ajola; "we went to and fro together; and I know some dogs from beyond the mountains, and some people too. I was never much of a talker; but, now that we most likely shall not be able to talk much longer together, I will tell you a little more than usual.

"I will tell you a story that I have kept to myself and

thought about for a long while. I don't understand it, and you won't understand it, but that does not matter; this much, at least, I have made out, that things are not quite equally divided in the world, either for dogs or for men.

"Not all sit on a lady's lap to drink milk: *I*'ve not been used to it, but I've seen one of those little lap-dogs, driving in the coach, and taking up a passenger's place in it; the lady, who was its mistress, had a little bottle of milk with her, out of which she gave the dog a drink; and she offered him sweet-meats, but he only sniffed at them, and would not even take them, and then she ate them herself.

"I was running along in the mud beside the carriage, as hungry as a dog can be, chewing my own thoughts, that this could not be quite right; but they say a good many things are going on that are not quite right. Should you like to sit in a lady's lap and ride in a coach? I should be glad if you did. But one can't manage that for oneself. I never could manage it, either by barking or howling."

These were Ajola's words; and Rudy embraced him and kissed him heartily on his wet nose; then he took the cat in his arms, but Puss struggled, saying—

"You're too strong for me, and I don't like to use my claws against you! Clamber away now over the mountains, for I have taught you how to climb. Don't think that you can fall, and then you will be sure to keep firm hold."

So saying, the cat ran away, not wishing Rudy to see that the tears were in his eyes.

To the goats he also said farewell; and they bleated "Meek! meek!" and wished to go with him, which made him feel very sorrowful.

Two brave guides from the neighbourhood, who were going across the mountains to the other side of the Gemmi, took him with them, and he followed them on foot. It was a tough march for such a little fellow, but Rudy was a strong boy, and his courage never gave way.

The road led across the foaming Lutchine, which pours forth in little streams from the black cleft of the Grindel glacier, and fallen trunks of trees and blocks of stone serve for a bridge. When they reached the forest opposite, they began to ascend the slope where the glacier had slipped away from the mountain, and now they strode across and around ice blocks over the glacier.

The glacier extended upwards like a mighty river of piled-up ice masses, shut in by steep rocks. Rudy thought for a moment of the tale once told him, how he and his mother had lain in one of those deep, cold-breathing fissures; but soon all such thoughts vanished from him, and the tale seemed only like others of the same kind which he had heard.

Rudy had never yet been so high; he had never yet stepped on the outspread sea of snow: here it lay with its motionless snowy billows, from which the wind every now and then blew off a flake, as it blows the foam from the waves of the sea. The glaciers stand here, so to speak, hand in hand; each one is a glass palace for the Ice Maiden, whose desire it is to catch and to bury.

The recollection of this whole journey—the night encampment in these lofty regions, the late walk, the deep, rocky chasms, where the water has pierced through the blocks of stone by the labour of ages—all this was firmly fixed upon Rudy's mind.

A deserted stone building beyond the snow sea gave them shelter for the night. Here they found fuel and pine branches, and soon a fire was kindled, and the bed made for the night, as comfortably as possible. The men seated themselves round the fire, smoked their pipes, and drank the warm, refreshing drink they had prepared for themselves.

Rudy received his share of the supper; and then the men began telling the strange stories of the Alpine land, to which Rudy listened attentively. At length, the men, remembering that Rudy was but a little lad, told him he might go to sleep; and, tired out with his toilsome march, he went to sleep on the instant, like a soldier obeying the word of command.

Very early next morning they resumed their journey. This day the sun shone on new mountains for Rudy, on fresh glaciers and new fields of snow: they had entered the Canton of Wallis, and had proceeded beyond the ridge which could be seen from the Grindelwald.

Then other charms came into view, new valleys, forests,

and mountain paths, and new houses also, and other people. The sight of strange, unfamiliar faces stirred up many thoughts in the little boy's mind, and, as the end of his journey drew near, he began wonderingly to think of the people whom he should find in his new home.

3. Uncle

THANK Heaven! the people in the house of Rudy's uncle, where the boy was now to live, looked like those he had been used to see. Uncle was still a stalwart huntsman, and, moreover, understood the craft of tub-making; his wife was a little lively woman with a face like a bird's. She had eyes like an eagle's, and her neck was covered with a fluffy down.

Everything here was new to Rudy—dress, manners, and habits, and even the language; but to the latter the child's ear would soon adapt itself. There was an appearance of wealth here, compared with grandfather's dwelling. The room was larger, the walls were hung with chamois horns, among which were polished rifles, and over the door was a picture of the Madonna, with fresh Alpine roses and a burning lamp in front of it.

Uncle was one of the best chamois hunters in the whole country, and one of the most trusted guides. In this household Rudy now became the pet child. "It is not bad living, here in the Canton of Wallis," said uncle; "and we have chamois here, who don't die so easily as the steinbock; and it is much better here now than in former days. They may say what they like in honour of the old times, but ours are better after all: the bog has been opened, and a fresh wind blows through our valley. Something better always comes up when the old is worn out."

When uncle was in a very talkative mood, he would tell of his youthful years, and of still earlier times, the strong times of his father, when Wallis was, as he said, a closed bog, full of sick people and miserable *cretins*.

"But the French soldiers came in," he said, "and they were the proper doctors, for they killed the disease at once, and they killed the people who had it too. They knew all about fighting, did the French, and they could fight in more than one way. Their girls made conquests too," and then uncle would laugh and nod to his wife, who was a Frenchwoman by birth.

Rudy for the first time heard them tell of France, and Lyons, the great town on the Rhone, where his uncle had been.

Not many years were to pass before Rudy should become an expert chamois hunter; his uncle said he had the stuff for it in him, and taught him to handle a rifle, to take aim, and shoot. In the hunting season he took the lad with him into the mountains, and initiated him into all the mysteries of the huntsmen's craft. The chamois were clever, he said—they sent out scouts; but the hunter should be more clever still, keep out of the line of scent, and lead them astray; and one day when Rudy was out hunting with uncle, the latter hung his coat and hat on the alpenstock, and the chamois took the coat for a man.

The rocky path was narrow; it was, properly speaking, not a path at all, but merely a narrow shelf beside the yawning abyss. The snow that lay here was half thawed, the stone crumbled beneath the tread, and therefore uncle lay down and crept forward. Every fragment that crumbled away from the rock fell down, jumping and rolling from one ledge of rock to another, until it was lost to sight in the darkness below.

About a hundred paces behind his uncle stood Rudy, on a firm point of rock; and from this station he saw a great "Lamb's Vulture" circling in the air and hovering over uncle, whom it evidently intended to hurl into the abyss with a blow of its wings, that it might make a prey of him.

Uncle's whole attention was taken up by the chamois which was to be seen, with its young one, on the other side of the cleft. Rudy kept his eyes firmly fixed upon the bird. He knew what the vulture intended to do, and accordingly stood with his rifle ready to fire.

Suddenly the chamois leaped up; uncle fired, and the creature fell, pierced by the deadly bullet; but the young one sprang away as if it had been accustomed all its life to flee from danger. Startled by the sound of the rifle, the great bird soared off in another direction, and uncle knew nothing of the danger in which he had stood, until Rudy informed him of it.

As they were returning homeward in the best spirits, uncle whistling one of the songs of his youth, they suddenly heard a peculiar noise not far from them; they looked around, and yonder, on the side of the mountain, the snow covering suddenly rose, and began to heave up and down like a piece of linen stretched on a field when the wind passes beneath it. The snowy waves, which had been smooth and hard as marble slabs, now broke to pieces, and the roar of waters sounded like rumbling thunder. An avalanche was falling, not over Rudy and uncle, but near where they stood, not at all far from them.

"Hold fast, Rudy!" cried uncle; "hold fast with all your strength."

Rudy clung to the trunk of the nearest tree. Uncle clambered up above him, and the avalanche rolled past, many feet from them, but the rush of the air, the stormy wings of the avalanche, broke trees and shrubs all around as if they had been frail reeds, and scattered the fragments headlong down.

Rudy lay crouched upon the earth, the trunk of the tree to which he clung was split through, and the crown hurled far away; and there among the broken branches lay uncle, with his head shattered: his hand was still warm, but his face could no longer be recognised. Rudy stood by him pale and trembling; it was the first fright of his life—the first time he felt a shudder run through him.

Late at night he brought the sorrowful news into his home, which was now a house of mourning. The wife could find no words, no tears for her grief; at last, when the corpse was brought home, her sorrow broke forth. It was Rudy's task to comfort and console her, and, when at length her grief had somewhat subsided, the widow turned and said—"Now thou art the prop of this house"; and Rudy became, in very truth the stay of his home.

4. Babette

WHO is the best marksman in the Canton of Wallis? The chamois knew well enough, and said to each other, "Beware of Rudy."

Who is the handsomest marksman? "Why, Rudy," said the girls; but *they* did not add, "Beware of Rudy."

How quick and merry he was! His cheeks were browned, his teeth regular and white, and his eyes black and shining; he was a handsome lad, and only twenty years old. The icy water could not harm him when he swam; he could turn and twist in the water like a fish, and climb better than any man in the mountains; he could cling like a snail to the rocky ledge, for he had good sinews and muscles of his own; and he showed that in his power of jumping, an art he had learned first from the cat and afterwards from the goats.

Rudy was the safest guide to whom any man could trust himself, and might have earned a fortune in that calling. His uncle had also taught him the craft of tub-making; but he did not take to that work, preferring chamois hunting, which also brought in money.

Rudy was what might be called a good match, if he did not look higher than his station. And he was such a dancer that the girls dreamed of him. Indeed more than one of them carried the thought of him in her waking hours.

"He kissed me once at the dance!" said the schoolmaster's daughter, Annette, to her dearest girl-friend; but she should not have said that, even to her dearest friend. A secret of that kind is hard to keep—it is like sand in a sieve, sure to run out; and soon it was known that Rudy, honest lad though he was, kissed his partner in the dance; and yet he had not kissed the one whom he would have liked best of all to kiss.

Down in the valley near Bex, among the great walnut-trees, by a little brawling mountain stream, lived the rich miller. The dwelling-house was a great building, three stories high, with little towers, roofed with planks and covered with plates of metal that shone in the sunlight and in the moon-light.

The mill looked pleasant and comfortable, and could be easily drawn and described; but the miller's daughter could neither be drawn nor described—so, at least, Rudy would have said; and yet she was pictured in his heart, where her eyes gleamed so brightly that they had lighted up a fire.

This had burst out quite suddenly; and the strangest thing

of all was, that the miller's daughter, pretty Babette, had no idea of the conquest she had made, for she and Rudy had never spoken a word together.

The miller was rich, and this wealth of his made Babette very difficult to get at, as if she had been high up in a tree. But nothing is so high that it may not be reached if a man will but climb; and he will not fall, if he is not afraid of falling.

Now it happened that on one occasion Rudy had some business to do in Bex. It was quite a journey thither, for in those days the railway had not yet been finished. From the Rhone glacier, along the foot of the Simplon, away among many changing mountain heights, the proud valley of Wallis extends, with its mighty river, the Rhone, which often overflows its banks and rushes across the fields and high roads, carrying destruction with it.

Between the little towns of Sion and St. Maurice the valley makes a bend, like an elbow, and becomes so narrow behind St. Maurice that it only affords room for the bed of the river and a narrow road. An old tower stands as a sentinel at the boundary of the Canton of Wallis, which ends here. The tower looks across over the stone bridge at the toll-house on the opposite side.

There begins the Canton of Waadt, and at a little distance is the first town of that canton, Bex. At every step the signs of fertility and plenty increase, and the traveller seems to be journeying through a garden of walnut-trees and chestnuts; here and there cypresses appear, and blooming pomegranates; and the climate has the southern warmth of Italy.

Rudy arrived in Bex, and did his business there; then he took a turn in the town; but not even a miller's lad, much less Babette, did he see. That was not as it should be.

Evening was coming on, and Rudy began to despair of seeing Babette when suddenly a thought rolled into his mind. "Never falter!" he cried. "Pay a visit to the mill, say 'Good-evening' to the miller and 'Good-evening' to Babette. He does not fall down who is not afraid of falling. Babette must see me sooner or later, if I am to be her husband."

The river, with its yellowish bed, foamed along, and the willows and lime-trees hung over the hurrying waters; Rudy walked along the path towards the miller's house. But, as the children's song has it—

> Nobody was at home to greet him,
> Only the house-cat came to meet him.

The house-cat stood on the step and said "Miaw," and arched her back; but Rudy paid no attention to this address. He knocked, but no one heard him, no one opened the door to him. "Miaw!" said the cat.

If Rudy had been still a child he would have understood her language, and have known that the cat was saying, "There's nobody at home here!" but, being a grown man, he must fain go over to the mill to make inquiries, and there he heard that the miller had gone far away to Interlaken, and Babette with him: a great shooting match was to come off there; it would begin to-morrow, and last a full week, and people from all the German cantons were to be there.

Poor Rudy! he might be said to have chosen an unlucky day for his visit to Bex, and now he must go home. He turned about accordingly, and marched over St. Maurice and Sion towards his own valley and the mountains of his home; but he was not cast down. When the sun rose next morning his good-humour already stood high, for it had never set.

"Babette is at Interlaken; many days' journey from here," he said to himself. "It is a long way if a man travels along the broad highroad, but it is not so far if one takes the short cut across the mountains, and the chamois hunter's path is straight forward. I've been that way already: yonder is my early home, where I lived as a child in grandfather's house; and there's a shooting match at Interlaken. I'll be there too, and be the best shot, and I'll be with Babette too, when once I have made her acquaintance."

With a light knapsack, containing his Sunday clothes, on his back, and his gun and hunting-bag across his shoulder, Rudy mounted the hill by the short cut, which was, nevertheless, fairly long; but the shooting match had only begun that day, and was to last a week or more; and they had told him that the miller and Babette would pass the whole time with their friends at Interlaken.

Fresh and merry, he walked on in the strengthening, light mountain-air. He passed along, in his journey, the mountain path where he had stood as a child with other little children, offering carved houses for sale. There among the pine-trees stood the house of his maternal grandfather; but strangers inhabited it now. Children came running along the road towards him to sell their wares, and one of them offered him an Alpine rose, which Rudy looked upon as a good omen; and he bought the rose, thinking of Babette.

Soon he crossed the bridge where the two branches of the Lutchine join: the woods became thicker there, and the walnut-trees gave a friendly shade. Now he saw the waving flags—the flags with the white cross in a red field—the national emblem of the Switzer and the Dane; and Interlaken lay before him.

This was certainly a town without equal, according to Rudy's idea, but in reality it was only a little Swiss town in its Sunday dress. What a crowd of people from the various cantons! What a number of richly-dressed ladies and gentlemen from foreign lands! Every marksman wore his number displayed in a wreath round his hat. There was music and singing, barrel-organs and trumpets, bustle and noise.

Houses and bridges were adorned with verses and emblems; flags and banners were waving; the rifles cracked merrily now and again; and in Rudy's ears the sound of the shots was the sweetest music; and in the bustle and tumult he had quite forgotten Babette, for whose sake he had come.

And now the marksmen went crowding to shoot at the target. Rudy took up his station among them, and proved to be the most skilful and the most fortunate of them all; each time his bullet struck the black spot in the centre of the target.

"Who may that stranger—that young marksman be?" asked some of the bystanders. "He speaks the French they talk in the Canton of Wallis."

"He can also make himself well understood in our German," said others.

"They say he lived as a child in the neighbourhood of Grindelwald," observed one of the marksmen.

And he was full of life, this stranger-youth. His eyes gleamed, and his glance and his arm were sure, and that is why he hit the mark so well. Fortune gives courage, but Rudy had courage enough of his own. He had soon assembled a circle of friends round him, who paid him honour, and showed respect for him; and Babette was quite forgotten for the moment. Then suddenly a heavy hand clapped him on the shoulder, and a deep voice addressed him in the French tongue—

"You are from the Canton of Wallis?"

Rudy turned round and saw a red, good humoured face, belonging to a portly person. The speaker was the rich miller of Bex; and his broad body almost hid the pretty, delicate Babette, who, however, soon peeped forth from behind him with her bright eyes.

When fellow-countrymen meet at a long distance from home, they are certain to talk and to make acquaintance with one another. By virtue of his good shooting, Rudy had become the first at the marksmen's meeting, just as the miller was the first at home in Bex on the strength of his money and of his good mill; and so the two men shook hands—a thing they had never done before; Babette also held out her hand frankly to Rudy, who pressed it so warmly, and gave her such an earnest look, that she blushed crimson to the roots of her hair.

The miller talked of the long distance they had come, and of the towns they had seen; according to his idea they had made quite a long journey of it, having travelled by railway, steamboat, and coach.

"I came the shortest way," observed Rudy. "I walked across the mountains. No road is so high but a man may get over it."

"And break his neck," quoth the miller with a laugh. "You look just the fellow to break your neck some of these days, so bold as you are, too."

The relatives of the miller at Interlaken, at whose house he and Babette were staying, invited Rudy to visit them, for he belonged to the same canton as the rich miller. That was a good offer for Rudy.

Rudy sat among the miller's relatives like one of the family. A glass was emptied to the health of the best marksman, and Babette clinked her glass with the rest, and Rudy returned thanks for the toast.

Towards evening they all took a walk, on the pretty road by the prosperous hotels, under the old walnut-trees, and so many people were there, and so much pushing, that Rudy was obliged to offer his arm to Babette.

They walked on together as if they had been old friends, and she talked and chattered away; and Rudy thought how charmingly she pointed out the ridiculous and absurd points in the costumes and manners of the foreign ladies; not that she did it to make game of them, for they might be very good, honourable people, as Babette well knew, for was not her own godmother one of these grand English ladies?

Eighteen years ago, when Babette was christened, this lady had been living in Bex, and had given Babette the costly brooch she now wore on her neck. Twice the lady had written and this year Babette had expected to meet her and her two daughters at Interlaken. "The daughters were old maids, nearly thirty years old," added Babette; but then she herself was only eighteen.

The sweet little mouth never rested for a moment; and everything that Babette said sounded in Rudy's ears like a matter of the utmost importance; and he, on his part, told all he had to tell. He said how fond he was of her, and that he had come thither on her account, and not for the sake of the marksmen's meeting. Babette was quite still while he said all this; it seemed to her as if he valued her far too highly.

And as they wandered on, the sun sank down behind the high rocky wall. Every one stood still to enjoy the glorious scene, and Rudy and Babette rejoiced in it too.

"It is nowhere more beautiful than here!" said Babette.

"Nowhere!" cried Rudy, and he looked at Babette. "To-morrow I must return home," he said, after a silence of a few moments.

"Come and see us at Bex," whispered Babette; "it will please my father."

5. The Visit to the Mill

OH, what a load Rudy had to carry when he went homeward across the mountains on the following day! Yes, he had three silver goblets, two handsome rifles, and a silver coffee-biggin. The coffee-biggin would be useful when he set up housekeeping. "What fine things you have brought home!" exclaimed the old aunt; and her strange eagle's eyes flashed, and her thin neck waved to and fro faster than ever. "You have luck, Rudy. I must kiss you, my darling boy!"

And Rudy allowed himself to be kissed, but with an expression in his face which told that he submitted to it as a necessary evil.

"How handsome you are, Rudy!" said the old woman admiringly.

"Don't put nonsense into my head," replied Rudy with a laugh; but still he was pleased to hear her say it.

"I repeat it," she cried. "Good luck attends upon you!"

"Perhaps you are right," he observed; and he thought of Babette.

Never had he felt such a longing to go down into the deep valley.

"They must have returned," he said to himself. "It is two days beyond the time when they were to have been back. I must go to Bex."

Accordingly, Rudy journeyed to Bex, and the people of the mill were at home. He was well received, and the people at Interlaken had sent a kind message to him. Babette did not say much: she had grown very silent, but her eyes spoke eloquently, and that was quite enough for Rudy.

It seemed as if the miller, who mostly led the conversation, and who always expected his hearers to laugh at his ideas and jokes because he was the rich miller—it seemed as if he would never tire of hearing Rudy's hunting adventures.

Rudy noticed clearly enough that with every fresh story he was more and more in the miller's favour; and the old man felt especially interested in what the young hunter told about the "Lamb's Vulture" and the royal eagle.

Among other things he mentioned how, not far off, in the Canton of Wallis, there was an eagle's nest built very cleverly under a steep overhanging rock, and in the nest was an eaglet which could not be captured. An Englishman had, a few days before, offered Rudy a handful of gold pieces if he would get the eaglet alive.

"But there is reason in all things," said Rudy; "that eaglet is not to be taken; it would be folly to make the attempt."

And the wine flowed and conversation flowed; but the evening appeared far too short for Rudy, although it was past midnight when he set out to go home after his first visit to the mill. The lights still gleamed for a short time through the windows of the mill among the green trees, and the Parlour Cat came forth from the open loophole in the roof, and met the Kitchen Cat walking along the rainspout.

"Do you know the news in the mill?" asked the Parlour Cat. "There's a secret betrothal going on in the house. Father knows nothing about it. Rudy and Babette are treading on each other's paws under the table all the evening. They trod upon me twice, but I would not mew for fear of exciting attention."

"*I* should have mewed," said the Kitchen Cat.

"What will pass in the kitchen will never do for the parlour," said the other cat; "but I'm curious to know what the miller will think about it when he hears of the affair."

Yes, indeed, what would the miller say? That is what Rudy would have liked to know, and, moreover he could not bear to remain long without knowing it. Accordingly, a few days afterwards, when the omnibus rattled across the Rhone bridge between Wallis and Waadt, Rudy sat in the vehicle, in good spirits as usual, and already basking in the sunny prospect of the consent he hoped to gain.

And when the evening came, and the omnibus was making its way back, Rudy once more sat in it as a passenger; but in the mill the Parlour Cat had important news to tell.

"Do you know it, you there out of the kitchen? The miller

has been told all about it. There was a fine end to it all. Rudy came here towards evening, and he and Babette had much to whisper to each other, standing in the passage outside the miller's room. I was lying at their feet, but they had neither eyes nor thoughts for me.

"'I shall go to your father without more ado,' said Rudy; 'that's the honest way to do it.' 'Shall I go with you?' asked Babette; 'It will give you courage.' 'I've courage enough,' replied Rudy; 'but if you are present he must be kind whether he likes it or not.' And they went in together. Rudy trod upon my tail most horribly. He's a very awkward fellow, is Rudy. I called out, but neither he nor Babette had ears to hear.

"They opened the door, and both went in, and I went on before them; but I sprang up on the back of a chair, for I could not know where Rudy would step."

"But what did they talk about? What did they say?" asked the Kitchen Cat.

"What did they say? Why, they said everything that people are accustomed to say when they come a-wooing. 'I love her and she loves me, and if there's milk enough in the pail for one, there's enough for two.' 'But she's perched too high for you,' said the miller.

"'Nothing is so high that a man can't reach it, if he has the will,' said Rudy, for he is a bold fellow. 'But you can't reach the eaglet; you said so yourself the other day, and Babette is higher than that.' 'I shall take both of them,' exclaimed Rudy. 'I'll give you Babette when you give me the young eaglet alive,' said the miller; and he laughed till the tears ran down his cheeks. 'But now I must thank you for your visit. Goodbye to you, Rudy.'"

"And Babette said good-bye too, as pitifully as a little kitten that can't see its mother yet. 'Your word is as good as your bond,' cried Rudy. 'Don't cry, Babette, I'll bring you the eaglet!' 'You'll break your neck first, I hope,' said the miller, 'and then we shall be rid of your dangling here!' That's what I call a capital kick!

"And now Rudy is gone, and Babette sits and weeps, but the miller sings German songs that he learned on his late journey. I don't like to be down-hearted about it, for that can do no good!"

"Well, after all, there's some chance for him still," observed the Kitchen Cat.

6. The Eagle's Nest

DOWN from the rocky path sounded a fresh song, merry and strong, full of courage and good spirits, and the singer was Rudy, who came to seek his friend Vesinaud.

"You must help me! We will have Nagli with us. I want to take the eaglet out of the nest on the rock."

"Would you not like to take the black spots out of the moon first?" replied Vesinaud. "That would be just as easy. You seem to be in a merry mood."

"Certainly I am, for I hope to be married soon. But let us speak seriously, and I will tell you what it is all about." And soon Vesinaud and Nagli knew what Rudy wanted.

At midnight they set out with poles, ladders, and ropes; their way led through forest, and thicket, over loose, rolling stones, ever upward, upward, through the dark night. The water rushed beneath them, water dripped down from above, and heavy clouds sailed through the air. The hunters reached the steep wall of rock. Here it was darker than ever.

The opposite sides of the chasm almost touched, and the sky could only be seen through a small cleft above them; while around them and beneath them was the great abyss with its foaming waters. The three sat on the rock waiting for the dawning of day, when the eagle should fly forth, for the old bird must be shot before they could think of capturing the young one, and a long time they had to wait.

Now there was a rushing, whirring sound above them, and a great soaring object darkened the air. Two guns were pointed as the black form of the eagle arose from the nest. A shot rang sharply out; for a moment the outstretched wings continued to move, and then the bird sank down into the abyss, breaking off twigs of trees and bushes in its descent.

And now the hunters began operations. Three of the longest ladders were bound together—those would reach high enough; they were reared on end on the last firm foothold of the edge of the abyss; but they did not reach far enough; and higher up, where the nest lay concealed under the shelter of the crag, the rock was as smooth as a wall.

After a short council, the men determined that two ladders should be tied together and let down from above into the cleft, and these tied to the three that had been fastened together below. With great labour the two ladders were dragged up and the rope made fast above; then the ladders were passed over the rock, so that they hung dangling above the abyss. Rudy had already taken his place on the lowest step.

Now he gave a swaying motion to the ladders, just as a spider sways itself to and fro, when, hanging at the end of its thread, it wishes to seize upon an object; and when Rudy for the fourth time touched the top of the ladder, the highest of the three that had been bound together, he seized it and held it firmly.

Then he bound the other two ladders with a strong hand to the first three, so that they reached up to the eagle's nest; but they rattled and swayed as if they had loose hinges.

The five long ladders thus bound together, and standing upright against the rocky wall, looked like a long swaying reed; and now came the most dangerous part of the business. There was climbing to be done as the cat climbs; but Rudy had learned to climb, and it was the cat who had taught him.

He knew nothing of the Spirit of Giddiness, who stood treading the air behind him and stretching out long arms towards him like the feelers of a polypus. Now he stood upon the highest step of the topmost ladder, and perceived that after all it was not high enough to let him look into the nest; he could only reach up into it with his hand.

He felt about to test the firmness of the thick plaited branches that formed the lower part of the nest, and when he had secured a thick, steady piece, he swung himself up by it from the ladder, and leaned against the branch, so that his head and shoulders were above the level of the nest. A stifling stench of carrion streamed towards him, for in the nest lay chamois, birds, and lambs, in a putrid state.

In a corner of the nest he saw the young one, which was not

yet fledged, sitting large and stately. Rudy fixed his eyes upon it, held himself fast with all the strength of one hand, while with the other he threw the noose over the young eagle. It was caught—caught alive!

Its legs were entangled in the tough noose, and Rudy threw the cord and the bird across his shoulder, so that the creature hung some distance beneath him, while he held fast by a rope they had lowered down to assist him, till his feet touched the topmost round of the ladder.

And now a whoop sounded strong and joyous, and Rudy stood safe and sound on the firm rock with the captured eaglet.

7. *What News the Parlour Cat had to Tell*

"HERE is what you wished for!" said Rudy as he entered the house of the miller at Bex.

Setting down a great basket on the ground, he lifted the cloth that covered it. Two yellow eyes, bordered with black, stared forth; they seemed to shoot forth sparks, and gleamed, burning and savage, as if they would burn all they looked at. The short strong beak was open, ready to snap, and the red neck was covered with wattles.

"The young eagle!" the miller cried. "*You're* not to be frightened off."

"And you always keep your word," answered Rudy. "Every man has his own character."

"But why did you not break your neck?" asked the miller.

"Because I held fast," replied Rudy. "I do that still. I hold Babette fast!"

"First see that you get her," said the miller; and he laughed.

But his laughter was a good sign, and Babette knew it. Rudy had to relate the adventure, at which the miller opened his eyes wider and wider.

"With your courage and good fortune you could gain a living for three wives," cried the miller at last.

"Thank you!" said Rudy.

"Still you have not Babette yet," continued the miller; and he tapped the young huntsman playfully on the shoulder.

"Do you know the latest news from the mill?" the Parlour Cat asked of the Kitchen Cat. "Rudy has brought us the eaglet, and is going to take Babette away in exchange. They have kissed each other, and let the old man see it. That's as good as a betrothal. The old man behaved quite politely; he drew in his claws, and took his nap, and let the two young ones sit together and purr. They've so much to tell each other that they won't have done till Christmas."

And they had not done till Christmas. The wind tossed up the brown leaves; the snow whirled through the valley and over the high mountains. The snowy covering reached almost down to Bex, and the Ice Maiden came thither also, and saw Rudy sitting in the mill; this winter he sat much more indoors than was his custom—he sat by Babette.

The wedding was to be next summer; his ears often buzzed, his friends spoke so much about it. In the mill there was sunshine—the loveliest Alpine rose bloomed there, the cheerful, smiling Babette, beautiful as the spring.

"How can those two sit and hang over each other?" said the Parlour Cat. "I am beginning to get quite tired of them."

8. Babette's Godmother

SPRING had unfolded its fresh green garland on the walnut and chestnut trees extending from the bridge at St. Maurice to the shore of the Lake of Geneva, along the Rhone, that rushed with headlong speed from its source beneath the green glacier, the ice palace where the Ice Maiden dwells, and whence she soars on the sharp wind up to the loftiest snow-field, there to rest upon her snowy couch.

At Montreux, the first of the towns which, with Clarens, Ferney, and Crini, form a garland round the north-eastern portion of the lake of Geneva, lived Babette's godmother, a high-born English lady, with her daughters and a young male relative. They had only lately arrived, but the miller had already waited upon them to tell them of Babette's betrothal, and the story of Rudy and the eaglet, and of his visit to Interlaken—in short, the whole story.

The visitors were much pleased to hear it, and showed

themselves very friendly towards Rudy, Babette, and the miller, who were all three urgently invited to come to Montreux.

By the little town of Villeneuve, at the extremity of the Lake of Geneva, lay the steamship which in its half-hour's trip to Ferney stops just below Montreux. The coast here has been sung by poets; here, under the walnut-trees, by the deep bluish-green lake, sat Byron, and wrote his melodious verses of the prisoner in the rocky fortress of Chillon. Yonder, where the weeping willows of Clarens are clearly mirrored in the water, Rousseau wandered, dreaming of Heloise.

The Rhone rolls onward among the lofty snow-clad mountains of Savoy; there, not far from its mouth, lies in the lake a little island, so small, that seen from the coast it appears like a ship upon the waters. It is a rock which a lady, about a century ago, caused to be walled round with stone and coated with earth. Three acacia-trees were planted there, and now they overshadow the whole island.

Babette was delighted with this spot, which seemed to her the prettiest point of all their journey, and she declared that they must land there. But the steamer glided past, and was moored, according to custom, at Ferney. Half-way up the hill was situated the hotel in which the English lady was staying.

The reception was very hearty. The English lady was a very friendly lady, with a round, smiling face; in her childhood her head must have been like one of Raphael's angels; but she had an old angel's head now, surrounded by curls of silvery white. The daughters were tall, slender, good-looking, lady-like girls.

The young cousin whom they had brought with them was dressed in white from head to foot. He had yellow hair, and enough of yellow whisker to have been shared among three or four gentlemen. He immediately showed the very greatest attention to Babette.

Rudy, who was generally frank, cheerful, and ready, felt very uncomfortable, and he moved as if he were walking on peas spread on a smooth surface. How long and wearisome the time seemed to him! And now they even went out to walk together; that was just as slow and wearisome as the rest.

They went down to Chillon, the old gloomy castle on the rocky island, to see the instruments of torture, the dreary dungeons, the rusty chains fastened to the walls, the stone benches on which men condemned to death had sat, and the trap-door through which the unhappy wretches were hurled down to be impaled below upon tipped iron stakes in the water.

They called it a pleasure to see all this. To Rudy it only brought the prison feeling with it, and he longed to be set free from the whole chattering company.

But Babette was in unusually good spirits. She declared she had enjoyed herself immensely, and told Rudy she considered the young cousin a complete gentleman. He had given her a little book in remembrance of Chillon. It was Byron's poem, "The Prisoner of Chillon," translated into French, so that Babette could read it.

"The book may be good," said Rudy, "but I don't like the combed and curled fellow who gave it to you."

9. The Cousin

A FEW days after these events, when Rudy went to pay a visit at the mill, he found the young Englishman there, and Babette was just about to offer her visitor some boiled trout, which she certainly must have garnished with parsley with her own hands, so tempting did they look—a thing that was not at all necessary.

What did the Englishman want here? And what business had Babette to treat him and pet him? Rudy was jealous, and that pleased Babette, for she liked to know all the points of his character—the weak as well as the strong.

Love was still only a game to her, and she played with Rudy's whole heart; yet he was, we must confess, her happiness, her whole life, her constant thought, the best and most precious possession she had on earth.

Still, the darker his glance became, the more did her eyes laugh, and she would have liked to kiss the fair Englishman with the yellow beard, if her doing this would have made Rudy wild and sent him raging away; for that would show how much he loved her. Now, this was not right of Babette but she was only nineteen years old.

The mill stood just where the high road from Bex leads down under the snow-covered mountain height, which in the language of the country is called Diablerets. It was not far from a rushing, mountain stream, whose waters were whitish-grey, like foaming soap-suds.

This stream did not work the mill; a smaller stream drove round the great wheel—one which fell from the rock some way beyond the main river, and whose power and fall were increased by a stone dam, and by a long wooden trough that carried it over the level of the great stream.

This trough was so full that the water poured over its sides, making a narrow, slippery path for those who chose to walk along it, that they might get to the mill by the shortest cut; and to whom of all people should the idea of reaching the mill by this road occur but to the young Englishman!

Dressed in white, like a miller's man, he climbed over at night, guided by the light that shone from Babette's chamber window; but he had not learned how to climb like Rudy, and was near falling headlong into the stream below, but he escaped with a pair of wet coat sleeves, and soiled trousers; and thus, wet and bespattered with mud, he came below Babette's window.

Here he climbed into the old elm-tree, and began to imitate the voice of the owl, the only bird whose cry he could manage. Babette heard the noise, and looked out of her window through the thin curtain; but when she saw the white form, and guessed who it was, her heart beat with fear and with anger.

She put out the light in a hurry, saw that all the bolts of the windows were well secured, and then let him whoop and tu-whoo to his heart's content.

It would be dreadful if Rudy were in the mill just now! But Rudy was not in the mill; no—what was worse still, he stood just under the elm-tree. Presently there were loud and angry voices, and there might be a fight and even murder. Babette

opened the window in a fright, and called Rudy by name,
begging him to go, and declaring that she would not allow
him to remain.

"You won't allow me to remain?" he shouted. "Then it's
a planned thing! You expect good friends, better men than I!
For shame, Babette!"

"You are odious!" cried Babette. "I hate you! Go, go!"

"I have not deserved this," he said, and went away, his face
burning like fire, and his heart burning as fiercely.

Babette threw herself on her bed and wept. "So dearly
as I love you, Rudy! And that you should think evil of
me!"

Then she broke out in anger; and that was good for her,
for otherwise she would have suffered too much from her
grief; and now she could sleep—the strengthening sleep of
health and youth.

10. Evil Powers

RUDY quitted Bex and took the way towards his home; he
went up the mountain, into the fresh, cool air, where the
snow lay on the ground, where the Ice Maiden ruled. A blue
gentian that stood by his path he crushed with a blow of his
rifle stock.

Higher up still two chamois came in view. Rudy's eyes
brightened, and his thoughts took a new direction; but he
was not near enough to be sure of his aim, so he mounted
higher, where nothing but scanty grass grew among the
blocks of stone.

The chamois were straying quietly along on the snow-field.
He hastened his steps till the veil of clouds began to cover him,
and suddenly he found himself in front of a steep wall of rock;
and now the rain began to pour down.

He felt a burning thirst, his head was hot, his limbs were
cold. He took his hunting flask, but it was empty—he had not
thought of filling it when he rushed out upon the mountains.

He had never been ill in his life, but now he had warnings
of such a state, for he was weary, and wished to lie down and
sleep, though the rain was pouring all around. He tried to

collect his thoughts, but all objects danced and trembled strangely before his eyes.

Then suddenly he beheld what he had never seen in that spot before, a new, low-browed house, that leaned against the rock. At the door stood a young girl, and she almost appeared to him like the school-master's daughter, Annette, whom he had once kissed at the dance.

"Whence do you come?" he asked.

"I am at home here. I am keeping my flock," was the reply.

"Your flock! Where does it graze? There is nothing here."

"Much you know about what is here," said the girl with a laugh. "Behind us, lower down, is a glorious pasture; my goats graze there. I tend them carefully, not one of them do I lose, and what is once mine remains mine."

"You are bold," said Rudy.

"And you too," replied the girl.

"If you have any milk in the house, pray give me some to drink; I am very thirsty."

"I've something better than milk," said the girl, "and I will give you that. Yesterday some travellers were here with their guide, who forgot a bottle of wine of a kind you have probably never tasted. They will not come back for it, and I do not drink it, therefore you must drink it."

And the girl brought the wine, and poured it into a wooden cup, which she gave to Rudy.

"That *is* good wine," said he. "I've never tasted any so strong or so fiery!"

And his eyes glistened, and a glowing, life-like feeling streamed through him, as if every care, every pressure, had melted into air, and the fresh bubbling human nature stirred within him.

"Why, this must be Annette!" he cried "Give me a kiss."

"Then give me the beautiful ring that you wear on your finger."

"My betrothal ring?"

"Yes, that very one," said the girl.

He looked at the young girl—it was Annette, and yet not Annette. The girl here on the mountain looked fresh as the white snow, blooming as an Alpine rose, and swift-footed as a kid; but still she looked as much a mortal as Rudy himself.

He looked into her wonderful clear eyes, only for a moment he looked into them, and—who shall describe it?—in that moment, whether it was the life of the spirit or death that filled him, he was borne upwards, or else he sank into the deep and deadly ice cleft, lower and lower. He saw the icy walls gleaming like blue-green glass, deep abysses yawned around, and the water dropped tinkling down like shining bells, clear as pearls, glowing with pale blue flames.

The Ice Maiden kissed him—a kiss that sent a shudder from neck to brow; a cry of pain escaped from him; he tore himself away, staggered, and—it was night before his eyes; but soon he opened them again. Evil powers had been playing their sport with him.

Vanished was the Alpine girl, vanished the sheltering hut; the water poured down the naked rocky wall, and snow lay all around. Rudy trembled with cold; he was wet to the skin, and his ring was gone—the betrothal ring which Babette had given him.

Babette sat in the mill and wept. Rudy had not been there for six days—he who was wrong, and who ought to come and beg her pardon, and whom she loved with her whole heart.

11. In the Mill

EVIL powers sport with us and in us; Rudy had felt that, and had thought much of it. What was all that which had happened to him and around him on the summit of the mountain? Were they spirits he had seen, or had he had a feverish vision? Never until now had he suffered from fever or any other illness.

But in judging Babette, he had looked into his own heart also. He had traced the wild whirlwind, the hot wind that had raged there. Would he be able to confess to Babette every thought he had had—thoughts that might become actions in the hour of temptation? He had lost her ring, and through this loss she had won him again.

Would she be able to confess to him? He felt as if his heart would burst when he thought of her. What a number of recollections arose within him! He saw her, as if she were standing bodily before him, laughing like a wayward child. Many a sweet word she had spoken out of the fullness of her heart now crept into his breast like a sunbeam, and soon there was nothing but sunshine within him when he thought of Babette.

Yes, she would be able to confess to him, and she should do so. Accordingly he went to the mill, and the confession began with a kiss, and ended in the fact that Rudy was declared to be the sinner. His great fault had been that he had doubted Babette's fidelity—it was wicked of him. Such distrust, such headlong anger, might bring sorrow upon them both.

Yes, certainly they could; and so Babette read him a short lecture to her own great contentment, and with charming grace. But in one point she agreed with Rudy; the nephew of her godmother was a booby, and she would burn the book he had given her, for she would not keep the slightest thing that reminded her of him.

The greatest happiness of Rudy and Babette—the fairest day, as they called it—the wedding-day, now approached rapidly.

The wedding was not to be celebrated at the church at Bex and in the mill. Babette's god-mother wished her godchild to be married from her house, and the service was to be read in the beautiful little church at Montreux.

The miller insisted upon having his way in this matter. He alone knew what the intentions of the English lady were with respect to her godchild, and declared that she intended making such a wedding present that they were bound to show some sense of gratitude.

The day was fixed. On the evening before it they were to travel to Villeneuve, so that they might drive over early to Montreux, where the young English ladies would dress the bride. To-morrow the journey would begin. And on this evening Rudy and Babette sat for the last time together in the mill as a betrothed pair.

Without, the Alps were glowing, the evening bells sounded, and the Daughters of the Sunbeams sang, "Let that happen which is best."

12. Conclusion

It was not yet evening when the three happy people entered Villeneuve, where they dined. Thereupon the miller sat in the arm-chair, smoked his pipe, and took a short nap. The betrothed pair went arm-in-arm out of the town; they walked along the road, under the green-clad rocks, beside the deep blue-green lake; the grey walls and heavy towers of gloomy Chillon were mirrored in the clear flood; the island of the three acacias lay still nearer to them, looking like a nosegay in the lake.

"It must be charming there!" said Babette.

She felt the greatest desire to go there; and as a boat lay by the shore it was an easy matter to loosen the rope by which it was fastened. No one was to be seen of whom leave could be asked to use the vessel, so they borrowed the boat without ceremony, for Rudy was a skilful rower.

The oars cut like fins into the water—the water that is so pliant and yet so strong—that has a back to bear burdens and a mouth to devour—that can smile, the very picture of mildness, and yet can terrify and crush. The water glistened in the wake of the boat, which in a few minutes carried the two over to the island, where they stepped ashore.

Rudy danced round it twice or thrice with Babette; then they sat down, hand in hand, upon the bench under the drooping acacias, looked into each other's eyes; and everything shone in the glory of the setting sun.

"So much beauty! So much happiness!" they both exclaimed.

"This earth has nothing more to give," said Rudy. "An evening like this seems to compromise a whole life! How often have I felt my happiness as I feel it now, and have thought, 'If everything were to end this moment, how happily I should have lived! How glorious is this world!' Then the day ended, and another began, and the new day seemed more beautiful to me than the last! How very good is God, Babette!"

"I am happy from the depth of my heart!" she said.

"This earth can offer me nothing more," said Rudy.

And the evening bells began to sound from the mountains of Savoy and from the Swiss hills, and in the west rose the black Jura range, crowned with a wreath of gold.

"May Heaven grant to thee what is happiest and best!" murmured Babette.

"It will," replied Rudy. "To-morrow I shall have it. To-morrow you will be mine entirely. My own sweet wife!"

"The boat!" exclaimed Babette suddenly.

The little skiff in which they were to return had broken loose and was drifting away from the island.

"I will bring it back," said Rudy.

He threw aside his coat, pulled off his boots, jumped into the lake, and swam with powerful strokes towards the boat.

Cold and deep was the clear blue-green ice water from the glacier of the mountain. Rudy looked down into its depths— one glance—and it seemed to him that he saw a golden ring, rolling, shining, and sparkling. He thought of his ring of betrothal—and the ring grew larger, and widened into a sparkling circle into which the glacier shone, and the water-drops rang like the chiming of bells, and glittered with white flames.

In a moment he beheld all that it has taken many words to describe. Young hunters and young girls, men and women who had at different times sunk down into the crevasses among the glaciers stood there living, with smiling mouths, and deep below them sounded the church bells of the sunken cities.

The congregation knelt beneath the church roof, the organ pipes were formed of great icicles, and beneath all the Ice Maiden sat on the clear, transparent ground. She raised herself towards Rudy and kissed his feet; then a cold, death-like numbness poured through his limbs, and an electric shock— ice and fire mingled! There is no difference to be felt between a sudden touch of these two.

"Mine! mine!" sounded around him and within him. "I

VERNON SOPER

kissed thee when thou wert little, kissed thee on thy mouth. Now I kiss thy feet, and thou art mine altogether!"

And he disappeared beneath the clear blue water.

All was silent; the chime of the church bells ceased, the last echoes died away with the last ruddy tints of the evening clouds.

"Thou art mine!" sounded from the depths. "Thou art mine!" sounded from the heights, from the regions of the Infinite.

Glorious! from love to love—to fly from earth to Heaven!

A chord broke, a sound of mourning was heard; the icy kiss of Death conquered that which was to pass away; the prologue ended that the true drama of life might begin, and discord was blended into harmony.

Do you call that a sorrowful story?

But poor Babette! Her grief was unspeakable. The boat drifted farther and farther away. No one on the mainland knew that the lovers had gone over to the little island. The sun went down and it became dark. She stood alone, weeping —despairing.

A storm came on; flash after flash lit up the Jura mountains: flash upon flash on all sides, the rolling thunder-clap mingling with clap for minutes together. The gleams of lightning were sometimes bright as the sun, showing every separate vine as at noonday, and the next moment all would be shrouded in darkness. On the mainland, people drew the boats high up on the shore; everything that had life hastened to get under shelter; and now the rain came pouring down.

"Where can Rudy and Babette be in this tempest?" said the miller.

Babette sat with folded hands, her head on her knees, speechless with grief; she no longer moaned or wept.

"In the deep waters!" was the one thought in her mind. "He is far down in the lake as if under the glacier."

And then arose the recollection of what Rudy had told about the death of his mother and his own rescue; how he had been borne forth, like a corpse, from the depths of the glacier.

"The Ice Maiden has got him again!"

A flash of lightning glared like sunshine over the white snow. Babette started up. The whole lake was at this moment like a shining glacier; and there stood the Ice Maiden, majestic, with a bluish-white light upon her, and at her feet lay Rudy's corpse.

"Mine!" she said.

Again there was darkness all around, and the crash of falling waters.

"How cruel!" groaned Babette. "Why must he die when the day of our happiness was about to dawn? O Lord, enlighten my understanding! Send Thy light into my heart! I understand not Thy ways, I grope in darkness, but submit myself to Thy power and Thy wisdom!"

The light for which she prayed was given to her. A gleam of thought, a ray of light, her dream of the past night in its living reality, flashed through her. She remembered the words, the wish she had uttered, concerning what would be "THE BEST" for her and for Rudy.

And she sat there in the dark night, lamenting. Through the thick darkness Rudy's words seemed to sound, the last words he had spoken on earth, "The earth has nothing more to give me!" They had sounded in the fullness of joy; they echoed now through the depths of distress.

Years have flown by since that time. The lake smiles and its shores smile; the grape-vine is covered with swelling branches; steamboats with waving flags glide along; pleasure boats with full sails flit across the waters like white butterflies; the railway has been opened past Chillon, and leads deep into the valley of the Rhone.

At every station strangers alight, with red-bound guide-books in their hands, and they read of the sights they have come to see. They visit Chillon, and in the lake they behold the little island with three acacias, and in the book they read about the lovers who, on an evening of the year 1856, sailed across thither, and of the death of the bridegroom, and how the despairing cries of the bride were not heard on the shore till the next morning.

BIBLIOGRAPHY

MAIN WORKS BY HANS CHRISTIAN ANDERSEN

1. *Travel Books*
      Silhouettes   1831
      Picture Book without Pictures   1840
      A Poet's Bazaar   1842
      In Sweden   1852
      In Spain   1863

2. *Fairy-Tales (Eventyr)*
      First Series   1835/37
                     1838/39
      Second Series   1839/42
      Third Series   1845
      New Fairy Tales   1847/48
      Later Fairy Tales (*Historier*)   1852/62
      Last Fairy Tales   1871/72

3. *Romances and Novels*
      The Improvisatore   1835
      O.T.   1836
      Only a Fiddler   1837
      The Two Baronesses   1848
      To Be or Not To Be   1857
      Fortunate Per   1870

4. *Autobiography*
      The Story of my Life   1855
      Andersen wrote another autobiography, which was
      not meant for publication, in 1832; it was first pub-
      lished in Denmark in 1926. He also wrote numerous
      plays, operetas, poems and vaudevilles.

5. Collected Works in 33 vols.   1854/79
                  in 15 vols.   1876/80

SOME ENGLISH WORKS ON HANS CHRISTIAN ANDERSEN

Hans Christian Andersen: A Biography by R. Nisbet Bain, 1895

The Life of Hans Christian Andersen by Signe Tokswig, 1933

The Shoemaker's Son: the Life of Hans Christian Andersen by C. B. Burnett, 1943

Hans Christian Andersen by Rumer Godden, 1956

Hans Christian Andersen and His Eventyr in England by Brian Alderson, 1982

An English Edition (Edited by W. F. Crawfort) of Andersen's correspondence was published in 1891.

There are numerous Danish Editions of his very extensive correspondence.